The Open Conspiracy

BY THE SAME AUTHOR
ALL PUBLISHED BY HOUSE OF STRATUS

The Open Conspiracy

And Other Writings

H G WELLS

HOUSE OF
STRATUS

The Open Conspiracy

Contents

CHAPTER ONE

The Present Crisis in Human Affairs

The world is undergoing immense changes. Never before have the conditions of life changed so swiftly and enormously as they have changed for mankind in the last fifty years. We have been carried along – with no means of measuring the increasing swiftness in the succession of events. We are only now beginning to realize the force and strength of the storm of change that has come upon us.

These changes have not come our world from without. No huge meteorite from outer space has struck our planet; there have been no overwhelming outbreaks of volcanic violence or strange epidemic diseases; the sun has not flared up to excessive heat or suddenly shrunken to plunge us into Arctic winter. The changes have come through men themselves. Quite a small number of people, heedless of the ultimate consequences of what they did, one man here and a group there, have made discoveries and produced and adopted inventions that have changed all the conditions of social life.

We are now just beginning to realize the nature of these changes, to find words and phrases for them and put them down. First they began to happen, and then we began to see that they were happening. And now we are beginning to see how these changes are connected together and to get the measure of their consequences. We are getting our minds so clear about them that soon we shall be able to demonstrate them and explain them to our children in our schools. We do not do so at present. We do not give our children a chance of discovering that they live in a world of universal change.

What are the broad lines upon which these alterations of condition are proceeding?

It will be most convenient to deal with them in the order in which they came to be realized and seen clearly, rather than by the order in which they came about or by their logical order. They are more or less interdependent changes; they overlap and interact.

It was only in the beginning of the twentieth century that people began to realize the real significance of that aspect of our changing conditions to which the phrase "*the abolition of distance*" has been applied. For a whole century before that there had been a continual increase in the speed and safety of travel and transport and the ease and swiftness with which messages could be transmitted, but this increase had not seemed to be a matter of primary importance. Various results of railway, steamship, and telegraph became manifest; towns grew larger, spreading into the countryside, once inaccessible lands became areas of rapid settlement and cultivation, industrial centres began to live on imported food, news from remote parts lost its time-lag and tended to become contemporary, but no one hailed these things as being more than "improvements" in existing conditions. They are not observed to be the beginnings of a profound revolution in the life of mankind. The attention of young people was not drawn to them; no attempt was made, or considered necessary, to adapt political and social institutions to this creeping enlargement of scale.

Until the closing years of the nineteenth century there was no recognition of the real state of affairs. Then a few observant people began, in a rather tentative, commentary sort of way, to call attention to what was happening. They did not seem to be moved by the idea that something had to be done about it; they merely remarked, brightly and intelligently, that it was going on. And then they went on to the realization that this "abolition of distance" was only one aspect of much more far-reaching advances.

Men were travelling about so much faster and flashing their communications instantly about the world because a progressive conquest of force and substance was going on. Improved transport was only one of a number of portentous consequences of that conquest; the first to be conspicuous and set men thinking; but not perhaps the first in importance. It dawned upon them that in the last hundred years there had been a stupendous progress in obtaining and utilizing mechanical power, a vast increase in the efficiency of mechanism, and associated with that an enormous increase in the substances available for man's purposes, from vulcanized rubber to the modern steels, and from petroleum and margarine to tungsten and aluminium. At first the general intelligence was disposed to regard these things as lucky "finds," happy chance discoveries. It was not apprehended that the shower of finds was systematic and continuous. Popular writers told about these things but they told of them at first as "Wonders" – "Wonders" like the Pyramids, the Colossus of Rhodes, and the Great Wall of China. Few realized how much more they were than any "Wonders". The "Seven Wonders of the World" left men free to go on living, toiling, marrying, and dying as they had been accustomed to for immemorial ages. If the "Seven Wonders" had vanished or been multiplied three score it would not have changed the lives of any large proportion of human beings. But these new powers and substances were modifying and transforming — unobtrusively, surely, and relentlessly — every particular of the normal life of mankind.

They increased the amount of production and the methods of production. They made possible "Big-Business", to drive the small producer and the small distributor out of the market. They swept away factories and evoked new ones. They changed the face of the fields. They brought into the normal life, thing by thing and day by day, electric light and heating, bright cities at night, better aeration, new types of clothing, a fresh cleanliness. They changed a world where there had never been enough into a world of potential plenty, into a world of excessive plenty. It dawned upon their minds after their realization of the "abolition of distance" that shortage of supplies had also been abolished and that irksome toil was no longer necessary to produce everything material that man might require. It is only in the last dozen years that this broader and profounder fact has come through to the intelligence of any considerable number of people. Most of them have still to carry their realization a step farther and see how complete is the revolution in the character of the daily life these things involve.

But there are still other changes outside this vast advance in the pace and power of material life. The biological sciences have undergone a corresponding extension. Medical art has attained a new level of efficiency, so that in all the modernizing societies of the world the average life is prolonged, and there is, in spite of a great fall in the birth rate, a steady, alarming increase in the world's population. The proportion of adults alive is greater than it has ever been before. Fewer and fewer human beings die young. This has changed the social atmosphere about us. The tragedy of lives cut short and ended prematurely is passing out of general experience. Health becomes prevalent. The continual toothaches, headaches, rheumatism, neuralgias, coughs, colds, indigestions that made up so large a part of the briefer lives of our grandfathers and grandmothers fade out of experience. We may all live now, we discover, without any great burthen of toil or fear, wholesomely and abundantly, for as long as the desire to live is in us.

But we do not do so. All this possible freedom of movement, this power and abundance, remains for most of us no more than possibility. There is a sense of profound instability about these achievements of our race. Even those who enjoy, enjoy without security, and for the great multitude of mankind there is neither ease, plenty, nor freedom. Hard tasks, insufficiency, and unending money worries are still the ordinary stuff of life. Over everything human hangs the threat of such war as man has never known before, war armed and reinforced by all the powers and discoveries of modern science.

When we demand why the achievement of power turns to distress and danger in our hands, we get some very unsatisfactory replies. The favourite platitude of the politician, excusing himself for the futilities of his business, is that "moral progress has not kept pace with material advance." That seems to satisfy him completely, but it can satisfy no other intelligent person. He says "moral." He leaves that word unexplained. Apparently he wants to shift the responsibility to our religious teachers. At the most he has made but the vaguest gesture towards a reply. And yet, when we consider it, charitably and sympathetically, there does seem to be a germ of reality in that phrase of his.

What does moral mean? *Mores* means manners and customs. Morality is the conduct of life. It is what we do with our social lives. It is how we deal with ourselves in relation to our fellow creatures. And there does seem to be a much greater discord now that there was (say) a couple of hundred years ago between the prevailing ideas of how to carry on life and the opportunities and dangers of the time. We are among to see more and more plainly that certain established traditions which have made up the frame of human relationships for ages are not merely no longer as convenient as they were, but are positively injurious and dangerous. And yet at present we do not know how to shake off these traditions, these habits of social behaviour which rule us. Still less are we able to state, and still less bring into operation, the new conceptions of conduct and obligation that must replace them.

For example, the general government of human affairs has hitherto been distributed among a number of sovereign states – there are about seventy of them now – and until recently that was a quite tolerable system of frameworks into which a general way of living could be fitted. The standard of living may not have been as high as our present standards, but the social stability and assurance were greater. The young were trained to be loyal, law-regarding, patriotic, and a defined system of crimes and misdemeanours with properly associated pains, penalties, and repressions, kept the social body together. Everyone was taught a history glorifying his own state, and patriotism was chief among the virtues. Now, with great rapidity, there has been that "abolition of distance", and everyone has become next-door neighbour to everyone else. States once separate, social and economic systems formerly remote from one another, now jostle each other exasperatingly. Commerce under the new conditions is perpetually breaking nationalist bounds and making militant raids upon the economic life of other countries. This exacerbates patriotism in which we have all been trained and with which we are all, with scarcely an exception, saturated. And meanwhile war, which was once a comparative slow bickering upon a front, has become war in three dimensions; it gets at the "non-combatant" almost as searchingly as at the combatant, and has acquired weapons of a stupendous cruelty and destructiveness. At present there exists no solution to this paradoxical situation. We are continually being urged by our training and traditions to antagonisms and conflicts that will impoverish, starve, and destroy both our antagonists and ourselves. We are all trained to distrust and hate foreigners, salute our flag, stiffen up in a wooden obedient way at our national anthem, and prepare to follow the little fellows in spurs and feathers who pose as the heads of our states into the most horrible common destruction. Our political and economic ideas of living are out of date, and we find great difficulty in adjusting them and reconstructing them to meet the huge and strenuous demands of the new times. That is really what our gramophone politicians have in mind – in the vague way in which they have anything in mind – when they put on that well-worn record about moral progress not having kept pace with material inventions.

Socially and politically we want a revised system of ideas about conduct, a view of social and political life brought up to date. We are not doing the effective thing with our lives, we are drifting, we are being hoodwinked and bamboozled and misled by those who trade upon the old traditions. It is preposterous that we should still be followed about and pestered by war, taxed for war preparations, and threatened bodily and in our liberties by this unnecessary and exaggerated and distorted survival of the disunited world of the pre-scientific era. And it is not simply that our political way of living is now no better than an inherited defect and malformation, but that our everyday life, our eating and drinking and clothing and housing and going about, is also cramped, thwarted, and impoverished, because we do not know how to set about shaking off the old ways and fitting the general life to our new opportunities. The strain takes the form of increased unemployment and a dislocation of spending power. We do not know whether to spend or save. Great swarms of us find ourselves unaccountably thrown out of work. Unjustly, irrationally. Colossal business reconstructions are made to increase production and accumulate profits, and meanwhile the customers with purchasing power dwindle in numbers and fade away. The economic machine creaks and makes every sign of stopping – and its stopping means universal want and starvation. It must not stop. There must be a reconstruction, a change-over. But what sort of a change-over?

Though none of us are yet clear as to the precise way in which this great change-over is to be effected, there is a world-wide feeling now that change-over or a vast catastrophe is before us. Increasing multitudes participate in that uneasy sense of insecure transition. In the course of one lifetime mankind has passed from a state of affairs that seems to us now to have been slow, dull, ill-provided, and limited, but at least picturesque and tranquil-minded, to a new phase of excitement, provocation, menace, urgency, and actual or potential distresses. Our lives are part of one another. We cannot get away from it. We are items in a social mass. What are we to do with our lives?

CHAPTER TWO

The Idea of the Open Conspiracy

I am a writer upon social and political matters. Essentially I am a very ordinary, undistinguished person. I have a mediocre brain, a very average brain, and the way in which my mind reacts to these problems is therefore very much the way in which most brains will react to them. But because it is my business to write and think about these questions, because on that account I am able to give more time and attention to them than most people, I am able to get rather ahead of my equals and to write articles and books just a little before the ideas I experience become plain to scores of thousands, and then to hundreds of thousands, and at last to millions of other people. And so it happened that a few years ago (round about 1927) I became very anxious to clear up and give form to a knot of suggestions that seemed to me to have in them the solution of this riddle of adapting our lives to the immense new possibilities and the immense new dangers that confront mankind.

It seemed to me that all over the world intelligent people were waking up to the indignity and absurdity of being endangered, restrained, and impoverished, by a mere uncritical adhesion to traditional governments, traditional ideas of economic life, and traditional forms of behaviour, and that these awaking intelligent people must constitute first a protest and then a creative resistance to the inertia that was stifling and threatening us. These people I imagined would say first, "We are drifting; we are doing nothing worth while with our lives. Our lives are dull and stupid and not good enough."

Then they would say, "What are we to do with our lives?"

And then, "Let us get together with other people of our sort and make over the world into a great world-civilization that will enable us to realize the promises and avoid the dangers of this new time."

It seemed to me that as, one after another, we woke up, that is what we should be saying. It amounted to a protest, first mental and then practical, it amounted to a sort of unpremeditated and unorganized conspiracy, against the fragmentary and insufficient governments and the wide-spread greed, appropriation, clumsiness, and waste that are now going on. But unlike conspiracies in general this widening protest and conspiracy against established things would, by its very nature, go on in the daylight, and it would be willing to accept participation and help from every quarter. It would, in fact, become an "Open Conspiracy", a necessary, naturally evolved conspiracy, to adjust our dislocated world.

I made various attempts to develop this idea. I published a little book called *The Open Conspiracy* as early as 1928, into which I put what I had in my mind at that time. It was an unsatisfactory little book even when I published it, not quite plain enough and not quite confident enough, and evidently unsure of its readers. I could not find out how to do it better at the time, and it seemed in its way to say something of living and current interest, and so I published it – but I arranged things so that I could withdraw it in a year or so. That I did, and this present book is a largely rewritten version, much clearer and more explicit. Since that first publication we have all got forward surprisingly. Events have hustled thought along and have been hustled along by thought. The idea of reorganizing the affairs of the world on quite a big scale, which was "Utopian", and so forth, in 1926 and 1927, and still "bold" in 1928, has now spread about the world until nearly everybody has it. It has broken out all over the place, thanks largely to the mental stimulation of the Russian Five Year Plan. Hundreds of thousands of people everywhere are now thinking upon the lines foreshadowed by my Open Conspiracy, not because they had ever heard of the book or phrase, but because that was the way thought was going.

The first *Open Conspiracy* conveyed the general idea of a world reconstructed, but it was very vague about the particular way in which this or that individual life could be lived in relation to that general idea. It gave a general answer to the question, "What are we to do with our lives?" It said, "Help to make over the New World amidst the confusions of the Old." But when the question was asked, "What am *I* to do with *my* life?" the reply was much less satisfactory.

The intervening years of thought and experience make it possible, now, to bring this general idea of a reconstructive effort, an attempt to build up a new world within the dangers and disharmonies of our present state, into a much closer and more explicit relation to the individual "Open Conspirator". We can present the thing in a better light and handle it with a surer touch.

Chapter Three

We Have to Clear and Clean Up Our Minds

Now, one thing is fairly plain to most of us who are waking up to the need of living our lives in a new way and of making over the state, which is the framework of our lives, to meet the new demands upon it, and that is, that we have to put our own minds in order. Why have we only awakened now to the crisis in human affairs? The changes in progress have been going on with a steady acceleration for a couple of centuries. Clearly we must all have been very unobservant, our knowledge as it came to us must have been very badly arranged in our minds, and our way of dealing with it must have been cloudy and muddled, or else we should surely have awakened long ago to the immense necessities that now challenge us. And if that is so, if it has taken decades to rouse us, then quite probably we are not yet completely awake. Even now we may not have realized the job before us in its completeness. We may still have much to get plain in our minds, and we certainly have much more to learn. One primary and permanent duty therefore is to go on with our thinking and to think as well as we can about the way in which we think and about the ways in which we get and use knowledge.

Fundamentally the Open Conspiracy must be an intellectual rebirth.

Human thought is still very much confused by the imperfection of the words and other symbols it employs and the consequences of this confused thinking are much more serious and extensive than is commonly realized. We still see the world through a mist of words; it is only the things immediately about us that are plain fact. Through symbols, and especially through words, man has raised himself above the level of the ape and come to a considerable mastery over his universe. But every step in his mental ascent has involved entanglement with these symbols and words he was using; they were at once helpful and very dangerous and misleading. A great part of our affairs, social, political, intellectual, is in a perplexing and dangerous state today because of our loose, uncritical, slovenly use of words.

All through the later Middle Ages there were great disputes among the schoolmen about the use of words and symbols. There is a queer disposition in the human mind to think that symbols and words and logical deductions are truer than actual experiences, and these great controversies were due to the struggle of the human intelligence against that disposition. On the one side were the Realists, who were so called because they believed, in effect, that names were more real than facts, and on the other side were the Nominalists, who from the first were pervaded by a suspicion about names and words generally; who thought there might be some sort of catch in verbal processes, and who gradually worked their way towards *verification by experiment* which is the fundamental thing about experimental science – experimental science which has given our human world all these immense powers and possibilities that tempt and threaten it today. These controversies of the schoolmen were of the utmost importance to mankind. The modern world could not begin to come into existence until the human mind had broken away from the narrow-minded verbalist way of thinking which the Realists followed.

But all through my education I never had this matter explained to me. The University of London intimated that I was a soundly educated young man by giving me a degree in first-class honours and the liberty to acquire and wear an elegant gown and hood, and the London College of Preceptors gave me and the world its highest assurances that I was fit to educate and train the minds of my fellow creatures, and yet I had still to discover that a Realist was not a novelist who put rather too highly flavoured sex appeal into his books, and a Nominalist, nothing in particular. But it had crept into my mind as I learnt about individuality in my biological work and about logic and psychology in my preparation as the perfect preceptor, that something very important and essential was being left out and that I wasn't at all as well equipped as my diplomas presently said I was, and in the next few years I found the time to clean up this matter pretty thoroughly. I made no marvellous discoveries, everything I found out was known already; nevertheless, I had to find out some of this stuff for myself quite over again, as though it had never been done; so inaccessible was any complete account of human thinking to an ordinary man who wanted to get his mind into proper working condition. And this was not that I had missed some recondite, precious refinements of philosophy; it was that my fundamental thinking, at the very root of my political and social conduct, was wrong. I was in a human community, and that community, and I with it, was thinking of phantoms and fantasies as though they were real and living things, was in a reverie of unrealities, was blind, slovenly, hypnotized, base and ineffective, blundering about in an extremely beautiful and an extremely dangerous world.

I set myself to re-educate myself, and after the practice of writers wrote it in various trial pamphlets, essays, and books. There is no need to refer to these books here. The gist of the matter is set out in three compilations, to which I shall refer again almost immediately. They are *The Outline of History* (Ch. XXI, Section 6, and Ch. XXXIII, Section 6), *The Science of Life* (Book VIII, on Thought and Behaviour) and *The Work, Wealth, and Happiness of Mankind* (Ch. II, Sections 1-4). In the last, it is shown quite plainly how man has had to struggle for the mastery of his mind, has discovered only after great controversies the proper and effective use of his intellectual tools, and has had to learn to avoid certain widespread traps and pitfalls before he could achieve his present mastery over matter. Thinking clearly and effectively does not come by nature. Hunting the truth is an art. We blunder naturally into a thousand misleading generalizations and false processes. Yet there is hardly any intelligent mental training done in the schools of the world today. We have to learn this art, if we are to practise it at all. Our schoolteachers have had no proper training themselves, they miseducate by example and precept, and so it is that our press and current discussions are more like an impromptu riot of crippled and deaf and blind minds than an intelligent interchange of ideas. What bosh one reads! What rash and impudent assumptions! What imbecile inferences!

But re-educating oneself, getting one's mind into health and exercising it and training it to think properly, is only the beginning of the task before the awakening Open Conspirator. He has not only to think clearly, but he has to see that his mind is equipped with the proper general ideas to form a true framework for his everyday judgments and decisions.

It was the Great War first brought home to me how ignorant I was, and how ill-finished and untidy my mind, about the most important things of life. That disastrous waste of life, material and happiness, since it was practically world wide, was manifestly the outcome of the processes that constitute the bulk of history, and yet I found I did not know – and nobody else seemed to know – history in such a fashion as to be able to explain how the Great War came about or what ought to come out of it. "Versailles", we all seem to be agreed nowadays, was silly, but how could Versailles be anything else than what it was in view of the imperfect, lopsided, historical knowledge and the consequent suspicion, emotion, and prejudice of those who assembled there. They did not know any better than the rest of us what the war was, and so how could they know what the peace ought to be? I perceived that I was in the same case with everyone else, and I set myself first of all for my own guidance to make a summary of all history and get some sort of map to more serviceable conclusions about the political state of mankind. This summary I made was *The Outline of History*, a shameless compilation and arrangement of the main facts of the world story, written without a touch of art or elegance, written indeed in a considerable hurry and excitement, and its sale, which is now in the third million, showed how much I had in common with a great dispersed crowd of ordinary people, all wanting to know, all disgusted with the patriotic, litigious twaddling gossipy stuff given them as history by their schoolmasters and schoolmistresses which had led them into the disaster of the war.

The Outline of History is not a whole history of life. Its main theme is the growth of human intercommunication and human communities and their rulers and conflicts, the story of how and why the myriads of little tribal systems of ten thousand years ago have fought and coalesced into the sixty- or seventy-odd governments of today and are now straining and labouring in the grip of forces that must presently accomplish their final unison. And even as I completed *The Outline,* I realized that there remained outside its scope wider and more fundamental, and closer, more immediate fields of knowledge which I still had to get in order for my own practical ends and the ends of like-minded people who wanted to use their lives effectively, if my existence was to escape futility.

I realized that I did not know enough about the life in my body and its relations to the world of life and matter outside it to come to proper decisions about a number of urgent matters – from race conflicts, birth control, and my private life, to the public control of health and the conservation of natural resources. And also, I found, I was astonishingly ignorant about the everyday business of life, the how and why of the miner who provided the coal to cook my dinner, and the banker who took my money in return for a cheque-book, and the shopkeeper from whom I bought things, and the policeman who kept the streets in order for me. Yet I was voting for laws affecting my relations with these people, paying them directly or indirectly, airing my ignorant opinions about them, and generally contributing by my behaviour to sustain and affect their lives.

So with the aid and direction of two very competent biologists I set to work to get out as plain and clear a statement as possible of what was known about the sources and nature of life and the relation of species to individuals and to other species, and the processes of consciousness and thought. This I published as *The Science of Life.* And while this was going on I set myself to the task of making a review of all human activities in relation to each other, the work of people and the needs of people, cultivation, manufacture, trade, direction, government, and all. This was the most difficult part of this attempt to get a rational account of the modern world, and it called for the help and counsel of a great variety of people. I had to ask and find some general answer to the question, "What are the nineteen hundred-odd million human beings who are alive today doing, and how and why are they doing it?" It was, in fact, an outline of economic, social, and political science, but since, after *The Outline of History*, the word "outline" has been a good deal cheapened by various enterprising publishers, I have called it, *The Work, Wealth, and Happiness of Mankind.*

Now, I find, by getting these three correlated compilations into existence, I have at last, in however rough a fashion, brought together a complete system of ideas upon which an Open Conspirator can go. Before anyone could hope to get on to anything like a practical working directive answer to "What are we to do with our lives?" it was necessary to know what our lives were – *The Science of Life;* what had led up to their present pattern – *The Outline of History;* and this third book, to tell what we were actually doing and supposed to be doing with our working lives, day by day, at the present time. By the time I was through with these books I felt I had really something sound and comprehensive to go upon, an "ideology", as people say, on which it was possible to think of building a new world without fundamental surprises, and, moreover, that I had got my mind stripped down and cleaned of many illusions and bad habits, so that it could handle life with an assurance it had never known before.

There is nothing marvellous about these compilations of mine. Any steady writer of average intelligence with the same will and the same resources, who could devote about nine or ten years to the task and get the proper sort of help, could have made them. It can be done, it is no doubt being done, all over again by other people, for themselves and perhaps for others, much more beautifully and adequately. But to get that amount of vision and knowledge, to achieve that general arrangement and understanding, was a necessary condition that had to be satisfied before any answer to the question, "What are we to do with our lives?" could even be attempted, and before one could become in any effective way an Open Conspirator.

There is nothing indispensable even now, I repeat, about these three particular books. I know about them and refer to them because I put them together myself and so they are handy for met to explain myself. But most of what they contain can be extracted from any good encyclopaedia. Any number of people have made similar outlines of history for themselves, have read widely, grasped the leading principles of biology and grappled with the current literature of business science and do not in the least need my particular summary. So far as history and biology are concerned there are parallel books, that are as good and serviceable. Van Loon's books for example. Yet even for highly-educated people these summaries may be useful in bringing things known with different degrees of thoroughness, into a general scheme. They correlate, and they fill up gaps. Between them they cover the ground; and in some fashion that ground has to be covered before the mind of a modern citizen is prepared to tackle the problems that confront it. Otherwise he is an incapable citizen, he does not know where he is and where the world is, and if he is rich or influential he may be a very dangerous citizen indeed. Presently there will be far better compilations to meet this need, or perhaps the gist of all the three divisions of knowledge, concentrated and made more lucid and attractive, may be available as the intellectual frame of modern education throughout the world, as a "General Account of Life" that should be given to everyone.

But certainly no one can possibly set about living properly and satisfactorily unless he knows what he is, where he is, and how he stands to the people and things about him.

Chapter Four

The Revolution in Education

Some sort of reckoning therefore between people awakened to the new world that dawns about us and the schools, colleges, and machinery of formal education is overdue. As a body the educated are getting nothing like that Account of Life which is needed to direct our conduct in this modern world.

It is the crowning absurdity in the world today that these institutions should go through a solemn parade of preparing the new generation for life and that then, afterwards, a minority of their victims, finding this preparation has left them almost totally unprepared, should have of their own accord to struggle out of our world heap of starved and distorted minds to some sort of real education. The world cannot be run by such a minority of escaped and re-educated minds alone, with all the rest of the heap against them. Our necessities demand the intelligence and services of everyone who can be trained to give them. The new world demands new schools, therefore, to give everyone a sound and thorough mental training and equip everyone with clear ideas about history, about life, and about political and economic relationships instead of the rubbishy head-content at present prevalent. The old-world teachers and schools have to be reformed or replaced. A vigorous educational reform movement arises as a natural and necessary expression of the awakening Open Conspirator. A revolution in education is the most imperative and fundamental part of the adaptation of life to its new conditions.

These various compendia of knowledge constituting a Modern Account of Life, on which we have laid stress in the previous section, these supplements to teaching, which are now produced and read outside the established formal educational world and in the teeth of its manifest hostility, arise because of the backwardness of that world, and as that world, and as that world yields slowly but surely to the pressure of the new spirit, so they will permeate and replace its text-books and disappear as a separate class of book. The education these new dangerous times in which we are now living demands, must start right, from the beginning and there must be nothing to replace and nothing to relearn in it. Before we can talk politics, finance, business, or morals, we must see that we have got the right mental habits and the right foundation of realized facts. There is nothing much to be done with our lives until we have seen to that.

CHAPTER FIVE

Religion in the New World

"Yes," objects a reader, "but does not our religion tell us what we are to do with our lives?"

We have to bring religion, as a fundamental matter, into this discussion. From our present point of view religion is that central essential part of education which determines conduct. Religion certainly should tell us what to do with our lives. But in the vast stir and occasions of modern life, so much of what we call religion remains irrelevant or dumb. Religion does not seem to "join on" to the main parts of the general problem of living. It has lost touch.

Let us try and bring this problem of the Open Conspiracy to meet and make the new world, into relation with the traditions of religion. The clear-minded Open Conspirator who has got his modern ideology, his lucidly arranged account of the universe in order, is obliged to believe that only by giving his life to the great processes of social reconstruction, and shaping his conduct with reference to that, can he do well with his life. But that merely launches him into the most subtle and unending of struggles, the struggle against the incessant gravitation of our interests to ourselves. He has to live the broad life and escape from the close narrow life. We all try to attain the dignity and happiness of magnanimity and escape from the tormenting urgencies of personal desire. In the past that struggle has generally assumed the form of a religious struggle. Religion is the antagonist of self.

In their completeness, in the life that was professionally *religious,* religions have always demanded great subordinations of self. Therein lay their creative force. They demanded devotion and gave reasons for that demand. They disentangled the will from the egotistical preoccupations – often very completely. There is no such thing as a self-contained religion, a private religious solo. Certain forms of Protestantism and some mystical types come near to making religion a secluded duet between the individual and his divinity, but here that may be regarded as a perversion of the religious impulse. Just as the normal sexual complex excites and stirs the individual out of his egotism to serve the ends of the race, so the normal religious process takes the individual out of his egotism for the service of the community. It is not a bargain, a "social contract", between the individual and the community; it is a subordination of both the existing individual and the existing community in relation to something, a divinity, a divine order, a standard, a righteousness, more important than either. What is called in the phraseology of certain religions "conviction of sin" and "the flight from the City of Destruction" are familiar instances of this reference of the self-centred individual and the current social life to something far better than either the one or the other.

This is the third element in the religious relationship, a hope, a promise, an objective which turns the convert not only from himself but from the "world", as it is, towards better things. First comes self-disregard, then service, and then this reconstructive creative urgency.

For the finer sort of mind this aspect of religion seems always to have been its primary attraction. One has to remember that there is a real will for religion scattered throughout mankind – a real desire to get away from self. Religion has never pursued its distinctive votaries; they have come to meet it. The desire to give oneself to greater ends than the everyday life affords, and to give oneself freely, is clearly dominant in that minority, and traceable in an incalculable proportion of the majority.

But hitherto religion has never been presented *simply* as a devotion to a universal cause. The devotion has always been in it, but it has been complicated by other considerations. The leaders in every great religious movement have considered it necessary that it should explain itself in the form of history and a cosmogony. It has been felt necessary to say *Why?* and *To what end?* Every religion therefore has had to adopt the physical conceptions, and usually also to assume many of the moral and social values, current at the time of its foundation. It could not transcend the philosophical phrases and attitudes that seemed then to supply the natural frame for a faith, nor draw upon anything beyond the store of scientific knowledge of its time. In this lurked the seed of the ultimate decay and supersession of every successive religion.

But as the idea of continual change, going farther and farther from existing realities and never returning to them, is a new one, as nobody until very recently has grasped the fact that the knowledge of today is the ignorance of tomorrow, each fresh development of religion in the world so far has been proclaimed in perfect good faith as the culminating and final truth.

This finality of statement has considerable immediate practical value. The suggestion of the possibility of further restatement is an unsettling suggestion; it undermines conviction and breaks the ranks of the believers, because there are enormous variations in the capacities of men to recognize the same spirit under a changing shape. Those variations cause endless difficulties today. While some intelligences can recognize the same God under a variety of names and symbols without any severe strain, others cannot even detect the most contrasted Gods one from the other, provided they wear the same mask and title. It appears a perfectly natural and reasonable thing to many minds to restate religion now in terms of biological and psychological necessity, while to others any variation whatever in the phrasing of the faith seems to be nothing less than atheistical misrepresentations of the most damnable kind. For these latter God, a God still anthropomorphic enough to have a will and purpose, to display preferences and reciprocate emotions, to be indeed a person, must be retained until the end of time. For others, God can be thought of as a Great First Cause, as impersonal and inhuman as atomic structure.

It is because of the historical and philosophical commitments they have undertaken, and because of concessions made to common human weaknesses in regard to such once apparently minor but now vital moral issues as property, mental activity, and public veracity – rather than of any inadequacy in their adaptation to psychological needs – that the present wide discredit of organized religions has come about. They no longer seem even roughly truthful upon issues of fact, and they give no imperatives over large fields of conduct in which perplexity is prevalent. People will say, "I could be perfectly happy leading the life of a Catholic devotee if only I could believe." But most of the framework of religious explanation upon which that life is sustained is too old-fashioned and too irrelevant to admit of that thoroughness of belief which is necessary for the devotion of intelligence people.

Great ingenuity has been shown by modern writers and thinkers in the adaptation of venerated religious expressions to new ideas. *Peccavi*. Have I not written of the creative will in humanity as "God the Invisible King" and presented it in the figure of a youthful and adventurous finite god?

The word "God" is in most minds so associated with the concept of religion that it is abandoned only with the greatest reluctance. The word remains, though the idea is continually attenuated. Respect for Him demands that He should have no limitations. He is pushed farther and farther from actually, therefore, and His definition becomes increasingly a bundle of negations, until at last, in His role of The Absolute, He becomes an entirely negative expression. While we can speak of good, say some, we can speak of God. God is the possibility of goodness, the good side of things. If phrases in which the name of God is used are to be abandoned, they argue, religion will be left speechless before many occasions.

Certainly there is something beyond the individual that is and the world that is; on that we have already insisted as a characteristic of all religions; that persuasion is the essence of faith and the key to courage. But whether that is to be considered, even after the most strenuous exercises in personification, as a greater person or a comprehensive person, is another matter. Personality is the last vestige of anthropomorphism. The modern

31

urge to a precise veracity is against such concessions to traditional expression.

On the other hand there is in many fine religious minds a desire amounting almost to a necessity for an object of devotion so individualized as to be capable at least of a receptive consciousness even if no definite response is conceded. One type of mind can accept a reality in itself which another must project and dramatize before it can comprehend it and react to it. The human soul is an intricate thing which will not endure elucidation when that passes beyond a certain degree of harshness and roughness. The human spirit has learnt love, devotion, obedience and humility in relation to other personalities, and with difficulty it takes the final step to a transcendent subordination, from which the last shred of personality has been stripped.

In matters not immediately material, language has to work by metaphors, and though every metaphor carries its own peculiar risks of confusion, we cannot do without them. Great intellectual tolerance is necessary, therefore – a cultivated disposition to translate and retranslate from one metaphysical or emotional idiom to another – if there is not to be a deplorable wastage of moral force in our world. Just now I wrote *Peccavi* because I had written God the Invisible King, but after all I do not think it was so much a sin to use that phrase, God the Invisible King, as an error in expression. If there is no sympathetic personal leader outside us, there is at least in us the attitude we should adopt towards a sympathetic personal leader.

Three profound differences between the new mental dispositions of the present time and those of preceding ages have to be realized if current developments of the religious impulse are to be seen in their correct relationship to the religious life

32

of the past. There has been a great advance in the analysis of psychic processes and the courage with which men have probed into the origins of human thought and feeling. Following upon the biological advances that have made us recognize fish and amphibian in the bodily structure of man, have come these parallel developments in which we see elemental fear and lust and self-love moulded, modified, and exalted, under the stress of social progress, into intricate human motives. Our conception of sin and our treatment of sin have been profoundly modified by this analysis. Our former sins are seen as ignorances, inadequacies and bad habits, and the moral conflict is robbed of three-fourths of its ego-centred melodramatic quality. We are no longer moved to be less wicked; we are moved to organize our conditioned reflexes and lead a life less fragmentary and silly.

Secondly, the conception of individuality has been influenced and relaxed by biological thought, so that we do not think so readily of the individual *contra mundum* as our fathers did. We begin to realize that we are egotists by misapprehension. Nature cheats the self to serve the purpose of the species by filling it with wants that war against its private interests. As our eyes are opened to these things, we see ourselves as beings greater or less than the definitive self. Man's soul is no longer his own. It is, he discovers, part of a greater being which lived before he was born and will survive him. The idea of a survival of the definite individual with all the accidents and idiosyncrasies of his temporal nature upon him dissolves to nothing in this new view of immortality.

The third of the main contrasts between modern and former thought which have rendered the general shapes of established religion old-fashioned and unserviceable is a reorientation of current ideas about time. The powerful disposition of the human mind to explain everything as the inevitable unfolding of a past event which, so to speak, sweeps the future helplessly before it, has been checked by a mass of subtle criticisms. The conception of progress as a broadening and increasing purpose, a conception which is taking hold of the human imagination more and more firmly, turns religious life toward the future. We think no longer of submission to the irrevocable decrees of absolute dominion, but of participation in an adventure on behalf of a power that gains strength and establishes itself. The history of our world, which has been unfolded to us by science, runs counter to all the histories on which religions have been based. There was no Creation in the past, we begin to realize, but eternally there is creation; there was no Fall to account for the conflict of good and evil, but a stormy ascent. Life as we know it is a mere beginning.

It seems unavoidable that if religion is to develop unifying and directive power in the present confusion of human affairs it must adapt itself to this forward-looking, individuality-analyzing turn of mind; it must divest itself of its sacred histories, its gross preoccupations, its posthumous prolongation of personal ends. *The desire for service, for subordination, for permanent effect, for an escape from the distressful pettiness and mortality of the individual life, is the undying element in every religious system.*

The time has come to strip religion right down to that, to strip it for greater tasks than it has ever faced before. The histories and symbols that served our fathers encumber and divide us. Sacraments and rituals harbour disputes and waste our scanty emotions. *The explanation of why things are is an unnecessary effort in religion.* The essential fact in religion is the desire for religion and not how it came about. If you do not want religion, no persuasions, no convictions about your place in the universe can give it to you. The first sentence in the modern creed must be, not "I believe," but "I give myself."

To what? And how? To these questions we will now address ourselves.

CHAPTER SIX

Modern Religion is Objective

To give oneself religiously is a continuing operation expressed in a series of acts. It can be nothing else. You cannot dedicate yourself and then go away to live just as you have lived before. It is a poor travesty of religion that does not produce an essential change in the life which embraces it. But in the established and older religions of our race, this change of conduct has involved much self-abasement merely to the God or Gods, or much self-mortification merely with a view to the moral perfecting of self. Christian devotion, for example, in these early stages, before the hermit life gave place to organized monastic life, did not to any extent direct itself to service except the spiritual service of other human beings. But as Christianity became a definite social organizing force, it took on a great service of healing, comforting, helping, and educational activities.

The modern tendency has been and is all in the direction of minimizing what one might call self-centred devotion and self-subjugation, and of expanding and developing external service. The idea of inner perfectibility dwindles with the diminishing importance attached to individuality. We cease to think of mortifying or exalting or perfecting ourselves and seek to lose

37

ourselves in a greater life. We think less and less of "conquering" self and more and more of escaping from self. If we attempt to perfect ourselves in any respect it is only as a soldier sharpens and polishes an essential weapon.

Our quickened apprehension of continuing change, our broader and fuller vision of the history of life, disabuse our minds of many limitations set to the imaginations of our predecessors. Much that they saw as fixed and determinate, we see as transitory and controllable. They saw life fixed in its species and subjected to irrevocable laws. We see life struggling insecurely but with a gathering successfulness for freedom and power against restriction and death. We see life coming at last to our tragic and hopeful human level. Unprecedented possibilities, mighty problems, we realize, confront mankind today. They frame our existences. The practical aspect, the material form, the embodiment of the modernized religious impulse is the direction of the whole life to the solution of these problems and the realization of their possibilities. The alternative before man now is either magnificence of spirit and magnificence of achievement, or disaster.

The modern religious life, like all forms of religious life, must needs have its own subtle and deep inner activities, its meditations, its self-confrontations, its phases of stress and search and appeal, its serene and prayerful moods, but these inward aspects do not come into the scope of this present inquiry, which is concerned entirely with the outward shape, the direction, and the organization of modern religious effort, with the question of what, given religious devotion, we have to do and how that has to be done.

Now, in the new and greater universe to which we are awakening, its immense possibilities furnish an entirely new frame and setting for the moral life. In the fixed and limited outlook of the past, practical good works took the form mainly of palliative measures against evils that were conceived of as incurable; the religious community nursed the sick, fed the hungry, provided sanctuary for the fugitive, pleaded with the powerful for mercy. It did not dream of preventing sickness, famine, or tyranny. Other-worldliness was its ready refuge from the invincible evil and confusion of the existing scheme of things.

But it is possible now to imagine an order in human affairs from which these evils have been largely or entirely eliminated. More and more people are coming to realize that such an order is a material possibility. And with the realization that this is a material possibility, we can no longer be content with a field of "good deeds" and right action restricted to palliative and consolatory activities. Such things are merely "first aid". The religious mind grows bolder than it has ever been before. It pushes through the curtain it once imagined was a barrier. It apprehends its larger obligations. The way in which our activities conduce to the realization of that conceivable better order in human affairs, becomes the new criterion of conduct. Other-worldliness has become unnecessary.

The realization of this possible better order brings us at once to certain definite lines of conduct. We have to make an end to war, and to make an end to war we must be cosmopolitan in our politics. It is impossible for any clear-headed person to suppose that the ever more destructive stupidities of war can be eliminated from human affairs until some common political control dominates the earth, and unless certain pressures due to the growth of population, due to the enlarging scope of economic operations or due to conflicting standards and traditions of life, are disposed of.

To avoid the positive evils of war and to attain the new levels of prosperity and power that now come into view, an effective world control, not merely of armed force, but of the production and main movements of staple commodities and the drift and expansion of population is required. It is absurd to dream of peace and world-wide progress without that much control. These things assured, the abilities and energies of a greatly increased proportion of human beings could be diverted to the happy activities of scientific research and creative work, with an ever-increasing release and enlargement of human possibility. On the political side it is plain that our lives must be given to the advancement of that union.

Such a forward stride in human life, the first stride in a mighty continuing advance, an advance to which no limit appears, is now not simply materially possible. It is urgent. The opportunity is plain before mankind. It is the alternative to social decay. But there is no certainty, no material necessity, that it should ever be taken. It will not be taken by mankind inadvertently. It can only be taken through such an organization of will and energy to take it as this world has never seen before.

These are the new imperatives that unfold themselves before the more alert minds of our generation. They will presently become the general mental background, as the modern interpretations of the history of life and of the material and mental possibilities about us establish themselves. Evil political, social, and economic usages and arrangements may seem obdurate and huge, but they are neither permanent nor uncontrollable. They can be controlled, however, only by an effort more powerful and determined than the instincts and inertias that sustain them. Religion, modern and disillusioned, has for its outward task to set itself to the control and direction of political, social, and economic life. If it does not do that, then it is no more than a drug for easing discomfort, "the opium of the people".

Can religion, or can it not, synthesize the needed effort to lift mankind out of our present disorders, dangers, baseness, frustrations, and futilities to a phase of relative security, accumulating knowledge, systematic and continuing growth in power and the widespread, deep happiness of hopeful and increasing life?

Our answer here is that the religious spirit, in the light of modern knowledge, can do this thing, and our subject now is to enquire what are the necessary opening stages in the synthesis of that effort. We write, from this point onward, for those who believe that it can, and who do already grasp the implications of world history and contemporary scientific achievement.

CHAPTER SEVEN

What Mankind Has to Do

Before we can consider the forms and methods of attacking this inevitable task of reconstruction it will be well to draw the main lines and to attempt some measure of the magnitude of that task. What are the new forms that it is thus proposed to impose upon human life, and how are they to be evolved from or imposed upon the current forms? And against what passive and active resistances has this to be done?

There can be no pause for replacement in the affairs of life. Day must follow day, and the common activities continue. The new world as a going concern must arise out of the old as a going concern.

Now the most comprehensive conception of this new world is of one politically, socially, and economically unified. Within that frame fall all the other ideas of our progressive ambition. To this end we set our faces and seek to direct our lives. Many there are at present who apprehend it as a possibility but do not *dare*, it seems, to desire it, because of the enormous difficulties that intervene, and because they see as yet no intimations of a way through or round these difficulties. They do not see a way of escape from the patchwork of governments that grips them and divides mankind. The great majority of human beings have still to see the human adventure as one whole; they are obsessed by the air of permanence and finality in established things; they accept current reality as ultimate reality. As the saying goes, they take the world as they find it.

But here we are writing for the modern-minded, and for them it is impossible to think of the world as secure and satisfactory until there exists a single world commonweal, preventing war and controlling those moral, biological, and economic forces and wastages that would otherwise lead to wars. And controlling them in the sense that science and man's realization and control of his powers and possibilities continually increase.

Let us make clear what sort of government we are trying to substitute for the patchwork of today. It will be a new sort of direction with a new psychology. The method of direction of such a world commonweal is not likely to imitate the methods of existing sovereign states. It will be something new and altogether different.

This point is not yet generally realized. It is too often assumed that the world commonweal will be, as it were, just the one heir and survivor of existing states, and that it will be a sort of megatherium of the same form and anatomy as its predecessors.

But a little reflection will show that this is a mistake. Existing states are primarily militant states, and a world state cannot be militant. There will be little need for president or king to lead the marshalled hosts of humanity, for where there is no war there is no need of any leader to lead hosts anywhere, and in a polyglot world a parliament of mankind or any sort of council that meets and talks is an inconceivable instrument of government. The voice will cease to be a suitable vehicle. World government, like scientific process, will be conducted by statement, criticism, and publication that will be capable of efficient translation.

The fundamental organization of contemporary states is plainly still military, and that is exactly what a world organization cannot be. Flags, uniforms, national anthems, patriotism sedulously cultivated in church and school, the brag, blare, and bluster of our competing sovereignties, belong to the phase of development the Open Conspiracy will supersede. We have to get clear of that clutter. The reasonable desire of all of us is that we should have the collective affairs of the world managed by suitably equipped groups of the most interested, intelligent, and devoted people, and that their activities should be subjected to a free, open, watchful criticism, restrained from making spasmodic interruptions but powerful enough to modify or supersede without haste or delay whatever is weakening or unsatisfactory in the general direction.

A number of readers will be disposed to say that this is a very vague, undefined, and complicated conception of world government. But indeed it is a simplification. Not only are the present governments of the world a fragmentary competitive confusion, but none of them is as simple as it appears. They seem to be simple because they have formal heads and definite forms, councils, voting assemblies, and so forth, for arriving at decisions. But the formal heads, the kings, presidents, and so forth, are really not the directive heads. They are merely the figure heads. They do not decide. They merely make gestures of potent and dignified acquiescence when decisions are put to them. They are complicating shams. Nor do the councils and assemblies really decide. They record, often very imperfectly and exasperatingly, the accumulating purpose of outer forces.

These outer really directive forces are no doubt very intricate in their operation; they depend finally on religious and educational forms and upon waves of gregarious feeling, but it does not in the least simplify the process of collective human activity to pretend that it is simple and to set up symbols and dummies in the guise of rulers and dictators to embody that pretence. To recognize the incurable intricacy of collective action is a mental simplification; to remain satisfied with the pretensions of existing governmental institutions, and to bring in all the problems of their procedure and interaction is to complicate the question.

The present rudimentary development of collective psychology obliges us to be vague and provisional about the way in which the collective mind may best define its will for the purpose of administrative action. We may know that a thing is possible and still be unable to do it as yet, just as we knew that aviation was possible in 1900. Some method of decision there must certainly be and a definite administrative machinery. But it may turn out to be a much slighter, less elaborate organization than a consideration of existing methods might lead us to imagine. It may never become one single interlocking administrative system. We may have systems of world control rather than a single world state. The practical regulations, enforcements, and officials needed to keep the world in good health, for example, may be only very loosely related to the system of controls that will maintain its communications in a state of efficiency. Enforcement and legal decisions, as we know them now, may be found to be enormously and needlessly cumbrous by our descendants. As the reasonableness of a thing is made plain, the need for its enforcement is diminished, and the necessity for litigation disappears.

The Open Conspiracy, the world movement for the supercession or enlargement or fusion of existing political, economic, and social institutions must necessarily, as it grows, draw closer and closer to questions of practical control. It is likely in its growth to incorporate many active public servants and many industrial and financial leaders and directors. It may also assimilate great masses of intelligent workers. As its activities spread it will work out a whole system of special methods of co-operation. As it grows, and by growing, it will learn the business of general direction and how to develop its critical function. A lucid, dispassionate, and immanent criticism is the primary necessity, the living spirit of a world civilization. The Open Conspiracy is essentially such a criticism, and the carrying out of such a criticism into working reality is the task of the Open Conspiracy. It will by its very nature be aiming not so much to set up a world direction as to become itself a world direction, and the educational and militant forms of its opening phase will evoke, step by step, as experience is gained and power and responsibility acquired, forms of administration and research and correlation.

The differences in nature and function between the world controls of the future and the state governments of the present age which we have just pointed out favours a hope that the Open Conspiracy may come to its own in many cases rather by the fading out of these state governments through the inhibition and paralysis of their destructive militant and competitive activities than by a direct conflict to overthrow them. As new world controls develop, it becomes the supreme business of the Open Conspiracy to keep them world wide and impartial, to save them by an incessant critical educational and propagandist activity from entanglement with the old traditional rivalries and feuds of states and nations. It is quite possible that such world controls should be able to develop independently, but it is highly probable, on the other hand, that they will continue to be entangled as they are today, and that they will need to be disengaged with a struggle. We repeat, the new directive organizations of men's affairs will not be of the same nature as old-fashioned governments. They will be in their nature biological, financial, and generally economic, and the old governments were primarily nothing of the sort. Their directive force will be (1) an effective criticism having the quality of science, and (2) the growing will in men to have things right. The directive force of the older governments was the uncriticized fantasies and wilfulness of an individual, a class, a tribe, or a majority.

The modernization of the religious impulse leads us straight to this effort for the establishment of the world state as a duty, and the close consideration of the necessary organization of that effort will bring the reader to the conclusion that a movement aiming at the establishment of a world directorate, however restricted that movement may be at first in numbers and power, must either contemplate the prospect of itself developing into a world directorate, and by the digestion and assimilation of superseded factors into an entire modern world community, or admit from the outset the futility, the spare-time amateurishness, of its gestures.

CHAPTER EIGHT

Broad Characteristics of a Scientific
World Commonweal

Continuing our examination of the practical task before the modern mind, we may next note the main lines of contemporary aspiration within this comprehensive outline of a world commonweal. Any sort of unification of human affairs will not serve the ends we seek. We aim at a particular sort of unification; a world Caesar is hardly better from the progressive viewpoint than world chaos; the unity we seek must mean a world-wide liberation of thought, experiment and creative effort.

A successful Open Conspiracy merely to seize governments and wield and retain world power would be at best only the empty frame of success. It might be the exact reverse of success. Release from the threat of war and from the waste of international economic conflicts is a poor release if it demands as its price the loss of all other liberties.

It is because we desire a unification of human direction, not simply for the sake of unity, but as a means of release to happiness and power, that it is necessary, at any cost – in delay, in loss of effective force, in strategic or tactical disadvantage – that the light of free, abundant criticism should play upon that direction and upon the movements and unifying organizations leading to the establishment of that unifying direction.

Man is an imperfect animal and never quite trustworthy in the dark. Neither morally nor intellectually is he safe from lapses. Most of us who are past our first youth know how little we can trust ourselves and are glad to have our activities checked and guarded by a sense of helpful inspection. It is for this reason that a movement to realize the conceivable better state of the world must deny itself the advantages of secret methods or tactical insincerities. It must leave that to its adversaries. We must declare our end plainly from the outset and risk no misunderstandings of our procedure.

The Open Conspiracy against the traditional and now cramping and dangerous institutions of the world must be an Open Conspiracy and cannot remain righteous otherwise. It is lost if it goes underground. Every step to world unity must be taken in the daylight with the understanding sympathy of as many people as possible, or the sort of unity that will be won will be found to be scarcely worth the winning. The essential task would have to be recommenced again within the mere frame of unity thus attained.

This candid attempt to take possession of the whole world, this Open Conspiracy of ours, must be made in the name of and for the sake of science and creative activity. Its aim is to release science and creative activity and every stage in the struggle must be watched and criticized, lest there be any sacrifice of these ends to the exigencies of conflict.

The security of creative progress and creative activity implies a competent regulation of the economic life in the collective interest. There must be food, shelter and leisure for all. The fundamental needs of the animal life must be assured before human life can have free play. Man does not live by bread alone; he eats that he may learn and adventure creatively, but unless he eats he cannot adventure. His life is primarily economic, as a house is primarily a foundation, and economic justice and efficiency must underlie all other activities; but to judge human society and organize political and social activities entirely on economic grounds is to forget the objectives of life's campaign in a preoccupation with supply.

It is true that man, like the animal world in general from which he has risen, in the creature of a struggle for sustenance, but unlike the animals, man can resort to methods of escape from that competitive pressure upon the means of subsistence, which has been the lot of every other animal species. He can restrain the increase in his numbers, and he seems capable of still quite undefined expansions of his productivity per head of population. He can escape therefore from the struggle for subsistence altogether with a surplus of energy such as no other kind of animal species has ever possessed. Intelligent control of population is a possibility which puts man outside competitive processes that have hitherto ruled the modification of species, and he can be released from these processes in no other way.

There is a clear hope that, later, directed breeding will come within his scope, but that goes beyond his present range of practical achievement, and we need not discuss it further here. Suffice it for us here that the world community of our desires, the organized world community conducting and ensuring its own progress, requires a deliberate collective control of population as a primary condition.

There is no strong instinctive desire for multitudinous offspring, as such, in the feminine make-up. The reproductive impulses operate indirectly. Nature ensures a pressure of population through passions and instincts that, given sufficient knowledge, intelligence, and freedom on the part of women, can be satisfactorily gratified and tranquillized, if need be, without the production of numerous children. Very slight adjustments in social and economic arrangements will, in a world of clear available knowledge and straightforward practice in these matters, supply sufficient inducement or discouragement to affect the general birth rate or the birth rate of specific types as the directive sense of the community may consider desirable. So long as the majority of human beings are begotten involuntarily in lust and ignorance, so long does man remain like any other animal under the moulding pressure of competition for subsistence. Social and political processes change entirely in their character when we recognize the possibility and practicability of this fundamental revolution in human biology.

In a world so relieved, the production of staple necessities presents a series of problems altogether less distressful than those of the present scramble for possessions and self-indulgence on the part of the successful, and for work and a bare living on the part of the masses. With the increase of population unrestrained, there was, as the end of the economic process, no practical alternative to a multitudinous equality at the level of bare subsistence, except through such an inequality of economic arrangements as allowed a minority to maintain a higher standard of life by withholding whatever surplus of production it could grasp, from consumption in mere proletarian breeding. In the past and at present, what is called the capitalist system, that is to say the unsystematic exploitation of production by private owners under the protection of the law, has, on the whole, in spite of much waste and conflict, worked beneficially by checking that gravitation to a universal low-grade consumption which would have been the inevitable outcome of a socialism oblivious of biological processes. With effective restraint upon the increase of population, however, entirely new possibilities open out before mankind.

The besetting vice of economic science, orthodox and unorthodox alike, has been the vice of beginning in the air, with current practice and current convictions, with questions of wages, prices, values, and possession, when the profounder issues of human association are really not to be found at all on these levels. The primary issues of human association are biological and psychological, and the essentials of economics are problems in applied physics and chemistry. The first thing we should examine is what we want to do with natural resources, and the next, how to get men to do what has to be done as pleasurably and effectively as possible. Then we should have a standard by which to judge the methods of today.

But the academic economists, and still more so Marx and his followers, refuse to deal with these fundamentals, and, with a stupid pose of sound practical wisdom, insist on opening up their case with an uncritical acceptance of the common antagonism of employers and employed and a long rigmarole about profits and wages. Ownership and expropriated labour are only one set of many possible sets of economic method.

The economists, however, will attend seriously only to the current set; the rest they ignore; and the Marxists, with their uncontrollable disposition to use nicknames in the place of judgements, condemn all others as "Utopian" – a word as final in its dismissal from the minds of the elect as that other pet counter in the Communist substitute for thought, "Bourgeois". If they can persuade themselves that an idea or a statement is "Utopian" or "Bourgeois", it does not seem to matter in the least to them whether it is right or wrong. It is disposed of. Just as in genteeler circles anything is disposed of that can be labelled "atheistical", "subversive" or "disloyal".

If a century and a half ago the world had submitted its problem of transport to the economists, they would have put aside, with as little wasted breath and ink as possible, all talk about railways, motorcars, steamships, and aeroplanes, and, with a fine sense of extravagance rebuked, set themselves to long neuralgic dissertations, disputations, and treatises upon highroads and the methods of connecting them, turnpike gates, canals, the influence of lock fees on bargemen, tidal landing places, anchorages, surplus carrying capacity, carriers, caravans, hand-barrows, and the pedestrianariat. There would have been a rapid and easy differentiation in feeling and requirements between the horse-owning minority and the walking majority; the wrongs of the latter would have tortured the mind of every philosopher who could not ride, and been minimized by every philosopher who could; and there would have been a broad rift between the narrow-footpath school, the no-footpath school, and the school which would look forward to a time when every horse would have to be led along one universal footpath under the dictatorship of the pedestrianariat. All with the profoundest gravity and dignity. These things, footpaths and roads and canals with their traffic, were "real", and "Utopian" projects for getting along at thirty or forty miles an hour or more uphill and against wind and tide, let alone the still more incredible suggestion of air transport, would have been smiled and sneered out of court. Life went about on its legs, with a certain assistance from wheels, or floated, rowed and was blown about on water; so it had been – and so it would always be.

The psychology of economic co-operation is still only dawning, and so the economists and the doctrinaire socialists have had the freest range for pedantry and authoritative pomp. For a hundred years they have argued and argued about "rent", about "surplus value", and so on, and have produced a literature ten thousand times as bulky, dreary, and foolish as the worst outpourings of the mediaeval schoolmen.

But as soon as this time-honoured preoccupation with the allotment of the shares of originators, organizers, workers, owners of material, credit dealers, and tax collectors in the total product, ceases to be dealt with as the primary question in economics; as soon as we liberate our minds from a pre-occupation which from the outset necessarily makes that science a squabble rather than a science, and begin our attack upon the subject with a survey of the machinery and other productive material required in order that the staple needs of mankind should be satisfied, if we go on from that to consider the way in which all this material and machinery can be worked and the product distributed with the least labour and the greatest possible satisfaction, we shift our treatment of economic questions towards standards by which all current methods of exploitation, employment, and finance can be judged rather than wrangled over. We can dismiss the question of the claims of this sort of participant or that, for later and subordinate consideration, and view each variety of human assistance in the general effort entirely from the standpoint of what makes that assistance least onerous and most effective.

The germs of such really scientific economics exist already in the study of industrial organization and industrial psychology. As the science of industrial psychology in particular develops, we shall find all this discussion of ownership, profit, wages, finance, and accumulation, which has been treated hitherto as the primary issues of economics, falling into place under the larger enquiry of what conventions in these matters, what system of money and what conceptions of property, yield the greatest stimulus and the least friction in that world-wide system of co-operation which must constitute the general economic basis to the activities of a unified mankind.

Manifestly the supreme direction of the complex of human economic activities in such a world must centre upon a bureau of information and advice, which will take account of all the resources of the planet, estimate current needs, apportion productive activities and control distribution. The topographical and geological surveys of modern civilized communities, their government maps, their periodic issue of agricultural and industrial statistics, are the first crude and unco-ordinated beginnings of such an economic world intelligence. In the propaganda work of David Lubin, a pioneer whom mankind must not forget, and in his International Institute of Agriculture in Rome, there were the beginnings of an impartial review month by month and year by year of world production, world needs and world transport. Such a great central organization of economic science would necessarily produce direction; it would indicate what had best be done here there, and everywhere, solve general tangles, examine, approve and initiate fresh methods and arrange the transitional process from old to new. It would not be an organization of will, imposing its will upon a reluctant or recalcitrant race; it would be a direction, just as a map is a direction.

A map imposes no will on anyone, breaks no one into its "policy". And yet we obey our maps.

The will to have the map full, accurate and up to date, and the determination to have its indications respected, would have to pervade the whole community. To nourish and sustain that will must be the task not of any particular social or economic division of the community but of the whole body of right-minded people in that community. The organization and preservation of that power of will is the primary undertaking, therefore, of a world revolution aiming at universal peace, welfare and happy activity. And through that will it will produce as the central organ the brain of the modern community, a great encyclopaedic organization, kept constantly up to date and giving approximate estimates and directions for all the material activities of mankind.

The older and still prevalent conception of government is bullying, is the breaking-in and subjugation of the "subject", to the God, or king, or lords of the community. Will-bending, the overcoming of the recalcitrant junior and inferior, was an essential process in the establishment of primitive societies, and its tradition still rules our education and law. No doubt there must be a necessary accommodation of the normal human will to every form of society; no man is innately virtuous; but compulsion and restraint are the friction of the social machine and, other being equal, the less compulsive social arrangement are, the more willingly, naturally, and easily they are accepted, the less wasteful of moral effort and the happier that community will be. The ideal state, other things being equal, is the state with the fewest possible number of will fights and will suppressions. This must be a primary consideration in arranging the economic, biological, and mental organization of the world community at which we aim.

We have advanced the opinion that the control of population pressure is practicable without any violent conflict with "human nature", that given a proper atmosphere of knowledge and intention, there need be far less suppression of will in relation to production than prevails today. In the same way, it is possible that the general economic life of mankind may be made universally satisfactory, that there may be an abundance out of all comparison greater than the existing supply of things necessary for human well-being, freedom, and activity, with not merely not more, but infinitely less subjugation and enslavement than now occurs. Man is still but half born out of the blind struggle for existence, and his nature still partakes of the infinite wastefulness of his mother Nature. He has still to learn how to price the commodities he covets in terms of human life. He is indeed only beginning to realize that there is anything to be learnt in that matter. He wastes will and human possibility extravagantly in his current economic methods.

We know nowadays that the nineteenth century expended a great wealth of intelligence upon a barren controversy between Individualism and Socialism. They were treated as mutually exclusive alternatives, instead of being questions of degree. Human society has been, is, and always must be an intricate system of adjustments between unconditional liberty and the disciplines and subordinations of co-operative enterprise. Affairs do not move simple from a more individualist to a more socialist state or vice versa; there may be a release of individual initiative going on here and standardization or restraint increasing there. Personal property never can be socially guaranteed and yet remain unlimited in action and extent as the extremer individualists desired, nor can it be "abolished" as the extremer socialists proposed. Property is not robbery, as Proudhon asserted; it is the protection of things against promiscuous and mainly wasteful use. Property is not necessarily personal. In some cases property may restrict or forbid a use of things that would be generally advantageous, and it may be and is frequently unfair in its assignment of initiative, but the remedy for that is not an abolition but a revision of property. In the concrete it is a form necessary for liberty of action upon material, while abstracted as money, which is a liquidated generalized form of property; it is a ticket for individual liberty of movement and individual choice of reward.

The economic history of mankind is a history of the operation of the idea of property; it relates the conflict of the unlimited acquisitiveness of egoistic individuals against the resentment of the disinherited and unsuccessful and the far less effective consciousness of a general welfare. Money grew out of a system of abstracting conventions and has been subjected to a great variety of restrictions, monopolizations, and regulations. It has never been an altogether logical device, and it has permitted the most extensive and complex developments of credit, debt, and dispossession. All these developments have brought with them characteristic forms of misuse and corruption. The story is intricate, and the tangle of relationships, of dependence, of pressure, of interception, of misdirected services, crippling embarrassments, and crushing obligations in which we live today admits of no such simple and general solutions as many exponents of socialism, for example, seem to consider possible.

But the thought and investigations of the past century or so have made it clear that a classification of property, according to the nature of the rights exercisable and according to the range of ownership involved, must be the basis of any system of social justice in the future.

Certain things, the ocean, the air, rare wild animals, must be the collective property of all mankind and cannot be altogether safe until they are so regarded, and until some concrete body exists to exercise these proprietary rights. Whatever collective control exists must protect these universal properties, the sea from derelicts, the strange shy things of the wild from extermination by the hunter and the foolish collector. The extinction of many beautiful creatures is one of the penalties our world is paying for its sluggishness in developing a collective common rule. And there are many staple things and general needs that now also demand a unified control in the common interest. The raw material of the earth should be for all, not to be monopolized by any acquisitive individual or acquisitive sovereign state, and not to be withheld from exploitation for the general benefit of any chance claims to territorial priority of this or that backward or bargaining person or tribe.

In the past, most of these universal concerns have had to be left to the competitive enterprise of profit-seeking individuals because there were as yet no collectivities organized to the pitch of ability needed to develop and control these concerns, but surely nobody in his senses believes that the supply and distribution of staple commodities about the earth by irresponsible persons and companies working entirely for monetary gain is the best possible method from the point of view of the race as a whole. The land of the earth, all utilizable natural products, have fallen very largely under the rules and usages of personal property because in the past that was the only recognized and practicable form of administrative proprietorship. The development both of extensive proprietary companies and of government departments with economic functions has been a matter of the last few countries, the development, that is to say, of communal, more or less impersonal ownership, and it is only through these developments that the idea of organized collectivity of proprietorship has become credible.

Even in quite modern state enterprises there is a tendency to recall the rôle of the vigilant, jealous, and primitive personal proprietor in the fiction of ownership by His Majesty the King. In Great Britain, for example, Georgius Rex is still dimly supposed to hover over the Postmaster General of his Post Office, approve, disapprove, and call him to account. But the Postal Union of the world which steers a registered letter from Chile to Norway or from Ireland to Pekin is almost completely divorced from the convention of an individual owner. It works; it is criticized without awe or malice. Except for the stealing and steaming of letters practised by the political police of various countries, it works fairly well. And the only force behind it to keep it working well is the conscious common sense of mankind.

But when we have stipulated for the replacement of individual private ownership by more highly organized forms of collective ownership, subject to free criticism and responsible to the whole republic of mankind, in the general control of sea and land, in the getting, preparation, and distribution of staple products and in transport, we have really named all the possible generalizations of concrete ownership that the most socialistic of contemporaries will be disposed to demand. And if we add to that the necessary maintenance of a money system by a central world authority upon a basis that will make money keep faith with the worker who earns it, and represent from first to last for him the value in staple commodities he was given to understand it was to have, and if we conceive credit adequately controlled in the general interest by a socialized world banking organization, we shall have defined the entire reason from which individual property and unrestricted individual enterprise have been excluded. Beyond that, the science of social psychology will probably assure us that the best work will be done for the world by individuals free to exploit their abilities as they wish. If the individual landowner or mineral-owner disappears altogether from the world, he will probably be replaced over large areas by tenants with considerable security of tenure, by householders and by licensees under collective proprietors. It will be the practice, the recognized best course, to allow the cultivator to profit as fully as possible by his own individual productivity and to leave the householder to fashion his house and garden after his own desire.

Such in the very broadest terms is the character of the world commonweal towards which the modern imagination is moving, so far as its direction and economic life are concerned. The organization of collective bodies capable of exercising these wider proprietorships, which cannot be properly used in the common interest by uncorrelated individual owners, is the positive practical problem before the intelligent portion of mankind today. The nature of such collective bodies is still a series of open questions, even upon such points as whether they will be elected bodies or groups deriving their authority from other sanctions. Their scope and methods of operations, their relations to one another and to the central bureau of intelligence, remain also to be defined. But before we conclude this essay we may be able to find precisions for at least the beginning of such definition.

Nineteenth-century socialism in its various forms, including the highly indurated formulae of communism, has been a series of projects for the establishment of such collective controls, for the most part very sketchy projects from which the necessary factor of a sound psychological analysis was almost completely wanting. Primarily movements of protest and revolt against the blazing injustices arising out of the selfishly individualistic exploitation of the new and more productive technical and financial methods of the eighteenth and nineteenth centuries, they have been apt to go beyond the limits of reasonable socialization in their demands and to minimize absurdly the difficulties and dangers of collective control. Indignation and impatience were their ruling moods, and if they constructed little they exposed much. We are better able to measure the magnitude of the task before us because of the clearances and lessons achieved by these pioneer movements.

CHAPTER NINE

No Stable Utopia is Now Conceivable

This unified world towards which the Open Conspiracy would direct its activities cannot be pictured for the reader as any static and stereotyped spectacle of happiness. Indeed, one may doubt if such a thing as happiness is possible without steadily changing conditions involving continually enlarging and exhilarating opportunities. Mankind, released from the pressure of population, the waste of warfare and the private monopolization of the sources of wealth, will face the universe with a great and increasing surplus of will and energy. Change and novelty will be the order of life; each day will differ from its predecessor in its great amplitude of interest. Life which was once routine, endurance, and mischance will become adventure and discovery. It will no longer be "the old, old story".

We have still barely emerged from among the animals in their struggle for existence. We live only in the early dawn of human self-consciousness and in the first awakening of the spirit of mastery. We believe that the persistent exploration of our outward and inward worlds by scientific and artistic endeavour will lead to developments of power and activity upon which at present we can set no limits nor give any certain form.

Our antagonists are confusion of mind, want of courage, want of curiosity and want of imagination, indolence, and spendthrift egotism. These are the enemies against which the Open Conspiracy arrays itself; these are the jailers of human freedom and achievement.

Chapter Ten

The Open Conspiracy is Not to be Thought of
as a Single Organization; It is a Conception
of Life out of which Efforts, Organizations,
and new Orientations Will Arise

This open and declared intention of establishing a world
order out of the present patchwork of particularist
governments, of effacing the militarist conceptions that
have hitherto given governments their typical form, and of re-
moving credit and the broad fundamental processes of economic
life out of reach of private profit-seeking and individual
monopolization, which is the substance of this Open Conspiracy
to which the modern religious mind must necessarily address its
practical activities, cannot fail to arouse enormous opposition. It
is not a creative effort in a clear field; it is a creative effort that
can hardly stir without attacking established things. It is the
repudiation of drift, of "leaving things alone". It criticizes
everything in human life from the top to the bottom and finds
everything not good enough. It strikes at the universal human
desire to feel that things are "all right".

One might conclude, and it would be a hasty, unsound conclusion, that the only people to whom we could look for sympathy and any passionate energy in forwarding the revolutionary change would be the unhappy, the discontented, the dispossessed, and the defeated in life's struggle. This idea lies at the root of the class-war dogmas of the Marxists, and it rests on an entirely crude conception of human nature. The successful minority is supposed to have no effective motive but a desire to retain and intensify its advantages. A quite imaginary solidarity to that end is attributed to it, a preposterous, base class activity. On the other hand, the unsuccessful mass – "proletariat" – is supposed to be capable of a clear apprehension of its disadvantages, and the more it is impoverished and embittered, the clearer-minded it becomes, and the nearer draws its uprising, its constructive "dictatorship", and the Millennium.

No doubt a considerable amount of truth is to be found in this theory of the Marxist revolution. Human beings, like other animals, are disposed to remain where their circumstances are tolerable and to want change when they are uncomfortable, and so a great proportion of the people who are "well off" want little or no change in present conditions, particularly those who are too dull to be bored by an unprogressive life, while a great proportion of those who actually feel the inconveniences of straitened means and population pressure, do. But much vaster masses of the rank and file of humanity are accustomed to inferiority and dispossession, they do not feel these things to the extent even of desiring change, or even if they do feel their disadvantages, they still fear change more than they dislike their disadvantages. Moreover, those who are sufficiently distressed to realize that "something ought to be done about it" are much more disposed to childish and threatening demands upon heaven and the government for redress and vindictive and punitive action against the envied fortunate with whom they happen to be in immediate contact, than to any reaction towards such complex, tentative, disciplined constructive work as alone can better the lot of mankind. In practice Marxism is found to work out in a ready resort to malignantly destructive activities, and to be so uncreative as to practically impotent in the face of material difficulties. In Russia, where – in and about the urban centres, at least – Marxism has been put to the test, the doctrine of the Workers' Republic remains as a unifying cant, a test of orthodoxy of as little practical significance there as the communism of Jesus and communion with Christ in Christendom, while beneath this creed a small oligarchy which has attained power by its profession does its obstinate best, much hampered by the suspicion and hostility of the Western financiers and politicians, to carry on a series of interesting and varyingly successful experiments in the socialization of economic life. Here we have no scope to discuss the NEP and the Five Year Plan. They are dealt with in *The Work, Wealth, and Happiness of Mankind.* Neither was properly Communist. The Five Year Plan is carried out as an autocratic state capitalism. Each year shows more and more clearly that Marxism and Communism are divagations from the path of human progress and that the line of advance must follow a course more intricate and less flattering to the common impulses of our nature.

The one main strand of truth in the theory of social development woven by Marx and Engels is that successful, comfortable people are disposed to dislike, obstruct and even resist actively any substantial changes in the current patchwork

69

of arrangements, however great the ultimate dangers of that patchwork may be or the privations and sufferings of other people involved in it. The one main strand of error in that theory is the facile assumption that the people at a disadvantage will be stirred to anything more than chaotic and destructive expressions of resentment. If now we reject the error and accept the truth, we lose the delusive comfort of belief in that magic giant, the Proletariat, who will dictate, arrange, restore, and create, but we clear the way for the recognition of an elite of intelligent, creative-minded people scattered through the whole community, and for a study of the method of making this creative element effective in human affairs against the massive oppositions of selfishness and unimaginative self-protective conservatism.

Now, certain classes of people such as thugs and burglars seem to be harmful to society without a redeeming point about them, and others, such as racecourse bookmakers, seem to provide the minimum of distraction and entertainment with a maximum of mischief. Wilful idlers are a mere burthen on the community. Other social classes again, professional soldiers, for example, have a certain traditional honourableness which disguises the essentially parasitic relationship of their services to the developing modern community. Armies and armaments are cancers produced by the malignant development of the patriotic virus under modern conditions of exaggeration and mass suggestion. But since there are armies prepared to act coercively in the world today, it is necessary that the Open Conspiracy should develop within itself the competence to resist military coercion and combat and destroy armies that stand in the way of its emergence. Possibly the first two types here instanced may be condemned as classes and excluded as classes from any participation in the organized effort to recast the world, but quite obviously the soldier cannot. The world commonweal will need its own scientific methods of protection so long as there are people running about the planet with flags and uniforms and weapons, offering violence to their fellow men and interfering with the free movements of commodities in the name of national sovereignty.

And when we come to the general functioning classes, landowners, industrial organizers, bankers, and so forth, who control the present system, such as it is, it should be still plainer that it is very largely from the ranks of these classes, and from their stores of experience and traditions of method, that the directive forces of the new order must emerge. The Open Conspiracy can have nothing to do with the heresy that the path of human progress lies through an extensive class war.

Let us consider, for example, how the Open Conspiracy stands to such a complex of activities, usages, accumulations, advantages as constitutes the banking world. There are no doubt many bankers and many practices in banking which make for personal or group advantage to the general detriment. They forestall, monopolize, constrain, and extort, and so increase their riches. And another large part of that banking world follows routine and established usage; it is carrying on and keeping things going, and it is neither inimical nor conducive to the development of a progressive world organization of finance. But there remains a residuum of original and intelligent people in banking or associated with banking or mentally interested in banking, who do realize that banking plays a very important and interesting part in the world's affairs, who are curious about their own intricate function and disposed towards a scientific investigation of its origins, conditions, and future possibilities. Such types move naturally towards the Open Conspiracy. Their enquiries carry them inevitably outside the bankers' habitual field to an examination of the nature, drift, and destiny of the entire economic process.

Now the theme of the preceding paragraph might be repeated with variations through a score of paragraphs in which appropriate modifications would adapt it to the industrial organizer, the merchant and organizer of transport, the advertiser, the retail distributor, the agriculturalist, the engineer, the builder, the economic chemist, and a number of other types functional in the contemporary community. In all we should distinguish firstly, a base and harmful section, than a mediocre section following established usage, and lastly, an active, progressive section to whom we turn naturally for developments leading towards the progressive world commonweal of our desires. And our analysis might penetrate further than separation into types of individuals. In nearly every individual instance we should find a mixed composition, a human being of fluctuating moods and confused purposes, sometimes base, sometimes drifting with the tide and sometimes alert and intellectually and morally quickened. The Open Conspiracy must be content to take a fraction of a man, as it appeals to fractions of many classes, if it cannot get him altogether.

This idea of drawing together a proportion of all or nearly all the functional classes in contemporary communities in order to weave the beginnings of a world community out of their selection is a fairly obvious one – and yet it has still to win practical recognition. Man is a morbidly gregarious and partisan creature; he is deep in his immediate struggles and stands by his own kind because in so doing he defends himself; the industrialist is best equipped to criticize his fellow industrialist, but he finds the root of all evil in the banker; the wages worker shifts the blame for all social wrongs on the "employing class". There is an element of exasperation in most economic and social reactions, and there is hardly a reforming or revolutionary movement in history which is not essentially an indiscriminate attack of one functioning class or type upon another, on the assumption that the attacked class is entirely to blame for the clash and that the attacking class is self-sufficient in the commonweal and can dispense with its annoying collaborator. A considerable element of justice usually enters into such recriminations. But the Open Conspiracy cannot avail itself of these class animosities for its driving force. It can have, therefore, no uniform method of approach. For each class it has a conception of modification and development, and each class it approaches therefore at a distinctive angle. Some classes, no doubt, it would supersede altogether; others – the scientific investigator, for example – it must regard as almost wholly good and seek only to multiply and empower, but it can no more adopt the prejudices and extravagances of any particular class as its basis than it can adopt the claims of any existing state or empire.

When it is clearly understood that the binding links of the Open Conspiracy we have in mind are certain broad general ideas, and that – except perhaps in the case of scientific workers – we have no current set of attitudes of mind and habits of activity which we can turn over directly and unmodified to the service of the conspiracy, we are in a position to realize that the movement we contemplate must from the outset be diversified in its traditions and elements and various in its methods. It must fight upon several fronts and with many sorts of equipment. It will have a common spirit, but it is quite conceivable that between many of its contributory factors there may be very wide gaps in understanding and sympathy. It is no sort of simple organization.

CHAPTER ELEVEN

Forces and Resistances in the Great Modern
Communities Now Prevalent, which are Antagonistic
to the Open Conspiracy. The War with Tradition

We have now stated broadly but plainly the idea of the world commonweal which is the objective of the Open Conspiracy, and we have made a preliminary examination of the composition of that movement, showing that it must be necessarily not a class development, but a convergence of many different sorts of people upon a common idea. Its opening task must be the elaboration, exposition, and propaganda of this common idea, a steady campaign to revolutionize education and establish a modern ideology in men's minds and, arising out of this, the incomparably vaster task of the realization of its ideas.

These are tasks not to be done *in vacuo;* they have to be done in a dense world of crowding, incessant, passionate, uncoordinated activities, the world of market and newspaper, seedtime and harvest, births, deaths, jails, hospitals, riots, barracks and army manoeuvres, false prophets and royal processions, games and shows, fire, storm, pestilence, earthquake, war. Every day and every hour things will be happening to help or thwart, stimulate or undermine, obstruct or defeat the creative effort to set up the world commonweal.

Before we go on to discuss the selection and organization of these heterogeneous and mainly religious impulses upon which we rest our hopes of greater life for mankind, before we plan how these impulses may be got together into a system of co-ordinated activities, it will be well to review the main antagonistic forces with which, from its very inception, the Open Conspiracy will be — is now — in conflict.

To begin with, we will consider these forces as they present themselves in the highly developed Western European States of today and in their American derivatives, derivatives which, in spite of the fact that in most cases they have far outgrown their lands of origin, still owe a large part of their social habits and political conceptions to Europe. All these States touch upon the Atlantic or its contributory seas; they have all grown to their present form since the discovery of America; they have a common tradition rooting in the ideas of Christendom and a generic resemblance of method. Economically and socially they present what is known in current parlance as the Capitalist system, but it will relieve us of a considerable load of disputatious matter if we call them here simply the "Atlantic" civilizations and communities.

The consideration of these Atlantic civilizations in relation to the coming world civilization will suffice for the present chapter. Afterwards we will consider the modification of the forces antagonistic to the Open Conspiracy as they display themselves beyond the formal confines of these now dominant states in the world's affairs, in the social systems weakened and injured by their expansion, and among such less highly organized communities as still survive from man's savage and barbaric past.

The Open Conspiracy is not necessarily antagonistic to any existing government. The Open Conspiracy is a creative, organizing movement and not an anarchistic one. It does not want to destroy existing controls and forms of human association, but either to supersede or amalgamate them into a common world directorate. If constitutions, parliaments, and kings can be dealt with as provisional institutions, trustees for the coming of age of the world commonweal, and in so far as they are conducted in that spirit, the Open Conspiracy makes no attacks upon them.

But most governments will not set about their business as in any way provisional; they and their supporters insist upon a reverence and obedience which repudiate any possibility of supersession. What should be an instrument becomes a divinity. In nearly every country of the world there is, in deference to the pretended necessities of a possible war, a vast degrading and dangerous cultivation of loyalty and mechanical subservience to flags, uniforms, presidents and kings. A president or king who does his appointed work well and righteously is entitled to as much subservience as a bricklayer who does his work well and righteously and to no more, but instead there is a sustained endeavour to give him the privileges of an idol above criticism or reproach, and the organized worship of flags has become – with changed conditions of intercourse and warfare – an entirely evil misdirection of the gregarious impulses of our race. Emotion and sentimentality are evoked in the cause of disciplines and co-operations that could quite easily be sustained and that are better sustained by rational conviction.

The Open Conspiracy is necessarily opposed to all such implacable loyalties, and still more so to the aggressive assertion and propaganda of such loyalties. When these things take the form of suppressing reasonable criticism and forbidding even the suggestion of other forms of government, they become plainly antagonists to any comprehensive project for human welfare. They become manifestly, from the wider point of view, seditious, and loyalty to "king and country" passes into plain treason to mankind. Almost everywhere, at present, educational institutions organize barriers in the path of progress, and there are only the feeblest attempts at any counter education that will break up these barriers. There is little or no effort to restrain the aggressive nationalist when he waves his flag against the welfare of our race, or to protect the children of the world from the infection of his enthusiasms. And this last is as true now of the American system as it is of any European State.

In the great mass of the modern community there is little more than a favourable acquiescence in patriotic ideas and in the worship of patriotic symbols, and that is based largely on such training. These things are not necessary things for the generality of today. A change of mental direction would be possible for the majority of people now without any violent disorganization of their intimate lives or any serious social or economic readjustments for them. Mental infection in such cases could be countered by mental sanitation. A majority of people in Europe, and a still larger majority in the United States and the other American Republics, could become citizens of the world without any serious hindrance to their present occupations, and with an incalculably vast increase of their present security.

But there remains a net of special classes in every community, from kings to custom-house officers, far more deeply involved in patriotism because it is their trade and their source of honour, and prepared in consequence with an instinctive resistance to any reorientation of ideas towards a broader outlook. In the case of such people no mental sanitation is possible without dangerous and alarming changes in their way of living. For the majority of these patriots by *métier*, the Open Conspiracy unlocks the gates leading from a fussy paradise of eminence, respect, and privilege, and motions them towards an austere wilderness which does not present even the faintest promise of a congenial, distinguished life for them. Nearly everything in human nature will dispose them to turn away from these gates which open towards the world peace, to bang-to and lock them again if they can, and to grow thickets as speedily as possible to conceal them and get them forgotten. The suggestion of being trustees in a transition will seem to most of such people only the camouflage of an ultimate degradation.

From such classes of patriots by *métier*, it is manifest that the Open Conspiracy can expect only opposition. It may detach individuals from them, but only by depriving them of their essential class loyalties and characteristics. The class as a class will remain none the less antagonistic. About royal courts and presidential residences, in diplomatic, consular, military, and naval circles, and wherever people wear titles and uniforms and enjoy pride and precedences based on existing political institutions, there will be the completest general inability to grasp the need for the Open Conspiracy. These people and their womankind, their friends and connections, their servants and dependents, are fortified by time-honoured traditions of social usage, of sentiment and romantic prestige. They will insist that they are reality and Cosmopolis a dream. Only individuals of exceptional liveliness, rare intellectual power, and innate moral force can be expected to break away from the anti-progressive habits such class conditions impose upon them.

This tangle of traditions and loyalties, of interested trades and professions, of privileged classes and official patriots, this complex of human beings embodying very easy and natural and time-honoured ideas of eternal national separation and unending international and class conflict, is the main objective of the Open Conspiracy in its opening phase. This tangle must be disentangled as the Open Conspiracy advances, and until it is largely disentangled and cleared up that Open Conspiracy cannot become anything very much more than a desire and a project.

This tangle of "necessary patriots", as one may call them, is different in its nature, less intricate and extensive proportionally in the United States and the States of Latin America, than it is in the old European communities, but it is none the less virulent in its action on that account. It is only recently that military and naval services have become important factors in American social life, and the really vitalizing contact of the interested patriot and the State has hitherto centred mainly upon the custom house and the concession. Instead of a mellow and romantic loyalty to "king and country" the American thinks simply of America and his flag.

The American exaggeration of patriotism began as a resistance to exploitation from overseas. Even when political and fiscal freedom were won, there was a long phase of industrial and financial dependence. The American's habits of mind, in spite of his recent realization of the enormous power and relative prosperity of the United States and of the expanding possibilities of their Spanish and Portuguese-speaking neighbours, are still largely self-protective against a now imaginary European peril. For the first three quarters of the nineteenth century the people of the American continent, and particularly the people of the United States, felt the industrial and financial ascendancy of Great Britain and had a reasonable fear of European attacks upon their continent. A growing tide of immigrants of uncertain sympathy threatened their dearest habits. Flag worship was imposed primarily as a repudiation of Europe. Europe no longer looms over America with over-powering intimations, American industries no longer have any practical justification for protection, American finance would be happier without it, but the patriotic interests are so established now that they go on and will go on. No American statesman who ventures to be cosmopolitan in his utterance and outlook is likely to escape altogether from the raucous attentions of the patriotic journalist.

We have said that the complex of classes in any country interested in the current method of government is sustained by traditions and impelled by its nature and conditions to protect itself against exploratory criticism. It is therefore unable to escape from the forms of competitive and militant nationalism in which it was evolved. It cannot, without grave danger of enfeeblement, change any such innate form. So that while parallel complexes of patriotic classes are found in greater or less intricacy grouped about the flags and governments of most existing states, these complexes are by their nature obliged to remain separate, nationalist, and mutually antagonistic. You cannot expect a world union of soldiers or diplomatists. Their existence and nature depend upon the idea that national separation is real and incurable, and that war, in the long run, is unavoidable. Their conceptions of loyalty involve an antagonism to all foreigners, even to foreigners of exactly the same types as themselves, and make for a continual campaign of annoyances, suspicions, and precautions – together with a general propaganda, affecting all other classes, of the necessity of an international antagonism – that creeps persistently towards war.

But while the methods of provoking war employed by the patriotic classes are traditional, modern science has made a new and enormously more powerful thing of warfare and, as the Great War showed, even the most conservative generals on both sides are unable to prevent the gigantic interventions of the mechanician and the chemist. So that a situation is brought about in which the militarist element is unable to fight without the support of the modern industrial organization and the acquiescence of the great mass of people. We are confronted therefore at the present time with the paradoxical situation that a patriotic tradition sustains in power and authority warlike classes who are quite incapable of carrying on war. The other classes to which they must go for support when the disaster of war is actually achieved are classes developed under peace conditions, which not only have no positive advantage in war, but must, as a whole, suffer great dislocation, discomfort, destruction, and distress from war. It is of primary importance therefore, to the formally dominant classes that these new social masses and powers should remain under the sway of the old social, sentimental, and romantic traditions, and equally important is it to the Open Conspiracy that they should be released.

Here we bring into consideration another great complex of persons, interests, traditions – the world of education, the various religious organizations, and, beyond these, the ramifying, indeterminate world of newspapers and other periodicals, books, the drama, art, and all the instruments of presentation and suggestion that mould opinion and direct action. The sum of the operations of this complex will be either to sustain or to demolish the old nationalist militant ascendancy. Its easiest immediate course is to accept it. Educational organizations on that account are now largely a conservative force in the community; they are in most cases directly controlled by authority and bound officially as well as practically to respect current fears and prejudices. It evokes fewer difficulties for them if they limit and mould rather than release the young. The schoolmaster tends, therefore, to accept and standardize and stereotype, even in the living, progressive fields of science and philosophy. Even there he is a brake on the forward movement. It is clear that the Open Conspiracy must either continually disturb and revivify him or else frankly antagonize him. Universities also struggle between the honourable past on which their prestige rests, and the need of adaptation to a world of enquiry, experiment, and change. It is an open question whether these particular organizations of intellectual prestige are of any real value in the living world. A modern world planned *de novo* would probably produce nothing like a contemporary university. Modern research, one may argue, would be stimulated rather than injured by complete detachment from the lingering mediaevalism of such institutions, their entanglement with adolescent education, and their ancient and contagious conceptions of precedence and honour.

Ordinary religious organizations, again, exist for self-preservation and are prone to follow rather than direct the currents of popular thought. They are kept alive, indeed, by revivalism and new departures which at the outset they are apt to resist, as the Catholic Church, for instance, resisted the Franciscan awakening, but their formal disposition is conservative. They say to religious development, thus far and no farther.

Here, in school, college, and church, are activities of thought and instruction which, generally speaking, drag upon the wheels of progress, but which need not necessarily do so. A schoolmaster may be original, stimulating, and creative, and if he is fortunate and a good fighter he may even achieve considerable worldly success; university teachers and investigators may strike out upon new lines and yet escape destruction by the older dons. Universities compete against other universities at home and abroad and cannot altogether yield to the forces of dullness and subservience. They must maintain a certain difference from vulgar opinion and a certain repute of intellectual virility.

As we pass from the more organized to the less organized intellectual activities, we find conservative influence declining in importance, and a freer play for the creative drive. Freshness is a primary condition of journalistic, literary, and artistic success, and orthodoxy has nothing new to say or do. But the desire for freshness may be satisfied all too readily by merely extravagant, superficial, and incoherent inventions.

The influence of this old traditional nationalist social and political hierarchy which blocks the way to the new world is not, however, exerted exclusively through its control over schools and universities. Nor is that indeed its more powerful activity. Would that it were! There is also a direct, less defined contact of the old order with the nascent powers, that plays a far more effective part in delaying the development of the modern world commonweal. Necessarily the old order has determined the established way of life, which is, at its best, large, comfortable, amusing, respected. It possesses all the entrances and exits and all the controls of the established daily round. It is able to exact, and it does exact, almost without design, many conformities. There can be no very ample social life, therefore, for those who are conspicuously dissentient. Again the old order has a complete provision for the growth, welfare, and advancement of its children. It controls the founts of honour and self-respect; it provides a mapped-out world of behaviour. The new initiatives make their appearance here and there in the form of isolated individuals, here an inventor, there a bold organizer or a vigorous thinker. Apart from his specific work the innovating type finds that he must fall in with established things or his womenfolk will be ostracized, and he will be distressed by a sense of isolation even in the midst of successful activities. The more intensely he innovates in particular, the more likely is he to be to busy to seek out kindred souls and organize a new social life in general. The new things and ideas, even when they arise abundantly, arise scattered and unorganized, and the old order takes them in its net. America for example – both on its Latin and on its English-speaking side – is in many ways a triumph of the old order over the new.

Men like Winwood Reade thought that the New World would be indeed a new world. They idealized its apparent emancipations. But as the more successful of the toiling farmers and traders of republican America rose one by one to affluence, leisure, and freedom, it was far more easy for them to adopt the polished and prepared social patterns and usages of Europe than to work out a new civilization in accordance with their equalitarian professions. Yet there remains a gap in their adapted "Society". Henry James, that acute observer of subtle social flavours, has pointed out the peculiar *headlessness* of social life in America because of the absence of court functions to "go on" to and justify the assembling and dressing. The social life has imitated the preparation for the Court without any political justification. In Europe the assimilation of the wealthy European industrialist and financier by the old order has been parallel and naturally more logically complete. He really has found a court to "go on" to. His social scheme was still undecapitated until kingdoms began to change into republics after 1917.

In this way the complex of classes vitally involved in the old militant nationalist order is mightily reinforced by much larger masses of imitative and annexed and more or less assimilated rich and active people. The great industrialist has married the daughter of the marquis and has a couple of sons in the Guards and a daughter who is a princess. The money of the American Leeds, fleeing from the social futility of its land of origin, helped bolster up a mischievous monarchy in Greece. The functional and private lives of the new men are thus at war with one another. The real interests of the great industrialist or financier lie in cosmopolitan organization and the material development of the world commonweal, but his womenfolk pin flags all over him, and his sons are prepared to sacrifice themselves and all his business creations for the sake of trite splendours and Ruritanian romance.

But just so far as the great business organizer is capable and creative, so far is he likely to realize and resent the price in frustration that the old order obliges him to pay for amusement, social interest, and domestic peace and comfort. The Open Conspiracy threatens him with no effacement; it may even appear with an air of release. If he had women who were interested in his business affairs instead of women who had to be amused, and if he realized in time the practical, intellectual, and moral kidnapping of his sons and daughters by the old order that goes on, he might pass quite easily from acquiescence to antagonism. But in this respect he cannot act single-handed. This is a social and not an individual operation. The Open Conspiracy, it is clear, must include in its activities a great fight for the souls of economically-functional people. It must carve out a Society of its own from Society. Only by the creation of a new and better social life can it resist the many advantages and attractions of the old.

This constant gravitation back to traditional uses on the part of what might become new social types applies not merely to big people but to such small people as are really functional in the modern economic scheme. They have no social life adapted to their new economic relationships, and they are forced back upon the methods of behaviour established for what were roughly their analogues in the old order of things. The various sorts of managers and foremen in big modern concerns, for example, carry on ways of living they have taken ready-made from the stewards, tradesmen, tenantry, and upper servants of an aristocratic territorial system. They release themselves and are released almost in spite of themselves, slowly, generation by generation, from habits of social subservience that are no longer necessary nor convenient in the social process, acquire an official pride in themselves and take on new conceptions of responsible loyalty to a scheme. And they find themselves under suggestions of class aloofness and superiority to the general mass of less cardinal workers, that are often unjustifiable under new conditions. Machinery and scientific organization have been and still are revolutionizing productive activity by the progressive elimination of the unskilled worker, the hack, the mere toiler. But the social organization of the modern community and the mutual deportment of the associated workers left over after this elimination are still haunted by the tradition of the lord, the middle-class tenant, and the servile hind. The development of self-respect and mutual respect among the mass of modern functional workers is clearly an intimate concern of the Open Conspiracy.

A vast amount of moral force has been wasted in the past hundred years by the antagonism of "Labour" to "Capital", as though this were the primary issue in human affairs. But this never was the primary issue, and it is steadily receding from its former importance. The ancient civilizations did actually rest upon a broad basis of slavery and serfdom. Human muscle was a main source of energy – ranking with sun, wind, and flood. But invention and discovery have so changed the conditions under which power is directed and utilized that muscle becomes economically secondary and inessential. We no longer want hewers of wood and drawers of water, carriers and pick and spade men. We no longer want that breeding swarm of hefty sweaty bodies without which the former civilizations could not have endured. We want watchful and understanding guardians and drivers of complex delicate machines, which can be mishandled and brutalized and spoilt all too easily. The less disposed these masters of our machines are to inordinate multiplication, the more room and food in the world for their ampler lives. Even to the lowest level of a fully-mechanicalized civilization it is required that the human element should be select. In the modern world, crowds are a survival, and they will presently be an anachronism, and crowd psychology therefore cannot supply the basis of a new order.

It is just because labour is becoming more intelligent, responsible, and individually efficient that it is becoming more audible and impatient in social affairs. It is just because it is no longer mere gang labour, and is becoming more and more intelligent co-operation in detail, that it now resents being treated as a serf, housed like a serf, and herded like a serf, and its pride and thoughts and feelings disregarded. Labour is in revolt because as a matter of fact it is, in the ancient and exact sense of the word, ceasing to be labour at all.

The more progressive elements of the directive classes recognize this, but, as we have shown, there are formidable forces still tending to maintain the old social attitudes when arrogance became the ruler and the common man accepted his servile status. A continual resistance is offered by large sections of the prosperous and advantaged to the larger claims of the modernized worker, and in response the rising and differentiating workers develop an angry antagonism to these directive classes which allow themselves to be controlled by their conservative and reactionary elements. Moreover, the increasing relative intelligence of the labour masses, the unprecedented imaginative stimulation they experience, the continually more widespread realization of the available freedoms and comforts and indulgences that might be and are not shared by all in a modern state, develop a recalcitrance where once there was little but fatalistic acquiescence. An objection to direction and obligation, always mutely present in the toiling multitude since the economic life of man began, becomes articulate and active. It is the taste of freedom that makes labour desire to be free. This series of frictions is a quite inevitable aspect of social reorganization, but it does not constitute a primary antagonism in the process.

The class war was invented by the classes; it is a natural tradition of the upper strata of the old order. It was so universally understood that there was no need to state it. It is implicit in nearly all the literature of the world before the nineteenth century – except the Bible, the Koran, and other sequelae. The "class war" of the Marxist is merely a poor snobbish imitation, a *tu quoque*, a pathetic, stupid, indignant reversal of and retort to the old arrogance, a pathetic *upward* arrogance.

These conflicts cut across rather than oppose or help the progressive development to which the Open Conspiracy devotes itself. Labour, awakened, enquiring, and indignant, is not necessarily progressive; if the ordinary undistinguished worker is no longer to be driven as a beast of burthen, he has – which also goes against the grain – to be educated to as high a level of co-operative efficiency as possible. He has to work better, even if he works for much shorter hours and under better conditions, and his work must be subordinated work still; he cannot become *en masse* sole owner and master of a scheme of things he did not make and is incapable of directing. Yet this is the ambition implicit in an exclusively "Labour" movement. Either the Labour revolutionary hopes to cadge the services of exceptional people without acknowledgment or return on sentimental grounds, or he really believes that anyone is as capable as anyone else – if not more so. The worker at a low level may be flattered by dreams of "class-conscious" mass dominion from which all sense of inferiority is banished, but they will remain dreams. The deep instinctive jealousy of the commonplace individual for outstanding quality and novel initiative may be organized and turned to sabotage and destruction, masquerading as and aspiring to be a new social order, but that will be a blind alley and not the road of progress. Our hope for the human future does not lie in crowd psychology and the indiscriminating rule of universal democracy.

The Open Conspiracy can have little use for mere resentments as a driving force towards its ends; it starts with a proposal not to exalt the labour class but to abolish it, its sustaining purpose is to throw drudges out of employment and eliminate the inept – and it is far more likely to incur suspicion and distrust in the lower ranks of the developing industrial order of today than to win support there. There, just as everywhere else in the changing social complexes of our time, it can appeal only to the exceptionally understanding individual who can without personal humiliation consider his present activities and relationships as provisional and who can, without taking offence, endure a searching criticism of his present quality and mode of living.

CHAPTER TWELVE

The Resistances of the Less Industrialized Peoples to the Drive of the Open Conspiracy

So far, in our accounting of the powers, institutions, dispositions, types, and classes which will be naturally opposed to the Open Conspiracy, we have surveyed only such territory in the domain of the future world commonweal as is represented by the complex, progressive, highly-industrialized communities, based on a preceding landlord-soldier, tenant, town-merchant, and tradesman system, of the Atlantic type. These communities have developed farthest in the direction of mechanicalization, and they are so much more efficient and powerful that they now dominate the rest of the world. India, China, Russia, Africa present *mélanges* of social systems, thrown together, outpaced, overstrained, shattered, invaded, exploited, and more or less subjugated by the finance, machinery, and political aggressions of the Atlantic, Baltic, and Mediterranean civilization. In many ways they have an air of assimilating themselves to that civilization, evolving modern types and classes, and abandoning much of their distinctive traditions. But what they take from the West is mainly the new developments, the material achievements, rather than the social and political achievements, that, empowered by modern inventions, have won their way to world predominance. They may imitate European nationalism to a certain extent; for them it becomes a convenient form of self-assertion against the pressure of a realized practical social and political inferiority; but the degree to which they will or can take over the social assumptions and habits of the long-established European-American hierarchy is probably very restricted. Their nationalism will remain largely indigenous; the social traditions to which they will try to make the new material forces subservient will be traditions of an Oriental life widely different from the original life of Europe. They will have their own resistances to the Open Conspiracy, therefore, but they will be different resistances from those we have hitherto considered. The automobile and the wireless set, the harvester and steel construction building, will come to the jungle rajah and the head hunter, the Brahmin and the Indian peasant, with a parallel and yet dissimilar message to the one they brought the British landowner or the corn and cattle farmers of the Argentine and the Middle West. Also they may be expected to evoke dissimilar reactions.

To a number of the finer, more energetic minds of these overshadowed communities which have lagged more or less in the material advances to which this present ascendancy of Western Europe and America is due, the Open Conspiracy may come with an effect of immense invitation. At one step they may go from the sinking vessel of their antiquated order, across their present conquerors, into a brotherhood of world rulers. They may turn to the problem of saving and adapting all that is rich and distinctive of their inheritance to the common ends of the race. But to the less vigorous intelligences of this outer world, the new project of the Open Conspiracy will seem no better than a new form of Western envelopment, and they will fight a mighty liberation as though it were a further enslavement to the European tradition. They will watch the Open Conspiracy for any signs of conscious superiority and racial disregard. Necessarily they will recognize it as a product of Western mentality and they may well be tempted to regard it as an elaboration and organization of current dispositions rather than the evolution of a new phase which will make no discrimination at last between the effete traditions of either East or West. Their suspicions will be sustained and developed by the clumsy and muddle-headed political and economic aggressions of the contemporary political and business systems, such as they are, of the West, now in progress. Behind that cloud of aggression Western thought has necessarily advanced upon them. It could have got to their attention in no other way.

Partly these resistances and criticisms of the decadent communities outside the Atlantic capitalist systems will be aimed, not at the developing methods of the coming world community, but at the European traditions and restrictions that have imposed themselves upon these methods, and so far the clash of the East and West may be found to subserve the aims of the Open Conspiracy. In the conflict of old traditions and in the consequent deadlocks lies much hope for the direct acceptance of the groups of ideas centring upon the Open Conspiracy. One of the most interesting areas of humanity in this respect is the great system of communities under the sway or influence of Soviet Russia. Russia has never been completely incorporated with the European system; she became a just passable imitation of a western European monarchy in the seventeenth and eighteenth centuries, and talked at last of constitutions and parliaments – but the reality of that vast empire remained an Asiatic despotism, and the European mask was altogether smashed by the successive revolutions of 1917. The ensuing system is a government presiding over an enormous extent of peasants and herdsmen, by a disciplined association professing the faith and dogmas of Marx, as interpreted and qualified by Lenin and Stalin.

In many ways this government is a novelty of extraordinary interest. It labours against enormous difficulties within itself and without. Flung amazingly into a position of tremendous power, its intellectual flexibility is greatly restricted by the urgent militant necessity for mental unanimity and a consequent repression of criticism. It finds itself separated, intellectually and morally, by an enormous gap from the illiterate millions over which it rules. More open perhaps to scientific and creative conceptions than any other government, and certainly more willing to experiment and innovate, its enterprise is starved by the economic depletion of the country in the Great War and by the technical and industrial backwardness of the population upon which it must draw for its personnel. Moreover, it struggles within itself between concepts of a modern scientific social organization and a vague anarchistic dream in which the "State" is to disappear, and an emancipated proletariat, breeding and expectorating freely, fills the vistas of time forevermore. The tradition of long years of hopeless opposition has tainted the world policy of the Marxist cult with a mischievous and irritating quality that focuses upon it the animosity of every government in the dominant Atlantic system. Marxism never had any but the vaguest fancies about the relation of one nation to another, and the new Russian government, for all its cosmopolitan phrases, is more and more plainly the heir to the obsessions of Tsarist imperialism, using the Communist party, as other countries have used Christian missionaries, to maintain a propagandist government to forward its schemes. Nevertheless, the Soviet government has maintained itself for more than twelve years, and it seems far more likely to evolve than to perish. It is quite possible that it will evolve towards the conceptions of the Open Conspiracy, and in that case Russia may witness once again a conflict between new ideas and Old Believers. So far the Communist party in Moscow has maintained a considerable propaganda of ideas in the rest of the world and especially across its western frontier. Many of these ideas are now trite and stale. The time may be not far distant when the tide of propaganda will flow in the reverse direction. It has pleased the vanity of the Communist party to imagine itself conducting propaganda of world revolution. Its fate may be to develop upon lines that will make its more intelligent elements easily assimilable to the Open Conspiracy for a world revolution. The Open Conspiracy as it spreads and grows may find a less encumbered field for trying out the economic developments implicit in its conceptions in Russia and Siberia than anywhere else in the world.

However severely the guiding themes and practical methods of the present Soviet government in Russia may be criticized, the fact remains that it has cleared out of its way many of the main obstructive elements that we find still vigorous in the more highly-organized communities in the West. It has liberated vast areas from the kindred superstitions of monarchy and the need for a private proprietary control of great economic interests. And it has presented both China and India with the exciting spectacle of a social and political system capable of throwing off many of

97

the most characteristic features of triumphant Westernism, and yet holding its own. In the days when Japan faced up to modern necessities there were no models for imitation that were not communities of the Atlantic type pervaded by the methods of private capitalism, and in consequence the Japanese reconstituted their affairs on a distinctly European plan, adopting a Parliament and bringing their monarchy, social hierarchy, and business and financial methods into a general conformity with that model. It is extremely doubtful whether any other Asiatic community will now set itself to a parallel imitation, and it will be thanks largely to the Russian revolution that this breakaway from Europeanization has occurred.

But it does not follow that such a breakaway will necessarily lead more directly to the Open Conspiracy. If we have to face a less highly organized system of interests and prejudices in Russia and China, we have to deal with a vastly wider ignorance and a vastly more formidable animalism. Russia is a land of tens of millions of peasants ruled over by a little band of the intelligentsia who can be counted only by tens of thousands. It is only these few score thousands who are accessible to ideas of world construction, and the only hope of bringing the Russian system into active participation in the world conspiracy is through that small minority and through its educational repercussion on the myriads below. As we go eastward from European Russia the proportion of soundly prepared intelligence to which we can appeal for understanding and participation diminishes to an even more dismaying fraction. Eliminate that fraction, and one is left face to face with inchoate barbarism incapable of social and political organization above the level of the war boss and the brigand leader. Russia itself is still by no means secure against a degenerative process in that direction, and the hope of China struggling out of it without some forcible directive interventions is a hope to which constructive liberalism clings with very little assurance.

We turn back therefore from Russia, China and the communities of central Asia to the Atlantic world. It is in that world alone that sufficient range and amplitude of thought and discussion are possible for the adequate development of the Open Conspiracy. In these communities it must begin and for a long time its main activities will need to be sustained from these necessary centres of diffusion. It will develop amidst incessant mental strife, and through that strife it will remain alive. It is no small part of the practical weakness of present-day communism that it attempts to centre its intellectual life and its directive activities in Moscow and so cuts itself off from the free and open discussions of the Western world. Marxism lost the world when it went to Moscow and took over the traditions of Tsarism, as Christianity lost the world when it went to Rome and took over the traditions of Caesar. Entrenched in Moscow from searching criticism, the Marxist ideology may become more and more dogmatic and unprogressive, repeating its sacred *credo* and issuing its disregarded orders to the proletariat of the world, and so stay ineffectively crystallized until the rising tide of the Open Conspiracy submerges, dissolves it afresh, and incorporates whatever it finds assimilable.

India, like Japan, is cut off from the main body of Asiatic affairs. But while Japan has become a formally Westernized nationality in the comity of such nations, India remains a world in itself. In that one peninsula nearly every type of community is to be found, from the tribe of jungle savages, through a great diversity of barbaric and mediaeval principalities, to the child and women-sweating factories and the vigorous modern commercialism of Bombay. Over it all the British imperialism prevails, a constraining and restraining influence, keeping the peace, checking epidemics, increasing the food supply by irrigation and the like, and making little or no effort to evoke responses to modern ideas. Britain in India is no propagandist of modern ferments: all those are left the other side of Suez. In India the Briton is a ruler as firm and self-assured and uncreative at the Roman. The old religious and social traditions, the complex customs, castes, tabus, and exclusions of a strangely-mixed but unamalgamated community, though a little discredited by this foreign predominance, still hold men's minds. They have been, so to speak, pickled in the preservative of the British raj.

The Open Conspiracy has to invade the Indian complex in conflict with the prejudices of both ruler and governed. It has to hope for individual breaches in the dull Romanism of the administration: here a genuine educationist, here a creative civil servant, here an official touched by the distant stir of the living homeland; and it has to try to bring these types into a co-operative relationship with a fine native scholar here or an active-minded prince or landowner or industrialist there. As the old methods of passenger transport are superseded by flying, it will be more and more difficult to keep the stir of the living homeland out of either the consciousness of the official hierarchy or the knowledge of the recalcitrant "native".

Very similar to Indian conditions is the state of affairs in the foreign possessions of France, the same administrative obstacles to the Open Conspiracy above, and below the same resentful subordination, cut off from the mental invigoration of responsibility. Within these areas of restraint, India and its lesser, simpler parallels in North Africa, Syria and the Far East, there goes on a rapid increase of low-grade population, undersized physically and mentally, and retarding the mechanical development of civilization by its standing offer of cheap labour to the unscrupulous entrepreneur, and possible feeble insurrectionary material to the unscrupulous political adventurer. It is impossible to estimate how slowly or how rapidly the knowledge and ideas that have checked the rate of increase of all the Atlantic populations may be diffused through these less alert communities.

We must complete our survey of the resistances against which the Open Conspiracy has to work by a few words about the Negro world and the regions of forest and jungle in which barbaric and even savage human life still escapes the infection of civilization. It seems inevitable that the development of modern means of communication and the conquest of tropical diseases should end in giving access everywhere to modern administration and to economic methods, and everywhere the incorporation of the former wilderness in the modern economic process means the destruction of the material basis, the free hunting, the free access to the soil, of such barbaric and savage communities as still precariously survive. The dusky peoples, who were formerly the lords of these still imperfectly assimilated areas, are becoming exploited workers, slaves, serfs, hut-tax payers, or labourers to a caste of white immigrants. The spirit of the plantation broods over all these lands. The Negro in America differs only from his subjugated brother in South Africa or Kenya Colony in the fact that he also, like his white master, is an immigrant. The situation in Africa and America adjusts itself therefore towards parallel conditions, the chief variation being in the relative proportions of the two races and the details of the methods by which black labour is made to serve white ends.

In these black and white communities which are establishing themselves in all those parts of the earth where once the black was native, or in which a sub-tropical climate is favourable to his existence at a low level of social development, there is – and there is bound to be for many years to come – much racial tension. The steady advance of birth-control may mitigate the biological factors of this tension later on, and a general amelioration of manners and conduct may efface that disposition to persecute dissimilar types, which man shares with many other gregarious animals. But meanwhile this tension increases and a vast multitude of lives is strained to tragic issues.

To exaggerate the dangers and evils of miscegenation is a weakness of out time. Man interbreeds with all his varieties and yet deludes himself that there are races of outstanding purity, the "Nordic", the "Semitic", and so forth. These are phantoms of the imagination. The reality is more intricate, less dramatic, and grips less easily upon the mind; the phantoms grip only too well and incite to terrible suppressions. Changes in the number of half-breeds and in the proportion of white and coloured are changes of a temporary nature that may become controllable and rectifiable in a few generations. But until this level of civilization is reached, until the colour of a man's skin or the kinks in a woman's hair cease to have the value of shibboleths that involve educational, professional, and social extinction or survival, a black and white community is bound to be continually preoccupied by a standing feud too intimate and persuasive to permit of any long views of the world's destiny.

We come to the conclusion therefore that it is from the more vigorous, varied, and less severely obsessed centres of the Atlantic civilizations in the temperate zone, with their abundant facilities for publication and discussion, their traditions of mental liberty and their immense variety of interacting free types, that the main beginnings of the Open Conspiracy must develop. For the rest of the world, its propaganda, finding but poor nourishment in the local conditions, may retain a missionary quality for many years.

CHAPTER THIRTEEN

Resistances and Antagonistic Forces in Our Conscious and Unconscious Selves

We have dealt in the preceding two chapters with great classes and assemblages of human beings as, in the mass, likely to be more or less antagonistic to the Open Conspiracy, and it has been difficult in those chapters to avoid the implication that "we", some sort of circle round the writer, were aloof from these obstructive and hostile multitudes, and ourselves entirely identified with the Open Conspiracy. But neither are these multitudes so definitely against, nor those who are with us so entirely for, the Open Conspiracy to establish a world community as the writer, in his desire for clearness and contrast and with an all too human disposition perhaps towards plain ego-centred combative issues, has been led to represent. There is no "we", and there can be no "we", in possession of the Open Conspiracy.

The Open Conspiracy is in partial possession of us, and we attempt to serve it. But the Open Conspiracy is a natural and necessary development of contemporary thought arising here, there, and everywhere. There are doubts and sympathies that weigh on the side of the Open Conspiracy in nearly everyone, and not one of us but retains many impulses, habits, and ideas in conflict with our general devotion, checking and limiting our service.

Let us therefore in this chapter cease to discuss classes and types and consider general mental tendencies and reactions which move through all humanity.

In our opening chapters we pointed out that religion is not universally distributed throughout human society. And of no one does it seem to have complete possession. It seizes upon some of us and exalts us for one hour now and then, for a day now and then; it may leave its afterglow upon our conduct for some time; it may establish restraints and habitual dispositions; sometimes it dominates us with but brief intermissions through long spells, and then we can be saints and martyrs. In all our religious phases there appears a desire to *hold* the phase, to subdue the rest of our life to the standards and exigencies of that phase. Our quickened intelligence sets itself to a general analysis of our conduct and to the problem of establishing controls over our unilluminated intervals.

And when the religious elements in the mind set themselves to such self-analysis, and attempt to order and unify the whole being upon this basis of the service and advancement of the race, they discover first a great series of indifferent moods, wherein the resistance to thought and word for the Open Conspiracy is merely passive and in the nature of inertia. There is a whole class of states of mind which may be brought together under the head of "everydayism". The dinner bell and the playing fields, the cinema and the newspaper, the week-end visit and the factory siren, a host of such expectant things calls to a vast majority of people in our modern world to stop thinking and get busy with the interest in hand, and so on to the next, without a thought for the general frame and drama in which these momentary and personal incidents are set. We are driven along these marked and established routes and turned this way or that by the accidents of upbringing, of rivalries and loves, of chance encounters and vivid experiences, and it is rarely for many of us, and never for some, that the phases of broad reflection and self-questioning arise. For many people the religious life now, as in the past, has been a quite desperate effort to withdraw sufficient attention and energy from the flood of events to get some sort of grasp, and keep whatever grip is won, upon the relations of the self to the whole. Far more recoil in terror from such a possibility and would struggle strenuously against solitude in the desert, solitude under the stars, solitude in a silent room or indeed any occasion for comprehensive thought.

But the instinct and purpose of the religious type is to keep hold upon the comprehensive drama, and at the heart of all the great religions of the world we find a parallel disposition to escape in some manner from the aimless drive and compulsion of accident and everyday. Escape is attempted either by withdrawal from the presence of crowding circumstance into a mystical contemplation and austere retirement, or – what is more difficult and desperate and reasonable – by imposing the mighty standards of enduring issues upon the whole mass of transitory problems which constitute the actual business of life. We have already noted how the modern mind turns from retreat as a recognizable method of religion, and faces squarely up to the second alternative. The tumult of life has to be met and conquered. Aim must prevail over the aimless. Remaining in normal life we must yet keep our wills and thoughts aloof from normal life and fixed upon creative processes. However busied we may be, however challenged, we must yet save something of our best mental activity for self-examination and keep ourselves alert against the endless treacheries within that would trip us back into everydayism and disconnected responses to the stimuli of life.

Religions in the past, though they have been apt to give a preference to the renunciation of things mundane, have sought by a considerable variety of expedients to preserve the faith of those whom chance or duty still kept in normal contact with the world. It would provide material for an interesting study to enquire how its organizations to do this have worked in the past and how far they may be imitated and paralleled in the progressive life of the future. All the wide-reaching religions which came into existence in the five centuries before and the five centuries after Christ have made great use of periodic meetings for mutual reassurance, of sacred books, creeds, fundamental heart-searchings, of confession, prayer, sacraments, seasons of withdrawal, meditation, fasting, and prayer. Do these methods mark a phase in the world's development, or are they still to be considered available?

This points to a very difficult tangle of psychological problems. The writer in his earlier draft of this book wrote that the modern religious individual leads, spiritually speaking, a life of extreme wasteful and dangerous isolation. He still feels that is true, but he realizes that the invention of corrective devices is not within his range. He cannot picture a secular Mass nor congregations singing hymns about the Open Conspiracy. Perhaps the modern soul in trouble will resort to the psychoanalysts instead of the confessional; in which case we need to pray for better psychoanalysts.

Can the modern mind work in societies? May the daily paper be slowly usurping the functions of morning prayer, a daily mental reminder of large things, with more vividness and, at present, lower standards? One of the most distressful facts of the spread of education in the nineteenth century was the unscrupulous exploitation of the new reading public by a group of trash-dealers who grew rich and mighty in the process. Is the popular publisher and newspaper proprietor always to remain a trash-dealer? Or are we to see, in the future, publications taking at times some or all of the influence of revivalist movements, and particular newspapers rising to the task of sustaining a common faith in a gathering section of the public?

The modern temple in which we shall go to meditate may be a museum; the modern religious house and its religious life may be a research organization. The Open Conspirator must see to it that the museums show their meaning plain. There may be not only literature presently, but even plays, shows, and music, to subserve new ideas instead of trading upon tradition.

It is plain that to read and be moved by great ideas and to form good resolutions with no subsequent reminders and moral stocktaking is not enough to keep people in the way of the Open Conspiracy. The relapse to everydayism is too easy. The contemporary Open Conspirator may forget, and he has nothing to remind him; he may relapse, and he will hear no reproach to warn him of his relapse. Nowhere has he recorded a vow. "Everyday" has endless ways of justifying the return of the believer to sceptical casualness. It is easy to persuade oneself that one is taking life or oneself "too seriously". The mind is very

109

self-protective; it has a disposition to abandon too great or too far-reaching an effort and return to things indisputably within its scope. We have an instinctive preference for thinking things are "all right"; we economize anxiety; we defend the delusions that we can work with, even though we half realize they are no more than delusions. We resent the warning voice, the critical question that robs our activities of assurance. Our everyday moods are not only the antagonists of our religious moods, but they resent all outward appeals to our religious moods, and they welcome every help against religious appeals. We pass very readily from the merely defensive to the defensive-aggressive, and from refusing to hear the word that might stir our consciences to a vigorous effort to suppress its utterance.

Churches, religious organizations, try to keep the revivifying phase and usage where it may strike upon the waning or slumbering faith of the convert, but modern religion as yet has no such organized rebinders. They cannot be improvised. Crude attempts to supply the needed corrective of conduct may do less good than harm. Each one of us for himself must do what he can to keep his high resolve in mind and protect himself from the snare of his own modes of fatigue or inadvertency.

But these passive and active defences of current things which operate in and through ourselves, and find such ready sympathy and assistance in the world about us, these massive resistance systems, are only the beginning of our tale of the forces antagonistic to the Open Conspiracy that lurk in our complexities.

Men are creatures with other faults quite beyond and outside our common disposition to be stupid, indolent, habitual, and defensive. Not only have we active creative impulses, but also acutely destructive ones. Man is a jealous animal. In youth and adolescence egotism is extravagant. It is natural for it to be extravagant, then, and there is no help for it. A great number of us at that stage would rather not see a beautiful or wonderful thing come into existence than have it come into existence disregarding us. Something of that jealous malice, that self-assertive ruthlessness, remains in all of us throughout life. At his worst man can be an exceedingly combative, malignant, mischievous and cruel animal. None of us are altogether above the possibility of such phases. When we consider the oppositions to the Open Conspiracy that operate in the normal personality, we appreciate the soundness of the catechism which instructs us to renounce not only the trivial world and the heavy flesh, but the active and militant devil.

To make is a long and wearisome business, with many arrests and disappointments, but to break gives an instant thrill. We all know something of the delight of the *Bang*. It is well for the Open Conspirator to ask himself at times how far he is in love with the dream of a world in order, and how far he is driven by hatred of institutions that bore or humiliate him. He may be no more than a revengeful incendiary in the mask of a constructive worker. How safe is he, then, from the reaction to some fresh humiliation? The Open Conspiracy which is now his refuge and vindication may presently fail to give him the compensation he has sought, may offer him no better than a minor rôle, may display irritating and incomprehensible preferences. And for a great number of things in overt antagonism to the great aim of the Open Conspiracy, he will still find within himself not simply acquiescence but sympathy and a genuine if inconsistent admiration. There they are, waiting for his phase of disappointment. Back he may go to the old loves with a new animus

111

against the greater scheme. He may be glad to be quit of prigs and humbugs, and back among the good fellowship of nothing in particular.

Man has pranced a soldier in reality and fancy for so many generations that few of us can altogether release our imaginations from the brilliant pretensions of flags, empire, patriotism, and aggression. Business men, especially in America, seem to feel a sort of glory in calling even the underselling and overadvertising of rival enterprises "fighting". Pill vendors and public departments can have their "wars", their heroisms, their desperate mischiefs, and so get that Napoleonic feeling. The world and our reveries are full of the sentimentalities, the false glories and loyalties of the old combative traditions, trailing after them, as they do, so much worth and virtue in a dulled and stupefied condition. It is difficult to resist the fine gravity, the high self-respect, the examples of honour and good style in small things, that the military and naval services can present to us, for all that they are now no more than noxious parasites upon the nascent world commonweal. In France not a word may be said against the army; in England, against the navy. There will be many Open Conspirators at first who will scarcely dare to say that word even to themselves.

But all these obsolete values and attitudes with which our minds are cumbered must be cleared out if the new faith is to have free play. We have to clear them out not only from our own minds but from the minds of others who are to become our associates. The finer and more picturesque these obsolescent loyalties, obsolescent standards of honour, obsolescent religious associations, may seem to us, the more thoroughly must we seek to release our minds and the minds of those about us from them and cut off all thoughts of a return.

We cannot compromise with these vestiges of the ancient order and be faithful servants of the new. Whatever we retain of them will come back to life and grow again. It is no good to operate for cancer unless the whole growth is removed. Leave a crown about and presently you will find it being worn by someone resolved to be a king. Keep the name and image of a god without a distinct museum label and sooner or later you will discover a worshipper on his knees to it and be lucky not to find a human sacrifice upon the altar. Wave a flag and it will wrap about you. Of yourself even more than of the community is this true; there can be no half measures. You have not yet completed your escape to the Open Conspiracy from the cities of the plain while it is still possible for you to take a single backward glance.

CHAPTER FOURTEEN

The Open Conspiracy Begins as a Movement of Discussion, Explanation, and Propaganda

A new and happier world, a world community, is awakening, within the body of the old order, to the possibility of its emergence. Our phrase, "the Open Conspiracy" is merely a name for that awakening. To begin with, the Open Conspiracy is necessarily a group of ideas.

It is a system of modern ideas which has been growing together in the last quarter of the century, and particularly since the war. It is the reaction of a rapidly progressing biological conception of life and of enlarged historical realizations upon the needs and urgencies of the times. In this book we are attempting to define this system and to give it this provisional name. Essentially at first it is a dissemination of this new ideology that must occur. The statement must be tried over and spread before a widening circle of people.

Since the idea of the Open Conspiracy rests upon and arises out of a synthesis of historical, biological, and sociological realizations, we may look for these realizations already in the case of people with sound knowledge in these fields; such people will be prepared for acquiescence without any explanatory work;

there is nothing to set out to them beyond the suggestion that it is time they became actively conscious of where they stand. They constitute already the Open Conspiracy in an unorganized solution, and they will not so much adhere as admit to themselves and others their state of mind. They will say, "We knew all that." Directly we pass beyond that comparatively restricted world, however, we find that we have to deal with partial knowledge, with distorted views, or with blank ignorance, and that a revision and extension of historical and biological ideas and a considerable elucidation of economic misconceptions have to be undertaken. Such people have to be brought up to date with their information.

I have told already how I have schemed out a group of writings to embody the necessary ideas of the new time in a form adapted to the current reading public; I have made a sort of provisional "Bible", so to speak, for some factors at least in the Open Conspiracy. It is an early sketch. As the current reading public changes, all this work will become obsolescent so far as its present form and method go. But not so far as its substantial method goes. That I believe will remain.

Ultimately this developing mass of biological, historical, and economic information and suggestion must be incorporated in general education if the Open Conspiracy is to come to its own. At present this propaganda has to go on among adolescents and adults because of the backwardness and political conservatism of existing educational organizations. Most real modern education now is done in spite of the schools and to correct the misconceptions established by the schools. But what will begin as adult propaganda must pass into a *kultur-kampf* to win our educational machinery from reaction and the conservation of outworn ideas and attitudes to the cause of world reconstruction. The Open Conspiracy itself can never be imprisoned and fixed in the form of an organization, but everywhere Open Conspirators should be organizing themselves for educational reform.

And also within the influence of this comprehensive project there will be all sorts of groupings for study and progressive activity. One can presuppose the formation of groups of friends, of family groups, of students and employees or other sorts of people, meeting and conversing frequently in the course of their normal occupations, who will exchange views and find themselves in agreement upon this idea of a constructive change of the world as the guiding form of human activities.

Fundamentally important issues upon which unanimity must be achieved from the outset are:

> *Firstly*, the entirely provisional nature of all existing governments, and the entirely provisional nature, therefore, of all loyalties associated therewith;
>
> *Secondly*, the supreme importance of population control in human biology and the possibility it affords us of a release from the pressure of the struggle for existence on ourselves; and
>
> *Thirdly*, the urgent necessity of protective resistance against the present traditional drift towards war.

People who do not grasp the vital significance of these test issues do not really begin to understand the Open Conspiracy. Groups coming into agreement upon these matters, and upon their general interpretation of history, will be in a position to seek adherents, enlarge themselves, and attempt to establish communication and co-operation with kindred groups for common ends. They can take up a variety of activities to develop a sense and habit of combined action and feel their way to greater enterprises.

We have seen already that the Open Conspiracy must be heterogeneous in origin. Its initial grouping and associations will be of no uniform pattern. They will be of a very different size, average age, social experience, and influence. Their particular activities will be determined by these things. Their diverse qualities and influences will express themselves by diverse attempts at organization, each effective in its own sphere. A group or movement of students may find itself capable of little more than self-education and personal propaganda; a handful of middle-class people in a small town may find its small resources fully engaged at first in such things as, for example, seeing that desirable literature is available for sale or in the local public library, protecting books and news vendors from suppression, or influencing local teachers. Most parents of school children can press for the teaching of universal history and sound biology and protest against the inculcation of aggressive patriotism. There is much scope for the single individual in this direction. On the other hand, a group of ampler experience and resources may undertake the printing, publication, and distribution of literature, and exercise considerable influence upon public opinion in turning education in the right direction. The League of Nations movement, the Birth Control movement, and most radical and socialist societies, are fields into which Open Conspirators may go to find adherents more than half prepared for their wider outlook. The Open Conspiracy is a fuller and ampler movement into which these incomplete activities must necessarily merge as its idea takes possession of men's imaginations.

From the outset, the Open Conspiracy will set its face against militarism. There is a plain present need for the organization now, before war comes again, of an open and explicit refusal to serve in any war – or at most to serve in war, directly or indirectly, only after the issue has been fully and fairly submitted to arbitration. The time for a conscientious objection to war service is manifestly before and not after the onset of war. People who have by their silence acquiesced in a belligerent foreign policy right up to the onset of war, have little to complain of if they are then compelled to serve. And a refusal to participate with one's country in warfare is a preposterously incomplete gesture unless it is rounded off by the deliberate advocacy of a world pax, a world economic control, and a restrained population, such as the idea of the Open Conspiracy embodies.

The putting upon record of its members' reservation of themselves from any or all of the military obligations that may be thrust upon the country by military and diplomatic effort, might very conceivably be the first considerable overt act of many Open Conspiracy groups. It would supply the practical incentive to bring many of them together in the first place. It would necessitate the creation of regional or national *ad hoc* committees for the establishment of a collective legal and political defensive for this dissent from current militant nationalism. It would bring the Open Conspiracy very early out of the province of discussion into the field of practical conflict. It would from the outset invest it with a very necessary quality of present applicability.

The anticipatory repudiation of military service, so far as this last may be imposed by existing governments in their factitious international rivalries, need not necessarily involve a denial of the need of military action on behalf of the world commonweal for the suppression of nationalist brigandage, nor need it prevent the military training of Open Conspirators. It is simply the practical form of assertion that the normal militant diplomacy and warfare of the present time are offences against civilization, processes in the nature of brigandage, sedition, and civil war, and that serious men cannot be expected to play anything but a rôle of disapproval, non-participation, or active prevention towards them. Our loyalty to our current government, we would intimate, is subject to its sane and adult behaviour.

These educational and propagandist groups drawing together into an organized resistance to militarism and to the excessive control of individuals by the makeshift governments of today, constitute at most only the earliest and more elementary grade of the Open Conspiracy, and we will presently go on to consider the more specialized and constructive forms its effort must evoke. Before doing so, however, we may say a little more about the structure and method of these possible initiatory groupings.

Since they are bound to be different and miscellaneous in form, size, quality, and ability, any early attempts to organize them into common general action or even into regular common gatherings are to be deprecated. There should be many types of groups. Collective action had better for a time – perhaps for a long time – be undertaken not through the merging of groups but through the formation of *ad hoc* associations for definitely specialized ends, all making for the new world civilization. Open

Conspirators will come into these associations to make a contribution very much as people come into limited liability companies, that is to say with a subscription and not with their whole capital. A comprehensive organization attempting from the first to cover all activities would necessarily rest upon and promote one prevalent pattern of activity and hamper or estrange the more original and interesting forms. It would develop a premature orthodoxy, it would cease almost at once to be creative, and it would begin to form a crust of tradition. It would become anchylosed. With the dreadful examples of Christianity and Communism before us, we must insist that the idea of the Open Conspiracy ever becoming a single organization must be dismissed from the mind. It is a movement, yes, a system of purposes, but its end is a free and living, if unified, world.

At the utmost seven broad principles may be stated as defining the Open Conspiracy and holding it together. And it is possible even of these, one, the seventh, may be, if not too restrictive, at least unnecessary. To the writer it seems unavoidable because it is so intimately associated with that continual dying out of tradition upon which our hopes for an unencumbered and expanding human future rest.

(1) The complete assertion, practical as well as theoretical, of the provisional nature of existing governments and of our acquiescence in them;

(2) The resolve to minimize by all available means the conflicts of these governments, their militant use of individuals and property, and their interferences with the establishment of a world economic system;

(3) The determination to replace private, local or national ownership of at least credit, transport, and staple production by a responsible world directorate serving the common ends of the race;

(4) The practical recognition of the necessity for world biological controls, for example, of population and disease;

(5) The support of a minimum standard of individual freedom and welfare in the world; and

(6) The supreme duty of subordinating the personal career to the creation of a world directorate capable of these tasks and to the general advancement of human knowledge, capacity, and power;

(7) The admission therewith that our immortality is conditional and lies in the race and not in our individual selves.

CHAPTER FIFTEEN

Early Constructive Work of the Open Conspiracy

In such terms we may sketch the practicable and possible opening phase of the Open Conspiracy.

We do not present it as a movement initiated by any individual or radiating from any particular centre. In this book we are not starting something; we are describing and participating in something which has started. It arises naturally and necessarily from the present increase of knowledge and the broadening outlook of many minds throughout the world, and gradually it becomes conscious of itself. It is reasonable therefore to anticipate its appearance all over the world in sporadic mutually independent groupings and movements, and to recognize not only that they will be extremely various, but that many of them will trail with them racial and regional habits and characteristics which will only be shaken off as its cosmopolitan character becomes imperatively evident.

The passage from the partial anticipations of the Open Conspiracy that already abound everywhere to its complete and completely self-conscious statement may be made by almost imperceptible degrees. Today it may seem no more than a visionary idea; tomorrow it may be realized as a world-wide force of opinion and will. People will pass with no great inconsistency from saying that the Open Conspiracy is impossible to saying that it has always been plain and clear to them, that to this fashion they have shaped their lives as long as they can remember.

In its opening phase, in the day of small things, quite minor accidents may help or delay the clear definition and popularization of its main ideas. The changing pattern of public events may disperse or concentrate attention upon it, or it may win the early adherence of men of exceptional resources, energy, or ability. It is impossible to foretell the speed of its advance. Its development may be slower or faster, direct or devious, but the logic of accumulating realizations thrusts it forward, will persist in thrusting it on, and sooner or later it will be discovered, conscious and potent, the working religion of most sane and energetic people.

Meanwhile our supreme virtues must be faith and persistence.

So far we have considered only two of the main activities of the Open Conspiracy, the one being its propaganda of confidence in the possible world commonweal, and the other its immediate practical attempt to systematize resistance to militant and competitive imperialism and nationalism. But such things are merely its groundwork undertakings; they do no more than clear the site and make the atmosphere possible for its organized constructive efforts.

Directly we turn to that, we turn to questions of special knowledge, special effort, and special organization.

Let us consider first the general advancement of science, the protection and support of scientific research, and the diffusion of scientific knowledge. These things fall within the normal scheme of duty for the members of the Open Conspiracy. The world of science and experiment is the region of origin of nearly all the great initiatives that characterize our times; the Open Conspiracy owes its inspiration, its existence, its form and direction entirely to the changes of condition these initiatives have brought about, and yet a large number of scientific workers live outside the sphere of sympathy in which we may expect the Open Conspiracy to materialize, and collectively their political and social influence upon the community is extraordinarily small. Having regard to the immensity of its contributions and the incalculable value of its promise to the modern community, science – research, that is, and the diffusion of scientific knowledge – is extraordinarily neglected, starved, and threatened by hostile interference. This is largely because scientific work has no strong unifying organization and cannot in itself develop such an organization.

Science is a hard mistress, and the first condition of successful scientific work is that the scientific man should stick to his research. The world of science is therefore in itself, at its core, a miscellany of specialists, often very ungracious specialists, and, rather than offer him help and co-operation, it calls for understanding, tolerance, and service from the man of more general intelligence and wider purpose. The company of scientific men is less like a host of guiding angels than like a swarm of marvellous bees – endowed with stings – which must be hived and cherished and multiplied by the Open Conspiracy.

But so soon as we have the Open Conspiracy at work, putting its case plainly and offering its developing ideas and activities to those most preciously preoccupied men, then reasonably, when it involves no special trouble for them, when it is the line of least resistance for them, they may be expected to fall in with its convenient and helpful aims and find in it what they have hitherto lacked, a common system of political and social concepts to hold them together.

When that stage is reached, we shall be saved such spectacles of intellectual prostitution as the last Great War offered, when men of science were herded blinking from their laboratories to curse one another upon nationalist lines, and when after the war stupid and wicked barriers were set up to the free communication of knowledge by the exclusion of scientific men of this or that nationality from international scientific gatherings. The Open Conspiracy must help the man of science to realize, what at present he fails most astonishingly to realize, that he belongs to a greater comity than any king or president represents today, and so prepare him for better behaviour in the next season of trial.

The formation of groups in, and not only in, but about and in relation to, the scientific world, which will add to those first main activities of the Open Conspiracy, propaganda and pacificism, a special attention to the needs of scientific work, may be enlarged upon with advantage here, because it will illustrate quite typically the idea of a special work carried on in relation to a general activity, which is the subject of this section.

The Open Conspiracy extends its invitation to all sorts and conditions of men, but the service of scientific progress is for these only who are specially equipped or who are sufficiently interested to equip themselves. For scientific work there is first of all a great need of endowment and the setting up of laboratories, observatories, experimental stations, and the like, in all parts of the world. Numbers of men and women capable of scientific work never achieve it for want of the stimulus of opportunity afforded by endowment. Few contrive to create their own opportunities. The essential man of science is very rarely an able collector or administrator of money, and anyhow, the detailed work of organization is a grave call upon his special mental energy. But many men capable of a broad and intelligent appreciation of scientific work, but not capable of the peculiar intensities of research, have the gift of extracting money from private and public sources, and it is for them to use that gift modestly and generously in providing the framework for those more especially endowed.

And there is already a steadily increasing need for the proper storage and indexing of scientific results, and every fresh worker enhances it. Quite a considerable amount of scientific work goes fruitless or is needlessly repeated because of the growing volume of publication, and men make discoveries in the field of reality only to lose them again in the lumber room of record. Here is a second line of activity to which the Open Conspirator with a scientific bias may direct his attention.

A third line is the liaison work between the man of science and the common intelligent man; the promotion of publications which will either state the substance, implications, and consequences of new work in the vulgar tongue, or, if that is impossible, train the general run of people to the new idioms and technicalities which need to be incorporated with the vulgar tongue if it is still to serve its ends as a means of intellectual intercourse.

Through special *ad hoc* organizations, societies for the promotion of Research, for Research Defence, for World Indexing, for the translation of Scientific Papers, for the Diffusion of New Knowledge, the surplus energies of a great number of Open Conspirators can be directed to entirely creative ends and a new world system of scientific work built up, within which such dear old institutions as the Royal Society of London, the various European Academies of Science and the like, now overgrown and inadequate, can maintain their venerable pride in themselves, their mellowing prestige, and their distinguished exclusiveness, without their present privilege of inflicting cramping slights and restrictions upon the more abundant scientific activities of today.

So in relation to science – and here the word is being used in its narrower accepted meaning for what is often spoken of as *pure* science, the search for physical and biological realities, uncomplicated by moral, social and "practical" considerations – we evoke a conception of the Open Conspiracy as producing groups of socially associated individuals, who engage primarily in the general basic activities of the Conspiracy and adhere to and promote the seven broad principles summarized at the end of Chapter Fourteen, but who work also with the larger part of their energies, through international and cosmopolitan societies and in a multitude of special ways, for the establishment of an enduring and progressive world organization of pure research. They will have come to this special work because their distinctive gifts, their inclinations, their positions and opportunities have indicated it as theirs.

Now a very parallel system of Open Conspiracy groups is conceivable, in relation to business and industrial life. It would necessarily be a vastly bulkier and more heterogeneous system of groups, but otherwise the analogy is complete. Here we imagine those people whose gifts, inclinations, positions and opportunities as directors, workers, or associates give them an exceptional insight into and influence in the processes of producing and distributing commodities, can also be drawn together into groups within the Open Conspiracy. But these groups will be concerned with the huge and more complicated problems of the processes by which even now the small isolated individual adventures in production and trading that constituted the economic life of former civilizations, are giving place to larger, better instructed, better planned industrial organizations, whose operations and combinational become at last world wide.

The amalgamations and combinations, the substitution of large-scale business for multitude of small-scale businesses, which are going on now, go on with all the cruelty and disregards of a natural process. If a man is to profit and survive, these unconscious blunderings – which now stagger towards but which may never attain world organization – must be watched, controlled, mastered, and directed. As uncertainty diminishes, the quality of adventure and the amount of waste diminish also, and large speculative profits are no longer possible or justifiable. The transition from speculative adventure to organized foresight in the common interest, in the whole world of economic life, is the substantial task of the Open Conspiracy. And it is these specially interested and equipped groups, and not the movement as a whole, which may best begin the attack upon these fundamental readjustments.

The various Socialist movements of the nineteenth and earlier twentieth centuries had this in common, that they sought to replace the "private owner" in most or all economic interests by some vaguely apprehended "public owner". This, following the democratic disposition of the times, was commonly conceived of as an elected body, a municipality, the parliamentary state or what not. There were municipal socialists, "nationalizing" socialists, imperial socialists. In the mystic teachings of the Marxist, the collective owner was to be "the dictatorship of the proletariat". Production for profit was denounced. The contemporary mind realizes the evils of production for profit and of the indiscriminate scrambling of private ownership more fully than ever before, but it has a completer realization and a certain accumulation of experience in the difficulties of organizing that larger ownership we desire. Private ownership may not be altogether evil as a provisional stage, even if it has no more in its favour than the ability to transcend political boundaries.

Moreover – and here again the democratic prepossessions of the nineteenth century come in – the Socialist movements sought to make every single adherent a reformer and a propagandist of economic methods. In order to do so, it was necessary to simplify economic processes to the crudity of nursery toys, and the intricate interplay of will and desire in enterprise, normal employment, and direction, in questions of ownership, wages, credit, and money, was reduced to a childish fable of surplus value wickedly appropriated. The Open Conspiracy is not so much a socialism as a more comprehensive offspring which has eaten and assimilated whatever was digestible of its socialist forbears. It turns to biology for guidance towards the regulation of quantity and a controlled distribution of the human population of the world, and it judges all the subsidiary aspects of property and pay by the criterion of most efficient production and distribution in relation to the indications thus obtained.

These economic groups, then, of the Open Conspiracy, which may come indeed to be a large part of the Open Conspiracy, will be working in that vast task of economic reconstruction – which from the point of view of the older socialism was the sole task before mankind. They will be conducting experiments and observing processes according to their opportunities. Through *ad hoc* societies and journals they will be comparing and examining their methods and preparing reports and clear information for the movement at large. The whole question of money and monetary methods in our modern communities, so extraordinarily disregarded in socialist literature, will be examined under the assumption that money is the token of the community's obligation, direct or indirect, to an individual, and credit its permission to deal freely with material.

The whole psychology of industry and industrial relationship needs to be revised and restated in terms of the collective efficiency and welfare of mankind. And just as far as can be contrived, the counsel and the confidences of those who now direct great industrial and financial operations will be invoked. The first special task of a banker, or a bank clerk for that matter, who joins the Open Conspiracy, will be to answer the questions: "What is a bank?" "What are you going to do about it?" "What have we to do about it?" The first questions to a manufacturer will be: "What are you making and why?" and "What are you and we to do about it?" Instead of the crude proposals to "expropriate" and "take over by the State" of the primitive socialism, the Open Conspiracy will build up an encyclopaedic conception of the modern economic complex as a labyrinthine pseudo-system progressively eliminating waste and working its way along multitudinous channels towards unity, towards clarity of purpose and method, towards abundant productivity and efficient social service.

Let us come back now for a paragraph or so to the ordinary adherent to the Open Conspiracy, the adherent considered not in relation to his special aptitudes and services, but in relation to the movement as a whole and to those special constructive organizations outside his own field. It will be his duty to keep his mind in touch with the progressing concepts of the scientific work so far as he is able and with the larger issues of the economic reconstruction that is afoot, to take his cues from the special groups and organizations engaged upon that work, and to help where he finds his opportunity and when there is a call upon him. But no adherent of the Open Conspiracy can remain merely and completely an ordinary adherent. There can be no pawns in the game of the Open Conspiracy, no "cannon fodder" in its war. A special activity, quite as much as a general understanding, is demanded from everyone who looks creatively towards the future of mankind.

We have instanced first the fine and distinctive world organization of pure science, and then the huge massive movement towards co-operating unity of aim in the economic life, until at last the production and distribution of staple necessities is apprehended as one world business, and we have suggested that this latter movement may gradually pervade and incorporate a very great bulk of human activities. But besides this fine current and this great torrent of evolving activities and relationships there are also a very considerable variety of other great functions in the community towards which Open Conspiracy groups must direct their organizing enquiries and suggestions in their common intention of ultimately assimilating all the confused processes of today into a world community.

For example, there must be a series of groups in close touch at one end with biological science and at the other with the complex of economic activity, who will be concerned specially with the practical administration of the biological interests of the race, from food plants and industrial products to pestilences and population. And another series of groups will gather together attention and energy to focus them upon the educational process. We have already pointed out that there is a strong disposition towards conservatism in normal educational institutions. They preserve traditions rather than develop them. They are likely to set up a considerable resistance to the reconstruction of the world outlook upon the threefold basis defined in Chapter Fourteen. This resistance must be attacked by special societies, by the establishment of competing schools, by help and promotion for enlightened teachers, and, wherever the attack is incompletely successful, it must be supplemented by the energetic diffusion of educational literature for adults, upon modern lines. The forces of the entire movement may be mobilized in a variety of ways to bring pressure upon reactionary schools and institutions.

A set of activities correlated with most of the directly creative ones will lie through existing political and administrative bodies. The political work of the Open Conspiracy must be conducted upon two levels and by entirely different methods. Its main political idea, its political strategy, is to weaken, efface, incorporate, or supersede existing governments. But there is also a tactical diversion of administrative powers and resources to economic and educational arrangements of a modern type. Because a country or a district is inconvenient as a division and destined to ultimate absorption in some more comprehensive and economical system of government, that is no reason why its administration should not be brought meanwhile into working co-operation with the development of the Open Conspiracy. Free Trade nationalism in power is better than high tariff nationalism, and pacificist party liberalism better than aggressive party patriotism.

This evokes the anticipation of another series of groups, a group in every possible political division, whose task it will be to organize the whole strength of the Open Conspiracy in that division as an effective voting or agitating force. In many divisions this might soon become a sufficiently considerable block to affect the attitudes and pledges of the national politicians. The organization of these political groups into provincial or national conferences and systems would follow hard upon their appearance. In their programmes they would be guided by meetings and discussions with the specifically economic, educational, biological, scientific and central groups, but they would also form their own special research bodies to work out the incessant problems of transition between the old type of locally centred administrations and a developing world system of political controls.

In the preceding chapter we sketched the first practicable first phase of the Open Conspiracy as the propaganda of a group of interlocking ideas, a propaganda associated with pacificist action. In the present chapter we have given a scheme of branching and amplifying development. In this scheme, this scheme of the second phase, we conceive of the Open Conspiracy as consisting of a great multitude and variety of overlapping groups, but now all organized for collective political, social, and educational as well as propagandist action. They will recognize each other much more clearly than they did at first, and they will have acquired a common name.

The groups, however, almost all of them, will still have specific work also. Some will be organizing a sounder setting for scientific progress, some exploring new social and educational possibilities, many concentrated upon this or that phase in the reorganization of the world's economic life, and so forth. The individual Open Conspirator may belong to one or more groups and in addition to the *ad hoc* societies and organizations which the movement will sustain, often in co-operation with partially sympathetic people still outside its ranks.

The character of the Open Conspiracy will now be plainly displayed. It will have become a great world movement as widespread and evident as socialism or communism. It will have taken the place of these movements very largely. It will be more than they were, it will be frankly a world religion. This large, loose assimilatory mass of movements, groups, and societies will be definitely and obviously attempting to swallow up the entire population of the world and become the new human community.

CHAPTER SIXTEEN

Existing and Developing Movements which are
Contributory to the Open Conspiracy and which Must
Develop a Common Consciousness. The Parable
of Provinder Island

A suggestion has already been made in an earlier chapter of this essay which may perhaps be expanded here a little more. It is that there already exist in the world a considerable number of movements in industry, in political life, in social matters, in education, which point in the same direction as the Open Conspiracy and are inspired by the same spirit. It will be interesting to discuss how far some of these movements may not become confluent with others and by a mere process of logical completion identify themselves consciously with the Open Conspiracy in its entirety.

Consider, for example, the movement for a scientific study and control of population pressure, known popularly as the Birth Control movement. By itself, assuming existing political and economic conditions, this movement lays itself open to the charge of being no better than a scheme of "race suicide". If a population in some area of high civilization attempts to restrict increase, organize its economic life upon methods of maximum individual productivity, and impose order and beauty upon its entire territory, that region will become irresistibly attractive to any adjacent festering mass of low-grade, highly reproductive population. The cheap humanity of the one community will make a constant attack upon the other, affording facile servility, prostitutes, toilers, hand labour. Tariffs against sweated products, restriction of immigration, tensions leading at last to a war of defensive massacre are inevitable. The conquest of an illiterate, hungry, and incontinent multitude may be almost as disastrous as defeat for the selecter race. Indeed, one finds that in discussion the propagandists of Birth Control admit that their project must be universal or dysgenic. But yet quite a number of them do not follow up these admissions to their logical consequences, produce the lines and continue the curves until the complete form of the Open Conspiracy appears. It will be the business of the early Open Conspiracy propagandists to make them do so, and to install groups and representatives at every possible point of vantage in this movement.

And similarly the now very numerous associations for world peace halt in alarm on the edge of their own implications. World Peace remains a vast aspiration until there is some substitute for the present competition of states for markets and raw material, and some restraint upon population pressure. League of Nation Societies and all forms of pacificist organization are either futile or insincere until they come into line with the complementary propositions of the Open Conspiracy.

The various Socialist movements again are partial projects professing at present to be self-sufficient schemes. Most of them involve a pretence that national and political forces are intangible phantoms, and that the primary issue of population pressure can be ignored. They produce one woolly scheme after another for transferring the property in this, that, or the other economic plant and interest from bodies of shareholders and company promoters to gangs of politicians or syndicates of workers – to be steered to efficiency, it would seem, by pillars of cloud by day and pillars of fire by night. The communist party has trained a whole generation of disciples to believe that the overthrow of a vaguely apprehended "Capitalism" is the simple solution of all human difficulties. No movement ever succeeded so completely in substituting phrases for thought. In Moscow communism has trampled "Capitalism" underfoot for ten eventful years, and still finds all the problems of social and political construction before it.

But as soon as the Socialist or Communist can be got to realize that his repudiation of private monopolization is not a complete programme but just a preliminary principle, he is ripe for the ampler concepts of the modern outlook. The Open Conspiracy is the natural inheritor of socialist and communist enthusiasms; it may be in control of Moscow before it is in control of New York.

The Open Conspiracy may achieve the more or less complete amalgamation of all the radical impulses in the Atlantic community of today. But its scope is not confined to the variety of sympathetic movements which are brought to mind by that loose word *radical*. In the past fifty years or so, while Socialists and Communists have been denouncing the current processes of economic life in the same invariable phrases and with the same undiscriminating animosity, these processes have been undergoing the profoundest and most interesting changes. While socialist thought has recited its phrases, with witty rather than substantial variations, a thousand times as many clever people have been busy upon industrial, mercantile and financial processes. The Socialist still reiterates that this greater body of intelligence has been merely seeking private gain, which has just as much truth in it as is necessary to make it an intoxicating lie. Everywhere competitive businesses have been giving way to amalgamated enterprises, marching towards monopoly, and personally owned businesses to organizations so large as to acquire more and more the character of publicly responsible bodies. In theory in Great Britain, banks are privately owned, and railway transport is privately owned, and they are run entirely for profit – in practice their profit making is austerely restrained and their proceedings are all the more sensitive to public welfare because they are outside the direct control of party politicians.

Now this transformation of business, trading, and finance has been so multitudinous and so rapid as to be still largely unconscious of itself. Intelligent men have gone from combination to combination and extended their range, year by year, without realizing how their activities were enlarging them to conspicuousness and responsibility. Economic organization is even now only discovering itself for what it is. It has accepted incompatible existing institutions to its own great injury. It has been patriotic and broken its shins against the tariff walls its patriotism has raised to hamper its own movements; it has been imperial and found itself taxed to the limits of its endurance, "controlled" by antiquated military and naval experts, and crippled altogether. The younger, more vigorous intelligences in the great business directorates of today are beginning to realize the uncompleted implications of their enterprise. A day will come when the gentlemen who are trying to control the oil supplies of the world without reference to anything else except as a subsidiary factor in their game will be considered to be quaint characters. The ends of Big Business must carry Big Business into the Open Conspiracy just as surely as every other creative and broadly organizing movement is carried.

Now I know that to all this urging towards a unification of constructive effort, a great number of people will be disposed to a reply which will, I hope, be less popular in the future than it is at the present time. They will assume first an expression of great sagacity, an elderly air. Then, smiling gently, they will ask whether there is not something preposterously ambitious in looking at the problem of life as one whole. Is it not wiser to concentrate our forces on more *practicable* things, to attempt one thing at a time, not to antagonize the whole order of established things against our poor desires, to begin tentatively, to refrain from putting too great a strain upon people, to trust to the growing common sense of the world to adjust this or that line of progress to the general scheme of things. Far better accomplish something definite here and there than challenge a general failure. That is, they declare, how reformers and creative things have gone on in the past; that is how they are going on now; muddling forward in a mild and confused and partially successful way. Why not trust them to go on like that? Let each man do his bit with a complete disregard of the logical interlocking of progressive effort to which I have been drawing attention.

Now I must confess that, popular as this style of argument is, it gives me so tedious a feeling that rather than argue against it in general terms I will resort to a parable. I will relate the story of the pig on Provinder Island.

There was, you must understand, only one pig on Provinder Island, and Heaven knows how it got there, whether it escaped and swam ashore or was put ashore from some vessel suddenly converted to vegetarianism, I cannot imagine. At first it was the only mammal there. But later on three sailors and a very small but observant cabin boy were wrecked there, and after subsisting for a time on shellfish and roots they became aware of this pig. And simultaneously they became aware of a nearly intolerable craving for bacon. The eldest of the three sailors began to think of a ham he had met in his boyhood, a beautiful ham for which his father had had the carving knife specially sharpened; the second of the three sailors dreamed repeatedly of a roast loin of pork he had eaten at his sister's wedding, and the third's mind ran on chitterlings – I know not why. They sat about their meagre fire and conferred and expatiated upon these things until their mouths watered and the shellfish turned to water within them. What dreams came to the cabin boy are unknown, for it was their custom to discourage his confidences. But he sat apart brooding and was at last moved to speech. "Let us hunt that old pig," he said, "and kill it."

Now it may have been because it was the habit of these sailors to discourage the cabin boy and keep him in his place, but anyhow, for whatever reason it was, all three sailors set themselves with one accord to oppose that proposal.

"Who spoke of killing the pig?" said the eldest sailor loudly, looking round to see if by any chance the pig was within hearing. "Who spoke of *killing* the pig? You're the sort of silly young devil who jumps at ideas and hasn't no sense of difficulties. What I said was *AM*. All I want is just a Am to go with my roots and sea salt. One Am. The Left Am. I don't want the right one, and I don't propose to get it. I've got a sense of proportion and a proper share of humour, and I know my limitations. I'm a sound, clear-headed, practical man. Am is what I'm after, and if I can get that, I'm prepared to say Quits and let the rest of the pig alone. Who's for joining me in a Left Am Unt – a simple reasonable Left Am Unt – just to get One Left Am?"

Nobody answered him directly, but when his voice died away, the next sailor in order of seniority took up the tale. "That Boy," he said, "will die of Swelled Ed, and I pity him. My idea is to follow up the pig and get hold of a loin chop. Just simply a loin chop. A loin chop is good enough for me. It's – feasible. Much more feasible than a great Am. Here we are, we've got no gun, we've got no wood of a sort to make bows and arrows, we've got nothing but our clasp knives, and that pig can run like Ell. It's ridiculous to think of killing that pig. But if one didn't trouble him, if one kind of got into his confidence and crept near him and just quietly and insidiously went for his loin – just sort of as if one was tickling him – one might get a loin chop almost before he knew of it."

The third sailor sat crumpled up and downcast with his lean fingers tangled in his shock of hair. "Chitterlings," he murmured, "chitterlings. I don't even want to *think* of the pig."

And the cabin boy pursued his own ideas in silence, for he deemed it unwise to provoke his elders further.

On these lines it was the three sailors set about the gratifying of their taste for pork, each in his own way, separately and sanely and modestly. And each had his reward. The first sailor, after weeks of patience, got within arm's length of the pig and smacked that coveted left ham loud and good, and felt success was near. The other two heard the smack and the grunt of dismay half a mile away. But the pig, in a state of astonishment, carried the ham off out of reach, there and then, and that was as close as the first sailor ever got to his objective. The roast loin hunter did no better. He came upon the pig asleep under a rock one day, and jumped upon the very loin he desired, but the pig bit him deeply and septically, and displayed so much resentment that the question of a chop was dropped forthwith and never again broached between them. And thereafter the arm of the second sailor was bandaged and swelled up and went from bad to worse. And as for the third sailor, it is doubtful whether he even got wind of a chitterling from the start to the finish of this parable. The cabin boy, pursuing notions of his own, made a pitfall for the whole pig, but as the others did not help him, and as he was an excessively small – though shrewd – cabin boy, it was a feeble and insufficient pitfall, and all it caught was the hunter of chitterlings, who was wandering distraught. After which the hunter of chitterlings, became a hunter of cabin boys, and the cabin boy's life, for all his shrewdness, was precarious and unpleasant. He slept only in snatches and learned the full bitterness of insight misunderstood.

When at last a ship came to Provinder Island and took off the three men and the cabin boy, the pig was still bacon intact and quite gay and cheerful, and all four castaways were in a very emaciated condition because at that season of the year shellfish were rare, and edible roots were hard to find, and the pig was very much cleverer than they were in finding them and digging them up – let alone digesting them.

From which parable it may be gathered that a partial enterprise is not always wiser or more hopeful than a comprehensive one.

And in the same manner, with myself in the rôle of that minute but observant cabin boy, I would sustain the proposition that none of these movements of partial reconstruction has the sound common sense quality its supporters suppose. All these movements are worthwhile if they can be taken into the world-wide movement; all in isolation are futile. They will be overlaid and lost in the general drift. The policy of the whole hog is the best one, the sanest one, the easiest, and the most hopeful. If sufficient men and women of intelligence can realize that simple truth and give up their lives to it, mankind may yet achieve a civilization and power and fullness of life beyond our present dreams. If they do not, frustration will triumph, and war, violence, and a drivelling waste of time and strength and desire, more disgusting even than war, will be the lot of our race down through the ages to its emaciated and miserable end.

For this little planet of ours is quite off the course of any rescue ships, if the will in our species fails.

CHAPTER SEVENTEEN

The Creative Home, Social Group, and School:
The Present Waste of Idealistic Will

Human society began with the family. The natural history of gregariousness is a history of the establishment of mutual toleration among human animals, so that a litter or a herd keeps together instead of breaking up. It is in the family group that the restraints, disciplines, and self-sacrifices which make human society possible were worked out and our fundamental prejudices established, and it is in the family group, enlarged perhaps in many respects, and more and more responsive to collective social influences, that our social life must be relearnt, generation after generation.

Now in each generation the Open Conspiracy, until it can develop its own reproductive methods, must remain a minority movement of intelligent converts. A unified progressive world community demands its own type of home and training. It needs to have its fundamental concepts firmly established in as many minds as possible and to guard its children from the infection of the old racial and national hatreds and jealousies, old superstitions and bad mental habits, and base interpretations of life. From its outset the Open Conspiracy will be setting itself to influence the existing educational machinery, but for a long time it will find itself confronted in school and college by powerful religious and political authorities determined to set back the children at the point or even behind the point from which their parents made their escape. At best, the liberalism of the state-controlled schools will be a compromise. Originally schools and colleges were transmitters of tradition and conservative forces. So they remain in essence to this day.

Organized teaching has always aimed, and will always tend to guide, train, and direct, the mind. The problem of reconstructing education so as to make it a releasing instead of a binding process has still to be solved. During the early phases of its struggle, therefore, the Open Conspiracy will be obliged to adopt a certain sectarianism of domestic and social life in the interests of its children, to experiment in novel educational methods and educational atmospheres, and it may even in many cases have to consider the grouping of its families and the establishment of its own schools. In many modern communities, the English-speaking states, for example, there is still liberty to establish educational companies, running schools of a special type. In every country where that right does not exist it has to be fought for.

There lies a great work for various groups of the Open Conspiracy. Successful schools would become laboratories of educational methods and patterns for new state schools. Necessarily for a time, but we may hope unconsciously, the Open Conspiracy children will become a social elite; from their first conscious moments they will begin to think and talk among clear-headed people speaking distinctly and behaving frankly, and it will be a waste and loss to put them back for the scholastic stage among their mentally indistinct and morally muddled contemporaries. A phase when there will be a special educational system for the Open Conspiracy seems, therefore, to be indicated. Its children will learn to speak, draw, think, compute lucidly and subtly, and into their vigorous minds they will take the broad concepts of history, biology, and mechanical progress, the basis of the new world, naturally and easily. Meanwhile, those who grow up outside the advancing educational frontier of the Open Conspiracy will never come under the full influence of its ideas, or they will get hold of them only after a severe struggle against a mass of misrepresentations and elaborately instilled prejudices. An adolescent and adult educational campaign, to undo the fixations and suggestions of the normal conservative and reactionary schools and colleges, is and will long remain an important part of the work of the Open Conspiracy.

Always, as long as I can remember, there have been a dispute and invidious comparisons between the old and the young. The young find the old prey upon and restrain them, and the old find the young shallow, disappointing, and aimless in vivid contrast to their revised memories of their own early days. The present time is one in which these perennial accusations flower with exceptional vigour. But there does seem to be some truth in the statement that the facilities to live frivolously are greater now than they have ever been for old and young alike. For example, in the great modern communities that emerge now from Christendom, there is a widespread disposition to regard Sunday as merely a holiday. But that was certainly not the original intention of Sunday. As we have noted already in an earlier chapter, it was a day dedicated to the greater issues of life. Now great multitudes of people do not even pretend to set aside any time at all to the greater issues of life. The greater issues are neglected altogether. The churches are neglected, and nothing of a unifying or exalting sort takes their place.

What the contemporary senior tells his junior today is perfectly correct. In his own youth, no serious impulse of his went to waste. He was not distracted by a thousand gay but petty temptations, and the local religious powers, whatever they happened to be, seemed to believe in themselves more and made a more comprehensive attack upon his conscience and imagination. Now the old faiths are damaged and discredited, and the new and greater one, which is the Open Conspiracy, takes shape only gradually. A decade or so ago, socialism preached its confident hopes, and patriotism and imperial pride shared its attraction for the ever grave and passionate will of emergent youth. Now socialism and democracy are "under revision" and the flags that once waved so bravely reek of poison gas, are stiff with blood and mud and shameful with exposed dishonesties. Youth is what youth has always been, eager for fine interpretations of life, capable of splendid resolves. It has no natural disposition towards the shallow and confused life. Its demand as ever is, "What am I to do with myself?" But it comes up out of its childhood today into a world of ruthless exposures and cynical pretensions. We are all a little ashamed of "earnestness". The past ten years have seen the shy and powerful idealism of youth at a loss and dismayed and ashamed as perhaps it has never been before. It is in the world still, but masked, hiding even from itself in a whirl of small excitements and futile, defiant depravities.

150

The old flags and faiths have lost their magic for the intelligence of the young; they can command it no more; it is in the mighty revolution to which Open Conspiracy directs itself that the youth of mankind must find its soul, if ever it is to find its soul again.

CHAPTER EIGHTEEN

Progressive Development of the Activities of
the Open Conspiracy into a World Control and
Commonweal: The Hazards of the Attempt

We have now sketched out in these Blue Prints the methods by which the confused radicalism and constructive forces of the present time may, can, and probably will be drawn together about a core of modernized religious feeling into one great and multifarious creative effort. A way has been shown by which this effort may be developed from a mere propagandist campaign and a merely resistant protest against contemporary militarism into an organized foreshadowing in research, publicity, and experiment in educational, economic, and political reconstructions, of that *Pax Mundi* which has become already the tantalized desire of great multitudes throughout the world. These foreshadowings and reconstructions will ignore and transcend the political boundaries of today. They will continually become more substantial as project passes into attempt and performance. In phase after phase and at point after point, therefore, the Open Conspiracy will come to grips with the powers that sustain these boundaries.

153

And it will not be merely topographical boundaries that will be passed. The Open Conspiracy will also be dissolving and repudiating many existing restrictions upon conduct and many social prejudices. The Open Conspiracy proposes to end and shows how an end may be put to that huge substratum of underdeveloped, undereducated, subjugated, exploited, and frustrated lives upon which such civilization as the world has known hitherto has rested, and upon which most of our social system still rest.

Whenever possible, the Open Conspiracy will advance by illumination and persuasion. But it has to advance, and even from the outset, where it is not allowed to illuminate and persuade, it must fight. Its first fights will probably be for the right to spread its system of ideas plainly and clearly throughout the world.

There is, I suppose, a flavour of treason about the assumption that any established government is provisional, and a quality of immorality in any criticism of accepted moral standards. Still more is the proposal, made even in times of peace, to resist war levies and conscription an offence against absolute conceptions of loyalty. But the ampler wisdom of the modern Atlantic communities, already touched by premonitions of change and futurity, has continually enlarged the common liberties of thought for some generations, and it is doubtful if there will be any serious resistance to the dissemination of these views and the early organization of the Open Conspiracy in any of the English-speaking communities or throughout the British Empire, in the Scandinavian countries, or in such liberal-minded countries as Holland, Switzerland, republican Germany or France. France, in the hasty years after the war, submitted to some repressive legislation against the discussion of birth control or hostile criticism of the militarist attitude; but such a check upon mental freedom is altogether contrary to the clear and open quality of the French mind; in practice it has already been effectively repudiated by such writers as Victor Margueritte, and it is unlikely that there will be any effective suppression of the opening phases of the Open Conspiracy in France.

This gives us a large portion of the existing civilized world in which men's minds may be readjusted to the idea that their existing governments are in the position of trustees for the greater government of the coming age. Throughout these communities it is conceivable that the structural lines of the world community may be materialized and established with only minor struggles, local boycotts, vigorous public controversies, normal legislative obstruction, social pressure, and overt political activities. Police, jail, expulsions, and so forth, let alone outlawry and warfare, may scarcely be brought into this struggle upon the high civilized level of the Atlantic communities. But where they are brought in, the Open Conspiracy, to the best of its ability and the full extent of its resources, must become a fighting force and organize itself upon resistant lines.

Non-resistance, the resistance of activities to moral suasion is no part of the programme of the Open Conspiracy. In the face of unscrupulous opposition creative ideas must become aggressive, must define their enemies and attack them. By its own organizations or through the police and military strength of governments amenable to its ideas, the movement is bound to find itself fighting for open roads, open frontiers, freedom of speech, and the realities of peace in regions of oppression. The Open Conspiracy rests upon a disrespect for nationality, and there is no reason why it should tolerate noxious or obstructive governments because they hold their own in this or that patch of human territory. It lies within the power of the Atlantic communities to impose peace upon the world and secure unimpeded movement and free speech from end to end of the earth. This is a fact on which the Open Conspiracy must insist. The English-speaking states, France, Germany, Holland, Switzerland, the Scandinavian countries, and Russia, given only a not very extravagant frankness of understanding between them, and a common disposition towards the ideas of the Open Conspiracy, could cease to arm against each other and still exert enough strength to impose disarmament and a respect for human freedom in every corner of the planet. It is fantastic pedantry to wait for all the world to accede before all the world is pacified and policed.

The most inconsistent factor in the liberal and radical thought of today is its prejudice against the interference of highly developed modern states in the affairs of less stable and less advanced regions. This is denounced as "imperialism", and regarded as criminal. It may have assumed grotesque and dangerous forms under the now decaying traditions of national competition, but as the merger of the Atlantic states proceeds, the possibility and necessity of bringing areas of misgovernment and disorder under world control increase. A great war like the war of 1914–1918 may never happen again. The common sense of mankind may suffice to avert that. But there is still much actual warfare before mankind, on the frontiers everywhere, against brigands, against ancient loyalties and traditions which will become at last no better than excuses for brigandage and obstructive exaction. All the weight of the Open Conspiracy will be on the side of the world order and against that sort of local independence which holds back its subject people from the citizenship of the world.

But in this broad prospect of far-reaching political amalgamations under the impulses of the Open Conspiracy lurk a thousand antagonisms and adverse chances, like the unsuspected gulleys and ravines and thickets in a wide and distant landscape. We know not what unexpected chasms may presently be discovered. The Open Conspirator may realize that he is one of an advancing and victorious force and still find himself outnumbered and outfought in his own particular corner of the battlefield. No one can yet estimate the possible strength of reaction against world unification; no one can foresee the extent of the divisions and confusions that may arise among ourselves. The ideas in this book may spread about without any serious resistance in most civilized countries, but there are still governments under which the persistent expression of such thoughts will be dealt with as crimes and bring men and women to prison, torment, and death. Nevertheless, they must be expressed.

While the Open Conspiracy is no more than a discussion it may spread unopposed because it is disregarded. As a mainly passive resistance to militarism it may still be tolerable. But as its knowledge and experience accumulate and its organization becomes more effective and aggressive, as it begins to lay hands upon education, upon social habits, upon business developments, as it proceeds to take over the organization of the community, it will marshal not only its own forces but its enemies. A complex of interests will find themselves restrained and threatened by it, and it may easily evoke that most dangerous of human mass

157

feelings, fear. In ways quite unpredictable it may raise a storm against itself beyond all our present imaginings. Our conception of an almost bloodless domination of the Atlantic communities may be merely the confident dream of a thinker whose thoughts have yet to be squarely challenged.

We are not even sure of the common peace. Across the path of mankind the storm of another Great War may break, bringing with it for a time more brutal repressions and vaster injuries even than its predecessor. The scaffoldings and work sheds of the Open Conspiracy may fare violently in that tornado. The restoration of progress may seem an almost hopeless struggle.

It is no part of modern religion to incur needless hardship or go out of the way to seek martyrdom. If we can do our work easily and happily, so it should be done. But the work is not to be shirked because it cannot be done easily and happily. The vision of a world at peace and liberated for an unending growth of knowledge and power is worth every danger of the way. And since in this age of confusion we must live imperfectly and anyhow die, we may as well suffer, if need be, and die for a great end as for none. Never has the translation of vision into realities been easy since the beginning of human effort. The establishment of the world community will surely exact a price – and who can tell what that price may be? – in toil, suffering, and blood.

CHAPTER NINETEEN

Human Life in the Coming World Community

The new life that the Open Conspiracy struggles to achieve through us for our race is first a life of liberations.

The oppression of incessant toil can surely be lifted from everyone, and the miseries due to a great multitude of infections and disorders of nutrition and growth cease to be a part of human experience. Few people are perfectly healthy nowadays except for brief periods of happiness, but the elation of physical well-being will some day be the common lot of mankind.

And not only from natural evils will man be largely free. He will not be left with his soul tangled, haunted by monstrous and irrational fears and a prey to malicious impulse. From his birth he will breathe sweetness and generosity and use his mind and hands cleanly and exactly. He will feel better, will better, think better, see, taste, and hear better than men do now. His undersoul will no longer be a mutinous cavern of ill-treated suppressions and of impulses repressed without understanding. All these releases are plainly possible for him. They pass out of his tormented desire now, they elude and mock him, because chance, confusion, and squalor rule his life. All the gifts of destiny are

159

overlaid and lost to him. He must still suspect and fear. Not one of us is yet as clear and free and happy within himself as most men will some day be. Before mankind lies the prospect not only of health but of magnanimity.

Within the peace and freedom that the Open Conspiracy is winning for us, all these good things that escape us now may be ensured. A graver humanity, stronger, more lovely, longer lived, will learn and develop the ever enlarging possibilities of its destiny. For the first time, the full beauty of this world will be revealed to its unhurried eyes. Its thoughts will be to our thoughts as the thoughts of a man to the troubled mental experimenting of a child. And all the best of us will be living on in that ampler life, as the child and the things it tried and learnt still live in the man. When we were children, we could not think or feel as we think and feel today, but today we can peer back and still recall something of the ignorances and guesses and wild hopes of these nigh forgotten years.

And so mankind, ourselves still living, but dispersed and reconstructed again in the future, will recall with affection and understanding the desperate wishes and troubled efforts of our present state.

How far can we anticipate the habitations and ways, the usages and adventures, the mighty employments, the ever increasing knowledge and power of the days to come? No more than a child with its scribbling paper and its box of bricks can picture or model the undertakings of its adult years. Our battle is with cruelties and frustrations, stupid, heavy, and hateful things from which we shall escape at last, less like victors conquering a world than like sleepers awaking from a nightmare in the dawn. From any dream, however dismal and horrible, one can escape by realizing that it is a dream; by saying, "I will awake."

The Open Conspiracy is the awaking of mankind from a nightmare, an infantile nightmare, of the struggle for existence and the inevitability of war. The light of day thrusts between our eyelids, and the multitudinous sounds of morning clamour in our ears. A time will come when men will sit with history before them or with some old newspaper before them and ask incredulously, "Was there ever such a world?"

First and Last Things

CONTENTS

BOOK ONE

METAPHYSICS

1

The Necessity for Metaphysics

A s a preliminary to that experiment in mutual confession from which this book arose, I found it necessary to consider and state certain truths about the nature of knowledge, about the meaning of truth and the value of words, that is to say I found I had to begin by being metaphysical. In writing out these notes now I think it is well that I should state just how important I think this metaphysical prelude is.

There is a popular prejudice against metaphysics as something at once difficult and fruitless, as an idle system of enquiries remote from any human interest. As a matter of fact metaphysical enquiries are a necessary condition to all clear thinking. I suppose this odd misconception arose from the vulgar pretensions of pedants, from their appeal to ancient names and their quotations in unfamiliar tongues, and from the easy fall into technicality of men struggling to be explicit where a high degree of explicitness is impossible. Metaphysics is a discussion of our general ideas, and naturally therefore intelligent metaphysical discussion is hardly possible except in the mother tongue in which those general ideas arose in our minds. But the interests and the pedantries that control higher education in Britain and influence it very powerfully in America, have imposed upon the proper study and teaching of metaphysics the absurd condition that it should be studied in connection with the badly-taught and little known language of Ancient Greece. So a naturally elementary discussion has been made into an intricate and allusive one. It needs erudition and accumulated and alien literature to make metaphysics obscure, and some of the most fruitful and able metaphysical discussion in the world was conducted by a number of unhampered men in small Greek cities, who knew no language but their own and had scarcely a technical term. The true metaphysician is after all only a person who says, "Now let us take thought for a moment before we fall into a discussion of the broad questions of life, lest we rush hastily into impossible and needless conflict. What is the exact value of these thoughts we are thinking and these words we are using?" He wants to take thought about thought. There are, of course, ardent spirits who, on the contrary, want to plunge into action or controversy or belief without taking thought; they feel that there is not time to examine thought. "While you argue," they say, "the house is burning." They are the kin of those who rush and struggle and make panics in theatre fires. But they are not likely to be among the readers of this book.

It seems to me that most of the troubles of humanity are really misunderstandings. Men's compositions and characters are, I think, more similar than their views, and if they had not needlessly different modes of expression upon many broad issues, they would be practically at one upon a hundred matters where now they widely differ.

Most of the great controversies of the world, most of the wide religious differences that keep men apart, arise from this: from differences in their way of thinking. Men imagine they stand on the same ground and mean the same thing by the same words, whereas they stand on slightly different grounds, use different terms for the same thing and express the same thing in different words. Logomachies, conflict about words, – into such death traps of effort do ardent spirits run and perish.

This has been said before by numberless people. It has been said before by numberless people, but it seems to me it has been realized by very few – and until it is realized to the fullest extent, we shall continue to live at intellectual cross-purposes and waste the forces of our species needlessly and abundantly.

This persuasion is a very important thing in my mind.

I think that the time has come when the modern mind must take up metaphysical discussion again – when it must resume those subtle but necessary and unavoidable problems which have been so markedly shirked for many years, when it must get to a common and general understanding upon what its ideas of truth, good, and beauty amount to, and upon the relation of the name to the thing, and of the relation of one mind to another mind in the matter of resemblance and the matter of difference – upon all those issues the young science student is apt to dismiss as Rot, and the young classical student as Gas. And the austere student of the science of Economics as Theorizing, unsuitable for his methods of research.

In our achievement of understandings in the place of these evasions about fundamental things lies the road, I believe, along which the human mind can escape, if ever it is to escape, from the confusion of purposes that distracts it at the present time.

2

Current Metaphysical Teaching Absurd

When the intellectual history of our time comes to be written I think that nothing will more impress the students of these years than the extraordinary evasion of metaphysical enlightenment in the education of our youth. Here were exercise and disciplines essential to the proper development of any good mind; here were questions intensely attractive to any intelligent youth; here were the common tests and filters for all knowledge and decision, and the youth of the big English-speaking community was almost deliberately kept away from and cheated out of this strengthening gymnastic. No wonder that the English-speaking mind had an understanding like a broken sieve and a will as capable of definite forms as a dropped egg. Philosophical study, the common material for every type of sound adolescent education, was stuck away into remote pretentious courses, behind barriers of Greek linguistic training, as if it were something too high for normal minds, too mystical for current speech. A general need was treated as a precious luxury. At Oxford instead of calling the philosophical course "Elements", the future historian will remark, with derision, they called it "Greats".

And when this student of things intellectual has done with the general preposterousness of a huge modern community treating philosophy as a remote special subject reserved for a small minority of university students, he will find still more matter for amazement and laughter in our way of teaching philosophy. We do not bring the young mind up against the few broad elemental questions that are *the questions of metaphysics*, the questions that provide *the* basis of all clear thinking. We do not make it discuss, correct it, elucidate it. That was the way of the Greeks, and we worship that divine people far too much to adopt their way. No, we lecture to our young people about not philosophy but philosophers, we put them through book after book, telling how other people have discussed these questions. We avoid the questions of metaphysics, but we deliver semi-digested half views of the discussions of, and answers to these questions made by men of all sorts and qualities, in various remote languages and under conditions quite different from our own. In their histories the essential questions are presently completely lost sight of. We give them compact (and indeed highly desiccated) accounts of the philosophy of Aristotle, Plato, Hegel, Locke, Descartes and so on and so on. It is as if we began teaching arithmetic by long lectures upon the origin of the Roman numerals and then went on to the lives and motives of the Arab mathematicians in Spain, or started with Roger Bacon in chemistry or Sir Richard Owen in comparative anatomy. A little while ago I had a most edifying conversation with two young women who had been "doing" and who had "done", bless them! "philosophy" in the Universities of London and Cambridge respectively. They had shared experiences of a lecturer, I forget his name, who lectures in both these radiant centres of wisdom. This incredible person lectures, they assured me, upon all philosophies ancient and modern. Poor Omniscience just knows everything, but this marvel knows what everybody has thought about everything. He told his classes what they all thought, all these wise men, and how they "derived" one from another. These two young people were in consequence more like bags of broken fragments from the ages than living

173

intelligences; they discussed glibly of the Platonic Ideal and the Golden Mean, of Categories and Imperatives, of Induction and Syllogism and Materialism; if you spoke of Plotinus they whispered "Mysticism", and if you said Lucretius, the atoms glittered in their eyes. Also they had a fine stock of lecture-room anecdotes. I tried them then upon one or two current questions. And on the whole they thought rather worse than if they had spent these same studious years upon embroidery.

It is time the educational powers began to realize that the questions of metaphysics, the elements of philosophy, are, here and now, to be done afresh in each mind. So far as the thought that has gone before us enlightens our present inquiry so far it lives still. The rest is for the museum and the special scholar. What is wanted is philosophy, and not a shallow smattering of the history of philosophy. Our children ask for bread and we give them worn millstones...

The proper way to discuss metaphysics, like the proper way to discuss mathematics or chemistry, is to discuss the accumulated and digested product of human thought in such matters. Only in creature literature and because of beauty are texts immortal. The reverence for texts and the "systems" of individuals in the case of philosophy is just as absurd and mischievous as it would be in the case of science. The only philosophy that a man is entitled to expound and discuss is that which he has made his own. I make no apology therefore in annexing every philosophical idea and phrase from the past that I have cared to assimilate. This is *my* system that I place before you in order that you should make *your* system. You can no more think about the world according to another man's system than you can look at it with a dead man's eyes.

The World of Fact

Necessarily when one begins an inquiry into the fundamental
nature of oneself and one's mind and its processes, one is forced
into biography. I begin by asking how the conscious mind with
which I identify myself, began.

It presents itself to me as a history of a perception of a world
of facts opening out from an accidental centre at which I
happened to begin.

I do not attempt to define this word fact. Fact expresses for me
something in its nature primary and unanalysable. I start from
that. I take as a typical statement of fact that I sit here at my desk
writing with a fountain pen on a pad of ruled scribbling paper,
that the sunlight falls upon me and throws the shadow of the
window mullion across the page, that Peter, my cat, sleeps on
the window-seat close at hand and that this agate paper-weight
with the silver top that once was Henley's holds my loose
memoranda together. Outside is a patch of lawn and then a fringe
of winter-bitten iris leaves and then the sea, greatly wrinkled and
astir under the south-west wind. There is a boat going out which
I think may be Jim Pain's, but of that I cannot be sure...

These are statements of a certain quality, a quality that
extends through a huge universe in which I find myself placed.

I try to recall how this world of fact arose in my mind. It
began with a succession of limited immediate scenes and of
certain minutely perceived persons; I recall an underground
kitchen with a drawered table, a window looking up at a grating, a
back yard in which, growing out by a dust-bin, was a grapevine;

a red-papered room with a bookcase, over my father's shop, the dusty aisles and fixtures, the regiments of wine-glasses and tumblers, the rows of hanging mugs and jugs, the towering edifices of jam-pots, the tea and dinner and toilet sets in that emporium, its brighter side of cricket goods, of pads and balls and stumps. Out of the window one peeped at the more exterior world, the High Street in front, the tailor's garden, the butcher's yard, the churchyard and Bromley church tower behind; and one was taken upon expeditions to fields and open places. This limited world was peopled with certain familiar presences, mother and father, two brothers, the evasive but interesting cat, and by intermittent people of a livelier but more transient interest, customers and callers.

Such was my opening world of fact, and each day it enlarged and widened and had more things added to it. I had soon won my way to speech and was hearing of facts beyond my visible world of fact. Presently I was at a Dame's school and learning to read.

From the centre of that little world, as primary, as the initiatory material, my perception of the world of fact widened and widened, by new sights and sounds, by reading and hearing descriptions and histories, by guesses and inferences; my curiosity and interest, my appetite for fact, grew by what it fed upon, I carried on my expansion of the world of fact until it took me through the mineral and fossil galleries of the Natural History Museum, through the geological drawers of the College of Science, through a year of dissection and some weeks at the astronomical telescope. So I built up my conceptions of a real world out of facts observed and out of inferences of a nature akin to fact, of a world immense and enduring, receding interminably into space and time. In that I found myself placed, a creature

176

relatively infinitesimal, needing and struggling. It was clear to me, by a hundred considerations, that I in my body upon this planet Earth, was the outcome of countless generations of conflict and begetting, the creature of natural selection, the heir of good and bad engendered in that struggle.

So my world of fact shaped itself. I find it altogether impossible to question or doubt that world of fact. Particular facts one may question as facts. For instance, I think I see an unseasonable yellow wallflower from my windows, but you may dispute that and show it is only a broken end of iris leaf accidentally lit to yellow. That is merely a substitution of fact for fact. One may doubt whether one is perceiving or remembering or telling facts clearly, but the persuasion that there are facts independent of one's interpretations and obdurate to one's will, remains invincible.

4

Scepticism of the Instrument

At first I took the world of fact as being exactly as I perceived it. I believed my eyes. Seeing was believing, I thought. Still more did I believe my reasoning. It was only slowly that I began to suspect that the world of fact could be anything different from the clear picture it made upon my mind.

I realized the inadequate of the senses first. Into that I will not enter here. Any proper textbook of physiology or psychology will supply a number of instances of the habitual deceptions of sight and touch and hearing. I came upon these things in my reading, in the laboratory, with microscope or telescope, lived with them as constant difficulties. I will only instance one trifling case of visual deception in order to lead to my next question. One draws two lines strictly parallel; so

Oblique to them one draws a series of lines; so

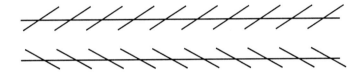

and instantly the parallelism seems to be disturbed. If the second figure is presented to any one without sufficient science to understand this delusion, the impression is created that these lines converge to the right and diverge to the left. The vision is deceived in its mental factor and judges wrongly of the thing seen.

In this case we are able to measure the distance of the lines, to find how the main lines looked before the cross ones were drawn, to bring the deception up against fact of a different sort and so correct the mistake. If the ignorant observer were unable to do that, he might remain permanently under the impression that the main lines were out of parallelism. And all the infirmities of eye and ear, touch and taste, are discovered and checked by the fact that the erroneous impressions presently strike against fact and discover an incompatibility with it. If they did not we should never have discovered them. If on the other hand they are so incompatible with fact as to endanger the lives of the beings labouring under such infirmities, they would tend to be eliminated from among our defects.

The presumption to which biological science brings one is that the senses and mind will work as well as the survival of the species may require, but that they will not work so very much better. There is no ground in matter-of-fact experience for assuming that there is any more inevitable certitude about purely intellectual operations than there is about sensory perceptions. The mind of a man may be primarily only a food-seeking, danger-avoiding, mate-finding instrument, just as the mind of a dog is, just as the nose of a dog is, or the snout of a pig.

You see the strong preparatory reason there is in this view of life for entertaining the suppositions that –

The senses seem surer than they are.

The thinking mind seems clearer than it is and is more positive than it ought to be.

The world of fact is not what it appears to be.

These preliminary assumptions were already strongly established in my mind before I began to philosophize at all.

5

The Classificatory Assumption

After I had studied science and particularly biological science for some years, I became a teacher in a school for boys. I found it necessary to supplement my untutored conception of teaching method by a more systematic knowledge of its principles and methods, and I took the courses for the diplomas of Licentiate and Fellow of the London College of Preceptors which happened to be convenient for me. These courses included some of the more elementary aspects of psychology and logic and set me thinking and reading further. From the first, Logic as it was presented to me impressed me as a system of ideas and methods remote and secluded from the world of fact in which I lived and with which I had to deal. As it came to me in the ordinary textbooks, it presented itself as the science of inference using the syllogism as its principal instrument. Now I was first struck by the fact that while my teachers in Logic seemed to be assuring me I always thought in this form:—

"M is P.
S is M.
S is P."

the method of my reasoning was almost always in this form:—

"S_1 is more or less P.
S_2 is very similar to S_1,
S_2 is very probably but not certainly more or less P.
Let us go on that assumption and see how it works."

That is to say, I was constantly reasoning by analogy and applying verification. So far from using the syllogistic form confidently, I habitually distrusted it as anything more than a test of consistency in statement. But I found the textbooks of logic disposed to ignore my customary method of reasoning altogether or to recognise it only where S_1, and S_2 could be lumped together under a common name. Then they put it something after this form as Induction:–

> "S_1, S_2, S_3 and S_4 are P.
> $S_1 + S_2 + S_3 + S_4 + \ldots$ are all S.
> All S is P."

I looked into the laws of thought and into the postulates upon which the syllogistic logic is based, and it slowly became clear to me that from my point of view, the point of view of one who seeks truth and reality, logic assumed a belief in the objective reality of classification of which my studies in biology and mineralogy had largely disabused me. Logic, it seemed to me, had taken a common innate error of the mind and had emphasized it in order to develop a system of reasoning that should be exact in its processes. I turned my attention to the examination of that. For in common with the general run of illiterate men I had supposed that logic professed to supply a trustworthy science and method for the investigation and expression of reality.

A mind nourished on anatomical study is of course permeated with the suggestion of the vagueness and instability of biological species. A biological species is quite obviously a great number of unique individuals which is separable from other biological species only by the fact that an enormous number of other linking individuals are inaccessible in time – are in other words dead and gone – and each new individual in that species does, in the distinction of its own individuality, break away in however infinitesimal degree from the previous average properties of the species. There is no property of any species, even the properties that constitute the specific definition, that is not a matter of more or less.

If, for example, a species be distinguished by a single large red spot on the back, you will find if you go over a great number of specimens that red spot shrinking here to nothing, expanding there to a more general redness, weakening to pink, deepening to russet and brown, shading into crimson, and so on and so on. And this is true not only of biological species. It is true of the mineral specimens constituting a mineral species, and I remember as a constant refrain in the lectures of Professor Judd upon rock classification, the words, "they pass into one another by insensible gradations." It is true, I hold, of all things.

You will think perhaps of atoms of the elements as instances of identically similar things, but these are things not of experience but of theory, and there is not a phenomenon in chemistry that is not equally well explained on the supposition that it is merely the immense quantities of atoms necessarily taken in any experiment that masks by the operation of the law of averages the fact that each atom also has its unique quality, its special individual difference.

This ideal of uniqueness in all individuals is not only true of the classifications of material science: it is true and still more evidently true of the species of common thought: it is true of common terms. Take the word *Chair*. When one says chair, one thinks vaguely of an average chair. But collect individual instances: think of armchairs and reading-chairs and dining-room chairs, and kitchen chairs, chairs that pass into benches, chairs that cross the boundary and become settees, dentist's chairs, thrones, opera stalls, seats of all sorts, those miraculous

182

fungoid growths that cumber the floor of the Arts and Crafts Exhibition, and you will perceive what a lax bundle in fact is this simple straightforward term. In co-operation with an intelligent joiner I would undertake to defeat any definition of chair or chairishness that you gave me. Chairs just as much as individual organisms, just as much as mineral and rock specimens, are unique things – if you know them well enough you will find an individual difference even in a set of machine-made chairs – and it is only because we do not possess minds of unlimited capacity, because our brain has only a limited number of pigeonholes for our correspondence with an unlimited universe of objective uniques, that we have to delude ourselves into the belief that there is a chairishness in this species common to and distinctive of all chairs.

Classification and number, which in truth ignore the fine differences of objective realities, have in the past of human thought been imposed upon things...

Greek thought impresses me as being over-much obsessed by an objective treatment of certain necessary preliminary conditions of human thought – number and definition and class and abstract form! But these things, – number, definition, class and abstract form, – I hold, are merely unavoidable conditions of mental activity – regrettable conditions rather than essential facts. *The forceps of our minds are clumsy forceps and crush the truth a little in taking hold of it...*

Let me give you a rough figure of what I am trying to convey in this first attack upon the philosophical validity of general terms. You have seen the result of those various methods of black and white reproduction that involve the use of a rectangular net. You know the sort of process picture I mean – it used to be employed very frequently in reproducing photographs. At a little distance you really seem to have a faithful reproduction of the original picture, but when you peer closely you find not the unique form and masses of the original, but a multitude of little rectangles, uniform in shape and size. The more earnestly you go into the thing, the closer you look, the more the picture is lost in reticulations. I submit, the world of reasoned inquiry has a very similar relation to the world of fact. For the rough purposes of every day the network picture will do, but the finer your purpose the less it will serve, and for an ideally fine purpose, for absolute and general knowledge that will be as true for a man at a distance with a telescope as for a man with a microscope, it will not serve at all.

It is true you can make your net of logical interpretation finer and finer, you can fine your classification more and more – up to a certain limit. But essentially you are working in limits, and as you come closer, as you look at finer and subtler things, as you leave the practical purpose for which the method exists, the element of error increases. Every species is vague, every term goes cloudy at its edges: and so in my way of thinking, relentless logic is only another name for a stupidity – for a sort of intellectual pigheadedness. If you push a philosophical or metaphysical inquiry through a series of valid syllogisms – never committing any generally recognized fallacy – you nevertheless leave behind you at each step a certain rubbing and marginal loss of objective truth, and you get deflections that are difficult to trace at each phase in the process. Every species waggles about in its definition, every tool is a little loose in its handle, every scale has its individual error. So long as you are reasoning for practical purposes about finite things of experiences, you can every now and then check your process and correct your adjustments. But not when you make what are called philosophical and theological inquiries, when you turn your implement towards the final absolute truth of things.

This real vagueness of class terms is equally true whether we consider those terms used extensively or intensively, that is to say whether in relation to all the members of the species or in relation to an imaginary typical specimen. The logician begins by declaring that S is either pink or not pink. In the world of fact it is the rarest thing to encounter this absolute alternative: S_1 is pink, but S_2 is pinker, S_3 is scarcely pink at all, and one is in doubt whether S_4 is not properly to be called scarlet. The finest type specimen you can find simply has the characteristic quality a little more rather than a little less. The neat little circles the logician uses to convey his idea of pink or not pink to the student are just pictures of boundaries in his mind, exaggerations of a natural mental tendency. They are required for the purpose of his science, but they are departures from the nature of fact.

6

Empty Terms

Classes in logic are not only represented by circles with a hard firm outline, whereas in fact they have no such definite limits, but also there is a constant disposition to think of all names as if they represented positive classes. With words just as with numbers and abstract forms there have been definite phases of human development. There was with regard to number, the phase when man could barely count at all, or counted in perfect good faith and sanity upon his fingers. Then there was the phase when he struggle with the development of number, when he began to elaborate all sorts of ideas about numbers, until at last he developed complex superstitions about perfect numbers and imperfect numbers, about threes and sevens and the like. The same was the case with abstract forms; and even today we are scarcely more than heads out of the vast subtle muddle of thinking about spheres and ideally perfect forms and so on, that was the price of this little necessary step to clear thinking. How large a part numerical and geometric magic, numerical and geometrical philosophy have played in the history of the mind! And the whole apparatus of language and mental communication is beset with like dangers. The language of the elemental savage is I suppose purely positive; the thing has a name, the name has a thing. This indeed is the tradition of language, even today, we, when we hear a name are predisposed – and sometimes it is a very vicious disposition – to imagine forthwith something answering to the name. *We are disposed, as an incurable mental vice, to accumulate intension in terms.* If I say to you Wodget or Crump, you find yourself passing over the fact that these are nothings, these are, so to speak, mere blankety blanks, and trying to think what sort of thing a Wodget or a Crump may be. You find yourself led insensibly by subtle associations of sound and ideas to giving these blank terms attributes.

Now this is true not only of quite empty terms but of terms that carry a meaning. It is a mental necessity that we should make classes and use general terms, and as soon as we do that we fall into immediate danger of unjustifiably increasing the intension of these terms. You will find a large proportion of human prejudice and misunderstanding arises from this universal proclivity.

7

Negative Terms

There is a particular sort of empty terms that has been and is conspicuously dangerous to the thinker, the class of negative terms. The negative term is in plain fact just nothing; "Not-A" is the absence of any trace of the quality that constitutes A, it is the rest of everything for ever. But there seems to be a real bias in the mind towards regarding "Not-A" as a thing mysteriously in the nature of A, as though "Not-A" and A were species of the same genus. When one speaks of Not-Pink one is apt to think of green things and yellow things and to ignore anger or abstract nouns or the sound of thunder. And logicians, following the normal bias of the mind, do actually present A and Not-A in this sort of diagram:–

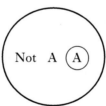

ignoring altogether the difficult case of the space in which these words are printed. Obviously the diagram that comes nearer experienced fact is:–

Not (A) A

with no outer boundary. But the logician finds it necessary for his processes[1] to present that outer Not-A as bonded, and to speak of the total area of A and Not-A as the Universe of Discourse; and the metaphysician and the common-sense thinker alike fall far too readily into the belief that this convention of method is an adequate representation of fact.

Let me try and express how in my mind this matter of negative terms has shaped itself. I think of something which I may perhaps best describe as being off the stage or out of court, or as the Void without Implications, or as Nothingness, or as Outer Darkness. This is a sort of hypothetical Beyond to the visible world of human thought, and thither I think all negative terms reach at last, and merge, and become nothing. Whatever positive class you make, whatever boundary you draw, straight away from that boundary begins the corresponding negative class and passes into the illimitable horizon of nothingness. You talk of pink things, you ignore, as the arbitrary postulates of Logic direct, the more elusive shades of pink, and draw your line. Beyond is the not-pink, known and knowable, and still in the not-pink region one comes to the Outer Darkness. Not blue, not happy, not iron, all the *not* classes meet in that Outer Darkness. That same Outer Darkness and nothingness is infinite space and infinite time and any being of infinite qualities; and all that region I rule out of court in my philosophy altogether. I will neither affirm nor deny if I can help it about any *not* things. I will not deal with *not* things at all, except by accident and inadvertence. If I use the word "infinite" I use it as one often uses "countless", "the countless hosts of the enemy" – or "immeasureable" – "immeasureable cliffs" – that is to say as the

1 *Vide e.g.* Keyne's *Formal Logic re* Euler's diagrams and Immediate Inferences.

limit of measurement, as a convenient equivalent to as many times this cloth yard as you can, and as many again, and so on and so on until you and your numerical system are beaten to a standstill.

Now a great number of apparently positive terms are, or have become, practically negative terms and are under the same ban with me. A considerable number of terms that have played a great part in the world of thought, seem to me to be invalidated by this same defect, to have no content or an undefined content or an unjustifiable content. For example, that word Omniscient, as implying infinite knowledge, impresses me as being a word with a delusive air of being solid and full, when it is really hollow with no content whatever. I am persuaded that knowing is the relation of a conscious being to something not itself, that the thing known is defined as a system of parts and aspects and relationships, that knowledge is comprehension, and so that only finite things can know or be known. When you talk of a being of infinite extension and infinite duration, omniscient and omnipotent and perfect, you seem to me to be talking in negatives of nothing whatever.

8

Logic Static and Life Kinetic

Not only are class terms vague with regard to these marginal instances, but they are also vague in time. The current syllogistic logic rests on the assumption that either A is B or it is not B. The practical reality is that nothing is permanent; A is always becoming more or less B or ceasing to be more or less B. But it would seem the human mind cannot manage with that. It has to hold a thing still for a moment before it can think it. It arrests the present moment for its struggle as Joshua stopped the sun. It cannot contemplate things continuously, and so it has to resort to a series of static snapshots. It has to kill motion in order to study it, as a naturalist kills and pins out a butterfly in order to study life.

You see the mind is really pigeon-holed and discontinuous in two respects, in respect to time and in respect to classification; whereas one has a strong persuasion that the world of fact is unbounded or continuous.

9

Planes and Dialects of Thought

Finally; the Logician, intent upon perfecting the certitudes of his methods rather than upon expressing the confusing subtleties of truth, has done little to help thinking men in the perpetual difficulty that arises from the fact that the universe can be seen in many different fashions and expressed by many different systems of terms, each expression within its limits true and yet incommensurable with expression upon a differing system. There is a sort of stratification in human ideas. I have it very much in mind that various terms in our reasoning lie, as it were, at different levels and in different planes, and that we accomplish a large amount of amount of error and confusion by reasoning terms together that do not lie or nearly lie in the same plane.

Let me endeavour to make myself a little less obscure by a flagrant instance from physical things. Suppose someone began to talk seriously of a man seeing an atom through a microscope, or better perhaps of cutting one in half with a knife. There are a number of non-analytical people who would be quite prepared to believe that an atom could be visible to the eye or cut in this manner. But say one at all conversant with physical conceptions would almost as soon think of killing the square root of 2 with a rook rifle as of cutting an atom in half with a knife. One's conception of an atom is reached through a process of hypothesis and analysis, and in the world of atoms there are no knives and no men to cut. If you have thought with a strong consistent mental movement, then when you have thought of your atom under the knife blade, your knife blade has itself become a cloud of swinging grouped atoms, and your microscope lens a little universe of oscillatory and vibratory molecules. If you think of the universe, thinking at the level of atoms, there is neither knife to cut, scale to weigh, nor eye to see. The universe at that plane to which the mind of the molecular physicist descends has none of the shapes or forms of our common life whatever. This hand with which I write is, in the universe of molecular physics, a cloud of warring atoms and molecules, combining and recombining, colliding, rotating, flying hither and thither in the universal atmosphere of ether.

You see, I hope, what I mean when I say that the universe of molecular physics is at a different level from the universe of common experience:– what we call stable and solid is in that world a freely moving system of interlacing centres of force, what we call colour and sound is there no more than this length of vibration or that. We have reached to a conception of that universe of molecular physics by a great enterprise of organized analysis, and our universe of daily experience stands in relation to that elemental world as if it were a synthesis of those elemental things.

I would suggest to you that this is only a very extreme instance of the general state of affairs, that there may be finer and subtler differences of level between one term and another, and that terms may very well be thought of as lying obliquely and as being twisted through different levels.

It will perhaps give a clearer idea of what I am seeking to convey if I suggest a concrete image for the whole world of a man's thought and knowledge. Imagine a large clear jelly, in which at all angles and in all states of simplicity or contortion his ideas are imbedded. They are all valid and possible ideas as they lie, none incompatible with any. If you imagine the direction of up or down in this clear jelly being as it were the direction in which one moves by analysis or by synthesis, if you go down for example from matter to atoms and centres of force and up to men and states and countries – if you will imagine the ideas lying in that manner – you will get the beginnings of my intention. But our instrument, our process of thinking, like a drawing before the discovery of perspective, appears to have difficulties with the third dimension, appears capable only of dealing with or reasoning about ideas by projecting them upon the same plane. It will be obvious that a great multitude of things may very well exist together in a solid jelly, which would be overlapping and incompatible and mutually destructive when projected together upon one plane. Through the bias in our instrument to do this, through reasoning between terms not in the same plane an enormous amount of confusion, perplexity, and mental deadlocking occurs.

The old theological deadlock between predestination and free will serves admirably as an example of the sort of deadlock I mean. Take life at the level of common sensation and common experience and there is no more indisputable fact than man's freedom of will, unless it is his complete moral responsibility. But make only the least penetrating of scientific analyses and you perceive a world of inevitable consequences, a rigid succession of cause and effect. Insist upon a flat agreement between the two, and there you are! The instrument fails.

So far as this particular opposition is concerned, I shall point out later the reasonableness and convenience of regarding the common-sense belief in free will as truer for one's personal life than determinism.

10

Practical Conclusions from these Considerations

Now what is the practical outcome of all these criticisms of the human mind? Does it fellow that thought is futile and discussion vain? By no means. Rather these considerations lead us towards mutual understanding. They clear up the deadlocks that come from the hard and fast use of terms, they establish mutual charity as an intellectual necessity. The common way of speech and thought which the old system of logic has simply systematized, is too glib and too presumptuous of certainty. We must needs use language, but we must use it always with the thought in our minds of its unreal exactness, its actual habitual deflection from fact. All propositions are approximations to an elusive truth, and we employ them as the mathematician studies the circle by supposing it to be a polygon of a very great number of sides.

We must make use of terms and sometimes of provisional terms. But we must guard against such terms and the mental danger of excessive intension they carry with them. The child takes a stick and says it is a sword and does not forget, he takes a shadow under the bed and says it is a bear and he half forgets. The man takes a set of emotions and says it is a God, and he gets excited and propagandist and does forget; he is involved in disputes and confusions with the old gods of wood and stone, and presently he is making his God a Great White Throne and fitting him up with a mystical family. Yet because he has made these extravagant extensions of his idea of God, it does not follow that his emotional reaction to a something greater than himself and personal like himself, was a deception.

Essentially we have to train our minds to think anew, if we are to think beyond the purposes for which the mind seems to have been evolved. We have to disabuse ourselves from the superstition of the binding nature of definitions and the exactness of logic. We have to cure ourselves of the natural tricks of common thought and argument. You know the way of it, how effective and foolish it is: the quotation of the exact statement of which every jot and tittle must be maintained, the challenge to be consistent, the deadlock between your terms and mine.

More and more as I grow older and more settled in my views am I bored by common argument, bored not because I am ceasing to be interested in the things argued about, but because I see more and more clearly the futility of the methods pursued.

How then are we to think and argue and what truth may we attain? Is not the method of the scientific investigator a valid one, and is there not truth to the world of fact in scientific laws? Decidedly there is. And the continual revision and testing against fact that these laws get is constantly approximating them more and more nearly to a trustworthy statement of fact. Nevertheless they are never true in that dogmatic degree in which they seem true to the unphilosophical student of science. Accepting as I do the validity of nearly all the general propositions of modern science, I have constantly to bear in mind that about them too clings the error of excessive claims to precision.

The man trained solely in science falls easily into a superstitious attitude; he is overdone with classification. He believes in the possibility of exact knowledge everywhere. What is not exact he declares is not knowledge. He believes in specialists and experts in all fields.

I dispute this universal range of possible scientific precision. There is, I allege, a not too clearly recognized order in the sciences which forms the gist of my case against this scientific pretension. There is a gradation in the importance of the individual instance as one passes from mechanics and physics and chemistry through the biological sciences to economics and sociology, a gradation whose correlations and implications have not yet received adequate recognition, and which does profoundly affect the method of study and research in each science.

Let me repeat in slightly altered terms some of the points raised in the preceding sections. I have doubted and denied that there are identically similar objective experiences: I consider all objective beings as individual and unique. It is now understood that conceivably only in the subjective world, and in theory and the imagination, do we deal with identically similar units, and with absolutely commensurable quantities. In the real world it is reasonable to suppose we deal at most with *practically* similar units and *practically* commensurable quantities. But there is a strong bias, a sort of labour-saving bias, in the normal human mind, to ignore this, and not only to speak but to think of a thousand bricks or a thousand sheep or a thousand Chinamen as though they were all absolutely true to sample. If it is brought before a thinker for a moment that in any special case this is not so, he slips back to the old attitude as soon as his attention is withdrawn. This type of error has, for instance, caught many of the race of chemists, and *atoms* and *ions* and so forth of the same species are tacitly assumed to be identically similar to one another.

Be it noted that, so far as the practical results of chemistry and physics go, it scarcely matters which assumption we adopt, the number of units is so great, the individual difference so drowned and lost. For purposes of inquiry and discussion the incorrect one is infinitely more convenient.

But this ceases to be true directly we emerge from the region of chemistry and physics. In the biological sciences of the eighteenth century, common sense struggled hard to ignore individuality in shells and plants and animals. There was an attempt to eliminate the more conspicuous departures as abnormalities, as sports, nature's weak moments; and it was only with the establishment of Darwin's great generalizations that the hard and fast classificatory system broke down and individuality came to its own. Yet there had always been a clearly felt difference between the conclusions of the biological sciences and those dealing with lifeless substance, in the relative vagueness, the insubordinate looseness and inaccuracy of the former. The naturalist accumulated facts and multiplied names, but he did not go triumphantly from generalization to generalization after the fashion of the chemist or physicist. It is easy to see, therefore, how it came about that the inorganic sciences were regarded as the true scientific bedrock. It was scarcely suspected that the biological sciences might perhaps after all be *truer* than the experimental, in spite of the difference in practical value in favour of the latter. It was, and is by the great majority of people to this day, supposed to be the latter that are invincibly true: and the former are regarded as a more complex set of problems merely, with obliquities and refractions that presently will be explained away. Comte and Herbert Spencer certainly seem to me to have taken that much for granted. Herbert Spencer no doubt talked of the unknown and unknowable, but not in this sense as an element of inexactness running through all things. He thought, it seems to me, of the unknown as the indefinable Beyond of an immediate world that might be quite clearly and definitely known.

There is a growing body of people which is beginning to hold the converse view – that counting, measurement, the whole fabric of mathematics, is subjective and untrue to the world of fact, and that the uniqueness of individuals is the objective truth. They realize that we see this world with "atmosphere". As the number of units taken diminishes, the amount of variety and inexactness of generalization increases, because individuality tells for more and more. Could you take men by the thousand billion, you could generalize about them as you do about atoms; could you take atoms singly, it may be you would find them as individual as your aunts and cousins. That concisely is the minority belief, and my belief.

Now what is called the scientific method in the physical sciences rests upon the ignoring of individualities; and like many mathematical conventions, its great practical convenience is no proof whatever of its final truth. Let me admit the enormous value, the wonder of its results in mechanics, in all the physical sciences, in chemistry, even in physiology, – but what is its value beyond that? Is the scientific method of value in biology? The great advances made by Darwin and his school in biology were not made, it must be remembered, by the scientific method, as it is generally conceived, at all. His was historical research. He conducted a research into pre-documentary history. He collected information along the lines indicated by certain interrogations; and the bulk of his work was the digesting and critical analysis of that. For documents and monuments he had fossils and anatomical structures and germinating eggs too innocent to lie. But, on the other hand, he had to correspond with breeders and travellers of various sorts; classes entirely analogous, from the point of view of evidence, to the writers of history and memoirs. I question profoundly whether the word "science", in current usage anyhow, ever means such patient disentanglement as Darwin pursued. It means the attainment of something positive and emphatic in the way of a conclusion, based on amply repeated experiments capable of infinite repetition, "proved", as they say, "up to the hilt".

It would be of course possible to dispute whether the word "science" should convey this quality of certitude, but to most people it certainly does at the present time. So far as the movements of comets and electric trams go, there is no doubt practically cock-sure science; and Comte and Herbert Spencer seem to me to have believed that cock-sure could be extended to every conceivable finite thing. The fact that Herbert Spencer called a certain doctrine Individualism reflects nothing on the

198

non-individualising quality of his primary assumptions and of his mental texture. He believed that individuality (heterogeneity) was and is an evolutionary product from an original homogeneity, begotten by folding and multiplying and dividing and twisting it, and still fundamentally *it*. It seems to me that the popular usage is entirely for the limitation of the word "science" to knowledge of a high degree of precision and the search after knowledge of a high degree of precision.

Now my contention is that we can arrange the fields of human thought and interest about the world of fact in a sort of scale. At one end the number of units is extreme and the methods almost exact, at the other we have the "humanities" in which there is no exactitude. The science of society stands at the extreme end of the scale from the molecular sciences. In these latter there is an infinitude of units; in sociology, as Comte perceived, there is only one unit. It is true that Herbert Spencer, in order to get classification somehow, did, as Professor Durkheim has pointed out, separate human society into societies, and made believe they competed one with another and died and reproduced just like animals, and that economists following List have for the purposes of fiscal controversy discovered economic types; but this is a transparent device, and one is surprised to find thoughtful and reputable writers off their guard against such bad analogy. But indeed it is impossible to isolate complete communities of men, or to trace any but rude general resemblances between group and group. These alleged units have as much individuality as pieces of cloud; they go, they fuse and separate. And we are forced to conclude that not only is the method of observation, experiment, and verification left far away down the scale, but that the method of classification under types, which has served so useful a purpose in the middle group of subjects, the subjects involving numerous but a finite number of units, has also to be abandoned in social science. We cannot put Humanity into a museum or dry it for examination; our one single still living specimen is all history, all anthropology, and the fluctuating world of men. There is no satisfactory means of dividing it, and nothing else in the real world with which to compare it. We have only the remotest ideas of its "life-cycle" and a few relics of its origin and dreams of its destiny.

This denial of scientific precision is true of all questions of general human relations and attitude. And in regard to all these matters affecting our personal motives, our self-control and our devotions, it is much truer.

From this it is an easy step to the statement that so far as the clear-cut confident sort of knowledge goes, the sort of knowledge one gets from a time-table or a text-book of chemistry, or seeks from a witness in a police court, I am, in relation to religious and moral questions, an agnostic. I do not think any general propositions partaking largely of the nature of fact can be known about these things. There is nothing possessing the general validity of fact to be stated or known.

11

Beliefs

Yet it is urgent practical necessity that we should have such propositions and beliefs. All those we conjure out of our mental apparatus and the world of fact dissolve and disappear again under scrutiny. It is clear we must resort to some other method for these necessities.

Now I make my beliefs as I want them. I do not attempt to distil them out of fact as physicists distil their laws. I make them thus and not thus exactly as an artist makes a picture so and not so. I believe that is how we all make our beliefs, but that many people do not see this clearly and confuse their beliefs with perceived and proven fact.

I draw my beliefs exactly as an artist draws lines to make a picture, to express my impression of the world and my purpose.

The artist cannot defend his expression as a scientific man defends his, and demonstrate that they are true upon any assumptions whatsoever. Any loud fool may stand in the front of a picture and call it inaccurate, untrustworthy, unbeautiful. That last, the most vital issue of all, is the one least assured. Loud fools always do do that sort of thing. Take quite ignorant people before almost any beautiful work of art and they will laugh at it as absurd. If one sits on a popular evening in that long room at South Kensington which contains Raphael's cartoons, one remarks that perhaps a third of those who stray through and look at all those fine efforts, titter. If one searches in the magazines of a little while ago, one finds in the angry and resentful reception of the Pre-Raphaelites another instance of the absolutely indefensible nature of many of the most beautiful propositions. And as a still more striking and remarkable case, take the onslaught made by Ruskin upon the works of Whistler. You will remember that a libel action ensued and that these pictures were gravely reasoned about by barristers and surveyed by jurymen to assess their merits...

In the end in these human matters it is the truth, however indefensible it may be, however open to blank denials, that lasts; it lasts because it works and serves. People come to it and remain and attract other understanding and inquiring people.

Now when I say I make my beliefs and that I cannot prove them to you and convince you of them, that does not mean that I make them wantonly and regardless of fact, that I throw them off as a child scribbles on a slate. Mr Ruskin, if I remember rightly, accused Whistler of throwing a pot of paint in the face of the public, – that was the essence of his libel. The artistic method in this field of beliefs, as in the field of visual renderings, is one of great freedom and initiative and great poverty of test, but of no wantonness; the conditions of rightness are none the less imperative because they are mysterious and indefinable. I adopt certain beliefs because I feel the need for them, because I feel an often quite unanalysable rightness in them; because the alternative of a chaotic life distresses me. My belief in them rests upon the fact that they *work* for me and satisfy my desire for harmony and beauty. They are arbitrary assumptions, if you will, that I see fit to impose upon my universe. But I am not able to go on imposing them upon my universe unless they stand the test of use. With my universe rests the power of veto.

But though my beliefs are really arbitrary in origin, they are not necessarily individual. Just so far as we all have a common likeness, just so far can we be brought under the same imperatives to think and believe. Other minds move as mine does.

And though my beliefs are arbitrary, each day they stand wear and tear, and each new person they satisfy, is another day and another voice towards showing they do correspond to something that is so far fact and real.

This is Pragmatism as I conceive it: the abandonment of infinite assumptions, the extension of the experimental spirit to all human interests.

12

The Aim and Method of Science

What I have said so far may seem a little ungracious to Science. It may be well to say a little more before leaving this metaphysical discussion altogether, about that new rich store of human knowledge, for the most part the achievement of the last three hundred years.

My qualification of the scope and exactitude of science must not be misread into an attack upon Science...

The scientific process of getting knowledge is really not different in kind from the method in which ordinary sensible men have always got knowledge and its aim has been very largely the same; the difference is that Science is systematic, co-operative and organized. Science is systematic Classification; the ordinary man spends his life working upon classifications unsystematically. But both sorts of judgments are classificatory judgments. The normal form of ordinary thought is, as I have already insisted in Section 5, not syllogism but something after this form:–

S_1 is P.
S_2 is probably classifiable with S_1.
So S_2 is probably more or less P.
Try it.

Ordinary mental life is constantly making experiments in classification, constantly trying whether S_2 does class in a proper workable way with S_1. Science only differs from this in its patient and systematic hunt for the most working classification, that is to say for the truest classification of things.

There are degrees of value in classification. Let me take a few instances to show what I mean by this.

Take first such a term as "Red Things" or "Old Things". We may speak of such a class as this for the purposes of some special discussion. We may say for instance that red things look black in a blue light. But such a term has scarcely any "intension" at all; its individuals carry no common property except the property stated in their definition. "Red things" may include a sunset, an angry baby, the planet Mars, a lacquer bowl, a drunkard's nose and so on and so on. The name, "Red things", is a mere link to hold all this miscellany together for a moment in our minds. Not so do we pack them for good in the pigeon holes of our brains. There are countless more convenient and useful ways than that.

Next take a term just a little less shallow, a term indicating not one attribute but a use, such as chair. Here the "intension" is a little greater. A small group of characteristics are imposed upon all "chairs" by the conditions of sitting down. Apart from that they are of the most diverse materials, forms, characters and qualities. There is something more real here in the name, in the "term" that holds this collection of things together, but it is still mainly a superficial link behind objects otherwise dissimilar.

The common nouns of our everyday speech record the classifications of everyday life. They record the verdict of the people to which we belong upon what they thought were the working kinds of things. "Science" is really a persistent criticism and rearrangement of these rule-of-thumb workaday classifications. It is a persistent attempt to get to truer and truer conceptions of the essential kinds of things. It studied "stuffs" for example; it attacked the classical idea that the stuffs of the world were made up of four elements: fire, air, earth and water. It broke down the idea that this was a primary classification and it replaced it with a far more accurate and secure list of elements. Its classification of fundamental stuffs, albeit it is still remote from any finality, into carbon, hydrogen, mercury and so on, has a far deeper mine of implication, a far keener statement of difference, than the old classification, and it has yielded such a human mastery over stuffs and materials, as men never dreamt of before the scientific age. But this newer classification was got by the organized armies of scientific research exactly after the fashion in which I get my individual judgments. I see S_2 and something about it suggests to my mind that it is to be classified with S_1. I know S_1 is P and so I try if S_2 is P. But while I do this individually and do not follow it up and forget about it presently, the organisation of research does it continuingly, records the judgment, confirms it, reconsiders it and makes sure of it for good. Just as I impose my arbitrary judgments on the universe, subject to the veto of the universe (Section 11), so does Science impose its theories upon the universe subject to "verification".

Now if the reader will consider the terms that are used in the sciences of chemistry and mineralogy he will find that they express a far intenser community of quality among their individuals and a far deeper difference in nature between these individuals and individuals of other species in the same classification, than is the case with the terms of such a use-classification as "Chair" and still more than the terms of such a quality-classification as "Red Things". The term, the name, is more real. A collection of quartz crystals for example have far more in common than a collection of chairs. It is a classification by kind.

Science is perpetually working away from provisional and empirical classifications to classifications of deeper and richer implication. For example it sets aside such obvious classes as Birds, Beasts and Fishes and distinguishes mammal from reptile and whale from fish. In the species of biology we get indeed to a maximum of classificatory intensity. The difference between an individual of this species and an individual of that is a difference in every detail and aspect through and through. The common cat and the common rabbit, except for some superficial resemblances, differ in everything; and every individual in each species agrees with every other individual in that same species upon a thousand matters over and above those specified in the definition, and differs from every individual in every other species. You can tell a cat's claw or hair or one of its small bones, you can tell even a little dried up drop of its blood from that of a rabbit. Here the term, the specific name, is at its very maximum of reality.

Biological Science does indeed assure us that the distinctness of biological species is exaggerated and emphasised by the disappearance of linking individuals that once bridged the gaps between now separated species. If we could go back in time we should realize that the present sharp distinction of existing biological species melts away in the past. This is a comparatively new idea in human thought. It was natural as well as convenient for man before the scientific era, dealing as he did chiefly with other men and beasts and plants to form an exaggerated idea of the fixity of classes by kind and to regard the terms, or specific names, that indicated things as having in themselves, *reality*.

This was the conception of Plato's Ideals. Besides individual men, Tom Jones, William Smith and so on, he held that there was an enduring reality, *Man*. Whether this was so or not, seem to have been a main subject for discussion in the middle ages; it is a discussion upon which modern biology throws a very strong light, a light so strong indeed as to bleach out many of its difficulties.

13

Nominalism and Realism

This discussion whether the name of a species expresses something in itself or whether it is merely a sort of verbal clutch holding together all the individuals of that species and of no other value at all, is one of the perennial questions of philosophy. It crops up in endless variations. It is unavoidable because upon our answer to it depends the meaning of all our religious formulae and most of our ideas about the relationships of our individual life to the world around it. What are called the "Realists" in the discussions of the middle ages, were essentially believers in a rather crude rendering of Platonic Idealism, and it is well to bear this in mind because in modern parlance "Realism" has come to mean something diametrically opposite to its proper significance. The Realists held that the name of a species of things did itself express a reality; the Nominalists held that the name was merely a link, the string of the bundle of individual things that alone were real.

It will be evident that Section 12 has been designed to lead up to the proposition that both these doctrines may be regarded as

more or less true according to the nature of the name considered.
If the name is the name of an attribute class such as "Red
things", it is obviously merely a link; about such names the
Nominalist is right. But as we pass up the scale to biological
species we begin to realize that there is a reality transcending the
individual and we begin to apprehend the justice of the Realist's
arguments so far as classification by kind is concerned. It was
chiefly of man that the Greek and mediaeval philosophers were
thinking; other things seemed of less significance. They could,
they perceived, think of "Man", quite apart from Tom Jones or
William Smith, and so far from thinking of the species man as
merely a crowd of individuals, they thought of these individuals
as a collection of failures, through this imperfection and that,
from the perfect thing Man. Now these discussions of these
matters are alien and perplexing to the modern student because
he has behind him a century and more of systematised
knowledge which makes his attitude to the idea of individuality
very different from that of an ancient Greek or a mediaeval
monk. He is accustomed to think of *Homo sapiens* or *Lepus
cuniculus* as the name of a being of a higher order, synthetically
speaking, than an individual man or rabbit, a multiple being that
maintains itself in its environment, resists adverse forces, and is
sustained, modified or exterminated by the outer forces of the
universe as time goes on. The reality of the species as a whole is
a commonplace in his thought. Having this idea very firmly
established in his mind, he is unable to see what these good
gentlemen are so earnestly disputing. He is in the position of a
far-sighted man who is asked to listen with attention to two
shorter-sighted but revered professors who are discussing very

profoundly whether a distant range of mountains is a bank of cloud or a dream figment.

14

What is a Being?

Human ideas are necessarily anthropocentred and man's first idea of unity was the unity of himself. By the standards of ordinary speech a being is an entity which can have an independent and complete relationship to a man, it is capable of a rôle in the drama of his life. It is unusual to speak of an arm or a finger or a hat or a ploughed field as a being. Still less does one think of them as individual beings. In common speech "an individual" means a human person. This very natural disposition of the human mind obsesses much philosophical discussion. On the other hand there is a pleasant disposition of venerable antiquity to accept individuality in the case of an animal or a tree or a shapely mountain. Roughly speaking the old idea of an individual was something to which you could pray or at which you could shake your fist.

Modern scientific work, particularly in the biological sciences, leads to a much keener criticism of the idea of individuality. Comparative anatomy leads straight to the discussion, "What is an individual?" A student drifts easily into the habit of considering all the larger animals, the metameric metazoa, as being not so much equivalent to one individual of the simpler metazoa as to a linear colony of reduced individuals, and of regarding the metazoa altogether as equivalent to multiples of protozoon individuals. He knows that the white corpuscles in his blood are singularly like individual amœbas and that the digestion of every big animal is dependent on the presence of great multitudes of individual bacteria in the intestine. Colonial organisations, the sponges and corals for example, add another aspect to this question. Vegetable individuality is still more disconcerting. What is the individual fungus, is it the toadstool springing from the spreading mycelium or the mycelium, and where is the individuality of a series of grafted trees? Is that three-bladed Irish yew that appeared as a sport years ago and which has been spread by cuttings all round and about the world one individual or many? The mind of the modern biological student is prepared by these things for the idea of individualities of a lower and of a higher order; it can contemplate the possibility of mergers and synthetic formations such as never entered into the heads of the ancient philosophers.

And it is his habit to think of a living species as a single whole, as a synthetic being, unique, conducting a unique struggle against the universe, made up of practically similar but still unique individuals, beings of a less complex grade. In that way also he comes to think of "Man".

15

The General and the Individual

In our consideration of every person we deal with two aspects. He is William Smith or what not and he is a man. And "William Smith" for him implies everything that is Man in him, but the stress is upon everything that is peculiar and distinctive in him. When we call him a "Man" we thrust these idiosyncrasies into the background and insist upon all those things that he possesses in common with the run of mankind. His individuality lies in his difference; apart from that he is a sample, a unit of the species. The life of every William Smith among us has that double strain; he is carried along the way of all flesh, he is a man like other men, and at the same time he is in every detail just a little different. By virtue of that difference and of individual accidents he succeeds or fails, he survives or is obliterated, he is accepted into or rejected from the heritage of the race.

At different hours in his life William Smith may be living with the utmost intensity as William Smith, or, self forgetful, as Man. When he lusts, when he boasts, when his vanity is bitterly hurt, he is William Smith in excelsis, when he discusses politics or philosophy or works with delight at a mathematical problem he is at his most generalised. His mind goes then with the mind of the species; he is Man… So perhaps in a quite parallel fashion the tissue cells in our bodies are sometimes full of local and individual stresses, sometimes altogether absorbed in their particular services in the common welfare of our beings.

BOOK TWO

OF BELIEFS

1

My Primary Act of Faith

And now having stated my conception of the true relationship between our thoughts and words on the one hand and facts on the other, having distinguished between the more accurate and frequently verified propositions of science and the more arbitrary and infrequently verified propositions of belief, and made clear the *spontaneous and artistic quality that inheres in all our moral and religious generalisations*, I may hope to go on to my confession of faith with less misunderstanding than would otherwise be inevitable.

Now my most comprehensive belief about the external and the internal and myself is that they make one universe in which I and every part are ultimately important. That is quite an arbitrary act of my mind. It is quite possible to maintain that everything is chaotic assembly, that any part might be destroyed without affecting any other part. I do not choose to argue against that. If you choose to say that, I am no more disposed to argue with you than if you choose to wear a mitre in Fleet Street or drink a bottle of ink, or declare the figure of Ally Sloper more dignified and beautiful than the head of Jove. There is no QED

215

that you cannot do so. You can. You will not like to go on with it, I think, and it will not answer, but that is a different matter.

I dismiss the idea that life is chaotic because it leaves my life ineffectual, and I cannot contemplate an ineffectual life patiently. I am by my nature impelled to refuse that. I assert that it is not so. I assert therefore that I am important in a scheme, that we all are important in that scheme, that the wheel-smashed frog in the road and the fly drowning in the milk are important and correlated with me. What the scheme as a whole is I do not clearly know; with my limited mind I cannot know. There I become a Mystic. I use the word scheme because it is the best word available, but I strain it in using it. I do not wish to imply a schemer, but only order and coordination as distinguished from haphazard. "All this is important, all this is profoundly significant." I say it of the universe as a child that has not learned to read might say it of a parchment agreement. I cannot read the universe, but I can believe that this is so.

And this unfounded and arbitrary declaration of the ultimate rightness and significance of things I call the Act of Faith. It is a voluntary and deliberate determination to believe, a choice made. I do not pretend to be able to prove it. I do not even assert that it is true. It is my working belief.

2

On Using the Name of God

You may say if you will that this scheme I talk about, this something that gives importance and .correlation and significance, is what is meant by God. You may embark upon a

216

logical wrangle here with me if you have failed to master what I have hitherto said about the meaning of words. If a Scheme, you will say, then there must be a Schemer.

But, I repeat, I am using scheme and importance and significance here only in a spirit of suggestion because they suggest order and because I can find no better words, and I will not allow myself to be entangled by an insistence upon their implications.

Yet let me confess I am greatly attracted by such fine phrases as the Will of God, the Hand of God, the Great Commander. These do most wonderfully express aspects of this belief I choose to hold. I think if there had been no gods before, I would call this God without hesitation. But there is a great danger in doing this sort of thing unguardedly. The run of people nowadays mean something more and something different when they say "God". They intend a personality exterior to them and limited, and they will instantly conclude I mean the same thing. To permit that misconception is, I feel, the first step on the slippery slope of meretricious complaisance, is to become in some small measure a successor of those who cried "Great is Diana of the Ephesians." Occasionally we may best serve the God of Truth by denying him.

Yet at times I admit the sense of personality in the universe is very strong. If I am confessing, I do not see why I should not confess up to the hilt. At times in the silence of the night and in rare lonely moments, I come upon a sort of communion of myself and something great that is not myself. It is perhaps poverty of mind and language obliges me to say that then this universal scheme takes on the effect of a sympathetic person – and my communion a quality of fearless worship. These moments happen, and they are the supreme fact in my religious life to me, they are the crown of my religious experiences.

Nonetheless, I do not usually speak of God even in regard to these moments, and where I do use that word it must be understood that I use it as a personification of something entirely different in nature from the personality of a human individual.

3

Free Will and Predestination

And now let me return to a point raised in the first Book in Section 9. Is the whole of this scheme of things settled and done? The whole trend of Science is to that belief. On the scientific plane one is a fatalist, the universe a system of inevitable consequences. But as I show in that section referred to, it is quite possible to accept as true in their several planes both predestination and free will.[1] If you ask me, I think I should say I incline to believe in predestination and do quite completely believe in free will. The important working belief is free will.

But does the whole universe of fact, the external world about me, the mysterious internal world from which my motives rise, form one rigid and fated system as determinists teach? Do I believe that, had one a mind ideally clear and powerful, the whole universe would seem orderly and absolutely predestined? I incline to that belief. I do not harshly believe it, but I admit its

1 I use free will in the sense of self-determinism and not as it is defined by Professor William James, and predestination as equivalent to the conception of a universe rigid in time and space.

large plausibility – that is all. I see no value whatever in jumping to a decision. One or two Pragmatists, so far as I can understand them, do not hold this view of predestination at all; but as a provisional assumption it underlies most scientific work.

I glance at this question rather to express a detachment than a view.

For me as a person this theory of predestination has no practical value. At the utmost it is an interesting theory like the theory that there is a fourth dimension. There may be a fourth dimension of space, but one gets along quite well by assuming there are just three. It may be knowable the next time I come to cross roads which I shall take. Possibly that knowledge actually exists somewhere. There are those who will tell you they can get intimations in the matter from packs of cards or the palms of my hands, or see by peering into crystals. Of such beliefs I am entirely free. The fact is I believe that neither I know nor anybody else who is practically concerned knows which I shall take. I hesitate, I choose just as though the thing was unknowable. For me and my conduct there is much wide practical margin of freedom.

I am free and freely and responsibly making the future – so far as I am concerned. You others are equally free. On that theory I find my life will work, and on a theory of mechanical predestination nothing works.

I take the former theory therefore for my everyday purposes, and as a matter of working experience so does everybody else. I regard myself as a free responsible person among free responsible persons.

4

A Picture of the World of Men

Now I have already given a first picture of the world of fact as it shaped itself upon my mind. Let me now give a second picture of this world in which I find myself, a picture in a rather different key and at a different level, in which I turn to a new set of aspects and bring into the foreground the other minds which are with me in the midst of his great spectacle.

What am I?

Here is a question to which in all ages men have sought to give a clear unambiguous answer, and to which a clear unambiguous answer is manifestly unfitted. Am I my body? Yes or no? It seems to me that I can externalise and think of as "not myself" nearly everything that pertains to my body, hands and feet, and even the most secret and central of those living and hidden parts, the pulsing arteries, the throbbing nerves, the ganglionic centres, that no eye, save for the surgeon's knife, has ever seen or ever will see until they coagulate in decay. So far I am not my body; and then as clearly, since I suffer through it, see the whole world through it and am always to be called upon where it is, I am it. Am I a mind mysteriously linked to this thing of matter and endeavour?

So I can present myself. I seem to be a consciousness, vague and insecure, placed between two worlds. One of these worlds seems clearly "not me", the other is more closely identified with me and yet is still imperfectly me. The first I called the exterior world, and it presents itself to me as existing in Time and Space. In a certain way I seem able to interfere with it and control it. The second is the interior world, having no forms in space and only a vague evasive reference to time, from which motives arise and storms of emotion, which acts and reacts constantly and in untraceable ways with my conscious mind. And that consciousness itself hangs and drifts about the region where the inner world and the outer world meet, much as a patch of limelight drifts about the stage, illuminating, affecting, following no manifest law except that usually it centres about the hero, my Ego.

It seems to me that to put the thing much more precisely than this is to depart from the reality of the matter.

But so departing a little, let me borrow a phrase from Herbart and identify myself more particularly with my mental self. It seems to me that I may speak of myself as a circle of thought and experience poised between these two imperfectly understood worlds of the internal and the external and passing imperceptibly into the former. The external world impresses me as being, as a practical fact, common to me and many other creatures similar to myself; the internal, I find similar but not identical with theirs. It is *mine*. It seems to me at times no more than something cut off from that external world and out into a sort of pit or cave, much as all the inner mystery of my body, those living, writhing, warm and thrilling organs are isolated, hidden from all eyes and interference so long as I remain alive. And I myself, the essential me, am the light and watcher in the mouth of the cave.

So I think of myself, and so I think of all other human beings, as circles of thought and experience, each a little different from the others. Each human being I see as essentially a circle of thought between an internal and an external world.

I figure these circles of thought as more or less imperfectly focussed pictures, all a little askew and vague as to margins and distances. In the internal world arise motives, and they pass

221

outward through the circle of thought and are modified and directed by it into external acts. And through speech, example, and a hundred various acts, one such circle, one human mind, lights and enlarges and plays upon another. That is the image under which the inter-relation of minds presents itself to me.

5

The Problem of Motives the Real Problem of Life

Now each self among us, for all its fluctuations and vagueness of boundary, is, as I have already pointed out, invincibly persuaded of Free Will. That is to say, it has a persuasion of responsible control over the impulses that teem from the internal world and tend to express themselves in act. The problem of that control and its solution is the reality of life. "What am I to do?" is the perpetual question of our existence. Our metaphysics, our beliefs are all sought as subsidiary to that and have no significance without it.

I confess I find myself a confusion of motives beside which my confusion of perceptions pales into insignificance.

There are many various motives and motives very variously estimated – some are called gross, some sublime, some – such as pride – wicked. I do not readily accept these classifications.

Many people seem to make a selection among their motives without much inquiry, taking those classifications as just; they seek to lead what they call pure lives or useful lives, and to set aside whole sets of motives which do not accord with this determination. Some exclude the seeking of pleasure as a permissible motive, some the love of beauty; some insist upon

222

one's "being oneself" and prohibit or limit responses to exterior opinions. Most of such selections strike me as wanton and hasty. I decline to dismiss any of my motives at all in that wholesale way. Just as I believe I am important in the scheme of things, so I believe are all my motives. Turning one's back on any set of them seems to me to savour of the headlong actions of stupidity. To suppress a passion or a curiosity for the sake of suppressing a passion is to my mind just the burial of a talent that has been entrusted to one's care. One has, I feel, to take all these things as weapons and instruments, material in the service of the scheme; one has to take them in the end gravely and do right among them unbiased in favour of any set. To take some poor appetite and fling it out is to my mind a cheap and unsatisfactory way of simplifying one's moral problems. One has to accept these things in oneself, I feel – even if one knows them to be dangerous things, even if one is sure they have an evil side.

Let me, however, in order to express my attitude better, make a rough grouping of the motives I find in myself and the people about me.

6

A Review of Motives

I cannot divide them into clearly defined classes, but I may perhaps begin with those that bring one into the widest sympathy with living things and go on to those one shares only with more intelligent and complex creatures.

There come first the desires one shares with those more limited souls the beasts, just as much as one does with one's fellow man. These are the bodily appetites and the crude emotions of fear and resentment. These first clamour for attention and must be assuaged or controlled before the other sets come into play.

Now in this matter of physical appetites I do not know whether to describe myself as a sensualist or an ascetic. If an ascetic is one who suppresses to a minimum all deference to these impulses, then certainly I am not an ascetic; if a sensualist is one who gives himself to heedless gratification, then certainly I am not a sensualist. But I find myself balanced in an intermediate position by something that I will speak of as the sense of Beauty. This sense of Beauty is something in me which demands not simply gratification but the best and keenest of a sense or continuance of sense impressions, and which refuses coarse quantitative assuagements. It ranges all over the senses, and just as I refuse to wholly cut off any of my motives, so do I refuse to limit its use to the plane of the eye or the ear.

It seems to me entirely just to speak of beauty in matters of scent and taste, to talk not only of beautiful skies and beautiful sounds but of beautiful beer and beautiful cheese! The balance as between asceticism and sensuality comes in, it seems to me, if we remember that to drink well one must not have drunken for some time, that to see well one's eye must be clear, that to make love well one must be fit and gracious and sweet and disciplined from top to toe, that the finest sense of all – the joyous sense of bodily well-being – comes only with exercises and restraints and fine living. There I think lies the way of my disposition. I do not want to live in the sensual sty, but also I do not want to scratch in the tub of Diogenes.

But I diverge a little in these comments from my present business of classifying motives.

Next I perceive hypertrophied in myself and many sympathetic human beings a passion that many animals certainly possess, the beautiful and fearless cousin of fear, Curiosity, that seeks keenly for knowing and feeling. Apart from appetites and bodily desires and blind impulses, I want most urgently to know and feel, for the sake of knowing and feeling. I want to go round corners and see what is there, to cross mountain ranges, to open boxes and parcels. Young animals at least have that disposition too. For me it is something that mingles with all my desires. Much more to me than the desire to live is the desire to taste life. I am not happy until I have done and felt things. I want to get as near as I can to the thrill of a dog going into a fight or the delight of a bird in the air. And not simply in the heroic field of war and the air do I want to understand. I want to know something of the jolly wholesome satisfaction that a hungry pig must find in its wash.

I do not think that in this I confess to any unusual temperament. I think that the more closely mentally animated people scrutinise their motives the less is the importance they will attach to mere physical and brute urgencies and the more to curiosity.

Next after curiosity come those desires and motives that one shares perhaps with some social beasts, but far more so as a conscious thing with men alone. These desires and motives all centre on a clearly apprehended "self" in relation to "others"; they are the essentially egotistical group. They are self-assertion in all its forms. I have dealt with motives towards gratification and motives towards experience; this set of motives is for the sake of oneself. Since they are the most acutely conscious motives in unthinking men, there is a tendency on the part of unthinking people to speak of them as though vanity, self-seeking, self-interest, were the only motives. But one has but to reflect on what has gone before to realize that this is not so. One finds these "self" motives vary with the mental power and training of the individual; here they are fragmentary and discursive, there drawn tight together into a coherent scheme. Where they are weak they mingle with the animal motives and curiosity like travellers in a busy market-place, but where the sense of self is strong they become rulers and regulators, self-seeking becomes deliberate and sustained in the case of the human being, vanity passes into pride.

Here again that something in the mind so difficult to define, so easy for all who understand to understand, that something which insists upon a best and keenest, the desire for beauty, comes into the play of motives. Pride demands a beautiful self and would discipline all other passions to its service. It also demands recognition for that beautiful self. Now pride, I know, is denounced by many as the essential quality of sin. We are taught that "self-abnegation" is the substance of virtue and self-forgetfulness the inseparable quality of right conduct. But indeed I cannot so dismiss egotism and that pride which was the first form in which the desire to rule oneself as a whole came to me. Through pride one shapes oneself towards a best, though at first it may be an ill-conceived best. Pride is not always arrogance and aggression. There is that pride that does not ape but learns humility.

And with the human imagination all these elementary instincts, of the flesh, of curiosity, of self-assertion, become only the basal substance of a huge elaborate edifice of secondary motive and intention. We live in a great flood of example and suggestion, our curiosity and our social quality impel us to a thousand imitations, to dramatic attitudes and subtly obscure ends. Our pride turns this way and that as we respond to new notes in the world about us. We are arenas for a conflict between suggestions flung in from all sources, from the most diverse and essentially incompatible sources. We live long hours and days in a kind of dream, negligent of self-interest, our elementary passions in abeyance, among these derivative things.

7

The Synthetic Motive

Such it seems to me are the chief masses of the complex of motives in us, the group of sense, the group of pride, curiosity and the imitative and suggested motives, making up the system of impulses which is our will. Such has been the common outfit of motives in every age, and in every age its mêlée has been found insufficient in itself. It is a heterogeneous system, it does not form in any sense a completed or balanced system, its constituents are variable and complete among themselves. They are not so much arranged about one another as superposed and higgledy-piggledy. The senses and curiosity war with pride and one another, the motives suggested to us fall into conflict with this element or that of our intimate and habitual selves. We find all our instincts are snares to excess. Excesses of indulgence lead to excesses of abstinence, and even the sense of beauty may be clouded and betray. So to us all, even for the most balanced of us, come disappointments, regrets, gaps; and for most of us who are ill-balanced, miseries and despairs. Nearly all of us want something to hold us together – something to dominate this swarming confusion and save us from the black misery of wounded and exploded pride, of thwarted desire, of futile conclusions. We want more oneness, some steadying thing that will afford an escape from fluctuations.

Different people, of differing temperament and tradition, have sought oneness, this steadying and universalising thing, in various manners. Some have attained it in this manner and some in that. Scarcely a religious system has existed that has not worked effectively and proved true for someone. To me it seems that the need is synthetic, that some synthetic idea and belief is needed to harmonise one's life, to give a law by which motive may be tried against motive and an effectual peace of mind achieved. I want an active peace and not a quiescence, and I do not want to suppress and expel any motive at all. But to many people the effort takes the form of attempts to cut off some part of oneself as it were, to repudiate altogether some straining or distressing or disappointing factor in the scheme of motives, and find a tranquillising refuge in the residuum. So we have men and women abandoning their share in economic development, crushing the impulses and evading the complications that arise out of sex and flying to devotions and simple duties in nunneries and monasteries; we have others cutting their lives down to a vegetarian dietary and scientific research, resorting to excesses of self-discipline, giving themselves up wholly to some "art" and making everything else subordinate to that, or, going in another direction, abandoning pride and love in favour of an acquired appetite for drugs or drink.

It seems to me that this desire to get the confused complex of life simplified is essentially what has been called the religious motive, and that the manner in which a man achieves that simplification, if he does achieve it, and imposes an order upon his life, is his religion. I find in the scheme of conversion and salvation as it is presented by many Christian sects, a very exact statement of the mental processes I am trying to express. In these systems this discontent with the complexity of life upon which religion is based, is called the conviction of sin, and it is the first phase in the process of conversion – of finding salvation. It leads through distress and confusion to illumination, to the act of faith and peace.

And after peace comes the beginning of right conduct. If you believe and you are saved, you will want to behave well, you will do your utmost to behave well and to understand what is behaving well and you will feel neither shame nor disappointment when after all you fail. You will say then: "so it is failure I had to achieve." And you will not feel bitterly because you seem unsuccessful beside others or because you are misunderstood or unjustly treated; you will not bear malice nor cherish anger nor seek revenge; you will never turn towards suicide as a relief from intolerable things; indeed there will be no intolerable things. You will have peace within you.

But if you do not truly believe and are not saved, you will know it because you will still suffer the conflict of motives; and in regrets, confusions, remorses and discontents, you will suffer the penalties of the unbeliever and the lost. You will know certainly your own salvation.

8

The Being of Mankind

I will boldly adopt the technicalities of the sects. I will speak as a person with experience and declare that I have been through the distresses of despair and the conviction of sin, and that I have found salvation.

I believe in the scheme, in the Project of all things, in the significance of myself and all life, and that my defects and uglinesses and failures, just as much as my powers and successes, are things that are necessary and important and contributory in that scheme, that scheme which passes my understanding – and that no thwarting of my conception, not even the cruelty of nature, now defeats or can defeat my faith, however much it perplexes my mind.

And though I say that scheme passes my understanding, nevertheless I hope you will see no inconsistency when I say that necessarily it has an aspect towards me that I find imperative.

It has an aspect that I can perceive, however dimly and fluctuatingly.

I take it that to perceive this aspect to the utmost of my mental power and to shape my acts according to that perception is my function in the scheme; that if I hold steadfastly to that conception, I am *saved*. I find in that idea of perceiving the scheme as a whole towards me and in this attempt to perceive, that something to which all my other emotions and passions may contribute by gathering and contributing experience, and through which the synthesis of my life becomes possible.

Let me try to convey to you what it is I perceive, what aspect this scheme seems to bear on the whole towards me.

The essential fact in man's history to my sense is the slow unfolding of a sense of community with his kind, of the possibilities of co-operations leading to scarce dreamt-of collective powers, of a synthesis of the species, of the development of a common general idea, a common general purpose out of a present confusion. In that awakening of the species, one's own personal being lives and moves – a part of it

230

and contributing to it. *One's individual existence is not so entirely cut off as it seems at first; one's entirely separate individuality is another, a profounder, among the subtle inherent delusions of the human mind.* Between you and me as we set our minds together, and between us and the rest of mankind, there is *something,* something real, something that rises through us and is neither you nor me, that comprehends us, that is thinking here and using me and you to play against each other in that thinking just as my finger and thumb play against each other as I hold this pen with which I write.

Let me point out that this is no sentimental or mystical statement. It is hard fact as any hard fact we know. We, you and I, are not only parts in a thought process, but parts of one flow of blood and life. Let me put that in a way that may be new to some readers. Let me remind you of what is sometimes told as a jest, the fact that the number of one's ancestors increases as we look back in time. Disregarding the chances of intermarriage, each one of us had two parents, four grandparents, eight great-grandparents, and so on backward, until very soon, in less than fifty generations, we should find that, but for the qualification introduced, we should have all the earth's inhabitants of that time as our progenitors. For a hundred generations it must hold absolutely true, that everyone of that time who has issue living now is ancestral to all of us. That brings the thing quite within the historical period. There is not a western European palaeolithic or neolithic relic of the present human race that is not a family relic for every soul alive. The blood in our veins has handled it.

And there is something more. We are all going to mingle our blood again. We cannot keep ourselves apart; the worst enemies will some day come to the Peace of Verona. All the Montagues and Capulets are doomed to intermarry. A time will come in less than fifty generations when all the population of the world will have my blood, and I and my worst enemy will not be able to say which child is his or mine.

But you may retort – perhaps you may die childless. Then all the sooner the whole species will get the little legacy of my personal achievement, whatever it may be.

You see that from this point of view – which is for me the vividly true and dominating point of view – our individualities, our nations and states and races are but bubbles and clusters of foam upon the great stream of the blood of the species, incidental experiments in the growing knowledge and consciousness of the race.

I think this real solidarity of humanity is a fact that is only being slowly apprehended, that it is an idea that we who have come to realize it have to assist in thinking into the collective mind. I believe the species is still as a whole unawakened, still sunken in the delusion of the permanent separateness of the individual and of races and nations, that so it turns upon itself and frets against itself and fails to see the stupendous possibilities of deliberate self-development that lie open to it now.

I see myself in life as part of a great physical being that strains and I believe grows towards beauty, and of a great mental being that strains and I believe grows towards knowledge and power. In this persuasion that I am a gatherer of experience, a mere tentacle that arranges thought beside thought for this being of the species, this being that grows beautiful and powerful, in this persuasion I find the ruling idea of which I stand in need, the ruling idea that reconciles and adjudicates among my warring motives. In it I find both concentration of myself and escape from myself; in a word, I find Salvation.

9

Individuality an Interlude

I would like in a parenthetical section to expand and render rather more concrete this idea of the species as one divaricating flow of blood, by an appeal to its arithmetical aspect. I do not know if it has ever occurred to the reader to compute the number of his living ancestors at some definite date, at, let us say, the year one of the Christian era. Everyone has two parents and four grandparents, most people have eight great-grandparents, and if we ignore the possibility of intermarriage we shall go on to a fresh power of two with every generation, thus –

Number of generations	Number of ancestors
3	8
4	16
5	32
7	128
10	1,024
20	1,048,576
30	1,073,741,824
40	1,099,511,627,776

I do not know whether the average age of the parent at the birth of a child under modern conditions can be determined from existing figures. There is, I should think, a strong presumption that it has been a rising age. There may have been a time in the past when most women were mothers in their early teens and bore most or all of their children before thirty, and when men had done the greater part of their procreation before thirty-five; this is still the case in many tropical climates, and I do not think I favour my case unduly by assuming that the average parent must be about, or even less than, five and twenty. This gives four generations to a century. At that rate and *disregarding intermarriage of relations* the ancestors living a thousand years ago needed to account for a living person would be double the estimated population of the world. But it is obvious that, if a person sprang from marriage of first cousins, the eight ancestors of the third generation are cut down to six; if of cousins at the next stage, to fourteen in the fourth. And every time that a common pair of ancestors appears in any generation, the number of ancestors in that generation must be reduced by two from our original figures, or if it is only one common ancestor, by one, and as we go back that reduction will have to be doubled, quadrupled and so on. I daresay that by the time anyone gets to the 8192 names of his Elizabethan ancestors he will find quite a large number repeated over and over again in the list and that he is cut down to perhaps two or three thousand separate persons. But this does not effectually invalidate my assumption that if we go back only to the closing years of the Roman Republic, we go back to an age in which nearly every person living within the confines of what was then the Roman Empire who left living offspring must have been ancestral to every person living within that area today. No doubt they were so in very variable measure. There must be for everyone some few individuals in that period who have so to speak intermarried with

234

themselves again and again and again down the genealogical series, and others who are represented by just one touch of their blood. The blood of the Jews, for example, has turned in upon itself again and again; but for all we know one Italian proselyte in the first year of the Christian era may have made by this time every Jew alive a descendant of some unrecorded bastard of Julius Caesar. The exclusive breeding of the Jews is in fact the most effectual guarantee that whatever does get into the charmed circle through either proselytism, the violence of enemies, or feminine unchastity, must ultimately pervade it universally.

It may be argued that as a matter of fact humanity has until recently been segregated in pools; that in the great civilisation of China, for example, humanity has pursued its own interlacing system of inheritances without admixture from other streams of blood. But such considerations only defer the conclusion; they do not stave it off indefinitely. It needs only that one philoprogenitive Chinaman should have wandered into those regions that are now Russia, about the time of Pericles, to link east and west in that matter; one Tartar chieftain in the Steppes may have given a daughter to a Roman soldier and sent his grandsons east and west to interlace the branches of every family tree in the world. If any race stands apart it is such an isolated group as that of the now extinct Tasmanian primitives or the Australian black. But even here, in the remote dawn of navigation, may have come some shipwrecked Malays, or some half-breed woman kidnapped by wandering Phoenicians have carried this link of blood back to the western world. The more one lets one's imagination play upon the incalculable drift and soak of population, the more one realizes the true value of that spreading relation with the past.

But now let us turn in the other direction, the direction of the future, because there it is that this series of considerations becomes most edifying. It is the commonest trick to think of a man's descendants as though they were his own. We are told that one of the dearest human motives is the desire to found a family, but think how much of a family one founds at the best. One's son is after all only half one's blood, one's grandson only a quarter, and so one goes on until it may be that in ten brief generations one's heir and namesake has but $1/1024$th of one's inherited self. Those other thousand odd unpredictable people thrust in and mingle with one's pride. The trend of all things nowadays – the ever-increasing ease of communication, the great and increasing drift of population, the establishment of a common standard of civilisation – is to render such admixture far more probable and facile in the future than in the past.

It is a pleasant fancy to imagine some ambitious hoarder of wealth, some egotistical founder of name and family, returning to find his descendants – *his* descendants – after the lapse of a few brief generations. His heir and namesake may have not a thousandth part of his heredity, while under some other name, lost to all the tradition and glory of him, enfeebled and degenerate through much intermarriage, may be a multitude of people who have as much as a fiftieth or even more of his quality. They may even be in servitude and dependence to the really alien person who is head of the family. Our founder will go through the spreading record of offspring and find it mixed with that of people he most hated and despised. The antagonists he wronged and overcame will have crept into his line and recaptured all they lost; have played the cuckoo in his blood and acquisitions, and turned out his diluted strain to perish.

And while I am being thus biological let me point out another queer aspect in which our egotism is overridden by physical facts. Men and women are apt to think of their children as being their very own, blood of their blood and bone of their bone. But indeed one of the most striking facts in this matter is the frequent want of resemblance between parents and children. It is one of the commonest things in the world for a child to resemble an aunt or an uncle, or to revive a trait of some grandparent that has seemed entirely lost in the intervening generation. The Mendelians have given much attention to facts of this nature; and though their general method of exposition seems to me quite unjustifiably exact and precise, it cannot be denied that it is often vividly illuminating. It is so in this connection. They distinguish between "dominant" and "recessive" qualities, and they establish cases in which parents with all the dominant characteristics produce offspring of recessive type. Recessive qualities are constantly being masked by dominant ones and emerging again in the next generation. It is not the individual that reproduces himself, it is the species that reproduces through the individual and often in spite of his characteristics.

The race flows through us, the race is the drama and we are the incidents. This is not any sort of poetical statement; it is a statement of fact. It so far as we are individuals, in so far as we seek to follow merely individual ends, we are accidental, disconnected, without significance, the sport of chance. In so far as we realize ourselves as experiments of the species for the species, just in so far do we escape from the accidental and the chaotic. We are episodes in an experience greater than ourselves.

Now none of this, if you read me aright, makes for the suppression of one's individual difference, but it does make for its correlation. We have to get everything we can out of ourselves for this very reason that we do not stand alone; we signify as parts of a universal and immortal development. Our separate selves are our charges, the talents of which much has to be made. It is because we are episodical in the great synthesis of life that we have to make the utmost of our individual lives and traits and possibilities.

10

The Mystic Element

What stupendous constructive mental and physical possibilities are there to which I feel I am contributing, you may ask, when I feel that I contribute to this greater Being; and at once I confess I become vague and mystical. I do not wish to pass glibly over this point. I call your attention to the fact that here I am mystical and arbitrary. I am what I am, an individual in this present phase. I can see nothing of these possibilities except that they will be in the nature of those indefinable and overpowering gleams of promise in our world that we call Beauty. Elsewhere (in my "Food of the Gods") I have tried to render my sense of our human possibility by monstrous images; I have written of those who will "stand on this earth as on a footstool and reach out their hands among the stars." But that is rhetoric at best, a straining image of unimaginable things. Things move to Power and Beauty; I say that much and I have said all that I can say.

But what is Beauty; you ask, and what will Power do? And here I reach my utmost point in the direction of what you are free to call the rhapsodical and the incomprehensible. I will not even attempt to define Beauty. I will not because I cannot. To me it is a final, quite indefinable thing. Either you understand it or you do not. Every true artist and many who are not artists know – they know there is something that shows suddenly – it may be in music, it may be in painting, it may be in the sunlight on a glacier or shadow cast by a furnace or the scent of a flower, it may be in the person or act of some fellow creature, but it is right, it is commanding, it is, to use theological language, the revelation of God. To this mystery of Power and Beauty, out of the earth that mothered us, we move.

I do not attempt to define Beauty nor even to distinguish it from Power. I do not think indeed that one can effectually distinguish these aspects of life. I do not know how far Beauty may not be simply fulness and clearness of sensation, a momentary unveiling of things hitherto seen but dully and darkly. As I have already said, there may be beauty in the feeling of beer in the throat, in the taste of cheese in the mouth; there may be beauty in the scent of earth, in the warmth of a body, in the sensation of waking from sleep. I use the word Beauty therefore in its widest possible sense, ranging far beyond the special beauties that art discovers and develops. Perhaps as we pass from death to life all things become beautiful. The utmost I can do in conveying what I mean by Beauty is to tell of things that I have perceived to be beautiful as beautifully as I can tell of them. It may be, as I suggest elsewhere, that Beauty is a thing synthetic and not simple; it is a common effect produced by a great medley of causes, a larger aspect of harmony.

But the question of what Beauty is does not very greatly concern me since I have known it when I met it and since almost every day in life I seem to apprehend it more and to find it more sufficient and satisfying. Objectively it may be altogether complex and various and synthetic, subjectively it is altogether simple. All analysis, all definition, must in the end rest upon and arrive at unanalysable and indefinable things. Beauty is light – I fall back upon that image – it is all things that light can be, beacon, elucidation, pleasure, comfort and consolation, promise, warning, the vision of reality.

11

The Synthesis

It seems to me that the whole living creation may be regarded as walking in its sleep, as walking in the sleep of instinct and individualised illusion, and that now out of it all rises the Spirit of Man, beginning to perceive his larger self, his collective synthetic purpose to increase Power and realize Beauty...

I write this down. It is the form of my belief, and that unanalysable something called Beauty is the light that falls upon that great figure.

It is only by such images, it is only by the use of what are practically parables, that I can in any way express these things in my mind. These two things, I say, are the two aspects of my belief; one is the form and the other the light. The former places me as it were in a scheme, the latter illuminates and inspires me. I am a member in that greater Being, and my function is, I take it, to develop my capacity for beauty and convey the perception of it to my fellows, to gather and store experience and increase the racial consciousness. I hazard no whys nor wherefores. That is how I see things; that is how the universe, in response to my demand for a synthesising aspect, presents itself to me. I see it as the scene of the great adventure of the human spirit, that God of Man, of which I am servant and part.

12

Of Personal Immortality

These are my beliefs. They begin with arbitrary assumptions; they end in mystery.

So do all beliefs that are not grossly utilitarian and material, promising houris and deathless appetite or endless hunting or a cosmic mortgage. The Peace of God passeth understanding, the Kingdom of Heaven within us and without can be presented only by parables. But the unapproachable distance and vagueness of these things makes them none the less necessary, just as a cloud upon a mountain, or sunlight remotely seen upon the sea, is as real as, and to many people far more necessary than, pork chops. The driven swine may root and take no heed, but man the dreamer drives. And because these things are vague and impalpable and wilfully attained, it is none the less important that they should be rendered with all the truth of one's being. To be atmospherically vague is one thing; to be haphazard, wanton and untruthful, quite another.

But here I may give a specific answer to a question that many find profoundly important, though indeed it is already implicitly answered in what has gone before.

I do not believe I have any personal immortality. I am part of an immortality perhaps; but that is different. I personally am not the continuing thing. I am experimental, incidental. I feel I have to do something, a number of things no one else could do, and then I am finished, and finished altogether. Then my substance returns to the common lot. I am a temporary enclosure for a temporary purpose; that served, and my skull and teeth, my idiosyncrasy and desire, will disperse, I believe, like the timbers of a booth after a fair.

Let me shift my ground a little and ask you to consider what is involved in the opposite belief.

My idea of the unknown scheme is of something so wide and deep that I cannot conceive it encumbered by my egotism perpetually. I shall serve my purpose and pass under the wheel and end. That distresses me not at all. Immortality would distress and perplex me. If I may put this in a mixture of theological and social language, I cannot respect, I cannot believe in a God who is always going about with me.

But this is after all what I feel is true and what I choose to believe. It is not a matter of fact. So far as that goes there is no evidence that I am immortal and none that I am not.

I may be altogether wrong in my beliefs; I may be misled by the appearance of things. I believe in the great and growing Being of the Species from which I rise, to which I return, and which, it maybe, will ultimately even transcend the limitation of the Species and grow into the Conscious Being, the undying conscious Being of all things. Believing that, I cannot also believe that my peculiar little thread will not undergo synthesis and vanish as a separate thing.

And what after all is my distinctive something, a few capacities, a few incapacities, an uncertain memory, a hesitating presence? It matters no doubt in its place and time, as all things matter in their place and time, but where in it all is the eternally indispensable? The great things of my life, love, faith, the intimation of beauty, the things most savouring of immortality, are the things most general, the things most shared and least distinctively me.

13

A Criticism of Christianity

And here perhaps, before I go on to the question of Conduct, is the place to define a relationship to that system of faith and religious observance out of which I and most of my readers have come. How do these beliefs on which I base may rule of conduct stand to Christianity?

They do not stand in any attitude of antagonism. A religious system so many-faced and so enduring as Christianity must necessarily be saturated with truth even if it be not wholly true. To assume, as the Atheist and Deist seem to do, that Christianity is a sort of disease that came upon civilisation, an unprofitable and wasting disease, is to deny that conception of a progressive scheme and rightness which we have taken as our basis of belief. As I have already confessed, the Scheme of Salvation, the idea of a process of sorrow and atonement, presents itself to me as adequately true. So far I do not think my new faith breaks with my old. But it follows as a natural consequence of my metaphysical preliminaries that I should find the Christian theology, Aristotelian, over defined and excessively personified. The painted figure of that bearded ancient upon the Sistine Chapel, or William Blake's wild-haired, wild-eyed Trinity, convey no nearer sense of God to me than some mother-of-pearl-eyed painted and carven monster from the worship of the South Sea Islanders. And the Miltonic fable of the offended creator and the sacrificial son! It cannot span the circle of my ideas; it is a little thing, and none the less little because it is intimate, flesh of my flesh and spirit of my spirit, like the drawings of my youngest boy. I put it aside as I would put aside the gay figure of a costumed officiating priest. The passage of time has made his canonicals too strange, too unlike my world of common thought and costume. These things helped, but now they hinder and disturb. I cannot bring myself back to them.

But the psychological experience and the theology of Christianity are only a ground-work for its essential feature, which is the conception of a relationship of the individual believer to a mystical being at once human and divine, the Risen Christ. This being presents itself to the modern consciousness as a familiar and beautiful figure, associated with a series of sayings and incidents that coalesce with a very distinct and rounded-off and complete effect of personality. After we have cleared off all the definitions of theology, He remains, mystically suffering for humanity, mystically asserting that love in pain and sacrifice in service are the necessary substance of Salvation. Whether he actually existed as a finite individual person in the opening of the Christian era seems to me a question entirely beside the mark. The evidence at this distance is of imperceptible force for or against. The Christ we know is quite evidently something different from any finite person, a figure, a conception, a synthesis of emotions, experiences and inspirations, sustained by and sustaining millions of human souls.

Now it seems to be the common teaching of almost all Christians, that Salvation, that is to say the consolidation and amplification of one's motives through the conception of a general scheme or purpose, is to be attained through the personality of Christ. Christ is made cardinal to the act of Faith. The act of Faith, they assert, is *belief in Him.*

We are dealing here, be it remembered, with beliefs deliberately undertaken and not with questions of fact. The only matters of fact material here are facts of experience. If in your experience Salvation is attainable through Christ, then certainly Christianity is true for you. And if a Christian asserts that my belief is a false light and that presently I shall "come to Christ", I cannot disprove his assertion. I can but disbelieve it. I hesitate even to make the obvious retort.

I hope I shall offend no susceptibilities when I assert that this great and very definite personality in the hearts and imaginations of mankind does not and never has attracted me. It is a fact I record about myself without aggression or regret. I do not find myself able to associate Him with the emotion of Salvation.

I admit the splendid imaginative appeal in the idea of a divine-human friend and mediator. If it were possible to have access by prayer, by meditation, by urgent outcries of the soul, to such a being whose feet were in the darknesses, who stooped down from the light, who was at once great and little, limitless in power and virtue and one's very brother; if it were possible by sheer will in believing to make and make one's way to such a helper, who would refuse such help? But I do not find such a being in Christ. To me the Christian Christ seems not so much a humanised God as an incomprehensibly sinless being neither God nor man. His sinlessness wears his incarnation like a fancy dress, all his white self unchanged. He had no petty weaknesses.

Now the essential trouble of my life is its petty weaknesses. If I am to have that love, that sense of understanding fellowship, which is, I conceive, the peculiar magic and merit of this idea of a personal Saviour, then I need someone quite other than this image of virtue, this terrible and incomprehensible Galilean with his crown of thorns, his blood-stained hands and feet. I cannot love him any more than I can love a man upon the rack. Even in the face of torments I do not think I should feel a need for him. I had rather then a hundred times have Botticelli's armed angel in his Tobit at Florence. (I hope I do not seem to want to shock in writing these things, but indeed my only aim is to lay my feelings bare.) I know what love for an idealised person can be. It happens that in my younger days I found a character in the history of literature who had a singular and extraordinary charm for me, of whom the thought was tender and comforting, who indeed helped me through shames and humiliations as though he held my hand. This person was Oliver Goldsmith. His blunders and troubles, his vices and vanities, seized and still hold my imagination. The slights of Boswell, the contempt of Gibbon and all his company save Johnson, the exquisite fineness of spirit in his *Vicar of Wakefield*, and that green suit of his and the doctor's cane and the love despised, these things together made him a congenial saint and hero for me, so that I thought of him as others pray. When I think of that youthful feeling for Goldsmith, I know what I need in a personal Saviour, as a troglodyte who has seen a candle can imagine the sun. But the Christian Christ in none of his three characteristic phases, neither as the magic babe (from whom I am cut off by the wanton and indecent purity of the Virgin Birth), nor as the white-robed, spotless miracle worker, nor as the fierce unreal torment of the cross, comes close to my soul. I do not understand the Agony in the Garden; to me it is like a scene from a play in an unknown tongue. The last cry of despair is the one human touch, discordant with all the rest of the story. One cry of despair does not suffice. The Christian's Christ is too fine for me, not incarnate enough, not flesh enough, not earth enough. He was never foolish and hot-eared and inarticulate, never vain, he never forgot things, nor tangled his miracles. I could love him I think more easily if the dead had not risen and if he had lain in peace in his sepulchre instead of coming back more enhaloed and whiter than ever, as a postscript to his own tragedy.

When I think of the Resurrection I am always reminded of the "happy endings" that editors and actor managers are accustomed to impose upon essentially tragic novels and plays...

You see how I stand in this matter, puzzled and confused by the Christian presentation of Christ. I know there are many will answer that what confuses me is the overlaying of the personality of Jesus by stories and superstitions and conflicting symbols; they will in effect ask me to disentangle the Christ I need from the accumulated material, choosing and rejecting. Perhaps one may do that. They do, I know, so present Him as a man inspired, and strenuously, inadequately and erringly presenting a dream of human brotherhood and the immediate Kingdom of Heaven on earth and so blundering to his failure and death. But that will be a recovered and restored person they would give me, and not the Christ the Christians worship and declare they love, in whom they find their Salvation.

When I write "declare they love" I throw doubt intentionally upon the universal love of Christians for their Saviour. I have watched men and nations in this matter. I am struck by the fact that so many Christians fall back upon more humanised figures, upon the tender figure of Mary, upon patron saints and such more erring creatures, for the effect of mediation and sympathy they need.

You see it comes to this: that I think Christianity has been true and is for countless people practically true, but that it is not true now for me, and that for most people it is true only with qualifications. Every believing Christian is, I am sure my spiritual brother, but if systematically I called myself a Christian I feel that to most men I should imply too much and so tell a lie.

14

Of Other Religions

In the same manner, in varying degree, I hold all religions to be in a measure true. Least comprehensible to me are the Indian formulae because they seem to stand not on common experience but on those intellectual assumptions my metaphysical analysis destroys. Transmigration of souls without a continuing memory is to my mind utter foolishness, the imagining of a race of children. The aggression, discipline and submission of Mahommedanism makes, I think, an intellectually limited but fine and honourable religion – for men. Its spirit if not its formulae is abundantly present in our modern world. Mr Rudyard Kipling, for example, manifestly preaches a Mahommedan God, a modernised Allah with a taste for engineering. I have no doubt that in devotion to a virile, almost national Deity and to the service of His Empire of stern Law and Order, efficiently upheld, men have found and will find Salvation.

All these religions are true for me as Canterbury Cathedral is a true thing and as a Swiss chalet is a true thing. There they are, and they have served a purpose, they have worked. Men and women have lived in and by them. Men and women still do. Only they are not true for me to live in them. I have, I believe, to live in a new edifice of my own discovery. They do not work for me.

These schemes are true, and also these schemes are false! In the sense that new things, new phrasings, have to replace them.

BOOK THREE
OF GENERAL CONDUCT

1

Conduct Follows from Belief

The broad direction of conduct follows necessarily from belief. The believer does not require rewards and punishments to direct him to the right. Motive and idea are not so separable. To believe truly is to want to do right. To get salvation is to be unified by a comprehending idea of a purpose and by a ruling motive.

The believer wants to do right, he naturally and necessarily seeks to do right. If he fails to do right, if he finds he has done wrong instead of right, he is not greatly distressed or terrified, he naturally and cheerfully does his best to correct his error. He can be damned only by the fading and loss of his belief. And naturally he recurs to and refreshes his belief.

I write in phrases that the evangelical Christianity of my childhood made familiar to me, because they are the most expressive phrases I have ever met for the psychological facts with which I am dealing.

But faith, though it banishes fear and despair and brings with it a real pervading desire to know and do the Good, does not in itself determine what is the Good or supply any simple guide to

253

the choice between alternatives. If it did there would be nothing more to be said, this book upon conduct would be unnecessary.

2

What is Good?

It seems to me one of the heedless errors of those who deal in philosophy, to suppose all things that have simple names or unified effects are in their nature simple and may be discovered and isolated as a sort of essence by analysis. It is natural to suppose – and I think it is also quite wrong to suppose – that such things as Good and Beauty can be abstracted from good and beautiful things and considered alone. But pure Good and pure Beauty are to me empty terms. It seems to me that these are in their nature synthetic things, that they arise out of the coming together of contributory things and conditions, and vanish at their dispersal; they are synthetic just as more obviously Harmony is synthetic. It is consequently not possible to give a definition of Good, just as it is not possible to give a definition of that other something which is so closely akin to it, Beauty. Nor is it to be maintained that what is good for one is good for another. But what is good of one's general relations and what is right in action must be determined by the nature of one's beliefs about the purpose in things. I have set down my broad impression of that purpose in respect to me, as the awakening and development of the consciousness and will of our species, and I have confessed my belief that in subordinating myself and all my motives to that idea lies my Salvation. It follows from that, that the good life is the life that most richly gathers and winnows and prepares experience and renders it available for the race, that contributes most effectively to the collective growth.

This is in general terms my idea of Good. So soon as one passes from general terms to the question of individual good, one encounters individuality; for everyone in the differing quality and measure of their personality and powers and possibilities, good and right must be different. We are all engaged, each contributing from his or her own standpoint, in the collective synthesis; whatever one can best do, one must do that; in whatever manner one can best help the synthesis, one must exert oneself; the setting apart of oneself, secrecy, the service of secret and personal ends, is the waste of life and the essential quality of Sin.

That is the general expression for right living as I conceive it. In such terms it may be expressed, but also it may be expressed in far more living words. For this collective "synthesis" is the adventure of humanity, the "purpose in things" is no more and no less than the enterprise of God the captain of mankind.

3

Socialism

In the study of God's will in us, it is very convenient to make a rough division of our subject into general and particular. There are first the interests and problems that affect us all collectively, in which we have a common concern and from which no one may legitimately seek exemption; of these interests and problems we may fairly say every man should do so and so, or so and so, or the law should be so and so, or so and so; and secondly there are those other problems in which individual difference and the interplay of one or two individualities is predominant. This is course no hard and fast classification, but it gives a method of approach. We can begin with the generalised person in ourselves and end with individuality.

In the world of ideas about me, I have found going on a great social and political movement that correlates itself with my conception of God's service as the aspect towards us of the general human scheme. This movement is Socialism. Socialism is to me no clear-cut system of theories and dogmas; it is one of those solid and extensive and synthetic ideas that are better indicated by a number of different formulae than by one, just as one only realizes a statue by walking round it and seeing it from a number of points of view. I do not think it is to be completely expressed by any one system of formulae or by any one man. Its common quality from nearly every point of view is the subordination of the will of the self-seeking individual to the idea of a racial well-being embodied in an organized state under God, organized for every end that can be best obtained collectively. Upon that I seize; that is the value of Socialism for me.

Socialism for me is a common step we are all taking in the realisation of God's purpose of human organisation and unity. It is the organisation of the general effort in regard to a great mass of common and fundamental interests that have hitherto been dispersedly served.

I see humanity scattered over the world, dispersed, conflicting unawakened... I see human life as avoidable waste and curable confusion. I see peasants living in wretched huts knee-deep in manure, mere parasites on their own pigs and cows; I see shy hunters wandering in primeval forests; I see the grimy millions who slave for industrial production; I see some who are extravagant and yet contemptible creatures of luxury, and some leading lives of shame and indignity; tens of thousands of wealthy people wasting lives in vulgar and unsatisfying trivialities, hundreds of thousands meanly chaffering themselves, rich or poor, in the wasteful byways of trade; I see gamblers, fools, brutes, toilers, martyrs. Their disorder of effort, the spectacle of futility is an offence against God, and fills the believer with a passionate desire to end waste, to create order, to develop understanding... All these people reflect and are part of the waste and discontent of life. The co-ordination of the species to common general end, and the quest for a personal salvation, are the two aspects, the outer and the inner, the social and the individual aspect of essentially the same desire...

And yet dispersed as all these people are, they are far more closely drawn together to common ends and a common effort than the filthy savages who ate food rotten and uncooked in the age of unpolished stone. They live in the mere opening phase of a synthesis of effort the end of which surpasses our imagination. Such intercourse and community as they have is only a dawn. We look towards the day, the day of the earthly Kingdom of God, the organized civilized world state. The first clear intimation of that conscious synthesis of human thought to which I look, the first edge of the dayspring, has arisen – as Socialism, as I conceive of Socialism. Socialism is to me no more and no less than the realisation of a common and universal loyalty in mankind, the awakening of a collective consciousness of duty in humanity, the awakening of a collective will and a collective mind out of which finer individualities may arise forever in a perpetual serious of fresh endeavours and fresh achievements for the race.

4

A Criticism of Certain Forms of Socialism

It seems to me one of the heedless errors arising in this way out of the conception of a synthesis of the will and thought of the species will necessarily differ from conceptions of Socialism arrived at in other and different ways. It is based on a self-discontent and self-abnegation and not on self-satisfaction, and it will be essentially a scheme of persistent thought and construction; it will support this or that method of law-making, or this or that method of economic exploitation, or this or that matter of social grouping, only incidentally and in relation to that.

Such a conception of Socialism is very remote in spirit, however it may agree in method, from that philanthropic administrative socialism one finds among the British ruling administrative class. That seems to me to be based on a pity which is largely unjustifiable and a pride that is altogether unintelligent. The pity is for the obvious wants and distresses of poverty, the pride appears in the arrogant and aggressive conception of raising one's fellows. I have no strong feeling for the horrors and discomforts of poverty as such, sensibilities can be hardened to endure the life led by the *Romans* in Dartmoor jail a hundred years ago[1], or softened to detect the crumpled rose-leaf; what disgusts me is the stupidity and warring purposes of which poverty is the outcome. When it comes to this idea of raising human beings, I must confess the only person I feel concerned about raising is H G Wells, and that even in his case

1 See *The Story of Dartmoor Prison* by Basil Thomson (Heinemann–1907).

my energies might be better employed. After all, presently he must die and the world will have done with him. His output for the species is more important than his individual elevation.

Moreover, all this talk of raising implies a classification I doubt. I find it hard to fix any standards that will determine who is above me and who below. Most people are different from me I perceive, but which among them is better, which worse? I have a certain power of communicating with other minds, but what experiences I communicate seem often far thinner and poorer stuff than those which others less expressive than I half fail to communicate and half display to me. My "inferiors", judged by the common social standards, seem indeed intellectually more limited than I and with a narrower outlook; they are often dirtier and more driven, more under the stress of hunger and animal appetites; but on the other hand have they not more vigorous sensations than I, and through sheer coarsening and hardening of fibre, the power to do more toilsome things and sustain intenser sensations than I could endure? When I sit upon the bench, a respectable magistrate, and commit some battered reprobate for trial for this lurid offence or that, or send him or her to prison for drunkenness or such-like indecorum, the doubt drifts into my mind which of us after all is indeed getting nearest to the keen edge of life. Are I and my respectable colleagues much more than successful evasions of *that*? Perhaps these people in the dock know more of the essential strains and stresses of nature, are more intimate with pain. At any rate I do not think I am justified in saying certainly that they do not know...

No, I do not want to raise people using my own position as a standard, I do not want to be one of a gang of consciously superior people, I do not want arrogantly to change the quality of other lives. I do not want to interfere with other lives, except incidentally – incidentally, in this way that I do want to get an understanding with them. I do want to share and feel with them in our commerce with the collective mind. I suppose I do not stretch language very much when I say I want to get rid of stresses and obstacles between our minds and personalities and to establish a relation that is understanding and sympathy and that will bring us at last to the harmonious service of God.

I want to make more generally possible a relationship of communication and interchange, that for want of a less battered and ambiguous word I must needs call love.

And if I disavow the Socialism of condescension, so also do I disavow the Socialism of revolt. There is a form of Socialism based upon the economic generalisations of Marx, an economic fatalistic Socialism that I hold to be rather wrong in its vision of facts, rather more distinctly wrong in its theory, and altogether wrong and hopeless in its spirit. It preaches, as inevitable, a concentration of property in hands of a limited number of property owners and the expropriation of the great proletarian mass of mankind, a concentration which is after all no more than a tendency conditional on changing and changeable conventions about property, and it finds its hope of a better future in the outcome of a class conflict between the expropriated Many and the expropriating Few. Both sides are to be equally swayed by self-interest, but the toilers are to be gregarious and mutually loyal in their self-interest – Heaven knows why, except that otherwise the Marxist dream will not work. The experience of contemporary events seems to show at least an equal power of combination for material ends among owners and employers as among workers.

260

Now this class-war idea is one diametrically opposed to that religious-spirited Socialism which supplies the form of my general activities. This class-war idea would exacerbate the antagonism of the interests of the many individuals against the few individuals, and I would oppose the service of the Whole to the self-seeking of the Individual. The spirit and constructive intention of the many today are no better than those of the few, poor and rich alike are over-individualised, self-seeking and non-creative; to organize the confused jostling competitions, over-reachings, envies and hatreds of today into two great class-hatreds and antagonisms will advance the reign of love at most only a very little, only so far as it will simplify and make plain certain issues. It may very possibly not advance the reign of love at all, but rather shatter the order we have. Socialism, as I conceive it, seeks to change economic arrangements only by the way, as an aspect and outcome of a great change, a change in the spirit and method of human intercourse, a change from an individual claim to a claim to serve the Spirit of Mankind fully and completely.

I know that here I go beyond the limits many Socialists in the past, and some who are still contemporary, have set for themselves. Much Socialism today seems to think of itself as fighting a battle against poverty and its concomitants alone. Now poverty is only a symptom of a profounder evil and is never to be cured by itself. It is one aspect of divided and dispersed purposes. If Socialism is only a conflict with poverty, Socialism is nothing. But I hold that Socialism is and must be a battle against human stupidity and egotism and disorder, a battle fought all through the forests and jungles of the soul of man. As we get intellectual and moral light and the realisation of brotherhood, so social and economic organisation will develop. But the Socialist may attack poverty for ever, disregarding the intellectual and moral factors that necessitate it, and he will remain until the end a purely economic doctrinaire crying in the wilderness in vain.

And if I antagonise myself in this way to the philanthropic Socialism of kindly prosperous people on the one hand and to the fierce class-hatred Socialism on the other, still more am I opposed to that furtive Socialism of the specialist which one meets most typically in the Fabian Society. It arises very naturally out of what I may perhaps call specialist fatigue and impatience. It is very easy for writers like myself to deal in the broad generalities of Socialism and urge their adoption as general principles; it is altogether another affair with a man who sets himself to work out the riddle of the complications of actuality in order to modify them in the direction of Socialism. He finds himself in a jungle of difficulties that strain his intellectual power to the utmost. He emerges at last with conclusions, and they are rarely the obvious conclusions, as to what needs to be done. Even the people of his own side he finds do not see as he sees; they are, he perceives, crude and ignorant.

Now I hold that his duty is to explain his discoveries and intentions until they see as he sees. But the specialist temperament is often not a generalising and expository temperament. Specialists are apt to measure minds by their speciality and underrate the average intelligence. The specialist is appalled by the real task before him, and he sets himself by tricks and misrepresentations, by benevolent scoundrelism in fact, to effect changes he desires. Too often he fails even in that.

Where he might have found fellowship he arouses suspicion. And even if a thing is done in this way, its essential merit is lost. For it is better, I hold, for a man to die of his disease than to be cured unwittingly. That is to cheat him of life and to cheat life of the contribution his consciousness might have given it.

The Socialism of my beliefs rests on a profounder faith and a broader proposition. It looks over and beyond the warring purposes of today as a general may look over and beyond a crowd of sullen, excited and confused recruits, to the day when they will be disciplined, exercised, trained, willing and convergent on a common end. It holds persistently to the idea of men increasingly working in agreement, doing things that are sane to do, on a basis of mutual helpfulness, temperance and toleration. It sees the great masses of humanity rising out of base and immediate anxieties, out of dwarfing pressures and cramped surroundings, to understanding and participation and fine effort. It sees the resources of the earth husbanded and harvested, economised and used with scientific skill for the maximum of result. It sees towns and cities finely built, a race of beings finely bred and taught and trained, open ways and peace and freedom from end to end of the earth. It sees beauty increasing in humanity, about humanity and through humanity. Through this great body of mankind goes evermore an increasing understanding, an intensifying brotherhood. As Christians have dreamt of the New Jerusalem so does Socialism, growing ever more temperate, patient, forgiving and resolute, set its face to the World City of Mankind.

5

Hate and Love

Before I go on to point out the broad principles of action that flow from this wide conception of Socialism, I may perhaps give a section to elucidating that opposition of hate and love I made when I dealt with the class war. I have already used the word love several times; it is an ambiguous word and it may be well to spend a few words in making clear the sense in which it is used here. I use it here in a broad sense to convey all that complex of motives, impulse, sentiments, that incline us to find our happiness and satisfactions in the happiness and sympathy of others and to merge ourselves emotionally in a design greater than ourselves. Essentially it is a synthetic force in human affairs, the merger tendency, a linking force, an expression in personal will and feeling of the common element and interest. It insists upon resemblances and shares and sympathies. And hate, I take it, is the emotional aspect of antagonism, it is the expression in personal will and feeling of the individual's separation from others. It is the competing and destructive tendency. So long as we are individuals and members of a species, we must needs both hate and love. But because I believe, as I have already confessed, that the oneness of the species is a greater fact than individuality, and that we individuals are temporary separations from a collective purpose, and since hate eliminates itself by eliminating its objects, whilst love multiplies itself by multiplying its objects, so love must be a thing more comprehensive and enduring than hate.

Moreover, hate must be in its nature a good thing. We individuals exist as such, I believe, for the purpose in things, and our separations and antagonisms serve that purpose. We play against each other like hammer and anvil. But the synthesis of a collective will in humanity, which is I believe our human and terrestrial share in that purpose, is an idea that carries with it a conception of a secular alteration in the scope and method of both love and hate. Both widen and change with man's widening and developing apprehension of the purpose he serves. The savage man loves in gusts a fellow creature or so about him, and fears and hates all other people. Every expansion of his scope and ideas widens either circle. The common man of our civilized world loves not only many of his friends and associates systematically and enduringly, but dimly he loves also his city and his country, his creed and his race; he loves it maybe less intensely but over a far wider field and much more steadily. But he hates also more widely if less passionately and vehemently than a savage, and since love makes rather harmony and peace and hate rather conflicts and events, one may easily be led to suppose that hate is the ruling motive in human affairs. Men band themselves together in leagues and loyalties, in cults and organisations and nationalities, and it is often hard to say whether the bond is one of love for the association or hatred of those to whom the association is antagonised. The two things pass insensibly into one another. London people have recently seen an instance of the transition, in the Brown Dog statue riots (1908). A number of people drawn together by their common pity for animal suffering, by love indeed of the most disinterested sort, had so forgotten their initial spirit as to erect a monument with an inscription at once recklessly untruthful, spiteful in spirit and particularly vexatious to one great medical school of London. They have provoked riots and placarded London with taunts and irritating misrepresentation of the spirit of medical research, and they have infected a whole fresh generation of London students with a bitter partisan contempt for the humanitarian effort that has so lamentably misconducted itself. Both sides vow they will never give in, and the antivivisectionists are busy manufacturing small china copies of the Brown Dog figure, inscription and all, for purposes of domestic irritation. Here hate, the evil ugly brother of effort, has manifestly slain love the initiator and taken the affair in hand. That is a little model of human conflicts. So soon as we become militant and play against one another, comes this danger of strain and this possible reversal of motive. The fight begins. Into a pit of heat and hate fall right and wrong together.

Now it seems to me that a religious faith such as I have set forth in the second Book, and a clear sense of our community of blood with all mankind, must necessarily affect both our loving and our hatred. It will certainly not abolish hate, but it will subordinate it altogether to love. We are individuals, so the Purpose presents itself to me, in order that we may hate the things that have to go, ugliness, baseness, insufficiency, unreality, that we may love and experiment and strive for the things that collectively we seek – power and beauty. Before our conversion we did this darkly and with our hate spreading to persons and parties from the things for which they stood. But the believer will hate lovingly and without fear. We are of one blood and substance with our antagonists, even with those that we desire keenly may die and leave no issue in flesh or persuasion. They all touch us and are part of one necessary experience. They are all necessary to the synthesis, even if they are necessary only as the potato-peel in the dust-bin is necessary to my dinner.

So it is, I disavow and deplore the whole spirit of class-war Socialism with its doctrine of hate, its envious assault upon the leisure and freedom of the wealthy. Without leisure and freedom and the experience of life they gave, the ideas of Socialism could never have been born. The true mission of Socialism is against darkness, vanity and cowardice, that darkness which hides from the property owner the intense beauty, the potentialities of interest, the splendid possibilities of life, that vanity and cowardice that make him clutch his precious holdings and fear and hate the shadow of change. It has to teach the collective organisation of society; and to that the class-consciousness and intense class-prejudices of the worker need to bow quite as much as those of the property owner. But when I say that Socialism's mission is to teach, I do not mean that its mission is a merely verbal and mental one; it must use all instruments and teach by example as well as precept. Socialism by becoming charitable and merciful will not cease to be militant. Socialism must, lovingly but resolutely, use law, use force, to dispossess the owners of socially disadvantageous wealth, as one coerces a lunatic brother or takes a wrongfully acquired toy from a spoiled and obstinate child. It must intervene between all who would keep their children from instruction in the business of citizenship and the lessons of fraternity. It must build and guard what it builds with laws and with that sword which is behind all laws. Non-resistance is for the non-constructive man, for the hermit in the cave and the naked saint in the dust; the builder and maker with the first stroke of his foundation spade uses force and opens war against the anti-builder.

6

The Preliminary Social Duty

The belief I have that contributing to the development of the collective being of man is the individual's general meaning and duty, and the formulae of the Socialism which embodies this belief so far as our common activities go, give a general framework and direction how a man or woman should live. (I do throughout all this book mean man or woman equally when I write of "man", unless it is manifestly inapplicable.)

And first in this present time he must see to it that he does live, that is to say he must get food, clothing, covering, and adequate leisure for the finer aspects of living. Socialism plans an organized civilization in which these things will be a collective solicitude, and the gaining of a subsistence an easy preliminary to the fine drama of existence, but in the world as we have it we are forced to engage much of our energy in scrambling for these preliminary necessities. Our problems of conduct lie in the world as it is and not in the world as we want it to be. First then a man must get a living, a fair, civilized living for himself. It is a fundamental duty. It must be a fair living, not pinched nor mean nor strained. A man can do nothing higher, he can be no service to any cause, until he himself is fed and clothed and equipped and free. He must earn this living or equip himself to earn it in some way not socially disadvantageous, he must contrive as far as possible that the work he does shall be constructive and contributory to the general well-being.

And these primary necessities of food, clothing and freedom being secured, one comes to the general disposition of one's surplus energy. With regard to that I think that a very simple proposition follows from the broad beliefs I have chosen to adopt. The general duty of a man, his existence being secured, is to educate, and chiefly to educate and develop himself. It is his duty to live, to make all he can out of himself and life, to get full of experience, to make himself fine and perceiving and expressive, to render his experience and perceptions honestly and helpfully to others. And in particular he has to educate himself and others with himself in Socialism. He has to make and keep this idea of synthetic human effort and of conscious constructive effort clear first to himself and then clear in the general mind. For it is an idea that comes and goes. We are all of us continually lapsing from it towards individual isolation again. He needs, we all need, constant refreshment in this belief if it is to remain a predominant living fact in our lives.

And that duty of education, of building up the collective idea and organisation of humanity, falls into various divisions depending in their importance upon individual quality. For all there is one personal work that none may evade, and that is thinking hard, criticizing strenuously and understanding as clearly as one can religion, socialism and the general principle of one's acts. The intellectual factor is of primary importance in my religion. I can see no more reason why salvation should come to the intellectually incapable than to the morally incapable. For simple souls thinking in simple processes, salvation perhaps comes easily, but there is none for the intellectual coward, for the mental sloven and sluggard, for the stupid and obdurate mind. The Believer will think hard and continue to grow and learn, to read and seek discussion as his needs determine.

Correlated with one's own intellectual activity, part of it and growing out of it for almost everyone, intellectual work with and upon others. By teaching we learn. Not to communicate one's thoughts to others, to keep one's thoughts to oneself as people say, is either cowardice or pride. It is a form of sin. A good man is an open man. It is a duty to talk, teach, explain, write, lecture, read and listen. Every truly religious man, every good Socialist, is a propagandist. Those who cannot write or discuss can talk, those who cannot argue can induce people to listen to others and read. We have a belief and an idea that we want to spread, each to the utmost of his means and measure, throughout all the world. We have a thought that we want to make humanity's thought. And it is a duty too that one should, within the compass of one's ability, make teaching, writing and lecturing possible where it has not existed before. This can be done in a hundred ways, by founding and enlarging schools and universities and chairs, for example; by making print and reading and all the material of thought cheap and abundant, by organizing discussion and societies for inquiry.

And talk and thought and study are but the more generalised aspects of duty. The Believer may find his own special aptitude lies rather among concrete things, in experimenting and promoting experiments in collective action. Things teach as well as words, and some of us are most expressive by concrete methods. The Believer will work himself and help others to his utmost in all those developments of material civilization, in organized sanitation for example, all those developments that force collective acts upon communities and collective realizations into the minds of men. And the whole field of scientific research is a field of duty calling to everyone who can enter it, to add to the permanent store of knowledge and new resources for the race.

The Mind of that Civilized State we seek to make by giving ourselves into its making, is evidently the central work before us. But while the writer, the publisher and printer, the bookseller and librarian and teacher and preacher, the investigator and experimenter, the reader and everyone who thinks, will be contributing themselves to this great organized mind and intention in the world, many sorts of specialised men will be more immediately concerned with parallel and more concrete aspects of the human synthesis. The medical worker and the medical investigator, for example, will be building up the body of a new generation, the body of the civilized state, and he will be doing all he can, not simply as an individual, but as a citizen, to *organize* his services of cure and prevention, of hygiene and selection. A great and growing multitude of men will be working out the apparatus of the civilized state; the organizers of transit and housing, the engineers in their incessantly increasing variety, the miners and geologists estimating the world's resources in metals and minerals, the mechanical inventors perpetually economising force. The scientific agriculturist again will be studying the food supply of the world as a whole, and how it may be increased and distributed and economised. And to the student of law comes the task of rephrasing his intricate and often quite beautiful science in relation to modern conceptions. All these and a hundred other aspects are integral to the wide project of Constructive Socialism as it shapes itself in my faith.

7

Wrong Ways of Living

When we lay down the proposition that it is one's duty to get one's living in some way not socially disadvantageous, and as far as possible by work that is contributory to the general well-being and development, when we state that one's surplus energies, after one's living is gained, must be devoted to experience, self-development and constructive work, it is clear we condemn by implication many modes of life that are followed today.

For example, it is manifest we condemn living in idleness or on non-productive sport, on the income derived from private property, and all sorts of ways of earning a living that cannot be shown to conduce to the constructive process. We condemn trading that is merely speculative, and in fact all trading and manufacture that is not a positive social service; we condemn living by gambling or by playing games for either stakes or pay. Much more do we condemn dishonest or fraudulent trading and every act of advertisement that is not punctiliously truthful. We must condemn too the taking of any income from the community that is neither earned nor conceded in the collective interest. But to this last point, and to certain issues arising out of it, I will return in the section next following this one.

And it follows evidently from our general propositions that every form of prostitution is a double sin, against one's individuality and against the species which we serve by the development of that individuality's preferences and idiosyncrasies.

And by prostitution I mean not simply the act of a woman who sells for money, and against her thoughts and preferences, her smiles and endearments and the secret beauty and pleasure of her body, but the act of anyone who, to gain a living, suppresses himself, does things in a manner alien to himself and subserves aims and purposes with which he disagrees. The journalist who writes against his personal convictions, the solicitor who knowingly assists the schemes of rogues, the barrister who pits himself against what he perceives is justice and the right, the artist who does unbeautiful things or less beautiful things than he might, simply to please base employers, the craftsman who makes instruments for foolish uses or bad uses, the dealer who sells and pushes an article because it fits the customer's folly; all these are prostitutes of mind and soul if not of body, with no right to lift an eyebrow at the painted disasters of the streets.

8

Social Parasitism and Contemporary Injustices

These broad principles about one's way of living are very simple; our minds move freely among them. But the real interest is with the individual case, and the individual case is almost always complicated by the fact that the existing social and economic system is based upon conditions that the growing collective intelligence condemns as unjust and undesirable, and that the constructive spirit in men now seeks to supersede. We have to live in a provisional State while we dream of and work for a better one.

The ideal life for the ordinary man in a civilized, that is to say a Socialist, State would be in public employment or in private enterprise aiming at public recognition. But in our present world only a small minority can have that direct and honourable relation of public service in the work they do; most of the important business of the community is done upon the older and more tortuous private ownership system, and the great mass of men in socially useful employment find themselves working only indirectly for the community and directly for the profit of a private owner, or they themselves are private owners. Every man who has any money put by in the bank, or any money invested, is a private owner, and in so far as he draws interest or profit from this investment he is a social parasite. It is in practice almost impossible to divest oneself of that parasitic quality however straightforward the general principle may be.

It is practically impossible for two equally valid sets of reasons. The first is that under existing conditions, saving and investment constitute the only way to rest and security in old age, to leisure, study and intellectual independence, to the safe upbringing of a family and the happiness of one's weaker dependents. These are things that should not be left for the individual to provide; in the civilized state, the state itself will insure every citizen against these anxieties that now make the study of the City Article almost a duty. To abandon saving and investment today, and to do so is of course to abandon all insurance, is to become a driven and uncertain worker, to risk one's personal freedom and culture and the upbringing and efficiency of one's children. It is to lower the standard of one's personal civilization, to think with less deliberation and less detachment, to fall away from that work of accumulating fine habits and beautiful and pleasant ways of living contributory to the coming State. And in the second place there is not only no return for such a sacrifice in anything won for Socialism, but for fine-thinking and living people to give up property is merely to let it pass into the hands of more egoistic possessors. Since at present things must be privately owned, it is better that they should be owned by people consciously working for social development and willing to use them to that end.

We have to live in the present system and under the conditions of the present system, while we work with all our power to change that system for a better one.

The case of Cadburys the cocoa and chocolate makers, and the practical slavery under the Portuguese of the East African negroes who grow the raw material for Messrs Cadbury, is an illuminating one in this connection. The Cadburys, like the Rowntrees, are well known as an energetic and public-spirited family, their social and industrial experiments at Bournville and their general social and political activities are broad and constructive in the best sense. But they find themselves in the peculiar dilemma that they must either abandon an important and profitable portion of their great manufacture or continue to buy produce grown under cruel and even horrible conditions. Their retirement from the branch of the cocoa and chocolate trade concerned would, under these circumstances, mean no diminution of the manufacture or of the horrors of this particular slavery; it would mean merely that less humanitarian manufacturers would step in to take up the abandoned trade. The self-righteous individualist would have no doubts about the question; he would keep his hands clean anyhow, retrench his social work, abandon the types of cocoa involved, and pass by on the other side. But indeed I do not believe we came into the mire of life simply to hold our hands up out of it. Messrs Cadbury follow a better line; they keep their business going, and exert themselves in every way to let light into the secrets of Portuguese East Africa and to organize a better control of these labour cruelties. That I think is altogether the right course in this difficulty.

We cannot keep our hands clean in this world as it is. There is no excuse indeed for a life of fraud or any other positive fruitless wrong-doing or for a purely parasitic non-productive life, yet all but the fortunate few who are properly paid and recognised state servants must in financial and business matters do their best amidst and through institutions tainted with injustice and flawed with unrealities. All Socialists everywhere are like expeditionary soldiers far ahead of the main advance. The organized state that should own and administer their possessions for the general good has not arrived to take them over; and in the meanwhile they must act like its anticipatory agents according to their lights and make things ready for its coming.

The Believer then who is not in the public service, whose life lies among the operations of private enterprise, must work always on the supposition that the property he administers, the business in which he works, the profession he follows, is destined to be taken over and organized collectively for the commonweal and must be made ready for the taking over; that the private outlook he secures by investment, the provision he makes for his friends and children, are temporary, wasteful, though at present unavoidable devices to be presently merged in and superseded by the broad and scientific previsions of the co-operative commonwealth.

9

The Case of the Wife and Mother

These principles give a rule also for the problem that faces the great majority of thinking wives and mothers today. The most urgent and necessary social work falls upon them; they bear, and largely educate and order the homes of, the next generation, and they have no direct recognition from the community for either of these supreme functions. They are supposed to perform them not for God or the world, but to please and satisfy a particular man. Our laws, our social conventions, our economic methods, so hem a woman about that, however fitted for and desirous of maternity she may be, she can only effectually do that duty in a dependent relation to her husband. Nearly always he is the paymaster, and if his payments are grudging or irregular, she has little remedy short of a breach and the rupture of the home. Her duty is conceived of as first to him and only secondarily to her children and the State. Many wives become under these circumstances, mere prostitutes to their husbands, often evading the bearing of children with their consent and even at their request, and "loving for a living". That is a natural outcome of the proprietary theory of the family out of which our civilisation emerges. But our modern ideas trend more and more to regard a woman's primary duty to be her duty to the children and to the world to which she gives them. She is to be a citizen side by side with her husband; no longer is he to intervene between her and the community. As a matter of contemporary fact he can do so and does so habitually, and most women have to square their ideas of life to that possibility.

Before any women who is clear-headed enough to perceive that this great business of motherhood is one of supreme public importance, there are a number of alternatives at the present time. She may, like Grant Allen's heroine in *The Woman Who Did*, declare an exaggerated and impossible independence, refuse the fetters of marriage and bear children to a lover. This, in the present state of public opinion in almost every existing social atmosphere, would be a purely anarchistic course. It would mean a fatherless home, and since the woman will have to play the double part of income-earner and mother, an impoverished and struggling home. It would mean also an unsocial because ostracised home. In most cases, and even assuming it to be right in idea, it would still be on all fours with that immediate abandonment of private property we have already discussed, a sort of suicide that helps the world nothing.

Or she may "strike", refuse marriage and pursue a solitary and childless career, engaging her surplus energies in constructive work. But that also is suicide; it is to miss the keenest experiences, the finest realities life has to offer.

Or she may meet a man whom she can trust to keep a treaty with her and supplement the common interpretations and legal insufficiencies of the marriage bond, who will respect her always as a free and independent person, will abstain absolutely from authoritative methods, and will either share and trust his income and property with her in a frank communism, or give her a sufficient and private income for her personal use. It is only fair under existing economic conditions, that at marriage a husband should insure his life in his wife's interest, and I do not think it would be impossible to bring our legal marriage contract into accordance with modern ideas in that matter. Certainly it should be legally imperative that at the birth of each child a new policy upon its father's life, as the income-getter, should begin. The latter provision at least should be a normal condition of marriage and one that a wife should have power to enforce when payments fall away. With such safeguards and under such conditions marriage ceases to be a haphazard dependence for a woman, and she may live, teaching and rearing and free, almost as though the co-operative commonwealth had come.

But in many cases, since great numbers of women marry so young and so ignorantly that their thinking about realities begins only after marriage, a woman will find herself already married to a man before she realizes the significance of these things. She may be already the mother of children. Her husband's ideas may not be her ideas. He may dominate, he may prohibit, he may intervene, he may default. He may, if he sees fit, burthen the family income with the charges of his illegitimate offspring. He may by his will deprive wife and children of any share of the family property.

We live in the world as it is and not in the world as it should be. That sentence becomes the refrain of this discussion.

The normal modern married woman has to make the best of a bad position, to do her best under the old conditions, to live as though she was under the new conditions, to make good citizens, to give her spare energies as far as she can to bringing about a better state of affairs. Like the private property owner and the official in a privately owned business, her best method of conduct is to consider herself an unrecognised public official, irregularly commanded and improperly paid. There is no good in flagrant rebellion. She has to study her particular circumstances and make what good she can out of them, keeping her face towards the coming time. I cannot better the image I have already used for the thinking and believing modern-minded people of today as an advance guard cut off from proper supplies, ill furnished so that makeshift prevails, and rather demoralised. We have to be wise as well as loyal; discretion itself is loyalty to the coming State.

10

Of Abstinences and Disciplines

I have already confessed that my nature is one that dislikes abstinences and is wearied by and wary of excess.

I do not feel that it is right to suppress altogether any part of one's being. In itself abstinence seems to me a refusal to experience, and that, upon the lines of thought I follow, is to say that abstinence for its own sake is evil. But for an end all abstinences are permissible, and if the kinetic type of believer finds both his individual and his associated efficiency enhanced by a systematic discipline, if he is convinced that he must specialize because of the discursiveness of his motives, because there is something he wants to do or be so good that the rest of them may very well be suppressed for its sake, then he must suppress. But the virtue is in what he gets done and not in what he does not do. Reasonable fear is a sound reason for abstinence, as when a man has a passion like a lightly sleeping maniac that the slightest indulgence will arouse. Then he must needs adopt heroic abstinence, and even more so must he take to preventive restraint if he sees any motive becoming unruly and urgent and troublesome. Fear is a sound reason for abstinence and so is love.

Many who have sensitive imaginations nowadays very properly abstain from meat because of butchery. And it is often needful, out of love and brotherhood, to abstain from things harmless to oneself because they are inconveniently alluring to others linked to us. The moderate drinker who sits at table sipping his wine in the sight of one he knows to be a potential dipsomaniac is at the best an unloving fool.

But mere abstinence and the doing of barren toilsome unrewarding things for the sake of the toil, is a perversion of one's impulses. There is neither honour nor virtue nor good in that.

I do not believe in negative virtues. I think the ideas of them arise out of the system of metaphysical errors I have roughly analysed in my first Book, out of the inherent tendency of the mind to make the relative absolute and to convert quantitative into qualitative differences. Our minds fall very readily under the spell of such unmitigated words as Purity and Chastity. Only death beyond decay, absolute non-existence, can be Pure and Chaste. Life is impurity, fact is impure. Everything has traces of alien matter; our very health is dependent upon parasitic bacteria; the purest blood in the world has a tainted ancestor, and not a saint but has evil thoughts. It was blindness to that which set men stoning the woman taken in adultery. They forgot what they were made of. This stupidity, this unreasonable idealism of the common mind, fills life today with cruelties and exclusions, with partial suicides and secret shames. But we are born impure, we die impure; it is a fable that spotless white lilies sprang from any saint's decay, and the chastity of monk or nun is but introverted impurity. We have to take life valiantly on these conditions and make such honour and beauty and sympathy

out of our confusions, gather such constructive experience, as
we may.

There is a mass of real superstition upon these points, a belief
in a magic purity, in magic personalities who can say –

> My strength is as the strength of ten
> Because my heart is pure.

and wonderful clairvoyant innocents like the young man in
Mr Kipling's *Finest Story in the World*.

There is a lurking disposition to believe, even among those
who lead the normal type of life, that the abstinent and chastely
celibate are exceptionally healthy, energetic, immune. The
wildest claims are made. But indeed it is true for all who can see
the facts of life simply and plainly, that man is an omnivorous,
versatile, various creature and can draw his strength from
a hundred varieties of nourishment. He has physiological
idiosyncrasies too that are indifferent to biological classifications
and moral generalities. It is not true that his absorbent
vessels begin their task as children begin the guessing game, by
asking, "Is it animal, vegetable or mineral?" He responds to
stimulation and recuperates after the exhaustion of his response,
and his being is singularly careless whether the stimulation
comes as a drug or stimulant, or as anger or music or noble
appeals.

Most people speak of drugs in the spirit of that admirable
firm of soap-boilers which assures its customers that the soap
they make "contains no chemicals". Drugs are supposed to be a
mystic diabolical class of substance, remote from and contrasting
in their nature with all other things. So people banish a tonic

282

from the house and stuff their children with manufactured cereals and chocolate creams. The drunken helot of this system of absurdities is the Christian Scientist who denies healing only to those who have studied pathology, and declares that anything whatever put into a bottle and labelled with directions for its use by a doctor is thereby damnable and damned. But indeed all drugs and all the things of life have their uses and dangers, and there is no wholesale truth to excuse us a particular wisdom and watchfulness in these matters. Unless we except smoking as an unclean and needless artificiality, all these matters of eating and drinking and habit are matters of more or less. It seems to me foolish to make anything that is stimulating and pleasurable into a habit, for that is slowly and surely to lose a stimulus and pleasure and create a need that it may become painful to check or control. The moral rule of my standards is irregularity. If I were a father confessor I should begin my catalogue of sins by asking; "are you a man of regular life?" And I would charge my penitent to go away forthwith and commit some practicable saving irregularity; to fast or get drunk or climb a mountain or sup on pork and beans or give up smoking or spend a month with publicans and sinners. Right conduct for the common unspecialised man lies delicately adjusted between defect and excess as a watch is adjusted and adjustable between fast and slow. We none of us altogether and always keep the balance or are altogether safe from losing it.

We swing, balancing and adjusting, along our path. Life is that, and abstinence is for the most part a mere evasion of life.

11

On Forgetting, and the Need of Prayer, Reading, Discussion and Worship

One aspect of life I had very much in mind when I planned those Samurai disciplines of mine. It was forgetting.

We forget. Even after we have found Salvation, we have to keep hold of Salvation; believing, we must continue to believe. We cannot always be at a high level of noble emotion. We have clambered on the ship of Faith and found our place and work aboard, and even while we are busied upon it, behold we are back and drowning in the sea of chaotic things.

Every religious body, every religious teacher, has appreciated this difficulty and the need there is of reminders and renewals. Faith needs restatement and revival as the body needs food. And since the Believer is to seek much experience and be a judge of less or more in many things, it is particularly necessary that he should keep hold upon a living Faith.

How may he best do this?

I think we may state it as a general duty that he must do whatever he can to keep his faith constantly alive. But beyond that, what a man must do depends almost entirely upon his own intellectual character. Many people of a regular type of mind can refresh themselves by some recurrent duty, by repeating a daily prayer, by daily reading or re-reading some devotional book. With others constant repetition leads to a mental and spiritual deadening, until beautiful phrases become unmeaning, eloquent statements inane and ridiculous, – matter for parody. All who can, I think, should pray and should read and re-read what they have found spiritually helpful, and if they know of others of kindred dispositions and can organize these exercises, they should do so. Collective worship again is a necessity for many Believers. For many, the public religious services of this or that form of Christianity supply an atmosphere rich in the essential quality of religion and abounding in phrases about the religious life, mellow from the use of centuries and almost immediately applicable. It seems to me that if one can do so, one should participate in such public worship and habituate oneself to read back into it that collective purpose and conscience it once embodied.

Very much is to be said for the ceremony of Holy Communion or the Mass, for those whom accident or intellectual scruples do not debar. I do not think young modern liberal thinkers quite appreciate the finer aspects of this, the one universal service of the Christian Church. Some of them are set forth very finely by a man who has been something of a martyr for conscience' sake, and is for me a hero as well as friend, in a world not rich in heroes,[1] the Rev. Stewart Headlam, in his book, *The Meaning of the Mass.*

With others again, Faith can be most animated by writing, by confession, by discussion, by talk with friends or antagonists.

One or other or all of these things the Believer must do, for the mind is a living and moving process, and the thing that lies inert in it is presently covered up by new interests and lost. If you make a sort of King Log of your faith, presently something else will be sitting upon it, pride or self-interest, or some rebel craving, King *de facto* of your soul, directing it back to anarchy.

1 Obviously written in 1908.

For many types that, however, is exactly what happens with public worship. They *do* get a King Log in Ceremony. And if you deliberately overcome and suppress your perception of and repugnance to the perfunctoriness of religion in nine-tenths of the worshippers about you, you may be destroying at the same time your own intellectual and moral sensitiveness. But I am not suggesting that you should force yourself to take part in public worship against your perceptions, but only that if it helps you to worship you should not hesitate to do so.

We deal here with a real need that is not to be fettered by any general prescription. I have one Cambridge friend who finds nothing so uplifting in the world as the atmosphere of the afternoon service in the choir of King's College Chapel, and another, a very great and distinguished and theologically sceptical woman, who accustomed herself for some time to hear from a distant corner the evening service in St Paul's Cathedral and who would go great distances to do that.

Many people find an exaltation and broadening of the mind in mountain scenery and the starry heavens and the wide arc of the sea; and as I have already said, it was part of the disciplines of these Samurai of mine that yearly they should go apart for at least a week of solitary wandering and meditation in lonely and desolate places. Music again is a frequent means of release from the narrow life as it closes about us. One man I know makes an anthology into which he copies to re-read any passage that stirs and revives in him the sense of broad issues. Others again seem able to refresh their nobility of outlook in the atmosphere of an intense personal love.

Some of us seem to forget almost as if it were an essential part of ourselves. Such a man as myself, irritable, easily fatigued and bored, versatile, sensuous, curious, and a little greedy for experience, is perpetually losing touch with his faith, so that indeed I sometimes turn over these pages that I have written and come upon my declarations and confessions with a sense of alien surprise.

It may be, I say, that for some of us forgetting is the normal process, that one has to believe and forget and blunder and learn something and regret and suffer and so come again to belief much as we have to eat and grow hungry and eat again. What these others can get in their temples we, after our own manner, must distil through sleepless and lonely nights, from unavoidable humiliations, from the smarting of bruised shins.

12

Democracy and Aristocracy

And now having dealt with the general form of a man's duty and with his duty to himself, let me come to his attitude to his individual fellow-men.

The broad principles determining that attitude are involved in things already written in this book. The belief in a collective being gathering experience and developing will, to which every life is subordinated, renders the cruder conception of aristocracy, the idea of a select life going on amidst a majority of trivial and contemptible persons who "do not exist", untenable. It abolishes contempt. Indeed to believe at all in a comprehensive purpose in things is to abandon that attitude and all the habits and acts that imply it. But a belief in universal significance does not altogether preclude a belief in an aristocratic method of progress, in the idea of the subordination of a number of individuals to others who can utilise their lives and help and contributory achievements in the general purpose. To a certain extent indeed, this last conception is almost inevitable. We must needs so think of ourselves in relation to plants and animals, and I see no reason why we should not think so of our relations to other men. There are clearly great differences in the capacity and range of experience of man and man and in their power of using and rendering their experiences for the racial synthesis. Vigorous persons do look naturally for help and service from persons of less initiative, and we are all more or less capable of admiration and hero-worship and pleased to help and give ourselves to those we feel to be finer or better or completer or more forceful and leaderly than ourselves. This is a natural and inevitable form of aristocracy.

For that reason aristocracy is not to be organized. We organize things that are not natural nor inevitable, but this is clearly a complex matter of accident and personalities for which there can be no general rule. All organized aristocracy is manifestly begotten by that fallacy of classification my Metaphysical book set itself to expose. Its effect is, and has been in all cases, to mask natural aristocracy, to draw the lines by wholesale and wrong, to bolster up weak and ineffectual persons in false positions and to fetter or hamper strong and vigorous people. The false aristocrat is a figure of pride and claims, a consumer followed by dupes. He is proudly secretive, pretending to aims beyond the common understanding. The true aristocrat is known rather than knows; he makes and serves. He exacts no deference. He is urgent to make others share what he knows and wants and achieves. He does not think of others as his but as God's as he also is God's.

There is a base democracy just as there is a base aristocracy, the swaggering, aggressive disposition of the vulgar soul that admits neither of superiors not leaders. Its true name is insubordination. It resents rules and refinements, delicacies, differences and organisation. It dreams that its leaders are its delegates. It takes refuge from all superiority, all special knowledge, in a phantom ideal, the People, the sublime and wonderful People. "You can fool some of the people all the time and all the people some of the time, but you can't fool all the people all the time," expresses I think quite the quintessence of this mystical faith, this faith in which men take refuge from the demand for order, discipline and conscious light. In England it has never been of any great account, but in America the vulgar individualist's self-protective exaltation of an idealised Common Man has worked and is working infinite mischief.

In politics the crude democratic faith leads directly to the submission of every question, however subtle and special its issues may be, to a popular vote. The community is regarded as a consultative committee of profoundly wise, alert and well-informed Common Men. Since the common man is, as Gustave le Bon has pointed out, a gregarious animal, collectively rather like a sheep, emotional, hasty and shallow, the practical outcome of political democracy in all large communities under modern conditions is to put power into the hands of rich newspaper proprietors, advertising producers and the energetic wealthy generally who are best able to flood the collective mind freely with the suggestions on which it acts.

But democracy has acquired a better meaning than its first crude intentions – there never was a theory started yet in the human mind that did not beget a finer offspring than itself – and

289

the secondary meaning brings it at last into entire accordance with the subtler conception of aristocracy. The test of this quintessential democracy is neither a passionate insistence upon voting and the majority rule, nor an arrogant bearing towards those who are one's betters in this aspect or that, but fellowship. The true democrat and the true aristocrat meet and are one in feeling themselves parts of one synthesis under one purpose and one scheme. Both realize that self-concealment is the last evil, both make frankness and veracity the basis of their intercourse. The general rightness of living for you and others and for others and you is to understand them to the best of your ability and to make them all, to the utmost limit of your capacity of expression and their understanding and sympathy, participators in your act and thought.

13

On Debts of Honour

My ethical disposition is all against punctilio and I set no greater value on unblemished honour than I do on purity. I never yet met a man who talked proudly of his honour who did not end by cheating or trying to cheat me, nor a code of honour that did not impress me as a conspiracy against the common welfare and purpose in life. There is honour among thieves, and I think it might well end there as an obligation in conduct. The soldier who risks a life he owes to his army in a duel upon some silly matter of personal pride is no better to me than the clerk who gambles with the money in his master's till. When I was a boy I once paid a debt of honour, and it is one of the things I am most ashamed of. I had played cards into debt and I still remember burningly how I went to my mother and got the money she could so ill afford to give me. I would not pay a debt of honour at such a price now. I would pay with my own skin or not at all. If I were to wake up one morning owing big sums that I had staked overnight I would set to work at once by every means in my power to evade and repudiate that obligation. I should be disgraced! Well and good, I should deserve it. Such money as I have I owe under our present system to wife and sons and my work and the world, and I see no valid reason why I should hand it over to Smith because he and I have played the fool and rascal and gambled. Better by far to accept that fact and be for my own part published fool and rascal than to rob these others or fall short of my tale of bricks.

I have never been able to understand the sentimental spectacle of sons toiling dreadfully and wasting themselves upon mere money-making to save the secret of a father's peculations and the "honour of the family", or men conspiring to weave a wide and mischievous net of lies to save the "honour" of a woman. In the conventional drama the preservation of the honour of a woman seems an adequate excuse for nearly any offence short of murder; the preservation that is to say of the appearance of something that is already gone. The honour of the family lies in every son and daughter doing his own service to the world in his own fashion. Here it is that I do definitely part company with the false aristocrat who is by nature and intent a humbug and fabricator of sham attitudes, and ally myself with democracy. Fact, valiantly faced, is of more value than any reputation. The false aristocrat is robed to the chin and unwashed beneath, the true goes stark as

Apollo. The false is ridiculous with undignified insistence upon his dignity; the true says like God, "I am that I am."

14

The Idea of Justice

One word has so far played a very little part in this book, and that is the word Justice.

Those who have read the opening book on Metaphysics will perhaps see that this is a necessary corollary of the system of thought developed therein. In my philosophy, with its insistence upon uniqueness and marginal differences and the provisional nature of numbers and classes, there is little scope for that blind-folded lady with the balances, seeking always exact equivalents. Nowhere in my system of thought is there work for the idea of Rights and conception of conscientious litigious-spirited people exactly observing nicely defined relationships.

You will note, for example, that I base my Socialism on the idea of a collective development and not on the "right" of every man to his own labour, or his "right" to work, or his "right" to subsistence. All these ideas of "rights" and of a social "contract" however implicit are merely conventional ways of looking at things, conventions that have arisen in the mercantile phase of human development.

Laws and rights, like common terms in speech, are provisional things, conveniences for taking hold of a number of cases that would otherwise be unmanageable. The appeal to Justice is a necessarily inadequate attempt to de-individualize a case, to eliminate the self's biassed attitude. I have declared that it is my wilful belief that everything that exists is significant and necessary. The idea of Justice seems to me a defective, quantitative application of the spirit of that belief to men and women. In every case you try and discover and act upon a plausible equity that must necessarily be based on arbitrary assumptions.

There is no equity in the universe, in the various spectacle outside our minds, and the most terrible nightmare the human imagination has ever engendered is a Just God, measuring, with himself as the Standard, against finite men. Ultimately there is no adequacy, we are all weighed in the balance and found wanting.

So, as the recognition of this has grown, Justice has been tempered with Mercy, which indeed is no more than an attempt to equalise things by making the factors of the very defect that is condemned, its condonation. The modern mind fluctuates uncertainly somewhere between these extremes, now harsh and now ineffectual.

To me there seems no validity in these quasi-absolute standards.

A man seeks and obeys standards of equity simply to economise his moral effort, not because there is anything true or sublime about justice, but because he knows he is too egoistic and weak-minded and obsessed to do any perfect thing at all, because he cannot trust himself with his own transitory emotions unless he trains himself beforehand to observe a predetermined rule. There is scarcely an eventuality in life what without the help of these generalisations would not exceed the average man's intellectual power and moral energy, just as there is scarcely an idea or an emotion that can be conveyed without the use of faulty and defective common names. Justice and Mercy are indeed not ultimately different in their nature from such other conventions as the rules of a game, the rules of etiquette, forms of address, cab tariffs and standards of all sorts. They are mere organisations of relationship either to economise thought or else to facilitate mutual understanding and codify common action. Modesty and self-submission, love and service are, in the system of my beliefs, far more fundamental rightnesses and duties.

We are not mercantile and litigious units such as making Justice our social basis would imply, we are not select responsible right persons mixed with and tending weak irresponsible wrong persons such as the notion of Mercy suggests, we are parts of one being and body, each unique yet sharing a common nature and a variety of imperfections and working together (albeit more or less darkly and ignorantly) for a common end.

We are strong and weak together and in one brotherhood. The weak have no essential rights against the strong, nor the strong against the weak. The world does not exist for our weaknesses but our strength. And the real justification of democracy lies in the fact that none of us are altogether strong nor altogether weak; for everyone there is an aspect wherein he is seen to be weak; for everyone there is a strength though it may be only a little peculiar strength or an undeveloped potentiality. The unconverted man uses his strength egotistically, emphasises himself harshly against the man who is weak where he is strong, and hates and conceals his own weakness. The Believer, in the measure of his belief, respects and seeks to understand the different strength of others and to use his own distinctive power with and not against his fellow men, in the common service of that synthesis to which each one of them is ultimately as necessary as he.

15

Of Love and Justice

Now here the friend who had read the first draft of this book falls into something like a dispute with me. She does not, I think, like this dismissal of Justice from a primary place in my scheme of conduct.

"Justice," she asserts, "is an instinctive craving very nearly akin to the physical craving for equilibrium. Its social importance corresponds. It seeks to keep the individual's claims in such a position as to conflict as little as possible with those of others. Justice is the root instinct of all social feeling, of all feeling which does not take account of whether we like or dislike individuals it is the feeling of an orderly position of our Ego towards others, merely considered *as* others, and of all the Egos merely *as* Egos towards each other. *Love* cannot be felt towards others *as* others. Love is the expression of individual suitability and preference, its positive existence in some cases implies its absolute negation in others. Hence Love can never be the essential and root of social feeling, and hence the necessity for the instinct of abstract justice which takes no account of preference or aversions. And here I may say that all application of the word *love* to unknown, distant creatures, to mere *others,* is a perversion and a wasting of the word love, which, taking its origin in sexual and parental preference, always implies a preference of one object to the other. To love everybody is simply not to love at all. And it is *just because* of the passionate preference instinctively felt for some individuals, that mankind requires the self-regarding and self-respecting passion of justice."

Now this is not altogether contradictory of what I hold. I disagree that because love necessarily expresses itself in preference, selecting this rather than that, that it follows necessarily that its absolute negation is implied in the non-selected cases. A man may go into the world as a child goes into a garden and gathers its hands full of the flowers that please it best and then desists, but only because its hands are full and not because it is at an end of the flowers that it can find delight in. So the man finds at last his memory and apprehensions glutted. It is not that he could not love those others. And I dispute that to love everybody is not to love at all. To love two people is surely to love more than to love just one person, and so by way of three and four to a very large number. Love is not an individual thing merely. One may love a class. I love the cheerful English soldier. I love smiling people. But if it is put that love must be a preference because of the mental limitations that forbid us to apprehend and understand more than a few of the multitudinous lovables of life, then I agree. For all the individuals and things and cases for which we have inadequate time and energy, we need a wholesale method – justice. That is exactly what I have said in the previous section. Justice is a time and energy saving device; nothing more.

16

The Weakness of Immaturity

One is apt to write and talk of strong and weak as though some were always strong, some always weak. But that is quite a misleading version of life. Apart from the fact that everyone is fluctuatingly strong and fluctuatingly weak, and weak and strong according to the quality we judge them by, we have to remember that we are all developing and learning and changing, gaining strength and at last losing it, from the cradle to the grave. We are all, to borrow the old scholastic term, pupil-teachers of Life; the term is none the less appropriate because the pupil-teacher taught badly and learned under difficulties.

It may seem to be a crowning feat of platitude to write that "we have to remember" this, but it is overlooked in a whole mass of legal, social and economic literature. Those extraordinary imaginary cases as between a man A and a man B who start level, on a desert island or elsewhere, and work or do not work, or save or do not save, become the basis of immense schemes of just arrangement which soar up confidently and serenely regardless of the fact that never did anything like that equal start occur; that from the beginning there were family groups and old heads and young heads, help, guidance and sacrifice, and those who had learned and those who had still to learn, jumbled together in confused transactions. Deals, tradings and so forth are entirely secondary aspects of these primaries, and the attempt to get an idea of abstract relationship by beginning upon a secondary issue is the fatal pervading fallacy in all these regions of thought. At the present moment the average age of the world is I suppose about 21 to 22, the normal death somewhen about 44 to 45, that is to say nearly half the world is "under age", green, inexperienced, demanding help, easily misled and put in the wrong and betrayed. Yet the younger moiety, if we do indeed assume life's object is a collective synthesis, is more important than the older, and every older person bound to be something of a guardian to the younger. It follows directly from the fundamental beliefs I have assumed that we are missing the most important aspects of life if we are not directly or indirectly serving the young, helping them individually or collectively. Just in the measure that one's living falls away from that, do we fall away from life into a mere futility of existence, and approach the state, the extraordinary and wonderful middle state of (for example) those extinct and entirely damned old gentlemen one sees and hears eating and sleeping in every comfortable London club.

17

Possibility of a New Etiquette

These two ideas, firstly the pupil-teacher parental idea and secondly the democratic idea (that is to say the idea of an equal ultimate significance), the second correcting any tendency in the first to pedagogic arrogance and tactful concealments, do I think give, when taken together, the general attitude a right-living man will take to his individual fellow creature. They play against each other, providing elements of contradiction and determining a balanced course. It seems to me to follow necessarily from my fundamental beliefs that the Believer will tend to be and want to be and seek to be friendly to, and interested in, all sorts of people, and truthful and helpful and hating concealment. To be that with any approach to perfection demands an intricate and difficult effort, introspection to the hilt of one's power, a saving natural gift; one has to avoid pedantry, aggression, brutality, amiable tiresomeness – there are pitfalls on every side. The more one thinks about other people the more interesting and pleasing they are; I am all for kindly gossip and knowing things about them, and all against the silly and limiting hardness of soul that will not look into one's fellows nor go out to them. The use and justification of most literature, of fiction, verse, history, biography, is that it lets us into understandings and the suggestion of human possibilities. The general purpose of intercourse is to get as close as one can to the realities of the people one meets, and to give oneself to them just so far as possible.

From that I think there arises naturally a new etiquette that would set aside many of the rigidities of procedure that keep people apart today. There is a fading prejudice against asking personal questions, against talking about oneself or one's immediate personal interests, against discussing religion and politics and any such keenly felt matter. No doubt it is necessary at times to protect oneself against clumsy and stupid familiarities, against noisy and inattentive egotists, against intriguers and liars, but only in the last resort do such breaches of patience seem justifiable to me; for the most part our traditions of speech and intercourse altogether overdo separations, the preservation of distances and protective devices in general.

18

Sex

So far I have ignored the immense importance of Sex in our lives and for the most part kept the discussion so generalized as to apply impartially to women and men. But now I have reached a point when this great boundary line between two halves of the world and the intense and intimate personal problems that play across it must be considered.

For not only must we bend our general activities and our intellectual life to the conception of a human synthesis, but out of our bodies and emotional possibilities we have to make the new world bodily and emotionally. To the test of that we have to bring all sorts of questions that agitate us today, the social and political equality and personal freedom of women, the differing code of honour for the sexes, the controls and limitations to set upon love and desire. If, for example, it is for the good of the species that a whole half of its individuals should be specialized and subordinated to the physical sexual life, as in certain phases of human development women have tended to be, then certainly we must do nothing to prevent that. We have set aside the conception of Justice as in any sense a countervailing idea to that of the synthetic process.

And it is well to remember that for the whole of sexual conduct there is quite conceivably no general simple rule. It is quite possible that, as Metchnikoff maintains in his extraordinarily illuminating *Nature of Man*, we are dealing with an irresolvable tangle of disharmonies. We have passions that do not insist upon their physiological end, desires that may be prematurely vivid in childhood, a fantastic curiosity, old needs of the ape but thinly overlaid by the acquisitions of the man, emotions that jar with physical impulses, inexplicable pains and diseases. And not only have we to remember that we are dealing with disharmonies that may at the very best be only patched together, but we are dealing with matters in which the element of idiosyncrasy is essential, insisting upon an incalculable flexibility in any rule we make, unless we are to take types and indeed whole classes of personality and write them down as absolutely bad and fit only for suppression and restraint. And on the mental side we are further perplexed by the extraordinary suggestibility of human beings. In sexual matters there seems to me – and I think I share a general ignorance here – to be no directing instinct at all, but only an instinct to do something generally sexual; there are almost equally powerful desires to do right and not to act under compulsion. The specific forms of conduct imposed upon these instincts and desires depend upon a vast confusion of suggestions, institutions, conventions, ways of putting things. We are dealing therefore with problems ineradicably complex, varying in their instances, and changing as we deal with them. I am inclined to think that the only really profitable discussion of sexual matters is in terms of individuality, through the novel, the lyric, the play, autobiography or biography of the frankest sort. But such generalisations as I can make I will.

To me it seems manifest that sexual matters may be discussed generally in at least three permissible and valid ways, of which the consideration of the world as a system of births and education is only the dominant chief. There is next the question of the physical health and beauty of the community and how far sexual rules and customs affect that, and thirdly the question of the mental and moral atmosphere in which sexual conventions and laws must necessarily be an important factor. It is alleged that probably in the case of men, and certainly in the case of women, some sexual intercourse is a necessary phase in existence; that without it there is an incompleteness, a failure in the life cycle, a real wilting and failure of energy and vitality and the development of morbid states. And for most of us half the friendships and intimacies from which we derive the daily interest and sustaining force in our lives draw mysterious elements from sexual attraction, and depend and hesitate upon our conception of the liberties and limits we must give to that force.

19

The Institution of Marriage

The individual attitudes of men to women and of women to men are necessarily determined to a large extent by certain general ideas of relationship, by institutions and conventions. One of the most important and debatable of these is whether we are to consider and treat women as citizens and fellows, or as beings differing mentally from men and grouped in positions of at least material dependence to individual men. Our decision in that direction will affect all our conduct from the larger matters down to the smallest points of deportment; it will affect even our manner of address and determine whether when we speak to a woman we shall be as frank and unaffected as with a man or touched with a faint suggestion of the reserves of a cat which does not wish to be suspected of wanting to steal the milk.

Now so far as that goes it follows almost necessarily from my views upon aristocracy and democracy that I declare for the conventional equality of women, that is to say for the determination to make neither sex nor any sexual characteristic a standard of superiority or inferiority, for the view that a woman is a person as important and necessary, as much to be consulted, and entitled to as much freedom of action as a man. I admit that this decision is a choice into which temperament enters, that I cannot produce compelling reasons why anyone else should adopt my view. I can produce considerations in support of my view, that is all. But they are so implicit in all that has gone before that I will not trouble to detail them here.

The conception of equality and fellowship between men and women is an idea at least as old as Plato and one that has recurred wherever civilisation has reached a phase in which men and women were sufficiently released from militant and economic urgency to talk and read and think. But it has never yet been, at least in the historical period and in any but isolated social groups, a working structural idea. The working structural idea is the Patriarchal Family in which the woman is inferior and submits herself and is subordinated to the man, the head of the family.

We live in a constantly changing development and modification of that tradition. It is well to bring that factor of constant change into mind at the outset of this discussion and to keep it there. To forget it, and it is commonly forgotten, is to falsify every issue. Marriage and the Family are perennially fluctuating institutions, and probably scarcely anything in modern life has changed and is changing so much; they are in their legal constitution or their moral and emotional quality profoundly different things from what they were a hundred years ago. A woman who marries nowadays marries, if one may put it quantitatively, far less than she did even half a century ago; the Married Women's Property Act, for example, has revolutionized the economic relationship; her husband has lost his right to assault her and he cannot even compel her to cohabit with him if she refuses to do so. Legal separations and divorces have come to modify the quality and logical consequences of the bond. The rights of parent over the child have been even more completely qualified. The State has come in as protector and educator of the children, taking over personal powers and responsibilities that have been essential to the family institution ever since the dawn of history. It inserts itself more and more between child and parent. It invades what were once the most sacred intimacies, and the Salvation Army is now promoting legislation to explore those overcrowded homes in which children (it is estimated to the number of thirty or forty thousand) are living as I write, daily witnesses of their mother's prostitution or in constant danger of incestuous attack from drunken fathers and brothers. And finally as another indication of profound differences, births were almost universally accidental a hundred years ago; they are now in an increasing number of families controlled and deliberate acts of will. In every one of their relations do Marriage and the Family change and continue to change.

But the inherent defectiveness of the human mind which my metaphysical book sets itself to analyse, does lead it constantly to speak of Marriage and the Family as things as fixed and unalterable as, let us say, the characteristics of oxygen. One is asked, Do you believe in Marriage and the Family? as if it was a case of either having or not having some definite thing. Socialists are accused of being "against the Family", as if it were not the case that Socialists, Individualists, high Anglicans and Roman Catholics are *all* against Marriage and the Family as these institutions exist at the present time. But once we have realized the absurdity of this absolute treatment, then it should become clear that with it goes most of the fabric of right and wrong, and nearly all those arbitrary standards by which we classify people into moral and immoral. Those last words are used when as a matter of fact we mean either conforming or failing to conform to changing laws and developing institutional customs we may or may not consider right or wrong. Their use imparts a flavour of essential wrong-doing and obliquity into acts and relations that may be in many cases no more than social indiscipline, which may be even conceivably a courageous act of defiance to an obsolescent limitation. Such, until a little while ago, was a man's cohabitation with his deceased wife's sister. This, which was scandalous yesterday, is now a legally honourable relationship, albeit I believe still regarded by the high Anglican as incestuous wickedness.

I am persuaded of the need of much greater facilities of divorce than exist at present, divorce on the score of mutual consent, of faithlessness, of simple cruelty, of insanity, habitual vice or the prolonged imprisonment of either party. And this being so I find it impossible to condemn on any ground, except that it is "breaking ranks" and making a confusion, those who by anticipating such wide facilities as I propose have sinned by existing standards. How far and in what manner such breaking of ranks is to be condoned I will presently discuss. But it is clear it is an offence of a different nature from actions one believes to be in themselves and apart from the law reprehensible things.

But my scepticisms about the current legal institutions and customary code are not exhausted by these modifications I have suggested. I believe firmly in some sort of marriage, that is to say an open declaration of the existence of sexual relations between a man and a woman, because I am averse to all unnecessary secrecies and because the existence of these peculiarly intimate relationships affects everybody about the persons concerned. It is ridiculous to say as some do that sexual relations between two people affect no one but themselves unless a child is born. They do, because they tend to break down barriers and set up a peculiar emotional partnership. It is a partnership that kept secret may work as antisocially as a secret business partnership or a secret preferential railway tariff. And I believe too in the general social desirability of the family group, the normal group of father, mother and children, and in the extreme efficacy in the normal human being of the blood link and pride link between parent and child in securing loving care and upbringing for the child. But this clear adhesion to Marriage and to the family grouping about mother and father does not close the door to a large series of exceptional cases which our existing institutions and customs ignore or crush.

For example, monogamy in general seems to me to be clearly indicated (as doctors say) by the fact that there are not several women in the world for every man, but quite as clearly does it seem necessary to recognise that the fact that there are (or were in 1901) 21,436,107 females to 20,172,984 males in our British community seems to condemn our present rigorous insistance upon monogamy, unless feminine celibacy has its own delights. But, as I have said, it is now largely believed that the sexual life of a woman is more important to her than his sexual life to a man and less easily ignored.

It is true also on the former side that for the great majority of people one knows personally, any sort of household but a monogamous one conjures up painful and unpleasant visions. The ordinary civilized woman and the ordinary civilized man are alike obsessed with the idea of meeting and possessing one peculiar intimate person, one special exclusive lover who is their very own, and a third person of either sex cannot be associated with that couple without an intolerable senses of privacy and confidence and possession destroyed. But if there are people so exceptionally constituted as not to feel in this way, I do not see what right we have to force conformity to our feelings upon them.

The peculiar defects of the human mind when they approach these questions of sex are reinforced by passions peculiar to the topic, and it is perhaps advisable to point out that to discuss these possibilities is not the same thing as to urge the reader to hazardous experiments. We are trained from the nursery to become secretive, muddle-headed and vehemently conclusive upon sexual matters, until at last the editors of magazines blush at the very phrase and long to put a petticoat over the page that bears it. Yet our rebellious natures insist on being interested by it. It seems to me that to judge these large questions from the personal point of view, to insist upon the whole world without exception living exactly in the manner that suits oneself or accords with one's emotional imagination and the forms of delicacy in which one has been trained, is not the proper way to deal with them. I want as a sane social organizer to get just as many contented and law-abiding citizens as possible; I do not want to force people who would otherwise be useful citizens into rebellion, concealments and the dark and furtive ways of vice, because they may not love and marry as their temperaments command, and so I want to make the meshes of the law as wide as possible. But the common man will not understand this yet, and seeks to make the meshes just as small as his own private case demands.

Then marriage, to resume my main discussion, does not necessarily mean cohabitation. All women who desire children do not want to be entrusted with their upbringing. Some women are sexual and philoprogenitive without being sedulously maternal, and some are maternal without much or any sexual passion. There are men and women in the world now, great allies, fond and passionate lovers who do not live nor want to live constantly together. It is at least conceivable that there are women who, while desiring offspring, do not want to abandon great careers for the work of maternity, women again who would be happiest managing and rearing children in manless households that they might even share with other women friends, and men to correspond with these who do not wish to live in a household with wife and children. I submit, these temperaments exist and have a right to exist in their own way. But one must recognise that the possibility of these departures from the normal type of household opens up other possibilities. The polygamy that is degrading or absurd under one roof assumes a different appearance when one considers it from the point of view of people whose habits of life do not centre upon an isolated home.

All the relations I have glanced at above do as a matter of fact exist today, but shamefully and shabbily, tainted with what seems to me an unmerited and unnecessary ignominy and frequently darkened by blackmail. A narrow, intolerant community is the blackmailer's paradise. The punishment for bigamy again, seems to me insane in its severity, contrasted as it is with our leniency to the common seducer. Better ruin a score of women, says the law, than marry two. I do not see why in these matters there should not be much ampler freedom than there is, and this being so I can hardly be expected to condemn with any moral fervour or exclude from my society those who have seen fit to behave by what I believe may be the standards of AD 2000 instead of by the standards of 1850. These are offences, so far as they are offences, on an altogether different footing from murder, or exacting usury, or the sweating of children, or cruelty, or transmitting diseases, or unveracity, or commercial or intellectual or physical prostitution, or any such essentially grave anti-social deeds. We must distinguish between sins on the one hand and mere errors of judgement and differences of taste from ourselves. To draw up harsh laws, to practise exclusions against everyone who does not see fit to duplicate one's own blameless home life, is to waste a number of courageous and exceptional persons in every generation, to drive many of them into a forced alliance with real crime and embittered rebellion against custom and the law.

20

Conduct in Relation to the Thing that Is

But the reader must keep clear in his mind the distinction between conduct that is right or permissible in itself and conduct that becomes either inadvisable or mischievous and wrong because of the circumstances about it. There is no harm under ordinary conditions in asking a boy with a pleasant voice to sing a song in the night, but the case is altered altogether if you have reason to supposes that a Red Indian is lying in wait a hundred yards off, holding a loaded rifle and ready to fire at the voice. It is a valid objection to many actions that I do not think objectionable in themselves, that to do them will discharge a loaded prejudice into the heart of my friend – or even into my own. I belong to the world and my work, and I must not lightly throw my time, my power, my influence away. For a splendid thing any risk or any defiance may be justifiable, but is it a sufficiently splendid thing? So far as he possibly can a man must conform to common prejudices, prevalent customs and all laws, whatever his estimate of them may be. But he must at the same time do his utmost to change what he thinks to be wrong.

And I think that conformity must be honest conformity. There is no more anti-social act than secret breaches, and only some very urgent and exceptional occasion justifies even the unveracity of silence about the thing done. If your personal convictions bring you to a breach, let it be an open breach, let there be no misrepresentation of attitudes, no meanness, no deception of honourable friends. Of course an open breach need not be an ostentatious breach; to do what is right to yourself without fraud or concealment is one thing, to make a challenge and aggression quite another. Your friends may understand and sympathize and condone, but it does not lie upon you to force them to identify themselves with your act and situation. But better too much openness than too little. Squalid intrigue was the shadow of the old intolerably narrow order; it is a shadow we want to illuminate out of existence. Secrets will be contraband in the new time.

And if it chances to you to feel called upon to make a breach with the institution or custom or prejudice that is, remember that doing so is your own affair. You are going to take risks and specialise as an experiment. You must not expect other people about you to share the consequences of your dash forward. You must not drag in confidants and secondaries. You must fight your little battle in front on your own responsibility, unsupported – and take the consequences without repining.

21

Conduct Towards Transgressors

So far as breaches of the prohibitions and laws of marriage go, to me it seems they are to be tolerated by us in others just in the measure that, within the limits set by discretion, they are frank and truthful and animated by spontaneous passion and pervaded by the quality of beauty. I hate the vulgar sexual intriguer, man or woman, and the smart and shallow atmosphere of unloving lust and vanity about the type as I hate few kinds of human life; I would as lief have a polecat in my home as this sort of person; and every sort of prostitute except the victim of utter necessity I despise, even though marriage be the fee. But honest lovers should be I think a charge and pleasure for us. We must judge each pair as we can.

One thing renders a sexual relationship incurably offensive to others and altogether wrong, and that is cruelty. But who can define cruelty? How far is the leaving of a third person to count as cruelty? There again I hesitate to judge. To love and not be loved is a fate for which it seems no one can be blamed; to lose love and to change one's loving belongs to a subtle interplay beyond analysis or control, but to be deceived or mocked or deliberately robbed of love, that at any rate is an abominable wrong.

In all these matters I perceive a general rule is in itself a possible instrument of cruelty. I set down what I can in the way of general principles, but it all leaves off far short of the point of application. Every case among those I know I think we moderns must judge for ourselves. Where there is doubt, there I hold must be charity. And with regard to strangers, manifestly our duty is to avoid inquisitorial and uncharitable acts.

This is as true of financial and economic misconduct as of sexual misconduct, of ways of living that are socially harmful and of political faith. We are dealing with people in a maladjusted world to whom absolute right living is practically impossible, because there are no absolutely right institutions and no simple choice of good or evil, and we have to balance merits and defects in every case.

Some people are manifestly and essentially base and self-seeking and regardless of the happiness and welfare of their fellows, some in business affairs and politics as others in love. Some wrong-doers again are evidently so through heedlessness, through weakness, timidity or haste. We have to judge and deal with each sort upon no clear issue, but upon impressions they have given us of their spirit and purpose. We owe it to them and ourselves not to judge too rashly or too harshly, but for all that we are obliged to judge and take sides, to avoid the malignant and exclude them for further opportunity, to help and champion the cheated and the betrayed, to forgive and aid the repentant blunderer and by mercy to save the lesser sinner from desperate alliance with the greater. That is the broad rule, and it is as much as we have to go upon until the individual case comes before us.

Book Four

Some Personal Things

1

Personal Love and Life

It has been most convenient to discuss all that might be generalized about conduct first, to put in the common background, the vistas and atmosphere of the scene. But a man's relations are of two orders, and these questions of rule and principle are over and about and round more vivid and immediate interests. A man is not simply a relationship between his individual self and the race, society and the world. Close about him are persons, friends and enemies and lovers and beloved people. He desires them, lusts after them, craves their affection, needs their presence, abhors them, hates and desires to limit and suppress them. This is for most of us the flesh and blood of life. We go through the scene of the world neither alone, nor alone with God, nor serving an undistinguishable multitude, but in a company of individualized people.

Here is a system of motives and passions, imperious and powerful, which follows no broad general rule and in which each man must needs be a light unto himself upon innumerable issues. I am satisfied that these personal urgencies are neither to be suppressed nor crudely nor ruthlessly subordinated to the general issues. Religious and moral teachers are apt to make this part of life either too detached or too insignificant. They teach it either as if it did not matter or as if it ought not to matter. Indeed our individual friends and enemies stand between us and hide or interpret for us all the larger things. Few can even worship alone. They must feel others, and those not strangers, kneeling beside them.

I have already spoken under the heading of Beliefs of the part that the idea of a Mediator has played and can play in the religious life. I have pointed out how the imagination of men has sought and found in certain personalities, historical or fictitious, a bridge between the blood-warm private life and the intolerable spaciousness of right and wrong. The world is full of such figures and their images, Christ and Mary and the Saints and all the lesser, dearer gods of heathendom. These things and the human passion for living leaders and heroes and leagues and brotherhoods all confess the mediatory rôle, the mediatory possibilities of personal love between the individual and the great synthesis of which he is a part and agent. The great synthesis may become incarnate in personal love, and personal love lead us directly to universal service.

I write *may* and temper that sentence to the quality of a possibility alone. This is only true for those who believe, for those who have faith, whose lives have been unified, who have found Salvation. For those whose lives are chaotic, personal loves must also be chaotic; this or that passion, malice, a jesting humour, some physical lust, gratified vanity, egotistical pride, will rule and limit the relationship and colour its ultimate futility. But the Believer uses personal love and sustains himself by personal love. It is his provender, the meat and drink of his campaign.

2

The Nature of Love

It is well perhaps to look a little into the factors that make up Love.

Love does not seem to me to be a simple elemental thing. It is, as I have already said, one of the vicious tendencies of the human mind to think that whatever can be given a simple name can be abstracted as a single something in a state of quintessential purity. I have pointed out that this is not true of Harmony or Beauty, and that these are synthetic things. You bring together this which is not beautiful and that which is not beautiful, and behold! Beauty! So also Love is, I think, a synthetic thing. One observes this and that, one is interested and stirred; suddenly the metal fuses, the dry bones live! One loves.

Almost every interest in one's being may be a factor in the love synthesis. But apart from the overflowing of the parental instinct that makes all that is fine and delicate and young dear to us and to be cherished, there are two main factors that bring us into love with our fellows. There is first the emotional elements in our nature that arise out of the tribal necessity, out of a fellowship in battle and hunting, drinking and feasting, out of the needs and excitements and delights of those occupations; and there is next the intenser narrower desirings and gratitudes, satisfactions and expectations that come from sexual intercourse. Now both these factors originate in physical needs and consummate in material acts, and it is well to remember that this great growth of love in life roots there, and, it may be, dies when its roots are altogether cut away.

At its lowest, love is the mere sharing of, or rather the desire to share, pleasure and excitement, the excitements of conflict or lust or what not. I think that the desire to partake, the desire to merge one's individual identity with another's, remains a necessary element in all personal loves. It is a way out of ourselves, a breaking down of our individual separation, just as hate is an intensification of that. Personal love is the narrow and intense form of that breaking down, just as what I call Salvation is its widest, most extensive form. We cast aside our reserves, our secrecies, our defences; we open ourselves; touches that would be intolerable from common people become a mystery of delight, acts of self-abasement and self-sacrifice are charged with symbolical pleasure. We cannot tell which of us is me, which you. Our imprisoned egoism looks out through this window, forgets its walls, and is for those brief moments released and universal.

For most of us the strain of primordial sexual emotion in our loves is very strong. Many men can love only women, many women only men, and some can scarcely love at all without bodily desire. But the love of fellowship is a strong one also, and for many, love is most possible and easy when the thought of physical love-making has been banished. Then the lovers will pursue other interests together, will work together or journey together. So we have the warm fellowships of men for men and women for women. But even then it may happen that men friends together will talk of women, and women friends of men. Nevertheless we have also the strong and altogether sexless glow of those who have fought well together, or drunk or jested together or hunted a common quarry.

Now it seems to me that the Believer must also be a Lover, that he will love as much as he can and as many people as he can, and in many moods and ways. As I have said already, many of those who have taught religion and morality in the past have been neglectful or unduly jealous of the intenser personal loves. They have been, to put it by a figure, urgent upon the road to the ocean. To that they would lead us, though we come to it shivering, fearful and unprepared, and they grudge it that we should strip and plunge into the wayside stream. But all streams, all rivers come from this ocean in the beginning, lead to it in the end.

It is the essential fact of love as I conceive it, that it breaks down the boundaries of self. That love is most perfect which does most completely merge its lovers. But no love is altogether perfect, and for most men and women love is no more than a partial and temporary lowering of the barriers that keep them apart. With many, the attraction of love seems always to fall short of what I hold to be its end, it draws people together in the most momentary of self-forgetfulnesses, and for the rest seems rather to enhance their egotisms and their difference. They are secret from one another even in their embraces. There is a sort of love that is egotistical lust almost regardless of its partner, a sort of love that is mere fleshless pride and vanity at a white heat. There is the love-making that springs from sheer boredom, like a man reading a story-book to fill an hour. These inferior loves seek to accomplish an agreeable act, or they seek the pursuit or glory of a living possession, they aim at gratification or excitement or conquest. True love seeks to be mutual and easy-minded, free of doubts, but these egotistical mockeries of love have always resentment in them and hatred in them and a watchful distrust. Jealousy is the measure of self-love in love.

True love is a synthetic thing, an outcome of life, it is not a universal thing. It is the individualised correlative of Salvation; like that it is a synthetic consequence of conflicts and confusions. Many people do not desire or need Salvation, they cannot understand it, much less achieve it; for them, chaotic life suffices. So too, many never, save for some rare moment of illumination, desire or feel love. Its happy abandonment, its careless self-giving, these things are mere foolishness to them. But much has been said and sung of faith and love alike, and in their confused greed these things also they desire and parody. So they act worship and make a fine fuss of their devotions. And also they must have a few half-furtive, half-flaunting fallen love-triumphs prowling the secret back-streets of their lives, they know not why.

(In setting this down be it remembered I am doing my best to tell what is in me because I am trying to put my whole view of life before the reader without any vital omissions. These are difficult matters to explain because they have no clear outlines; one lets in a hard light suddenly upon things that have lurked in warm intimate shadows, dim inner things engendering motives. I am not only telling quasi-secret things but exploring them for myself. They are none the less real and important because they are elusive.)

True love I think is not simply felt but known. Just as Salvation as I conceive it demands a fine intelligence and mental activity, so love calls to brain and body alike and all one's powers. There is always elaborate thinking and dreaming in love. Love will stir imaginations that have never stirred before.

Love may be, and is for the most part, one-sided. It is the going out from oneself that is love, and not the accident of its return. It is the expedition whether it fail or succeed.

320

But an expedition starves that comes to no port. Love always seeks mutuality and grows by the sense of responses, or we should love beautiful inanimate things more passionately than we do. Failing a full return, it makes the most of an inadequate return. Failing a sustained return it welcomes a temporary coincidence. Failing a return it finds support in accepted sacrifices. But it seeks a full return, and the fullness of life has come only to those who, loving, have met the lover.

I am trying to be as explicit as possible in thus writing about Love. But the substance in which one works here is emotion that evades definition, poetic flashes and figures of speech are truer than prosaic statements. Body and the most sublimated ecstasy pass into one another, exchange themselves and elude every net of words we cast.

I have put out two ideas of unification and self-devotion, extremes upon a scale one from another; one of these ideas is that devotion to the Purpose in things I have called Salvation; the other that devotion to some other most fitting and satisfying individual which is passionate love, the former extensive as the universe, the latter the intensest thing in life. These, it seems to me, are the boundary and the living capital of the empire of life we rule.

All empires need a comprehending boundary, but many have not one capital but many chief cities, and all have cities and towns and villages beyond the capital. It is an impoverished capital that has no dependent towns, and it is a poor love that will not overflow in affection and eager kindly curiosity and sympathy and the search for fresh mutuality. To love is to go living radiantly through the world. To love and be loved is to be fearless of experience and rich in the power to give.

3

The Will to Love

Love is a thing to a large extent in its beginnings voluntary and controllable, and at last quite involuntary. It is so hedged about by obligations and consequences, real and artificial, that for the most part I think people are overmuch afraid of it. And also the tradition of sentiment that suggests its forms and guides it in the world about us, is far too strongly exclusive. It is not so much when love is glowing as when it is becoming habitual that it is jealous for itself and others. Lovers a little exhausting their mutual interest find a fillip in an alliance against the world. They bury their talent of understanding and sympathy to return it duly in a clean napkin. They narrow their interest in life lest the other lover should misunderstand their amplitude as disloyalty.

Our institutions and social customs seem all to assume a definiteness of preference, a singleness and a limitation of love, which is not psychologically justifiable. People do not, I think, fall naturally into agreement with these assumptions; they train themselves to agreement. They take refuge from experiences that seem to carry with them the risk at least of perplexing situations, in a theory of barred possibilities and locked doors. How far this shy and cultivated irresponsive lovelessness towards the world at large may not carry with it the possibility of compensating intensities, I do not know. Quite equally probable is a starvation of one's emotional nature.

The same reasons that make me decide against mere wanton abstinences make me hostile to the common convention of emotional indifference to most of the charming and interesting people one encounters. In pleasing and being pleased, in the mutual interest, the mutual opening out of people to one another, is the key of the door to all sweet and mellow living.

4

Love and Death

For him who has faith, death, so far as it is his own death, ceases to possess any quality of terror. The experiment will be over, the rinsed beaker returned to its shelf, the crystals gone dissolving down the waste-pipe; the duster sweeps the bench. But the deaths of those we love are harder to understand or bear.

It happens that of those very intimate with me I have lost only one, and that came slowly and elaborately, a long gradual separation wrought by the accumulation of years and mental decay, but many close friends and many whom I have counted upon for sympathy and fellowship have passed out of my world. I miss such a one as Bob Stevenson, that luminous, extravagant talker, that eager fantastic mind. I miss him whenever I write. It is less pleasure now to write a story since he will never read it, much less give me a word of praise for it. And I miss York Powell's friendly laughter and Henley's exuberant welcome. They made a warmth that has gone, those men. I can understand why I, with my fumbling lucidities and explanations, have to finish up presently and go, expressing as I do the mood of a type and of a time; but not those radiant presences.

And the gap these men have left, these men with whom after all I only sat now and again, or wrote to in a cheerful mood or got a letter from at odd times, gives me some measure of the thing that happens, that may happen when the mind that is always near one's thoughts, the person who moves to one's movement and lights nearly all the common flow of events about one with the remainder of fellowship and meaning – ceases.

Faith which feeds on personal love must at last prevail over it. If Faith has any virtue it must have it here when we find ourselves bereft and isolated, facing a world from which the light has fled leaving it bleak and strange. We live for experience and the race; these individual interludes are just helps to that; the warm inn in which we lovers met and refreshed was but a halt on a journey. When we have loved to the intensest point we have done our best with each other. To keep to that image of the inn, we must not sit overlong at our wine beside the fire. We must go on to new experiences and new adventures. Death comes to part us and turn us out and set us on the road again.

But the dead stay where we leave them.

I suppose that is the real good in death, that they do stay; that it makes them immortal for us. Living they were mortal. But now they can never spoil themselves or be spoiled by change again. They have finished – for us indeed just as much as themselves. There they sit for ever, rounded off and bright and done. Beside these clear and certain memories I have of my dead, my impressions of the living are vague provisional things.

And since they are gone out of the world and become immortal memories in me, I feel no need to think of them as in some disembodied and incomprehensible elsewhere, changed and yet not done. I want actual immortality for those I love as little as I desire it for myself.

Indeed I dislike the idea that those I have loved are immortal in any real sense; it conjures up dim uncomfortable drifting phantoms, that have no kindred with the flesh and blood I knew. I would as soon think of them trailing after the tides up and down the Channel outside my window. Bob Stevenson for me is a presence utterly concrete, slouching, eager, quick-eyed, intimate and profound, carelessly dressed (at Sandgate he commonly wore a felt hat that belonged to his little son) and himself, himself, indissoluble matter and spirit, down to the heels of his boots. I cannot conceive of his as any but a concrete immortality. If he lives, he lives as I knew him and clothed as I knew him and with his unalterable voice, in a heaven of daedal flowers or a hell of ineffectual flame; he lives, dreaming and talking and explaining, explaining it all very earnestly and preposterously, so I picture him, into the ear of the amused incredulous, principal person in the place.

I have a real hatred for those dreary fools and knaves who would have me suppose that Henley, that crippled Titan, may conceivably be tapping at the underside of a mahogany table or scratching stifled incoherence into a locked slate! Henley tapping! – for the professional purposes of Sludge! If he found himself among the circumstances of a spiritualist séance he would, I know, instantly smash the table with that big fist of his. And as the splinters flew, surely York Powell, out of the dead past from which he shines on me, would laugh that hearty laugh of his back into the world again.

Henley is nowhere now except that, red-faced and jolly like an October sunset, he leans over a gate at Worthing after a long day of picnicking at Chanctonbury Ring, or sits at his Woking table praising and quoting *The Admirable Bashville*, or blue-shirted and wearing the hat that Nicholson has painted, is thrust and lugged, laughing and talking aside in his bath-chair, along the Worthing esplanade...

And Bob Stevenson walks for ever about a garden in Chiswick talking in the dusk.

5

The Consolation of Failure

That parable of the talents I have made such free use of in this book has one significant defect. It gives but two cases, and three are possible. There was first the man who buried his talent, and of his condemnation we are assured. But those others all took their talents and used them courageously and came back with gain. Was that gain inevitable? Does courage always ensure us victory? Because if that is so we can all be heroes and valour is the better part of discretion. Alas! the faith in such magic dies. What of the possible case of the man who took his two or three talents and invested them as best he could and was deceived or heedless and lost them, interest and principal together?

There is something harder to face than death, and that is the realisation of failure and misdirected effort and wrong-doing. Faith is no Open Sesame to right-doing, much less is it the secret of success. The service of God on earth is no processional triumph. What if one does wrong so extremely as to condemn one's life, to make oneself part of the refuse and not of the building? Or what if one is misjudged, or it may be too pitilessly judged, and one's co-operation despised and the help one brought becomes a source of weakness? Or suppose that the fine scheme one made lies shattered or wrecked by one's own act, or through some hidden blemish one's offering is rejected and flung back and one is thrust out?

So in the end it may be you or I will find we have been anvil and not hammer in the Purpose of God.

Then indeed will come the time for Faith, for the last word of Faith, to say still steadfastly, disgraced or dying, defeated or discredited, that all is well:–

'This and not that was my appointed work, and this I had to be."

6

The Last Confession

So these broken confessions and statements of mood and attitude come to an end.

But at this end, since I have, I perceive, run a little into a pietistic strain, I must repeat again how provisional and personal I know all these things to be. I began by disavowing ultimates. My beliefs, my dogmas, my rules, they are made for my campaigning needs, like the knapsack and water-bottle of a Cockney soldier invading some stupendous mountain gorge. About him are fastnesses and splendours, torrents and cataracts, glaciers and untrodden snows. He comes tramping on heel-worn boots and ragged socks. Beauties and blue mysteries shine upon him and appeal to him, the enigma of beauty smiling the faint strange smile of Leonardo's Mona Lisa. He sees a light on the grass like music; and the blossom on the trees against the sky brings him near weeping. Such things come to him, give themselves to him. I do not know why he should not in response fling his shabby gear aside and behave like a god; I only know that he does not do so. His grunt of appreciation is absurd, his speech goes like a crippled thing – and withal, and partly by virtue of the knapsack and water-bottle, he is conqueror of the valley. The valley is his for the taking.

There is a duality in life that I cannot express except by such images as this, a duality so that we are at once absurd and full of sublimity, and most absurd when we are most anxious to render the real splendours that pervade us. This duplicity in life seems to me at times ineradicable, at times like the confusing of something essentially simple, like the duplication when one looks through a doubly refracting medium. You think in this latter mood that you have only to turn the crystal of Iceland spar about in order to have the whole thing plain. But you never get it plain. I have been doing my halting utmost to get down sincerely and simply my vision of life and duty. I have permitted myself no defensive restraints; I have shamelessly written my starkest, and it is plain to me that a smile that is not mine plays over my most urgent passages. There is a rebellious rippling of the grotesque under our utmost tragedy and gravity. One's martialled phrases grimace as one turns, and wink at the reader. Nonetheless they signify. Do you note how in this that I have written, such a word as Believer will begin to wear a capital letter and give itself solemn ridiculous airs? It does not matter. It carries its message for all that necessary superficial absurdity.

Thought has made me shameless. It does not matter at last at all if one is a little harsh or indelicate or ridiculous if that also is in the mystery of things.

Behind everything I perceive the smile that makes all effort and discipline temporary, all the stress and pain of life endurable.

In the last resort I do not care whether I am seated on a throne or drunk or dying in a gutter. I follow my leading. I am more than myself for I myself am Man. In the ultimate I know, though I cannot prove my knowledge in any way whatever, that everything is right and all things mine.

Russia in the Shadows

CONTENTS

CHAPTER ONE

Petersburg in Collapse

In January 1914 I visited Petersburg and Moscow for a couple of weeks; in September 1920 I was asked to repeat this visit by Mr Kamenev, of the Russian Trade Delegation in London. I snatched at this suggestion, and went to Russia at the end of September with my son, who speaks a little Russian. We spent a fortnight and a day in Russia, passing most of our time in Petersburg, where we went about freely by ourselves, and were shown nearly everything we asked to see. We visited Moscow, and I had a long conversation with Mr Lenin, which I shall relate. In Petersburg I did not stay at the Hotel International, to which foreign visitors are usually sent, but with my old friend, Maxim Gorky. The guide and interpreter assigned to assist us was a lady I had met in Russia in 1914, the niece of a former Russian Ambassador to London. She was educated at Newnham, she has been imprisoned five times by the Bolshevist Government, she is not allowed to leave Petersburg because of an attempt to cross the frontier to her children in Esthonia, and she was, therefore, the last person likely to lend herself to any attempt to hoodwink me. I mention this because on every hand at home and in Russia I had been told that the most elaborate

335

camouflage of realities would go on, and that I should be kept in blinkers throughout my visit.

As a matter of fact, the harsh and terrible realities of the situation in Russia cannot be camouflaged. In the case of special delegations, perhaps, a certain distracting tumult of receptions, bands, and speeches may be possible, and may be attempted. But it is hardly possible to dress up two large cities for the benefit of two stray visitors, wandering observantly often in different directions. Naturally, when one demands to see a school or a prison one is not shown the worst. Any country would in the circumstances show the best it had, and Soviet Russia is no exception. One can allow for that.

Our dominant impression of things Russian is an impression of a vast irreparable breakdown. The great monarchy that was here in 1914, the administrative, social, financial, and commercial systems connected with it have, under the strains of six years of incessant war, fallen down and smashed utterly. Never in all history has there been so great a *débâcle* before. The fact of the Revolution is, to our minds, altogether dwarfed by the fact of this downfall. By its own inherent rottenness and by the thrusts and strains of aggressive imperialism the Russian part of the old civilized world that existed before 1914 fell, and is now gone. The peasant, who was the base of the old pyramid, remains upon the land, living very much as he has always lived. Everything else is broken down, or is breaking down. Amid this vast disorganisation an emergency Government, supported by a disciplined party of perhaps 150,000 adherents – the Communist Party – has taken control. It has – at the price of much shooting – suppressed brigandage, established a sort of order and security in the exhausted towns, and set up a crude rationing system.

It is, I would say at once, the only possible Government in Russia at the present time. It is only idea, it supplies the only solidarity, left in Russia. But it is a secondary fact. The dominant fact for the Western reader, the threatening and disconcerting fact, is that a social and economic system very like our own and intimately connected with our own has crashed.

Nowhere in all Russia is the fact of that crash so completely evident as it is in Petersburg. Petersburg was the artificial creation of Peter the Great; his bronze statue in the little garden near the Admiralty still prances amid the ebbing life of the city. Its palaces are still and empty, or strangely refurnished with the typewriters and tables and plank partitions of a new Administration which is engaged chiefly in a strenuous struggle against famine and the foreign invader. Its streets were streets of busy shops. In 1914 I loafed agreeably in the Petersburg streets – buying little articles and watching the abundant traffic. All these shops have ceased. There are perhaps half a dozen shops still open in Petersburg. There is a Government crockery shop where I bought a plate or so as a souvenir, for seven or eight hundred roubles each, and there are a few flower shops. It is a wonderful fact, I think, that in this city, in which most of the shrinking population is already nearly starving, and hardly anyone possesses a second suit of clothes or more than a single change of worn and patched linen, flowers can be and are still bought and sold. For five thousand roubles, which is about six and eightpence at the current rate of exchange, one can get a very pleasing bunch of big chrysanthemums.

I do not know if the words "all the shops have ceased" convey any picture to the Western reader of what a street looks like in Russia. It is not like Bond Street or Piccadilly on a Sunday, with the blinds neatly drawn down in a decorous sleep, and ready to wake up and begin again on Monday. The shops have an utterly wretched and abandoned look; paint is peeling off, windows are cracked, some are broken and boarded up, some still display a few fly-blown relics of stock in the window, some have their windows covered with notices; the windows are growing dim, the fixtures have gathered two years' dust. They are dead shops. They will never open again.

All the great bazaar-like markets are closed, too, in Petersburg now, in the desperate struggle to keep a public control of necessities and prevent the profiteer driving up the last vestiges of food to incredible prices. And this cessation of shops makes walking about the streets seem a silly sort of thing to do. Nobody "walks about" any more. One realizes that a modern city is really nothing but long alleys of shops and restaurants and the like. Shut them up, and the meaning of a street has disappeared. People hurry past – a thin traffic compared with my memories of 1914. The electric street cars are still running and busy – until six o'clock. They are the only means of locomotion for ordinary people remaining in town – the last legacy of capitalist enterprise. They became free while we were in Petersburg. Previously there had been a charge of two or three roubles – the hundredth part of the price of an egg. Freeing them made little difference in their extreme congestion during the home-going hours. Everyone scrambles on the tramcar. If there is no room inside you cluster outside. In the busy hours festoons of people hand outside by any handhold; people are frequently pushed off, and accidents are frequent. We saw a crowd collected round a child cut in half by a tramcar, and two people in the little circle in which we moved in Petersburg had broken their legs in tramway accidents.

The roads along which these tramcars run are in a frightful condition. They have not been repaired for three or four years; they are full of holes like shell-holes, often two or three feet deep. Frost has eaten out great cavities, drains have collapsed, and people have torn up the wood pavement for fires. Only once did we see any attempt to repair the streets in Petrograd. In a side street some mysterious agency had collected a load of wood blocks and two barrels of tar. Most of our longer journeys about the town were done in official motor-cars – left over from the former times. A drive is an affair of tremendous swerves and concussions. These surviving motor-cars are running now on kerosene. They disengage clouds of pale blue smoke, and start up with a noise like a machine-gun battle. Every wooden house was demolished for firing last winter, and such masonry as there was in those houses remains in ruinous gaps, between the houses of stone.

Every one is shabby; every one seems to be carrying bundles in both Petersburg and Moscow. To walk into some side street in the twilight and see nothing but ill-clad figures, all hurrying, all carrying loads, gives one an impression as though the entire population was setting out in flight. That impression is not altogether misleading. The Bolshevik statistics I have seen are perfectly frank and honest in the matter. The population of Petersburg has fallen from 1,200,000 (before 1919) to a little over 700,000, and it is still falling. Many people have returned to peasant life in the country, many have gone abroad, but hardship has taken an enormous toll of this city. The death-rate in Petersburg is over 81 per 1,000; formerly it was high among

339

European cities at 22. The birth-rate of the underfed and profoundly depressed population is about 15. It was formerly about 30.

These bundles that every one carries are partly the rations of food that are doled out by the Soviet organisation, partly they are the material and results of illicit trade. The Russian population has always been a trading and bargaining population. Even in 1914 there were but few shops in Petersburg whose prices were really fixed prices. Tariffs were abominated; in Moscow taking a droshky meant always a haggle, ten kopecks at a time. Confronted with a shortage of nearly every commodity, a shortage caused partly by the war strain, – for Russia has been at war continuously now for six years – partly by the general collapse of social organisation, and partly by the blockade, and with a currency in complete disorder, the only possible way to save the towns from a chaos of cornering, profiteering, starvation, and at last a mere savage fight for the remnants of food and common necessities, was some sort of collective control and rationing.

The Soviet Government rations on principle, but any Government in Russia now would have to ration. If the war in the West had lasted up to the present time London would be rationing too – food, clothing, and housing. But in Russia this has to be done on a basis of uncontrollable peasant production, with a population temperamentally indisciplined and self-indulgent. The struggle is necessarily a bitter one. The detected profiteer, the genuine profiteer who profiteers on any considerable scale, gets short shrift; he is shot. Quite ordinary trading may be punished severely. All trading is called "speculation", and is now illegal. But a queer street-corner trading in food and so forth is winked at in Petersburg, and quite openly practised in Moscow, because only by permitting this can the peasants be induced to bring in food.

There is also much underground trade between buyers and sellers who know each other. Every one who can supplements his public rations in this way. And every railway station at which one stops is an open market. We would find a crowd of peasants at every stopping-place waiting to sell milk, eggs, apples, bread, and so forth. The passengers clamber down and accumulate bundles. An egg or an apple costs 300 roubles.

The peasants look well fed, and I doubt if they are very much worse off than they were in 1914. Probably they are better off. They have more land than they had, and they have got rid of their landlords. They will not help in any attempt to overthrow the Soviet Government because they are convinced that while it endures this state of things will continue. This does not prevent their resisting whenever they can the attempts of the Red Guards to collect food at regulation prices. Insufficient forces of Red Guards may be attacked and massacred. Such incidents are magnified in the London Press as peasant insurrections against the Bolsheviks. They are nothing of the sort. It is just the peasants making themselves comfortable under the existing *régime*.

But every class above the peasants – including the official class – is now in a state of extreme privation. The credit and industrial system that produced commodities has broken down, and so far the attempts to replace it by some other form of production have been ineffective. So that nowhere are there any new things. About the only things that seem to be fairly well supplied are tea, cigarettes, and matches. Matches are more abundant in Russia than they were in England in 1917, and the Soviet State match is quite a good match. But such things as collars, ties, shoelaces, sheets and blankets, spoons and forks, all the haberdashery and crockery of life, are unattainable. There is no replacing a broken cup or glass except by a sedulous search and illegal trading. From Petersburg to Moscow we were given a sleeping car deluxe, but there were no water-bottles, glasses, or, indeed, any loose fittings. They have all gone. Most of the men one meets strike one at first as being carelessly shaven, and at first we were inclined to regard that as a sign of a general apathy, but we understood better how things were when a friend mentioned to my son quite casually that he had been using one safety razor blade for nearly a year.

Drugs and any medicines are equally unattainable. There is nothing to take for a cold or a headache; no packing off to bed with a hot-water bottle. Small ailments develop very easily therefore into serious trouble. Nearly everybody we met struck us as being uncomfortable and a little out of health. A buoyant, healthy person is very rare in this atmosphere of discomforts and petty deficiencies.

If anyone falls into a real illness the outlook is grim. My son paid a visit to the big Obuchovskaya Hospital, and he tells me things were very miserable there indeed. There was an appalling lack of every sort of material, and half the beds were not in use through the sheer impossibility of dealing with more patients if they came in. Strengthening and stimulating food is out of the question unless the patient's family can by some miracle procure it outside and send it in. Operations are performed only on one day in the week, Dr Federoff told me, when the necessary preparations can be made. On other days they are impossible, and the patient must wait.

Hardly anyone in Petersburg has much more than a change of raiment, and in a great city in which there remains no means of communication but a few overcrowded tramcars,[1] old, leaky, and ill-fitting boots are the only footwear. At times one sees astonishing makeshifts by way of costume. The master of a school to which we paid a surprise visit struck me as unusually dapper. He was wearing a dinner suit with a blue serge waistcoat. Several of the distinguished scientific and literary men I met had no collars and wore neck-wraps. Gorky possesses only the one suit of clothes he wears.

At a gathering of literary people in Petersburg, Mr Amphiteatroff, the well-known writer, addressed a long and bitter speech to me. He suffered from the usual delusion that I was blind and stupid and being hoodwinked. He was for taking off the respectable-looking coats of all the company present in order that I might see for myself the rags and tatters and pitiful expedients beneath. It was a painful and, so far as I was concerned, an unnecessary speech, but I quote it here to emphasise this effect of general destitution. And this underclad town population in this dismantled and ruinous city is, in spite of all the furtive trading that goes on, appallingly underfed. With the best will in the world the Soviet Government is unable to produce a sufficient ration to sustain a healthy life. We went to a district kitchen and saw the normal food distribution going on. The place seemed to us fairly clean and fairly well run, but that does not compensate for a lack of material. The lowest grade ration consisted of a basinful of thin skilly and about the same quantity of stewed apple compote. People have bread cards and

1 I saw one passenger steamboat on the Neva crowded with passengers. Usually the river was quite deserted except for a rare Government tug or a solitary boatman picking up drift timber.

wait in queues for bread, but for three days the Petersburg bakeries stopped for lack of flour. The bread varies greatly in quality; some was good coarse brown bread, and some I found damp, clay-like, and uneatable.

I do not know how far these disconnected details will suffice to give the Western reader an idea of what ordinary life in Petersburg is at the present time. Moscow, they say, is more overcrowded and shorter of fuel than Petersburg, but superficially it looked far less grim than Petersburg. We saw these things in October, in a particularly fine and warm October. We saw them in sunshine in a setting of ruddy and golden foliage. But one day there came a chill, and the yellow leaves went whirling before a drive of snowflakes. It was the first breath of the coming winter. Everyone shivered and looked out of the double windows – already sealed up – and talked to us of the previous year. Then the glow of October returned.

It was still glorious sunshine when we left Russia. But when I think of that coming winter my heart sinks. The Soviet Government in the commune of the north has made extraordinary efforts to prepare for the time of need. There are piles of wood along the quays, along the middle of the main streets, in the courtyards, and in every place where wood can be piled. Last year many people had to live in rooms below the freezing point; the water-pipes froze up, the sanitary machinery ceased to work. The reader must imagine the consequences. People huddled together in the ill-lit rooms, and kept themselves alive with tea and talk. Presently some Russian novelist will tell us all that this has meant to heart and mind in Russia. This year it may not be quite so bad as that. The food situation also, they say, is better, but this I very much doubt. The railways are now in an extreme state of deterioration; the wood-stoked engines are wearing out; the bolts start and the rails shift as the trains rumble along at a maximum of twenty-five miles per hour. Even were the railways more efficient, Wrangel has got hold of the southern food supplies. Soon the cold rain will be falling upon these 700,000 souls still left in Petersburg, and then the snow. The long nights extend and the daylight dwindles.

And this spectacle of misery and ebbing energy is, you will say, the result of Bolshevist rule! I do not believe it is. I will deal with the Bolshevist Government when I have painted the general scenery of our problem. But let me say here that this desolate Russia is not a system that has been attacked and destroyed by something vigorous and malignant. It is an unsound system that has worked itself out and fallen down. It was not communism which built up these great, impossible cities, but capitalism. It was not communism that plunged this huge, creaking, bankrupt empire into six years of exhausting war. It was European imperialism. Nor is it communism that has pestered this suffering and perhaps dying Russia with a series of subsidized raids, invasions, and insurrections, and inflicted upon it an atrocious blockade. The vindictive French creditor, the journalistic British oaf, are far more responsible for these deathbed miseries than any communist. But to these questions I will return after I have given a little more description of Russia as we saw it during our visit. It is only when one has some conception of the physical and mental realities of the Russian collapse that one can see and estimate the Bolshevist Government in its proper proportions.

CHAPTER TWO

Drift and Salvage

Among the things I wanted most to see amid this tremendous spectacle of social collapse in Russia was the work of my old friend Maxim Gorky. I had heard of this from members of the returning labour delegation, and what they told me had whetted my desire for a closer view of what was going on. Mr Bertrand Russell's description of Gorky's health had also made me anxious on his own account; but I am happy to say that upon that score my news is good. Gorky seems as strong and well to me now as he was when I knew him first in 1906. And as a personality he has grown immensely. Mr Russell wrote that Gorky is dying and that perhaps culture in Russia is dying too. Mr Russell was, I think, betrayed by the artistic temptation of a dark and purple concluding passage. He found Gorky in bed and afflicted by a fit of coughing, and his imagination made the most of it.

Gorky's position in Russia is a quite extraordinary and personal one. He is no more of a communist than I am, and I have heard him argue with the utmost freedom in his flat against the extremist positions with such men as Bokaiev, recently the head of the Extraordinary Commission in Petersburg, and

Zalutsky, one of the rising leaders of the Communist party. It was a very reassuring display of free speech, for Gorky did not so much argue as denounce – and this in front of two deeply interested English enquirers.

But he has gained the confidence and respect of most of the Bolshevik leaders, and he has become by a kind of necessity the semi-official salvage man under the new *régime*. He is possessed by a passionate sense of the value of Western science and culture, and by the necessity of preserving the intellectual continuity of Russian life through these dark years of famine and war and social stress, with the general intellectual life of the world. He has found a steady supporter in Lenin. His work illuminates the situation to an extraordinary degree because it collects together a number of significant factors and makes the essentially catastrophic nature of the Russian situation plain.

The Russian smash at the end of 1917 was certainly the completest that has ever happened to any modern social organisation. After the failure of the Kerensky Government to make peace and of the British naval authorities to relieve the situation upon the Baltic flank, the shattered Russian armies, weapons in hand, broke up and rolled back upon Russia, a flood of peasant soldiers making for home, without hope, without supplies, without discipline. That time of *débâcle* was a time of complete social disorder. It was a social dissolution. In many parts of Russia there was a peasant revolt. There was château-burning, often accompanied by quite horrible atrocities. It was an explosion of the very worst side of human nature in despair, and for most of the abominations committed the Bolsheviks are about as responsible as the Government of Australia. People would be held up and robbed even to their shirts in open daylight in the streets of Petersburg and Moscow, no one interfering. Murdered bodies lay disregarded in the gutters sometimes for a whole day, with passengers on the footwalk going to and fro. Armed men, often professing to be Red Guards, entered houses and looted and murdered. The early months of 1918 saw a violent struggle of the new Bolshevik Government not only with counter-revolutions but with robbers and brigands of every description. It was not until the summer of 1918, and after thousands of looters and plunderers had been shot, that life began to be ordinarily safe again in the streets of the Russian great towns. For a time Russia was not a civilisation, but a torrent of lawless violence, with a weak central Government of inexperienced rulers, fighting not only against unintelligent foreign intervention but against the completest internal disorder. It is from such chaotic conditions that Russia still struggles to emerge.

Art, literature, science, all the refinements and elaboration of life, all that we mean by "civilisation", were involved in this torrential catastrophe. For a time the stablest thing in Russian culture was the theatre. There stood the theatres, and nobody wanted to loot them or destroy them; the artists were accustomed to meet and work in them and went on meeting and working; the tradition of official subsidies held good. So quite amazingly the Russian dramatic and operatic life kept on through the extremest storms of violence, and keeps on to this day. In Petersburg we found there were more than forty shows going on every night; in Moscow we found very much the same state of affairs. We heard Shalyapin, greatest of actors and singers, in *The Barber of Seville* and in *Chovanchina*; the admirable orchestra was variously attired, but the conductor still held out valiantly in swallow tails

349

and a white tie; we saw a performance of *Sadko*, we saw Monachof in *The Tsarevitch Alexei* and as Iago in *Othello* (with Madame Gorky – Madame Andreievna – as Desdemona). When one faced the stage, it was as if nothing had changed in Russia; but when the curtain fell and one turned to the audience one realized the revolution. There were now no brilliant uniforms, no evening dress in boxes and stalls. The audience was an undifferentiated mass of people, the same sort of people everywhere, attentive, good-humoured, well-behaved and shabby. Like the London Stage Society, one's place in the house is determined by ballot. And for the most part there is no paying to enter the theatre. For one performance the tickets go, let us say, to the professional unions, for another to the Red Army and their families, for another to the school children, and so on. A certain selling of tickets goes on, but it is not in the present scheme of things.

I had heard Shalyapin in London, but I had not met him personally there. We made his acquaintance this time in Petersburg, we dined with him and saw something of his very jolly household. There are two stepchildren almost grown up, and two little daughters, who speak a nice, stiff, correct English, and the youngest of whom dances delightfully. Shalyapin is certainly one of the most wonderful things in Russia at the present time. He is the Artist, defiant and magnificent. Off the stage he has much the same vitality and abounding humour that made an encounter with Beerbohm Tree so delightful an experience. He refuses absolutely to sing except for pay – 200,000 roubles a performance, they say, which is nearly £15 – and when the markets get too tight, he insists upon payment in flour or eggs or the like. What he demands he gets, for Shalyapin on strike would leave too dismal a hole altogether in the theatrical world of Petersburg. So it is that he maintains what is perhaps the last fairly comfortable home in Russia. And Madame Shalyapin we found so unbroken by the revolution that she asked us what people were wearing in London. The last fashion papers she had seen – thanks to the blockade – dated from somewhere early in 1918.

But the position of the theatre among the arts is peculiar. For the rest of the arts, for literature generally and for the scientific worker, the catastrophe of 1917-18 was overwhelming. There remained no one to buy books or pictures, and the scientific worker found himself with a salary of roubles that dwindled rapidly to less than the five-hundredth part of their original value. The new crude social organisation, fighting robbery, murder, and the wildest disorder, had no place for them; it had forgotten them. For the scientific men at first the Soviet Government had as little regard as the first French revolution, which had "no need for chemists". These classes of worker, vitally important to every civilized system, were reduced, therefore, to a state of the utmost privation and misery. It was to their assistance and salvation that Gorky's first efforts were directed. Thanks very largely to him and to the more creative intelligences in the Bolshevik Government, there has now been organized a group of salvage establishments, of which the best and most fully developed is the House of Science in Petersburg, in the ancient palace of the Archduchess Marie Pavlova. Here we saw the headquarters of a special rationing system which provides as well as it can for the needs of four thousand scientific workers and their dependants – in all perhaps for ten thousand people. At this centre they not only draw their food rations, but they can get baths and barber, tailoring, cobbling and the like conveniences. There is even a small stock of boots and clothing. There are bedrooms, and a sort of hospital accommodation for cases of weakness and ill-health.

It was to me one of the strangest of my Russian experiences to go to this institution and to meet there, as careworn and unprosperous-looking figures, some of the great survivors of the Russian scientific world. Here were such men as Oldenburg the orientalist, Karpinsky the geologist, Pavloff the Nobel prizeman, Radloff, Bielopolsky, and the like, names of world-wide celebrity. They asked me a multitude of questions about recent scientific progress in the world outside Russia, and made me ashamed of my frightful ignorance of such matters. If I had known that this would happen I would have taken some sort of report with me. Out blockade has cut them off from all scientific literature outside Russia. They are without new instruments, they are short of paper, the work they do has to go on in unwarmed laboratories. It is amazing they do any work at all. Yet they are getting work done; Pavloff is carrying on research of astonishing scope and ingenuity upon the mentality of animals; Manuchin claims to have worked out an effectual cure for tuberculosis, even in advanced cases; and so on. I have brought back abstracts of Manuchin's work for translation and publication here and they are now being put into English. The scientific spirit is a wonderful spirit. If Petersburg starves this winter, the House of Science – unless we make some special effort on its behalf – will starve too, but these scientific men said very little to me about the possibility of sending them in supplies. The House of Literature and Art talked a little of want and miseries, but not the scientific men. What they were all keen about was the possibility of getting

352

scientific publications; they value knowledge more than bread. Upon that matter I hope I may be of some help to them. I got them to form a committee to make me out a list of all the books and publications of which they stood in need, and I have brought this list back to the Secretary of the Royal Society of London, which had already been stirring in this matter. Funds will be needed, three or four thousand pounds perhaps (the address of the Secretary of the Royal Society is Burlington House, W.), but the assent of the Bolshevik Government and our own to this mental provisioning of Russia has been secured, and in a little time I hope the first parcel of books will be going through to these men, who have been cut off for so long from the general mental life of the world.

If I had no other reason for satisfaction about this trip to Russia, I should find quite enough in the hope and comfort our mere presence evidently gave to many of these distinguished men in the House of Science and in the House of Literature and Art. Upon many of them there had settled a kind of despair of ever seeing or hearing anything of the outer world again. They had been living for three years, very grey and long years indeed, in a world that seemed sinking down steadily through one degree of privation after another into utter darkness. Possibly they had seen something of one or two of the political deputations that have visited Russia – I do not know; but manifestly they had never expected to see again a free and independent individual walk in, with an air of having come quite easily and unofficially from London, and of its being quite possible not only to come but to go again into the lost world of the West. It was like an unexpected afternoon caller strolling into a cell in a gaol.

All musical people in England know the work of Glazounov; he has conducted concerts in London and is an honorary doctor both of Oxford and Cambridge. I was very deeply touched by my meeting with him. He used to be a big florid man, but now he is pallid and much fallen away, so that his clothes hang loosely on him. He came and talked of his friends Sir Hubert Parry and Sir Charles Villiers Stanford. He told me he still composed, but that his stock of music paper was almost exhausted. "Then there will be no more." I said there would be much more, and that soon. He doubted it. He spoke of London and Oxford; I could see that he was consumed by an almost intolerable longing for some great city full of life, a city with abundance, with pleasant crowds, a city that would give him stirring audiences in warm, brightly-lit places. While I was there, I was a sort of living token to him that such things could still be. He turned his back on the window which gave on the cold grey Neva, deserted in the twilight, and the low lines of the fortress prison of St Peter and St Paul. "In England there will be no revolution – no? I had many friends in England – many good friends in England..." I was loth to leave him, and he was very loth to let me go.

Seeing all these distinguished men living a sort of refugee life amidst the impoverished ruins of the fallen imperialist system has made me realize how helplessly dependent the man of exceptional gifts is upon a securely organized civilisation. The ordinary man can turn from this to that occupation; he can be a sailor or a worker in a factor or a digger or what not. He is under a general necessity to work, but he has no internal demon which compels him to do a particular thing and nothing else, which compels him to be a particular thing or die. But a Shalyapin must be Shalyapin or nothing, Pavloff is Pavloff and Glazounov,

Glazounov. So long as they can go on doing their particular thing, such men will live and flourish. Shalyapin still acts and sings magnificently – in absolute defiance of every Communist principle; Pavloff still continues his marvellous researches – in an old coat and with his study piled up with the potatoes and carrots he grows in his spare time; Glazounov will compose until the paper runs out. But many of the others are evidently stricken much harder. The mortality among the intellectually distinguished men of Russia has been terribly high. Much, no doubt, has been due to the general hardship of life, but in many cases I believe that the sheer mortification of great gifts become futile has been the determining cause. They could no more live in the Russia of 1919 than they could have lived in a Kaffir kraal.

Science, art, and literature are hothouse plants demanding warmth and respect and service. It is the paradox of science that it alters the whole world and is produced by the genius of men who need protection and help more than any other class of worker. The collapse of the Russian imperial system has smashed up all the shelters in which such things could exist. The crude Marxist philosophy which divides all men into bourgeoisie and proletariat, which sees all social life as a stupidly simple "class war", had no knowledge of the conditions necessary for the collective mental life. But it is to the credit of the Bolshevik Government that it has now risen to the danger of a universal intellectual destruction in Russia, and that, in spite of the blockade and the unending struggle against the subsidised revolts and invasions with which we and the French plague Russia, it is now permitting and helping these salvage organizations. Parallel with the House of Science is the House of Literature and Art. The writing of new books, except for some poetry, and the painting of pictures have ceased in Russia. But the bulk of the writers and artists have been found employment upon a grandiose scheme for the publication of a sort of Russian encyclopaedia of the literature of the world. In this strange Russia of conflict, cold, famine and pitiful privations there is actually going on now a literary task that would be inconceivable in the rich England and the rich America of today. In England and America the production of good literature at popular prices has practically ceased now – "because of the price of paper." The mental food of the English and American masses dwindles and deteriorates, and nobody in authority cares a rap. The Bolshevik Government is at least a shade above that level. In starving Russia hundreds of people are working upon translations, and the books they translate are being set up and printed, work which may presently give a new Russia such a knowledge of world thought as no other people will possess. I have seen some of the books and the work going on. "May" I write, with no certainty. Because, like everything else in this ruined country, this creative work is essentially improvised and fragmentary. How this world literature is to be distributed to the Russian people I do not know. The bookshops are closed and bookselling, like every other form of trading, is illegal. Probably the books will be distributed to schools and other institutions.

In this matter of book distribution the Bolshevik authorities are clearly at a loss. They are at a loss upon very many such matters. In regard to the intellectual life of the community one discovers that Marxist Communism is without plans and without ideas. Marxist Communism has always been a theory of revolution, a theory not merely lacking in creative and constructive ideas, but hostile to creative and constructive ideas. Every Communist

356

orator has been trained to contemn "Utopianism", that is to say, has been trained to contemn intelligent planning. Not even a British business man of the older type is quite such a believer in things righting themselves and in "muddling through" as these Marxists. The Russian Communist Government now finds itself face to face, among a multiplicity of other constructive problems, with the problem of sustaining scientific life, of sustaining thought and discussion, of promoting artistic creation. Marx the Prophet and his Sacred Book supply it with no lead at all in the matter. Bolshevism, having no schemes, must improvise therefore – clumsily, and is reduced to these pathetic attempts to salvage the wreckage of the intellectual life of the old order. And that life is very sick and unhappy and seems likely to die on its hands.

It is not simply scientific and literary work and workers that Maxim Gorky is trying to salvage in Russia. There is a third and still more curious salvage organisation associated with him. This is the Expertise Commission, which has its headquarters in the former British Embassy. When a social order based on private property crashes, when private property is with some abruptness and no qualification abolished, this does not abolish and destroy the things which have hitherto constituted private property. Houses and their gear remain standing, still being occupied and used by the people who had them before – except when those people have fled. When the Bolshevik authorities requisition a house or take over a deserted palace, they find themselves faced by this problem of the gear. Anyone who knows human nature will understand that there has been a certain amount of quiet annexation of desirable things by inadvertent officials and, perhaps less inadvertently, by their wives. But the general spirit

357

of Bolshevism is quite honest, and it is set very stoutly against looting and suchlike developments of individual enterprise. There has evidently been comparatively little looting either in Petersburg or Moscow since the days of the *débâcle*. Looting died against the wall in Moscow in the spring of 1918. In the guest houses and suchlike places we noted that everything was numbered and listed. Occasionally we saw odd things astray, fine glass or crested silver upon tables where it seemed out of place, but in many cases these were things which had been sold for food or suchlike necessities on the part of the original owners. The sailor courier who attended to our comfort to and from Moscow was provided with a beautiful little silver teapot that must once have brightened a charming drawing-room. But apparently it had taken to a semi-public life in a quite legitimate way.

For greater security there has been a gathering together and a cataloguing of everything that could claim to be a work of art by this Expertise Commission. The palace that once sheltered the British Embassy is now like some congested second-hand art shop in the Brompton Road. We went through room after room piled with the beautiful lumber of the former Russian social system. There are big rooms crammed with statuary; never have I seen so many white marble Venuses and sylphs together, not even in the Naples Museum. There are stacks of pictures of every sort, passages choked with inlaid cabinets piled up to the ceiling; a room full of cases of old lace, piles of magnificent furniture. This accumulation has been counted and catalogued. And there it is. I could not find out that anyone had an idea of what was ultimately to be done with all this lovely and elegant litter. The stuff does not seem to belong in any way to the new world, if it is indeed a new world that the Russian Communists are organising. They never anticipated that they would have to deal with such things. Just as they never really thought of what they would do with the shops and markets when they had abolished shopping and marketing. Just as they had never thought out the problem of converting a city of private palaces into a Communist gathering-place. Marxist theory had led their minds up to the "dictatorship of the class-conscious proletariat" and then intimated – we discover now how vaguely – that there would be a new heaven and a new earth. Had that happened it would indeed have been a revolution in human affairs. But as we saw Russia there is still the old heaven and the old earth, covered with the ruins, littered with the abandoned furnishings and dislocated machinery of the former system, with the old peasant tough and obstinate upon the soil – and Communism, ruling in the cities quite pluckily and honestly, and yet, in so many matters, like a conjurer who has left his pigeon and his rabbit behind him, and can produce nothing whatever from the hat.

Ruin; that is the primary Russian fact at the present time. The revolution, the Communist rule, which I will proceed to describe in my next paper, is quite secondary to that. It is something that has happened in the ruin and because of the ruin. It is of primary importance that people in the West should realize that. If the Great War had gone on for a year or so more, Germany and then the Western Powers would probably have repeated, with local variations, the Russian crash. The state of affairs we have seen in Russia is only the intensification and completion of the state of affairs towards which Britain was drifting in 1918. Here also there are shortages such as we had in England, but they are relatively monstrous; here also is rationing, but it is relatively feeble and inefficient: the profiteer in Russia is not fined but

359

shot, and for the English DORA you have the Extraordinary Commission. What were nuisances in England are magnified to disasters in Russia. That is all the difference. For all I know, Western Europe may be still drifting even now towards a parallel crash. I am not by any means sure that we have turned the corner. War, self-indulgence, and unproductive speculation may still be wasting more than the Western world is producing; in which case our own crash – currency failure, a universal shortage, social and political collapse and all the rest of it – is merely a question of time. The shops of Regent Street will follow the shops of the Nevsky Prospect, and Mr Galsworthy and Mr Bennett will have to do what they can to salvage the art treasures of Mayfair. It falsifies the whole world situation, it sets people altogether astray in their political actions, to assert that the frightful destitution of Russia today is to any large extent the result merely of Communist effort; that the wicked Communists have pulled down Russia to her present plight, and that if you can overthrow the Communists every one and everything in Russia will suddenly become happy again. Russia fell into its present miseries through the world war and the moral and intellectual insufficiency of its ruling and wealthy people. (As our own British State – as presently even the American State – may fall.) They had neither the brains nor the conscience to stop warfare, stop waste of all sorts, and stop taking the best of everything and leaving every one else dangerously unhappy, until it was too late. They ruled and wasted and quarrelled, blind to the coming disaster up to the very moment of its occurrence. And then, as I describe in the next chapters, the Communist came in...

CHAPTER THREE

The Quintessence of Bolshevism

In the two preceding chapters I have tried to give the reader my impression of Russian life as I saw it in Petersburg and Moscow, as a spectacle of collapse, as the collapse of a political, social, and economic system, akin to our own but weaker and more rotten than our own, which has crashed under the pressure of six years of war and misgovernment. The main collapse occurred in 1917 when Tsarism, brutishly incompetent, became manifestly impossible. It has wasted the whole land, lost control of its army and the confidence of the entire population. Its police system had degenerated into a *régime* of violence and brigandage. It fell inevitably.

And there was no alternative government. For generations the chief energies of Tsarism had been directed to destroying any possibility of an alternative government. It had subsisted on that one fact that, bad as it was, there was nothing else to put in its place. The first Russian Revolution, therefore, turned Russia into a debating society and a political scramble. The liberal forces of the country, unaccustomed to action or responsibility, set up a clamorous discussion whether Russia was to be a constitutional monarchy, a liberal republic, a socialist republic, or what not.

Over the confusion gesticulated Kerensky in attitudes of the finest liberalism. Through it loomed various ambiguous adventurers, "strong men", sham strong men, Russian Monks and Russian Bonapartes. What remained of social order collapsed. In the closing months of 1917 murder and robbery were common street incidents in Petersburg and Moscow, as common as an automobile accident in the streets of London, and less heeded. On the Reval boat was an American who had formerly directed the affairs of the American Harvester Company in Russia. He had been in Moscow during this phase of complete disorder. He described hold-ups in open daylight in busy streets, dead bodies lying for hours in the gutter – as a dead kitten might do in a western town – while crowds went about their business along the side-walk.

Through this fevered and confused country went the representatives of Britain and France, blind to the quality of the immense and tragic disaster about them, intent only upon *the* war, badgering the Russians to keep on fighting and make a fresh offensive against Germany. But when the Germans made a strong thrust towards Petersburg through the Baltic provinces and by sea, the British Admiralty, either through sheer cowardice or through Royalist intrigues, failed to give any effectual help to Russia. Upon this matter the evidence of the late Lord Fisher is plain. And so this unhappy country, mortally sick and, as it were, delirious, staggered towards a further stage of collapse.

From end to end of Russia, and in the Russian-speaking community throughout the world, there existed only one sort of people who had common general ideas upon which to work, a common faith and a common will, and that was the Communist party. While all the rest of Russia was either apathetic like the peasantry or garrulously at sixes and sevens or given over to violence or fear, the Communists believed and were prepared to act. Numerically they were and are a very small part of the Russian population. At the present time not one per cent of the people in Russia are Communists; the organized party certainly does not number more than 600,000 and has probably not much more than 150,000 active members. Nevertheless, because it was in those terrible days the only organisation which gave men a common idea of action, common formulae, and mutual confidence, it was able to seize and retain control of the smashed empire. It was and it is the only sort of administrative solidarity possible in Russia. These ambigious adventurers who have been and are afflicting Russia, with the support of the Western Powers, Deniken, Kolchak, Wrangel and the like, stand for no guiding principle and offer no security of any sort upon which men's confidence can crystallise. They are essentially brigands. The Communist party, however one may criticize it, does embody an idea and can be relied upon to stand by its idea. So far it is a thing morally higher than anything that has yet come against it. It at once secured the passive support of the peasant mass by permitting them to take land from the estates and by making peace with Germany. It restored order – after a frightful lot of shooting – in the great towns. For a time everybody found carrying arms without authority was shot. This action was clumsy and bloody but effective. To retain its power this Communist Government organized Extraordinary Commissions, with practically unlimited powers, and crushed out all opposition by a Red Terror. Much that that Red Terror did was cruel and frightful, it was largely controlled by narrow-mined men, and many of its officials were inspired by social hatred and the fear of counter-revolution, but if it was fanatical it was honest. Apart from individual atrocities it did on the whole kill for a reason and to an end. Its bloodshed was not like the silly aimless butcheries of the Deniken *régime,* which would not even recognise, I was told, the Bolshevik Red Cross. And today the Bolshevik Government sits, I believe, in Moscow as securely established as any Government in Europe, and the streets of the Russian towns are as safe as any streets in Europe.

It not only established itself and restored order, but – thanks largely to the genius of that ex-pacifist Trotsky – it re-created the Russian army as a fighting force. That we must recognise as a very remarkable achievement. I saw little of the Russian army myself, it was not what I went to Russia to see, but Mr Vanderlip, the enterprising American financier, whom I found in Moscow engaged in some mysterious negotiations with the Soviet Government, had been treated to review of several thousand troops, and was very enthusiastic about their spirit and equipment. My son and I saw a number of drafts going to the front, and also bodies of recruits joining up, and our impression is that the spirit of the men was quite as good as that of similar bodies of British recruits in London in 1917–18.

Now who are these Bolsheviki who have taken such an effectual hold upon Russia? According to the crazier section of the British Press they are the agents of a mysterious racial plot, a secret society, in which Jews, Jesuits, Freemasons, and Germans are all jumbled together in the maddest fashion. As a matter of fact, nothing was ever quite less secret than the ideas and aims and methods of the Bolsheviks, nor anything quite less like a secret society than their organisation. But in England we cultivate a peculiar style of thinking, so impervious to any general ideas that it must needs fall back upon the notion of a conspiracy to explain the simplest reactions of the human mind. If, for instance, a day labourer in Essex makes a fuss because he finds that the price of his children's boots has risen out of all proportion to the increase in weekly wages, and declares that he and his fellow-workers are being cheated and underpaid, the editors of *The Times* and of the *Morning Post* will trace his resentment to the insidious propaganda of some mysterious society at Königsberg or Pekin. They cannot conceive how otherwise he should get such ideas into his head. Conspiracy mania of this kind is so prevalent that I feel constrained to apologise for my own immunity. I find the Bolsheviks very much what they profess to be. I find myself obliged to treat them as fairly straightforward people. I do not agree with either their views or their methods, but that is another question.

The Bolsheviks are Marxist Socialists. Marx died in London nearly forty years ago; the propaganda of his views has been going on for over half a century. It has spread over the whole earth and finds in nearly every country a small but enthusiastic following. It is a natural result of world-wide economic conditions. Everywhere it expresses the same limited ideas in the same distinctive phrasing. It is a cult, a world-wide international brotherhood. No one need learn Russian to study the ideas of Bolshevism. The enquirer will find them all in the London *Plebs* or the New York *Liberator* in exactly the same phrases as in the Russian *Pravda*. They hide nothing. They say everything. And just precisely what these Marxists write and say, so they attempt to do.

It will be best if I write about Marx without any hypocritical deference. I have always regarded him as a Bore of the extremest sort. His vast unfinished work, *Das Kapital*, a cadence of wearisome volumes about such phantom unrealities as the *bourgeoisie* and the *proletariat*, a book for ever maundering away into tedious secondary discussions, impresses me as a monument of pretentious pedantry. But before I went to Russia on this last occasion I had no active hostility to Marx. I avoided his works, and when I encountered Marxists I disposed of them by asking them to tell me exactly what people constituted the proletariat. None of them knew. No Marxist knows. In Gorky's flat I listened with attention while Bokaiev discussed with Shalyapin the fine question of whether in Russia there was a proletariat at all, distinguishable from the peasants. As Bokaiev has been head of the Extraordinary Commission of the Dictatorship of the Proletariat in Petersburg, it was interesting to note the fine difficulties of the argument. The "proletarian" in the Marxist jargon is like the "producer" in the jargon of some political economists, who is supposed to be a creature absolutely distinct and different from the "consumer". So the proletarian is a figure put into flat opposition to something called capital. I find in large type outside the current number of the *Plebs*, "The working class and the employing class have nothing in common." Apply this to a works foreman who is being taken in a train by an engine-driver to see how the house he is having built for him by a building society is getting on. To which of these immiscibles does he belong, employer or employed? The stuff is sheer nonsense.

In Russia I must confess my passive objection to Marx has changed to a very active hostility. Wherever we went we encountered busts, portraits, and statues of Marx. About two-thirds of the face of Marx is beard, a vast solemn woolly uneventful beard that must have made all normal exercise impossible. It is not the sort of beard that happens to a man, it is a beard cultivated, cherished, and thrust patriarchally upon the world. It is exactly like *Das Kapital* in its inane abundance, and the human part of the face looks over it owlishly as if it looked to see how the growth impressed mankind. I found the omnipresent images of that beard more and more irritating. A gnawing desire grew upon me to see Karl Marx shaved. Some day, if I am spared, I will take up shears and a razor against *Das Kapital;* I will write *The Shaving of Karl Marx.*

But Marx is for the Marxists merely an image and a symbol, and it is with the Marxist and not with Marx that we are now dealing. Few Marxists have read much of *Das Kapital.* The Marxist is very much the same sort of person in all modern communities, and I will confess that by my temperament and circumstances I have the very warmest sympathy for him. He adopts Marx as his prophet simply because he believes that Marx wrote of the class war, an implacable war of the employed against the employer, and that he prophesied a triumph for the employed person, a dictatorship of the world by the leaders of these liberated employed persons (dictatorship of the proletariat), and a Communist millennium arising out of that dictatorship. Now this doctrine and this prophecy have appealed in every country with extraordinary power to young persons, and particularly to young men of energy and imagination who have found themselves at the outset of life imperfectly educated, ill-equipped, and caught into hopeless wages slavery in our existing economic system. They realize in their own persons the social injustice, the stupid negligence, the colossal incivility of our system; they realize that they are insulted and sacrificed by it; and they devote themselves to break it and emancipate themselves from it. No insidious propaganda is needed to make such rebels; it is the faults of a system that half-educates and then enslaves them which have created the Communist movement wherever industrialism has developed. There would have been Marxists if Marx had never lived. When I was a boy of fourteen I was a complete Marxist, long before I had heard the name of Marx. I had been cut off abruptly from education, caught in a detestable shop, and I was being broken in to a life of mean and dreary toil. I was worked too hard and for such long hours that all thoughts of self-improvement seemed hopeless. I would have set fire to that place if I had not been convinced it was over-insured. I revived the spirit of those bitter days in a conversation I had with Zorin, one of the leaders of the Commune of the North. He is a young man who has come back from unskilled work in America, a very likeable human being and a humorous and very popular speaker in the Petersburg Soviet. He and I exchanged experiences, and I found that the thing that rankled most in his mind about America was the brutal incivility he had encountered when applying for a job as packer in a big dry goods store in New York. We told each other stories of the way our social system wastes and breaks and maddens decent and willing men. Between us was the freemasonry of a common indignation.

It is that indignation of youth and energy, thwarted and misused, it is that and no mere economic theorising, which is the living and linking inspiration of the Marxist movement throughout the world. It is not that Marx was profoundly wise, but that our economic system has been stupid, selfish, wasteful, and anarchistic. The Communistic organisation has provided for this angry recalcitrance certain shibboleths and passwords;

"Workers of the World unite," and so forth. It has suggested to them an idea of a great conspiracy against human happiness concocted by a mysterious body of wicked men called capitalists. For in this mentally enfeebled world in which we live today conspiracy mania on one side finds its echo on the other, and it is hard to persuade a Marxist that capitalists are in their totality no more than a scrambling disorder of mean-spirited and short-sighted men. And the Communist propaganda had knitted all these angry and disinherited spirits together into a world-wide organisation of revolt – and hope – formless though that hope proves to be on examination. It has chosen Marx for its prophet and red for its colour... And so when the crash came in Russia, when there remained no other solidarity of men who could work together upon any but immediate selfish ends, there came flowing back from America and the West to rejoin their comrades a considerable number of keen and enthusiastic young and youngish men, who had in that more bracing Western world lost something of the habitual impracticability of the Russian and acquired a certain habit of getting things done, who all thought in the same phrases and had the courage of the same ideas, and who were all inspired by the dream of a revolution that should bring human life to a new level of justice and happiness. It is these young men who constitute the living force of Bolshevism. Many of them are Jews, because most of the Russian emigrants to America were Jews; but few of them have any strong racial Jewish feeling. They are not out for Jewry but for a new world. So far from being in continuation of the Jewish tradition the Bolsheviks have put most of the Zionist leaders in Russia in prison, and they have proscribed the teaching of Hebrew as a "reactionary" language. Several of the most interesting

Bolsheviks I met were not Jews at all, but blond Nordic men. Lenin, the beloved leader of all that is energetic in Russia today, has a Tartar type of face and is certainly no Jew.

This Bolshevik Government is at once the most temerarious and the least experienced governing body in the world. In some directions its incompetence is amazing. In most its ignorance is profound. Of the diabolical cunning of "capitalism" and of the subtleties of reaction it is ridiculously suspicious, and sometimes it takes fright and is cruel. But essentially it is honest. It is the most simple-minded Government that exists in the world today.

Its simple-mindedness is shown by one question that I was asked again and again during this Russian visit. "When is the social revolution going to happen in England?" Lenin asked me that, Zenovieff, who is the head of the Commune of the North, Zorin, and many others.

Because it is by the Marxist theory all wrong that the social revolution should happen first in Russia. That fact is bothering every intelligent man in the movement. According to the Marxist theory the social revolution should have happened first in the country with the oldest and most highly developed industrialism, with a large, definite, mainly propertyless, mainly wages-earning working class (proletariat). It should have begun in Britain, and spread to France and Germany, then should have come America's turn and so on. Instead they find Communism in power in Russia, which really possesses no specialised labouring class at all, which has worked its factories with peasant labourers who come and go from the villages, and so has scarcely any "proletariat" – to unite with the workers of the world and so forth – at all. Behind the minds of many of these Bolsheviks with whom I talked I saw clearly that there dawns now a chill suspicion of the reality of the case, a realisation that what they have got in Russia is not truly the promised Marxist social revolution at all, that in truth they have not captured a State but got aboard a derelict. I tried to assist the development of this novel and disconcerting discovery. And also I indulged in a little lecture on the absence of a large "class-conscious proletariat" in the Western communities. I explained that in England there were two hundred different classes at least, and that the only "class-conscious proletarians" known to me in the land were a small band of mainly Scotch workers kept together by the vigorous leadership of a gentleman named MacManus. Their dearest convictions struggled against my manifest candour. They are clinging desperately to the belief that there are hundreds of thousands of convinced Communists in Britain, versed in the whole gospel of Marx, a proletarian solidarity, on the eve of seizing power and proclaiming a British Soviet Republic. They hold obstinately to that after three years of waiting – but their hold weakens.

Among the most amusing things in this queer intellectual situation are the repeated scoldings that come by wireless from Moscow to Western Labour because it does not behave as Marx said it would behave. It isn't red – and it ought to be. It is just yellow.

My conversation with Zenovieff was particularly curious. He is a man with the voice and animation of Hilaire Belloc, and a lot of curly coal-black hair. "You have civil war in Ireland," he said. "Practically," said I. "Which do you consider are the proletarian, the Sinn Feiners or the Ulstermen?" We spent some time while Zenovieff worked like a man with a jigsaw puzzle trying to get the Irish situation into the class war formula. That jigsaw puzzle remained unsolved, and we then shifted our attention to Asia. Impatient at the long delay of the Western proletarians to emerge and declare themselves, Zenovieff, assisted by Bela Kun, our Mr Tom Quelch, and a number of other leading Communists, has recently gone on a pilgrimage to Baku to raise the Asiatic proletariat. They went to beat up the class-conscious wages slaves of Persia and Turkestan. They sought out factory workers and slum dwellers in the tents of the steppes. They held a congress at Baku, at which they gathered together a quite wonderful accumulation of white, black, brown, and yellow people, Asiatic costumes and astonishing weapons. They had a great assembly in which they swore undying hatred of Capitalism and British imperialism; they had a great procession in which I regret to say certain batteries of British guns, which some careless, hasty empire-builder had left behind him, figured; they disinterred and buried again thirteen people whom this British empire-builder seems to have shot without trial, and they burnt Mr Lloyd George, M. Millerand, and President Wilson in effigy. I not only saw a five-part film of this remarkable festival when I visited the Petersburg Soviet, but, thanks to Zorin, I have brought the film back with me. It is to be administered with caution and to adults only. There are parts of it that would make Mr Gwynne of the *Morning Post* or Mr Rudyard Kipling scream in their sleep. If so be they ever slept again after seeing it.

I did my best to find out from Zenovieff and Zorin what they thought they were doing in the Baku Conference. And frankly I do not think they know. I doubt if they have anything clearer in their minds than a vague idea of hitting back at the British Government through Mesopotamia and India, because it has been hitting them through Kolchak, Deniken, Wrangel, and the Poles. It is a counter-offensive almost as clumsy and stupid as the offensives it would counter. It is inconceivable that they can hope for any social solidarity with the miscellaneous discontents their congress assembled. One item "featured" on this Baku film is a dance by a gentleman from the neighbourhood of Baku. He is in fact one of the main features of this remarkable film. He wears a fur-trimmed jacket, high boots, and a high cap, and his dancing is a very rapid and dexterous step dancing. He produces two knives and puts them between his teeth, and then two others which he balances perilously with the blades dangerously close to his nose on either side of it. Finally he poises a fifth knife on his forehead, still stepping it featly to the distinctly Oriental music. He stoops and squats, arms akimbo, sending his nimble boots flying out and back like the Cossacks in the Russian ballet. He circles slowly as he does this, clapping his hands. He is now rolled up in my keeping, ready to dance again when opportunity offers. I tried to find out whether he was a specimen Asiatic proletarian or just what he symbolised, but I could get no light on him. But there are yards and yards of film of him. I wish I could have resuscitated Karl Marx, just to watch that solemn stare over the beard, regarding him. The film gives no indication of the dancer's reception by Mr Tom Quelch.

I hope I shall not offend Comrade Zorin, for whom I have a real friendship, if I thus confess to him that I cannot take his Baku Conference very seriously. It was an excursion, a pageant, a Beano. As a meeting of Asiatic proletarians it was preposterous. But if it was not very much in itself, it was something very important in its revelation of shifting intentions. Its chief significance to me is this, that it shows a new orientation of the Bolshevik mind as it is embodied in Zenovieff. So long as the Bolsheviki held firmly with unshaken conviction to the Marxist formula they looked westward, a little surprised that the "social revolution" should have begun so far to the east of its indicated centre. Now as they begin to realize that it is not that prescribed social revolution at all but something quite different which has brought them into power, they are naturally enough casting about for a new system of relationships. The ideal figure of the Russian republic is still huge western "Worker" with a vast hammer or a sickle. A time may come, if we maintain the European blockade with sufficient stringency and make any industrial recuperation impossible, when that ideal may give place altogether to a nomadic-looking gentleman from Turkestan with a number of knives. We may drive what will remain of Bolshevik Russia to the steppes and the knife. If we help some new Wrangel to pull down the by no means firmly established Government in Moscow, under the delusion that thereby we shall bring about "representative institutions" and a "limited monarchy", we may find ourselves very much out in our calculations. Anyone who destroys the present law and order of Moscow will, I believe, destroy what is left of law and order in Russia. A brigand monarchist government will leave a trail of fresh blood across the Russian scene, show what gentlemen can do when they are roused, in a tremendous pogrom and White Terror, flourish horribly for a time, break up and vanish. Asia will resume. The simple ancient rhythm of the horseman plundering the peasant and the peasant waylaying the horseman will creep back across the plains to the Niemen and the Dniester.

The cities will become clusters of ruins in the waste; the roads and railroads will rot and rust; the river traffic will decay...

This Baku Conference has depressed Gorky profoundly. He is obsessed by a nightmare of Russia going east. Perhaps I have caught a little of his depression.

CHAPTER FOUR

The Creative Effort in Russia

In the previous three chapters I have tried to give my impression of the Russian spectacle as that of a rather ramshackle modern civilization completely shattered and overthrown by misgovernment, under-education, and finally six years of war strain. I have shown science and art starving and the comforts and many of the decencies of life gone. In Vienna the overthrow is just as bad; and there too such men of science as the late Professor Margules starve to death. If London had had to endure four more years of war, much the same sort of thing would be happening in London. We should have now no coal in our grates and no food for our food tickets, and the shops in Bond Street would be as desolate as the shops in the Nevsky Prospect. Bolshevik government in Russia is neither responsible for the causation nor for the continuance of these miseries.

I have also tried to get the facts of Bolshevik rule into what I believe is their proper proportions in the picture. The Bolsheviks, albeit numbering less than five per cent of the population, have been able to seize and retain power in Russia because they were and are the only body of people in this vast spectacle of Russian ruin with a common faith and a common spirit. I disbelieve in their faith, I ridicule Marx, their prophet, but I understand and respect their spirit. They are – with all their faults, and they have abundant faults – the only possible backbone now to a renascent Russia. The recivilizing of Russia must be done with the Soviet Government as the starting phase. The great mass of the Russian population is an entirely illiterate peasantry, grossly materialistic and politically indifferent. They are superstitious, they are for ever crossing themselves and kissing images, – in Moscow particularly they were at it – but they are not religious. They have no will in things political and social beyond their immediate satisfactions. They are roughly content with Bolshevik rule. The Orthodox priest is quite unlike the Catholic priest in Western Europe; he is himself typically a dirty and illiterate peasant with no power over the wills and consciences of his people. There is no constructive quality in either peasant or Orthodoxy. For the rest there is a confusion of more or less civilized Russians, in and out of Russia, with no common political ideas and with no common will. They are incapable of producing anything but adventurers and disputes.

The Russian refugees in England are politically contemptible. They rehearse endless stories of "Bolshevik outrages"; château-burnings by peasants, burglaries and murders by disbanded soldiers in the towns, back street crimes – they tell them all as acts of the Bolshevik Government. Ask them what government they want in its place, and you will get rubbishy generalities – usually adapted to what the speaker supposes to be your particular political obsession. Or they sicken you with the praise of some current super-man, Deniken or Wrangel, who is to put everything right – God knows how. They deserve nothing better than a Tsar, and they are incapable even of deciding which Tsar they desire. The better part of the educated people still in Russia are – for the sake of Russia – slowly drifting into a reluctant but honest co-operation with Bolshevik rule.

The Bolsheviks themselves are Marxists and Communists. They find themselves in control of Russia, in complete contradiction, as I have explained, to the theories of Karl Marx. A large part of their energies have been occupied in an entirely patriotic struggle against the raids, invasions, blockades, and persecutions of every sort that our insensate Western Governments have rained upon their tragically shattered country. What is left over goes in the attempt to keep Russia alive, and to organize some sort of social order among the ruins. These Bolsheviks are, as I have explained, extremely inexperienced men, intellectual exiles from Geneva and Hampstead, or comparatively illiterate manual workers from the United States. Never was there so amateurish a government since the early Moslim found themselves in control of Cairo, Damascus, and Mesopotamia.

I believe that in the minds of very many of them there is a considerable element of dismay at the tremendous tasks they find before them. But one thing has helped them and Russia enormously, and that is their training in Communistic ideas. As the British found out during the submarine war, so far as the urban and industrial population goes there is nothing for it during a time of tragic scarcity but collapse or collective control. We in England had to control and ration, we had to suppress profiteering by stringent laws. These Communists came into power in Russia and began to do at once, on principle, the first most necessary thing in that chaos of social wreckage. Against all the habits and traditions of Russia, they began to control and ration – exhaustively. They have now a rationing system that is, on paper, admirable beyond cavil; and perhaps it works as well as the temperament and circumstances of Russian production and consumption permit. It is easy to note defects and failures, but not nearly so easy to show how in this depleted and demoralised Russia they could be avoided. And things are in such a state in Russia now that even if we suppose the Bolsheviks overthrown and any other Government in their place, it matters not what, that Government would have to go on with the rationing the Bolsheviks have organized, with the suppression of vague political experiments, and the punishment and shooting of profiteers. The Bolsheviki in this state of siege and famine have done upon principle what any other Government would have had to do from necessity.

And in the face of gigantic difficulties they are trying to rebuild a new Russia among the ruins. We may quarrel with their principles and methods, we may call their schemes Utopian and so forth, we may sneer at or we may dread what they are doing, but it is no good pretending that there is no creative effort in Russia at the present time. A certain section of the Bolsheviks are hard-minded, doctrinaire and unteachable men, fanatics who believe that the mere destruction of capitalism, the disuse of money and trading, the effacement of all social differences, will in itself bring about a sort of bleak millennium. There are Bolsheviki so stupid that they would stop the teaching of chemistry in schools until they were assured it was "proletarian" chemistry, and who would suppress every decorative design that was not an elaboration of the letters RSFSR (Russian Socialist Federal Soviet Republic) as reactionary art. I have told of the suppression of Hebrew studies because they are "reactionary";

and while I was with Gorky I found him in constant bitter disputes with extremist officials who would see no good in any literature of the past except the literature of revolt. But there were other more liberal minds in this new Russian world, minds which, given an opportunity, will build and will probably build well. Among men of such constructive force I would quote such names as Lenin himself, who has developed wonderfully since the days of his exile, and who has recently written powerfully against the extravagances of his own extremists; Trotsky, who has never been an extremist, and who is a man of very great organising ability; Lunacharsky, the Minister for Education; Rikoff, the head of the Department of People's Economy; Madame Lilna of the Petersburg Child Welfare Department; and Krassin, the head of the London Trade Delegation. These are names that occur to me; it is by no means an exhaustive list of the statesmanlike elements in the Bolshevik Government. Already they have achieved something, in spite of blockade and civil and foreign war. It is not only that they work to restore a country depleted of material to an extent almost inconceivable to English and American readers, but they work with an extraordinarily unhelpful personnel. Russia today stands more in need of men of the foreman and works-manager class than she does of medicaments or food. The ordinary work in the Government offices of Russia is shockingly done; the slackness and inaccuracy are indescribable. Everybody seems to be working in a muddle of unsorted papers and cigarette ends. This again is a state of affairs no counter-revolution could change. It is inherent in the present Russian situation. If one of these military adventurers the Western Powers patronise were, by some disastrous accident, to get control of Russia, his success would only add strong drink, embezzlement and a great squalor of kept mistresses to the general complication. For whatever else we may say to the discredit of the Bolshevik leaders, it is undeniable that the great majority lead not simply laborious but puritanical lives.

I write of this general inefficiency in Russia with the more asperity because it was the cause of my not meeting Lunacharsky. About eighty hours of my life were consumed in travelling, telephoning, and waiting about in order to talk for about an hour and a half with Lenin and for the same time with Tchitcherin. At that rate, and in view of the intermittent boat service from Reval to Stockholm, to see Lunacharsky would have meant at least a week more in Russia. The whole of my visit to Moscow was muddled in the most irritating fashion. A sailor-man carrying a silver kettle who did not know his way about Moscow was put in charge of my journey, and an American who did not know enough Russian to telephone freely was set to make my appointments in the town. Although I had heard Gorky arrange for my meeting with Lenin by long-distance telephone days before, Moscow declared that it had had no notice of my coming. Finally I was put into the wrong train back to Petersburg, a train which took twenty-two hours instead of fourteen for the journey. These may seem petty details to relate, but when it is remembered that Russia was really doing its best to impress me with its vigour and good order, they are extremely significant. In the train, when I realized that it was a slow train and that the express had gone three hours before while we had been pacing the hall of the guest house with our luggage packed and nobody coming for us, the spirit came upon me and my lips were unsealed. I spoke to my guide, as one mariner might speak to another, and told him what I thought of Russian methods. He listened with the profoundest respect to my rich incisive phrases. When at last I paused, he replied – in words that are also significant of certain weaknesses of the present Russian state of mind. "You see," he said, "the blockade – "

But if I saw nothing of Lunacharsky personally, I saw something of the work he has organized. The primary material of the educationist is human beings, and of these at least there is still no shortage in Russia, so that in that respect Lunacharsky is better off than most of his colleagues. And beginning with an initial prejudice and much distrust, I am bound to confess that, in view of their enormous difficulties, the educational work of the Bolsheviks impresses me as being astonishingly good.

Things started badly. Directly I got to Petersburg I asked to see a school, and on the second day of my visit I was taken to one that impressed me very unfavourably. It was extremely well equipped, much better than an ordinary English grammar school, and the children were bright and intelligent; but our visit fell in the recess. I could witness no teaching, and the behaviour of the youngsters I saw indicated a low standard of discipline. I formed an opinion that I was probably being shown a picked school specially prepared for me, and that this was all that Petersburg had to offer. The special guide who was with us then began to question these children upon the subject of English literature and the writers they liked most. One name dominated all others. My own. Such comparatively trivial figures as Milton, Dickens, Shakespeare ran about intermittently between the feet of that literary colossus. Being questioned further, these children produced the titles of perhaps a dozen of my books. I said I was completely satisfied by what I had seen and heard, that I wanted to see nothing more – for indeed what more could I possibly require? – and I left that school smiling with difficulty and thoroughly cross with my guides.

Three days later I suddenly scrapped my morning's engagements and insisted upon being taken at once to another school – any school close at hand. I was convinced that I had been deceived about the former school, and that now I should see a very bad school indeed. Instead I saw a much better one than the first I had seen. The equipment and building were better, the discipline of the children was better, and I saw some excellent teaching in progress. Most of the teachers were women, very competent-looking middle-aged women, and I chose elementary geometrical teaching to observe because that on the blackboard is in the universal language of the diagram. I saw also a heap of drawings and various models the pupils had done, and they were very good. The school was supplied with abundant pictures. I noted particularly a well-chosen series of landscapes to assist the geographical teaching. There was plenty of chemical and physical apparatus, and it was evidently put to a proper use. I also saw the children's next meal in preparation – for children eat at school in Soviet Russia – and the food was excellent and well cooked, far above the standard of the adult rations we had seen served out. All this was much more satisfactory. Finally by a few questions we tested the extraordinary vogue of H G Wells among the young people of Russia. None of these children had ever heard of him. The school library contained none of his books. This did much to convince me that I was seeing a quite normal school. I had, I now begin to realize, been taken to the previous one not, as I had supposed in my wrath, with any elaborate intention of deceiving me about the state of education in the country, but after certain kindly intrigues and preparations by a literary friend, Mr Chukovsky the critic, affectionately anxious to make me feel myself beloved in Russia, and a little oblivious of the real gravity of the business I had in hand.

Subsequent enquiries and comparison of my observations with those of other visitors to Russia, and particularly those of Dr Haden Guest, who also made surprise visits to several schools in Moscow, have convinced me that Soviet Russia, in the face of gigantic difficulties, has made and is making very great educational efforts, and that in spite of the difficulties of the general situation the quality and number of the schools *in the towns* has risen absolutely since the Tsarist *régime*. (The peasant, as ever, except in a few "show" localities, remains scarcely touched by these things.) The schools I saw would have been good middle schools in England. They are open to all, and there is an attempt to make education compulsory. Of course Russia has its peculiar difficulties. Many of the schools are understaffed, and it is difficult to secure the attendance of unwilling pupils. Numbers of children prefer to keep out of the schools and trade upon the streets. A large part of the illicit trading in Russia is done by bands of children. They are harder to catch than adults, and the spirit of Russian Communism is against punishing them. And the Russian child is, for a northern child, remarkably precocious.

The common practice of co-educating youngsters up to fifteen or sixteen, in a country as demoralised as Russia is now, has brought peculiar evils in its train. My attention was called to this by the visit of Bokaiev, the former head of the Petersburg Extraordinary Commission, and his colleague Zalutsky to Gorky to consult him in the matter. They discussed their business in front of me quite frankly, and the whole conversation was translated to me as it went on. The Bolshevik authorities have collected and published very startling, very shocking figures of the moral condition of young people in Petersburg, which I have seen. How far they would compare with the British figures – if there are any British figures – of such bad districts for the young as are some parts of East London or such towns of low type employment as Reading I do not know. (The reader should compare the Fabian Society's report on prostitution, *Downward Paths,* upon this question.) Nor do I know how they would show in comparison with preceding Tsarist conditions. Nor can I speculate how far these phenomena in Russia are the mechanical consequence of privation and overcrowding in a home atmosphere bordering on despair. But there can be no doubt that in the Russian towns, concurrently with increased educational effort and an enhanced intellectual stimulation of the young, there is also an increased lawlessness on their part, especially in sexual matters, and that this is going on in a phase of unexampled sobriety and harsh puritanical decorum so far as adult life is concerned. This hectic moral fever of the young is the dark side of the educational spectacle in Russia. I think it is to be regarded mainly as an aspect of the general social collapse; every European country has noted a parallel moral relaxation of the young under the war strain; but the revolution itself, in sweeping a number of the old experienced teachers out of the schools and in making every moral standard a subject of debate, has no doubt contributed also to an as yet incalculable amount in the excessive disorder of these matters in present-day Russia.

Faced with this problem of starving and shattered homes and a social chaos, the Bolshevik organizers are *institutionalising* the town children of Russia. They are making their schools residential. The children of the Russian urban population are going, like the children of the British upper class, into boarding schools. Close to this second school I visited stood two big buildings which are the living places of the boys and of the girls respectively. In these places they can be kept under some sort of hygienic and moral discipline. This again happens to be not only in accordance with Communist doctrine, but with the special necessities of the Russian crisis. Entire towns are sinking down towards slum conditions, and the Bolshevik Government has had to play the part of a gigantic Dr Barnardo.

We went over the organisation of a sort of reception home to which children are brought by their parents who find it impossible to keep them clean and decent and nourished under the terrible conditions outside. This reception home is the old Hotel de l'Europe, the scene of countless pleasant little dinner-parties under the old *régime*. On the roof there is still the summertime roof garden, where the string quartette used to play, and on the staircase we passed a frosted glass window still bearing in gold letters the words *Coiffure des Dames*.

Slender gilded pointing hands directed us to the "Restaurant", long vanished from the grim Petersburg scheme of things. Into this place the children come; they pass into a special quarantine section for infectious diseases and for personal cleanliness – nine-tenths of the newcomers harbour unpleasant parasites – and then into another section, the moral quarantine, where for a time they are watched for bad habits and undesirable tendencies. From this section some individuals may need to be weeded out and sent to special schools for defectives. The rest pass on into the general body of institutionalised children, and so on to the boarding schools.

Here certainly we have the "break-up of the family" in full progress, and the Bolshevik net is sweeping wide and taking in children of the most miscellaneous origins. The parents have reasonably free access to their children in the daytime, but little or no control over their education, clothing, or the like. We went among the children in the various stages of this educational process, and they seemed to us to be quite healthy, happy, and contented children. But they get very good people to look after them. Many men and women, political suspects or openly discontented with the existing political conditions, and yet with a desire to serve Russia, have found in these places work that they can do with a good heart and conscience. My interpreter and the lady who took us round this place had often dined and supped in the Hotel de l'Europe in its brilliant days, and they knew each other well. This lady was now plainly clad, with short cut hair and a grave manner; her husband was a White and serving with the Poles; she had two children of her own in the institution, and she was mothering some scores of little creatures. But she was evidently keenly proud of the work of her organization, and she said that she found life – in this city of want, under the shadow of a coming famine – more interesting and satisfying than it had ever been in the old days.

I have no space to tell of other educational work we saw going on in Russia. I can give but a word or so to the Home of Rest for Workmen in the Kamenni Ostrof. I thought that at once rather fine and not a little absurd. To this place workers are sent to live a life of refined ease for two or three weeks. It is a very beautiful country house with big gardens, an orangery, and subordinate

388

buildings. The meals are served on white cloths with flowers upon the table and so forth. And the worker has to live up to these elegant surroundings. It is a part of his education. If in a forgetful moment he clears his throat in the good old resonant peasant manner and spits upon the floor, an attendant, I was told, chalks a circle about his defilement and obliges him to clean the offended parquetry. The avenue approaching this place has been adorned with decoration in the futurist style, and there is a vast figure of a "worker" at the gates resting on his hammer, done in gypsum, which was obtained from the surgical reserves of the Petersburg hospitals... But after all, the idea of civilising your workpeople by dipping them into pleasant surroundings is, in itself, rather a good one...

I find it difficult to hold the scales of justice upon many of these efforts of Bolshevism. Here are these creative and educational things going on, varying between the admirable and the ridiculous, islands at least of cleanly work and, I think, of hope, amidst the vast spectacle of grisly want and wide decay. Who can weigh the power and possibility of their thrust against the huge gravitation of this sinking system? Who can guess what encouragement and enhancement they may get if Russia can win through to a respite from civil and foreign warfare and from famine and want? It was of this re-created Russia, this Russia that may be, that I was most desirous of talking when I went to the Kremlin to meet Lenin. Of that conversation I will tell in my final chapter.

CHAPTER FIVE

The Petersburg Soviet

O n Thursday the 7th of October we attended a meeting of the Petersburg Soviet. We were told that we should find this a very different legislative body from the British House of Commons, and we did. Like nearly everything else in the arrangements of Soviet Russia it struck us as extraordinarily unpremeditated and improvised. Nothing could have been less intelligently planned for the functions it had to perform or the responsibilities it had to undertake.

The meeting was held in the old Winter Garden of the Tauride Palace, the former palace of Potemkin, the favourite of Catherine the Second. Here the Imperial Duma met under the Tsarist *régime,* and I visited it in 1914 and saw a languid session in progress. I went then with Mr Maurice Baring and one of the Benckendorffs to the strangers' gallery, which ran round three sides of the hall. There was accommodation for perhaps a thousand people in the hall, and most of it was empty. The president with his bell sat above a rostrum, and behind him was a row of women reporters. I do not now remember what business was in hand on that occasion; it was certainly not very exciting business. Baring, I remember, pointed out the large proportion of priests elected to the third Duma; their beards and cassocks made a distinctive feature of that scattered gathering.

On this second visit we were no longer stranger onlookers, but active participants in the meeting; we came into the body of the hall behind the president's bench, where on a sort of stage the members of the Government, official visitors, and so forth find accommodation. The presidential bench, the rostrum, and the reporters remained, but instead of an atmosphere of weary parliamentarianism, we found ourselves in the crowding, the noise, and the peculiar thrill of a mass meeting. There were, I should think, some two hundred people or more packed upon the semi-circular benches round about us on the platform behind the president, comrades in naval uniforms and in middle-class and working-class costume, numerous intelligent-looking women, one or two Asiatics and a few unclassifiable visitors, and the body of the hall beyond the presidential bench was densely packed with people who filled not only the seats but the gangways and the spaces under the galleries. There may have been two or three thousand people down there, men and women. They were all members of the Petersburg Soviet, which is really a sort of conjoint meeting of its constituent soviets. The visitors' galleries above were equally full.

Above the rostrum, with his back to us, sat Zenovieff, his right-hand man Zorin, and the president. The subject under discussion was the proposed peace with Poland. The meeting was smarting with the sense of defeat and disposed to resent the Polish terms. Soon after we came in Zenovieff made a long and, so far as I could judge, a very able speech, preparing the minds of this great gathering for a Russian surrender. The Polish demands were outrageous, but for the present Russia must submit. He was followed by an oldish man who made a bitter attack upon the irreligion of the people and government of Russia; Russia was suffering for her sins, and until she repented and returned to religion she would continue to suffer one disaster after another. His opinions were not those of the meeting, but he was allowed to have his say without interruption. The decision to make peace with Poland was then taken by a show of hands. Then came my little turn. The meeting was told that I had come from England to see the Bolshevik *régime*; I was praised profusely; I was also exhorted to treat that *régime* fairly and not to emulate those other recent visitors (these were Mrs Snowden and Guest and Bertrand Russell) who had enjoyed the hospitality of the republic and then gone away to say unfavourable things of it. This exhortation left me cold; I had come to Russia to judge the Bolshevik Government and not to praise it. I had then to take possession of the rostrum and address this big crowd of people. This rostrum I knew had proved an unfortunate place for one or two previous visitors, who had found it hard to explain away afterwards the speeches their translators had given the world through the medium of the wireless reports. Happily, I had had some inkling of what was coming. To avoid any misunderstanding I had written out a short speech in English, and I had had this translated carefully into Russian. I began by saying clearly that I was neither Marxist nor Communist, but a Collectivist, and that it was not to a social revolution in the West that Russians should look for peace and help in their troubles, but to the liberal opinion of the moderate mass of Western people. I declared that the people of the Western States were determined to give Russia peace, so that she might develop upon her own lines. Their own line of development might be very

393

different from that of Russia. When I had done I handed a translation of my speech to my interpreter, Zorin, which not only eased his task but did away with any possibility of a subsequent misunderstanding. My speech was reported in the *Pravda* quite fully and fairly.

Then followed a motion by Zorin that Zenovieff should have leave to visit Berlin and attend the conference of the Independent Socialists there. Zorin is a witty and humorous speaker, and he got his audience into an excellent frame of mind. His motion was carried by a show of hands, and then came a report and a discussion upon the production of vegetables in the Petersburg district. It was a practical question upon which feeling ran high. Here speakers rose in the body of the hall, discharging brief utterances for a minute or so and subsiding again. There were shouts and interruptions. The debate was much more like a big labour mass meeting in the Queen's Hall than anything that a Western European would recognise as a legislature.

This business disposed of, a still more extraordinary thing happened. We who sat behind the rostrum poured down into the already very crowded body of the hall and got such seats as we could find, and a white sheet was lowered behind the president's seat. At the same time a band appeared in the gallery to the left. A five-part cinematograph film was then run, showing the Baku Conference to which I have already alluded. The pictures were viewed with interest but without any violent applause. And at the end the band played the *Internationale,* and the audience – I beg its pardon! – the Petersburg Soviet dispersed singing that popular chant. It was in fact a mass meeting incapable of any real legislative activities; capable at the utmost of endorsing or not endorsing the Government in control of the platform. Compared with the British Parliament it has about as much organisation, structure, and working efficiency as a big bagful of miscellaneous wheels might have, compared to an old-fashioned and inaccurate but still going clock.

CHAPTER SIX

The Dreamer in the Kremlin

My chief purpose in going from Petersburg to Moscow was to see and talk to Lenin. I was very curious to see him, and I was disposed to be hostile to him. I encountered a personality entirely different from anything I had expected to meet.

Lenin is not a writer; his published work does not express him. The shrill little pamphlets and papers issued from Moscow in his name, full of misconceptions of the labour psychology of the West and obstinately defensive of the impossible proposition that it is the prophesied Marxist social revolution which has happened in Russia, display hardly anything of the real Lenin mentality as I encountered it. Occasionally there are gleams of an inspired shrewdness, but for the rest these publications do no more than rehearse the set ideas and phrases of doctrinaire Marxism. Perhaps that is necessary. That may be the only language Communism understands; a break into a new dialect would be disturbing and demoralizing. Left Communism is the backbone of Russia today; unhappily it is a backbone without flexible joints, a backbone that can be bent only with the utmost difficulty and which must be bent by means of flattery and deference.

Moscow under the bright October sunshine, amidst the fluttering yellow leaves, impressed us as being altogether more lax and animated than Petersburg. There is much more movement of people, more trading, and a comparative plenty of droshkys. Markets are open. There is not the same general ruination of streets and houses. There are, it is true, many traces of the desperate street fighting of early 1918. One of the domes of that absurd cathedral of St Basil just outside the Kremlin gate was smashed by a shell and still awaits repair. The tramcars we found were not carrying passengers; they were being used for the transport of supplies of food and fuel. In these matters Petersburg claims to be better prepared than Moscow.

The ten thousand crosses of Moscow still glitter in the afternoon light. On one conspicuous pinnacle of the Kremlin the imperial eagles spread their wings; the Bolshevik Government has been too busy or too indifferent to pull them down. The churches are open, the kissing of ikons is a flourishing industry, and beggars still woo casual charity at the doors. The celebrated miraculous shrine of the Iberian Madonna outside the Redeemer Gate was particularly busy. There were many peasant women, unable to get into the little chapel, kissing the stones outside.

Just opposite to it, on a plaster panel on a house front, is that now celebrated inscription put up by one of the early revolutionary administrations in Moscow: "Religion is the Opium of the People". The effect this inscription produces is greatly reduced by the fact that in Russia the people cannot read.

About that inscription I had a slight but amusing argument with Mr Vanderlip, the American financier, who was lodged in the same guest house as ourselves. He wanted to have it effaced. I was for retaining it as being historically interesting, and because

I think that religious toleration should extent to atheists. But Mr Vanderlip felt too strongly to see the point of that.

The Moscow Guest House, which we shared with Mr Vanderlip and an adventurous English artist who had somehow got though to Moscow to execute busts of Lenin and Trotsky, was a big, richly-furnished house upon the Sofiskaya Naberezhnaya (No. 17), directly facing the great wall of the Kremlin and all the clustering domes and pinnacles of that imperial inner city. We felt much less free and more secluded here than in Petersburg. There were sentinels at the gates to protect us from casual visitors, whereas in Petersburg all sorts of unauthorized persons could and did stray in to talk to me. Mr Vanderlip had been staying here, I gathered, for some weeks, and proposed to stay some weeks more. He was without valet, secretary, or interpreter. He did not discuss his business with me beyond telling me rather carefully once or twice that it was strictly financial and commercial and in no sense political. I was told that he had brought credentials from Senator Harding to Lenin, but I am temperamentally incurious and I made no attempt whatever to verify this statement or to pry into Mr Vanderlip's affairs. I did not even ask how it could be possible to conduct business or financial operations in a Communist State with anyone but the Government, nor how it was possible to deal with a Government upon strictly non-political lines. These were, I admitted, mysteries beyond my understanding. But we ate, smoked, drank our coffee and conversed together in an atmosphere of profound discretion. By not mentioning Mr Vanderlip's "mission", we made it a portentous, omnipresent fact.

The arrangements leading up to my meeting with Lenin were tedious and irritating, but at last I found myself under way for the Kremlin in the company of Mr Rothstein, formerly a figure in London Communist circles, and an American comrade with a large camera who was also, I gathered, an official of the Russian Foreign Office.

The Kremlin as I remembered it in 1914 was a very open place, open much as Windsor Castle is, with a thin trickle of pilgrims and tourists in groups and couples flowing through it. But now it is closed up and difficult of access. There was a great pother with passes and permits before we could get through even the outer gates. And we were filtered and inspected through five or six rooms of clerks and sentinels before we got into the presence. This may be necessary for the personal security of Lenin, but it puts him out of reach of Russia, and, what perhaps is more serious, if there is to be an effectual dictatorship, it puts Russia out of his reach. If things must filter up to him, they must also filter down, and they may undergo very considerable changes in the process.

We got to Lenin at last and found him, a little figure at a great desk in a well-lit room that looked out upon palatial spaces. I thought his desk was rather in a litter. I sat down on a chair at a corner of the desk, and the little man – his feet scarcely touch the ground as he sits on the edge of his chair – twisted round to talk to me, putting his arms round and over a pile of papers. He spoke excellent English, but it was, I thought, rather characteristic of the present condition of Russian affairs that Mr Rothstein chaperoned the conversation, occasionally offering footnotes and other assistance. Meanwhile the American got to work with his camera, and unobtrusively but persistently exposed plates. The talk, however, was too interesting for that to be an annoyance. One forgot about that clicking and shifting about quite soon.

400

I had come expecting to struggle with a doctrinaire Marxist. I found nothing of the sort. I had been told that Lenin lectured people; he certainly did not do so on this occasion. Much has been made of his laugh in the descriptions, a laugh which is said to be pleasing at first and afterwards to become cynical. This laugh was not in evidence. His forehead reminded me of someone else – I could not remember who it was, until the other evening I saw Mr Arthur Balfour sitting and talking under a shaded light. It is exactly the same domed, slightly one-sided cranium. Lenin has a pleasant, quick-changing, brownish face, with a lively smile and a habit (due perhaps to some defect in focussing) of screwing up one eye as he pauses in his talk; he is not very like the photographs you see of him because he is one of those people whose change of expression is more important than their features; he gesticulated a little with his hands over the heaped papers as he talked, and he talked quickly, very keen on his subject, without any posing or pretences or reservations, as a good type of scientific man will talk.

Our talk was threaded throughout and held together by two – what shall I call them? – *motifs*. One was from me to him: "What do you think you are making of Russia? What is the state you are trying to create?" The other was from him to me: "Why does not the social revolution begin in England? Why do you not work for the social revolution? Why are you not destroying Capitalism and establishing the Communist State?" These *motifs* interwove, reacted on each other, illuminated each other. The second brought back the first: "But what are you making of the social revolution? Are you making a success of it?" And from that we got back to two again with: "To make it a success the Western world must join in. Why doesn't it?"

In the days before 1918 all the Marxist world thought of the social revolution as an end. The workers of the world were to unite, overthrow Capitalism, and be happy ever afterwards. But in 1918 the Communists, to their own surprise, found themselves in control of Russia and challenged to produce their millennium. They have a colourable excuse for a delay in the production of a new and better social order in their continuation of war conditions, in the blockade and so forth, nevertheless it is clear that they begin to realize the tremendous unpreparedness which the Marxist methods of thought involve. At a hundred points – I have already put a finger upon one or two of them – they do not know what to do. But the commonplace Communist simply loses his temper if you venture to doubt whether everything is being done in precisely the best and most intelligent way under the new *régime*. He is like a tetchy housewife who wants you to recognise that everything is in perfect order in the middle of an eviction. He is like one of those now forgotten suffragettes who used to promise us an earthly paradise as soon as we escaped from the tyranny of "man-made laws". Lenin, on the other hand, whose frankness must at times leave his disciples breathless, has recently stripped off the last pretence that the Russian revolution is anything more than the inauguration of an age of limitless experiment. "Those who are engaged in the formidable task of overcoming capitalism," he has recently written, "must be prepared to try method after method until they find the one which answers their purpose best."

We opened our talk with a discussion of the future of the great towns under Communism. I wanted to see how far Lenin contemplated the dying out of the towns in Russia. The desolation of Petersburg had brought home to me a point I had never realized before, that the whole form and arrangement of a town is determined by shopping and marketing, and that the abolition of these things renders nine-tenths of the buildings in an ordinary town directly or indirectly unmeaning and useless. "The towns will get very much smaller," he admitted. "They will be different. Yes, quite different." That, I suggested, implied a tremendous task. It meant the scrapping of the existing towns and their replacement. The churches and great buildings of Petersburg would become presently like those of Novgorod the Great or like the temples of Paestum. Most of the town would dissolve away. He agreed quite cheerfully. I think it warmed his heart to find someone who understood a necessary consequence of collectivism that many even of his own people fail to grasp. Russia has to be rebuilt fundamentally, has to become a new thing...

And industry has to be reconstructed – as fundamentally?

Did I realize what was already in hand with Russia? The electrification of Russia?

For Lenin, who like a good orthodox Marxist denounces all "Utopians", has succumbed at last to a Utopia, the Utopia of the electricians. He is throwing all his weight into a scheme for the development of great power stations in Russia to serve whole provinces with light, with transport, and industrial power. Two experimental districts he said had already been electrified. Can one imagine a more courageous project in a vast flat land of forests and illiterate peasants, with no water power, with no technical skill available, and with trade and industry at the last gasp? Projects for such an electrification are in process of development in Holland and they have been discussed in England, and in those densely-populated and industrially highly-developed centres one can imagine them as successful, economical, and altogether beneficial. But their application to Russia is an altogether greater strain upon the constructive imagination. I cannot see anything of the sort happening in this dark crystal of Russia, but this little man at the Kremlin can; he sees the decaying railways replaced by a new electric transport, sees new roadways spreading throughout the land, sees a new and happier Communist industrialism arising again. While I talked to him he almost persuaded me to share his vision.

"And you will go on to these things with the peasants rooted in your soil?"

But not only are the towns to be rebuilt; every agricultural landmark is to go.

"Even now," said Lenin, "all the agricultural production of Russia is not peasant production. We have, in places, large scale agriculture. The Government is already running big estates with workers instead of peasants, where conditions are favourable. That can spread. It can be extended first to one province, then another. The peasants in the other provinces, selfish and illiterate, will not know what is happening until their turn comes…"

It may be difficult to defeat the Russian peasant *en masse;* but in detail there is no difficulty at all. At the mention of the peasant Lenin's head came nearer to mine; his manner became confidential. As if after all the peasant *might* overhear.

It is not only the material organisation of society you have to build, I argued, it is the mentality of a whole people. The Russian people are by habit and tradition traders and individualists; their very souls must be remoulded if this new world is to be achieved. Lenin asked me what I had seen of the

404

educational work afoot. I praised some of the things I had seen. He nodded and smiled with pleasure. He has an unlimited confidence in his work.

"But these are only sketches and beginnings," I said.

"Come back and see what we have done in Russia in ten years' time," he answered.

In him I realized that Communism could after all, in spite of Marx, be enormously creative. After the tiresome class-war fanatics I had been encountering among the Communists, men of formulae as sterile as flints, after numerous experiences of the trained and empty conceit of the common Marxist devotee, this amazing little man, with his frank admission of the immensity and complication of the project of Communism and his simple concentration upon its realisation, was very refreshing. He at least has a vision of a world changed over and planned and built afresh.

He wanted more of my Russia impressions. I told him that I thought that in many directions, and more particularly in the Petersburg Commune, Communism was pressing too hard and too fast, and destroying before it was ready to rebuild. They did broken down trading before they were ready to ration; the co-operative organisation had been smashed up instead of being utilised, and so on. That brought us to our essential difference, the difference of the Evolutionary Collectivist and Marxist, the question whether the social revolution is, in its extremity, necessary, whether it is necessary to overthrow one economic system completely before the new one can begin. I believe that through a vast sustained educational campaign the existing Capitalist system can be *civilized* into a Collectivist world system; Lenin on the other hand tied himself years ago to the Marxist

405

dogmas of the inevitable class war, the downfall of Capitalist order as a prelude to reconstruction, the proletarian dictatorship, and so forth. He had to argue, therefore, that modern Capitalism is incurably predatory, wasteful, and unteachable, and that until it is destroyed it will continue to exploit the human heritage stupidly and aimlessly, that it will fight against and prevent any administration of natural resources for the general good, and that, because essentially it is a scramble, it will inevitably make wars.

I had, I will confess, a very uphill argument. He suddenly produced Chiozza Money's new book, *The Triumph of Nationalisation,* which he had evidently been reading very carefully. "But you see directly you begin to have a good working collectivist organisation of any public interest, the Capitalists smash it up again. They smashed your national shipyards; they won't let you work your coal economically." He tapped the book. "It is all here."

And against my argument that wars sprang from nationalist imperialism and not from a Capitalist organisation of society he suddenly brought: "But what do you think of this new Republican Imperialism that comes to us from America?"

Here Mr Rothstein intervened in Russian with an objection that Lenin swept aside.

And regardless of Mr Rothstein's plea for diplomatic reserve, Lenin proceeded to explain the projects with which one American at least was seeking to dazzle the imagination of Moscow. There was to be economic assistance for Russia and recognition of the Bolshevik Government. There was to be a defensive alliance against Japanese aggression in Siberia. There was to be an American naval station on the coast of Asia, and leases for long terms of sixty or fifty years of the natural resources of Khamskhatka and possibly of other large regions of Russian Asia. Well, did I think that made for peace? Was it anything more than the beginning of a new world scramble? How would the British Imperialists like this sort of thing?

Always, he insisted, Capitalism competes and scrambles. It is the antithesis of collective action. It cannot develop into social unity or into world unity.

But some industrial power had to come in and help Russia, I said. She cannot reconstruct now without such help...

Our multifarious argumentation ended indecisively. We parted warmly, and I and my companion were filtered out of the Kremlin through one barrier after another in much the same fashion as we had been filtered in.

"He is wonderful," said Mr Rothsein. "But it was an indiscretion – "

I was not disposed to talk as we made our way, under the glowing trees that grow in the ancient moat of the Kremlin, back to our Guest House. I wanted to think Lenin over while I had him fresh in my mind, and I did not want to be assisted by the expositions of my companion. But Mr Rothstein kept on talking.

He was still pressing me not to mention this little sketch of the Russian–American outlook to Mr Vanderlip long after I assured him that I respected Mr Vanderlip's veil of discretion far too much to pierce it by any careless word.

And so back to No. 17 Sofiskaya Naberezhnaya, and lunch with Mr Vanderlip and the young sculptor from London. The old servant of the house waited on us, mournfully conscious of the meagreness of our entertainment and reminiscent of the great days of the past when Caruso had been a guest and had sung to all that was brilliant in Moscow in the room upstairs.

Mr Vanderlip was for visiting the big market that afternoon – and later going to the Ballet, but my son and I were set upon returning to Petersburg that night and so getting on to Reval in time for the Stockholm boat.

CHAPTER SEVEN

The Envoy

In the preceding chapters I have written in the first person and in a familiar style because I did not want the reader to lose sight for a moment of the shortness of our visit to Russia and of my personal limitations. Now in conclusion, if the reader will have patience with me for a few final words, I would like in the less personal terms and very plainly to set down my main convictions about the Russian situation. They are deep-seated convictions, and they concern not merely Russia but the whole present outlook of our civilisation. They are merely one man's opinion, but as I feel them strongly, so I put them without weakening qualifications.

First, then, Russia, which was a modern civilization of the Western type, least disciplined and most ramshackle of all the Great Powers, is now a modern civilisation *in extremis*. The direct cause of its downfall has been modern war leading to physical exhaustion. Only through that could the Bolsheviks have secured power. Nothing like this Russian downfall has ever happened before. If it goes on for a year or so more the process of collapse will be complete. Nothing will be left of Russia but a country of peasants; the towns will be practically deserted and in ruins, the railways will be rusting in disuse. With the railways will go the last vestiges of any general government. The peasants are absolutely illiterate and collectively stupid, capable of resisting interference but incapable of comprehensive foresight and organisation. They will become a sort of human swamp in a state of division, petty civil war, and political squalor, with a famine whenever the harvests are bad; and they will be breeding epidemics for the rest of Europe. They will lapse towards Asia.

The collapse of the civilized system in Russia into peasant barbarism means that Europe will be cut off for many years from all the mineral wealth of Russia, and from any supply of raw products from this area, from its corn, flax, and the like. It is an open question whether the Western Powers can get along without these supplies. Their cessation certainly means a general impoverishment of Western Europe.

The only possible Government that can stave off such a final collapse of Russia now is the present Bolshevik Government, if it can be assisted by America and the Western Powers. There is now no alternative to that Government possible. There are of course a multitude of antagonists – adventurers and the like – ready, with European assistance, to attempt the overthrow of that Bolshevik Government, but there are no signs of any common purpose and moral unity capable of replacing it. And moreover there is no time now for another revolution in Russia. A year more of civil war will make the final sinking of Russia out of civilisation inevitable. We have to make what we can, therefore, of the Bolshevik Government, whether we like it or not.

The Bolshevik Government is inexperienced and incapable to an extreme degree; it has had phases of violence and cruelty; but it is on the whole honest. And it includes a few individuals of real creative imagination and power, who may with opportunity, if their hands are strengthened, achieve great reconstructions. The Bolshevik Government seems on the whole to be trying to act up to its professions, which are still held by most of its supporters with a quite religious passion. Given generous help, it may succeed in establishing a new social order in Russia of a civilized type with which the rest of the world will be able to deal. It will probably be a mitigated Communism, with a large-scale handling of transport, industry, and (later) agriculture.

It is necessary that we should understand and respect the professions and principles of the Bolsheviks if we Western peoples are to be of any effectual service to humanity in Russia. Hitherto these professions and principles have been ignored in the most extraordinary way by the Western Governments. The Bolshevik Government is, and says it is, a Communist Government. And it means this, and will make this the standard of its conduct. It has suppressed private ownership and private trade in Russia, not as an act of expediency but as an act of right; and in all Russia there remain now no commercial individuals and bodies with whom we can deal who will respect the conventions and usages of Western commercial life. The Bolshevik Government, we have to understand, has, by its nature, an invincible prejudice against individual business men; it will not treat them in a manner that they will consider fair and honourable; it will distrust them and, as far as it can, put them at the completest disadvantage. It regards them as pirates – or at best as privateers. It is hopeless and impossible therefore for individual persons and firms to think of going into Russia to trade. There is only one being in Russia with whom the Western world can deal, and that is the Bolshevik Government itself, and there is no way of dealing with that one being safely and effectually except through some national or, better, some international Trust. This latter body, which might represent some single Power or group of Powers, or which might even have some titular connection with the League of Nations, would be able to deal with the Bolshevik Government on equal terms. It would have to recognise the Bolshevik Government and, in conjunction with it, to set about the now urgent task of the material restoration of civilized life in European and Asiatic Russia. It should resemble in its general nature one of the big buying and controlling trusts that were so necessary and effectual in the European States during the Great War. It should deal with its individual producers on the one hand, and the Bolshevik Government would deal with its own population on the other. Such a Trust could speedily make itself indispensable to the Bolshevik Government. This indeed is the only way in which a capitalist State can hold commerce with a Communist State. The attempts that have been made during the past year and more to devise some method of private trading in Russia without recognition of the Bolshevik Government were from the outset as hopeless as the search for the North-West passage from England to India. The channels are frozen up.

Any country or group of countries with adequate industrial resources which goes into Bolshevik Russia with recognition and help will necessarily become the supporter, the right hand, and the consultant of the Bolshevik Government. It will react upon that Government and be reacted upon. It will probably become more collectivist in its methods, and, on the other hand, the rigours of extreme Communism in Russia will probably be greatly tempered through its influence.

412

The only Power capable of playing this *rôle* of eleventh-hour helper to Russia single-handed is the United States of America. That is why I find the adventure of the enterprising and imaginative Mr Vanderlip very significant. I doubt the conclusiveness of his negotiations; they are probably only the opening phase of a discussion of the Russian problem upon a new basis that may lead it at last to a comprehensive world treatment of this situation. Other Powers than the United States will, in the present phase of world-exhaustion, need to combine before they can be of any effective use to Russia. Big business is by no means antipathetic to Communism. The larger big business grows the more it approximates to Collectivism. It is the upper road of the few instead of the lower road of the masses to Collectivism.

The only alternative to such a helpful intervention in Bolshevik Russia is, I firmly believe, the final collapse of all that remains of modern civilization throughout what was formerly the Russian Empire. It is highly improbable that the collapse will be limited to its boundaries. Both eastward and westward other great regions may, one after another, tumble into the big hole in civilisation thus created. Possible all modern civilisation may tumble in.

These propositions do not refer to any hypothetical future; they are an attempt to state the outline facts and possibilities of what is going on – and going on with great rapidity – in Russia and in the world generally now, as they present themselves to my mind. This in general terms is the frame of circumstance in which I would have the sketches of Russia that have preceded this set and read. So it is I interpret the writing on the Eastern wall of Europe.

H G Wells

The History of Mr Polly

Mr Polly is one of literature's most enduring and universal creations. An ordinary man, trapped in an ordinary life, Mr Polly makes a series of ill-advised choices that bring him to the very brink of financial ruin. Determined not to become the latest victim of the economic retrenchment of the Edwardian age, he rebels in magnificent style and takes control of his life once and for all.

ISBN 0-7551-0404-8

H G Wells

In the Days of the Comet

Revenge was all Leadford could think of as he set out to find the unfaithful Nettie and her adulterous lover. But this was all to change when a new comet entered the earth's orbit and totally reversed the natural order of things. The Great Change had occurred and any previous emotions, thoughts, ambitions, hopes and fears had all been removed. Free love, pacifism and equality were now the name of the game. But how would Leadford fare in this most utopian of societies?

ISBN 0-7551-0406-4

H G Wells

The Invisible Man

On a cold wintry day in the depths of February a stranger appeared in The Coach and Horses requesting a room. So strange was this man's appearance, dressed from head to foot with layer upon layer of clothing, bandages and the most enormous glasses, that the owner, Mrs Hall, quite wondered what accident could have befallen him. She didn't know then that he was invisible – but the rumours soon began to spread…

H G Wells' masterpiece *The Invisible Man* is a classic science-fiction thriller showing the perils of scientific advancement.

ISBN 0-7551-0407-2

H G WELLS

THE ISLAND OF DR MOREAU

A shipwreck in the South Seas brings a doctor to an island paradise. Far from seeing this as the end of his life, Dr Moreau seizes the opportunity to play God and infiltrate a reign of terror in this new kingdom. Endless cruel and perverse experiments ensue and see a series of new creations – the 'Beast People' – all of which must bow before the deified doctor.

Originally a Swiftian satire on the dangers of authority and submission, Wells' *The Island of Dr Moreau* can now just as well be read as a prophetic tale of genetic modification and mutability.

ISBN 0-7551-0408-0

H G Wells

Men Like Gods

Mr Barnstaple was ever such a careful driver, careful to indicate before every manoeuvre and very much in favour of slowing down at the slightest hint of difficulty. So however could he have got the car into a skid on a bend on the Maidenhead road?

When he recovered himself he was more than a little relieved to see the two cars that he had been following still merrily motoring along in front of him. It seemed that all was well – except that the scenery had changed, rather a lot. It was then that the awful truth dawned: Mr Barnstaple had been hurled into another world altogether.

How would he ever survive in this supposed Utopia, and more importantly, how would he ever get back?

ISBN 0-7551-0413-7

H G WELLS

THE WAR OF THE WORLDS

'No one would have believed in the last years of the nineteenth century that this world was being watched keenly and closely by intelligences greater than man's...'

A series of strange atmospheric disturbances on the planet Mars may raise concern on Earth but it does little to prepare the inhabitants for imminent invasion. At first the odd-looking Martians seem to pose no threat for the intellectual powers of Victorian London, but it seems man's superior confidence is disastrously misplaced. For the Martians are heading towards victory with terrifying velocity.

The War of the Worlds is an expertly crafted invasion story that can be read as a frenzied satire on the dangers of imperialism and occupation.

ISBN 0-7551-0426-9

OTHER TITLES BY H G WELLS AVAILABLE DIRECT
FROM HOUSE OF STRATUS

Quantity	£	$(US)	$(CAN)	€
FICTION				
ANN VERONICA	9.99	14.95	22.95	16.50
APROPOS OF DOLORES	9.99	14.95	22.95	16.50
THE AUTOCRACY OF MR PARHAM	9.99	14.95	22.95	16.50
BABES IN THE DARKLING WOOD	9.99	14.95	22.95	16.50
BEALBY	9.99	14.95	22.95	16.50
THE BROTHERS *AND*				
THE CROQUET PLAYER	7.99	12.95	19.95	14.50
BRYNHILD	9.99	14.95	22.95	16.50
THE BULPINGTON OF BLUP	9.99	14.95	22.95	16.50
THE DREAM	9.99	14.95	22.95	16.50
THE FIRST MEN IN THE MOON	9.99	14.95	22.95	16.50
THE FOOD OF THE GODS	9.99	14.95	22.95	16.50
THE HISTORY OF MR POLLY	9.99	14.95	22.95	16.50
THE HOLY TERROR	9.99	14.95	22.95	16.50
IN THE DAYS OF THE COMET	9.99	14.95	22.95	16.50
THE INVISIBLE MAN	7.99	12.95	19.95	14.50
THE ISLAND OF DR MOREAU	7.99	12.95	19.95	14.50
KIPPS: THE STORY OF A SIMPLE SOUL	9.99	14.95	22.95	16.50
LOVE AND MR LEWISHAM	9.99	14.95	22.95	16.50
MARRIAGE	9.99	14.95	22.95	16.50
MEANWHILE	9.99	14.95	22.95	16.50
MEN LIKE GODS	9.99	14.95	22.95	16.50
A MODERN UTOPIA	9.99	14.95	22.95	16.50
MR BRITLING SEES IT THROUGH	9.99	14.95	22.95	16.50

ALL HOUSE OF STRATUS BOOKS ARE AVAILABLE FROM GOOD BOOKSHOPS
OR DIRECT FROM THE PUBLISHER:

Internet: www.houseofstratus.com including synopses and features.

Email: sales@houseofstratus.com
info@houseofstratus.com
(please quote author, title and credit card details.)